Neurodivergent
by

Jeff Scott

Copyright 2025

Neurodivergent

Jeff Scott

Copyright 2025

This novel is a work of fiction created by Jeff Scott. Names, characters, places, businesses, events, and all other descriptions are products of the author's imagination. Any resemblance to real people, places, or things is purely coincidental.

All rights are reserved. No part of this book may be used or reproduced in any way without written permission from the author. However, brief quotations or excerpts may be used in critical reviews and articles.

ISBN: 9798267100564

Kindle Edition ASIN: B006YXEJ0E

First Edition, October 2025

Edits with assistance from Grammarly Professional

Neurodivergent

Matthew was born a prisoner of an extraordinary mind. A brilliant neurodivergent, his personality is made whole by an experimental cure that was as dangerous as it was miraculous. Having since forged a more normal life from a void-less childhood, with a loving wife and a beautiful child. But the fragile peace he has so carefully constructed is about to shatter. The shadows from a life he tried to bury are returning, whispering his name and threatening to claim more than just his past.

The nightmare he thought he escaped in the wreckage of his early life was just the beginning. A ghost from his past returns, cloaked in a new face, a man who sees Matthew not as a person, but as the final triumph of his mad genius. The spectral figure of Dr. Meacham, a sinister genetic architect, has come back to reclaim his ultimate creation. Matthew is drawn into a clandestine world of human echoes, chilling conspiracies, and a truth so terrifying it could unravel the very fabric of his identity and destroy his family.

Now, the two halves of Matthew's life are about to collide. The peaceful world he created is at risk, and the only way to save his family lies in a world he never knew existed. As the founder of a monstrous new reality tightens his hold, Matthew must step out of the light and into the dark corners of genetic manipulation and rogue clones. Can he outsmart the man who made him and protect those he loves, or will he become a pawn in a game that decides the future of humanity?

Contents

1 *THE SPINDLY MAN* 6
2 *A STAR IS BORN* 26
3 *ILLUMINATION* 36
4 *SIDE SHOW FREAK* 41
5 *GRAVITY* 51
6 *SENSORY OVERLOAD* 55
7 *THE SECRET KEY* 59
8 *SURREAL LIFE* 64
9 *REUNION* 76
10 *DROPPING ANCHOR* 84
11 *TIES THAT BIND* 91
12 *NEW BEGINNINGS* 92
13 *ROSETTA'S STONE* 95
14 *ARDUOUS ENDEAVORS* 104
15 *BLACK TIE AFFAIR* 112
16 *FANDANGLORIOUS* 128
17 *GROWING PANGS* 140
18 *CALAMITY FALLS* 146
19 *BERLIN* 167
20 *IVORY TOWER* 178
21 *GUIDEING LIGHT* 190
22 *HOUSTON, WE ARE GO FOR LAUNCH* 203
23 *REVOLVING WHEEL* 228
24 *BINDINGS* 237
25 *OSLO* 258
26 *ENLIGHTENMENT* 280
27 *PERSISTENCE OF TIME* 292
28 *SPANDAU BALLET* 299

29 *WOLFS DEN*	307
30 *MIND OVER MATTER*	314
31 *NIGHT OF THE LONG KNIVES*	322
32 *SIDE SHOW FREAK RETURNS*	336

1 *THE SPINDLY MAN*

Robert Duvet teetered ponderously into the Green Room, arriving early so he could stake his claim on the oversized black leather chair across from the complimentary victuals. His arthritis had been acting up recently, so the stiff cushions made it easier for him to get up when it was time to go on stage. Being a fan favorite, he was a veteran of the Ida Winthrop show, and having a new movie out meant playing the role of marketing agent for the network Execs. Not his favorite part of the job, leaving his wife at home while he did the talk show circuit to promote his latest work, but this movie was already generating Oscar buzz. Not bad for an old timer.

Entering the Green Room, he was startled by a constant, melodic humming sound and the squeak of leather rubbing like a rider on a horse saddle. He paused, looking down at a spindly young man sitting in *his* chair. *Well, I'll be damned*, he huffed to himself. He quickly scanned the room, looking for some other seating option. Not finding any to his liking, he chose the love seat across from the spindly man.

Robert's indignation increased with obvious inconvenience. *Just who the hell is this guy, anyway? He's sitting in my chair, for Chrissakes!* Rosie knew the setup by now. This place was getting a little too complacent, considering the number of times he'd helped Ida jump-start her ratings. Maybe this guy was lost or something, an observer, a make-a-wish-come-true recipient, or something. He looked a little off. *And what's up with that rocking and humming?*

Robert studied the spindly man's posture for a few minutes as he watched him rock like he was riding a hobby horse. Then he gathered the courage to speak to him, trying not to startle him—or himself, for that matter.

"Hey there, fella. Almost sat on you. What's your name?"

The spindly man abruptly stopped rocking, slowly turned his head, and then cocked it sideways, assuming an odd position. The movement was smooth and methodical, like an animatronic robot. An expressionless face peered back at him. Spindly man's eyes were like fish's eyes, with no feeling or thought about them. The hair stood up on the back of Robert's neck.

A seasoned actor like Robert had learned many expressions and could execute them on camera even though he simulated most of them. The expression on his face after seeing the way the spindly man moved was most likely one of horror. What he had just witnessed was not only unsettling but just a little bit creepy.

"Matthew Le'Dain," spindly man replied, his voice a monotone.

Robert drew a blank. Usually a good judge of people, he was taken aback. The voice didn't match the body. He had the voice of a very powerful man, but in a frail container. The rocking, Robert thought, must be the spindly man's nerves at the thought of going on television.

First impressions could be deceiving, he knew, but so far Robert felt that spindly man, named Matthew Le'Dain, was nothing more than a basket-case retard. Harsh thoughts for Robert under normal circumstances, but this spindly man had claimed his property! Once Robert made up his mind, it was hard to get him to change. He was a WWII kid. The world back then was much different than now, and people in his generation were resolute with their opinions. Taking that chair was a complete breach of etiquette, an assault on his seniority, if nothing else.

Sitting a few more minutes and studying the spindly man, Robert decided he was being much too harsh on the boy without any notable cause.

"Bit nervous, aintcha?" Robert lowered himself onto the loveseat, feeling his hips pop as he sank down in the too-soft cushion, like a boat being lowered into the water.

The spindly man named Matthew continued rocking, humming even louder than before. Robert grimaced at the noise, hoisting an eyebrow in defiance. Then, deciding to embrace the situation, he tried to establish a rapport with the spindly man.

"Hey, kid, I've done this a thousand times. Never gets any easier. Hell, I'm eighty-two years old, and I still get nervous before I go on stage. You ever been on television before?"

Without missing a beat, the spindly man continued to rock, this time giving the impression he was not interested in conversation. In fact, if Robert were younger, he would have taken the spindly man's lack of eye contact as disrespect.

"Yes." Rock, rock, rock. Hmm, hmm, hmm.

"You're an enigma wrapped in quiet, are' ya? Trying to get in the right state of mind to tackle your stage fright, then, huh? You do know this is a daytime talk show, right?" Robert lay on the sarcasm, trying to get a rise out of the spindly man, but not getting any response; he decided it was a waste of effort.

"Yes." Rock, rock, rock. Hmm, hmm, hmm.

"Oookay," Robert sighed, mumbling under his breath and adjusting his legs as he tried to prevent sinking deeper into the cushions. Keeping a conversation with this guy is like trying to catch wind with a soup ladle. So after more uncomfortable minutes of rocking and humming, Robert decided to try a little harder. He extended his right hand and said, "Robert Duvet, by the way. I act, if you can call it that." He said, trying to appear humble. "You know any actors, Matt?"

His hand hung in the air like a broken tree limb over a fast-running stream, unnoticed by the water traveling underneath. Under normal circumstances, Robert would not have even considered making such a move, but normal was far removed this morning.

"No. I like to be addressed as Matthew." Rock, rock, rock. Hmm, hmm, hmm.

Robert recoiled his arm and leaned back into the soft, cushioned sofa. He struggled to make friendly conversation with the spindly man named Matthew.

Alrighty then, Robert thought. *This one is a lit fuse with no boom, for sure. A little on the strange end of the unsettling spectrum of personalities.* "I can give you a few tips, if you'd like."

Matthew continued rocking back and forth, his head cocked sideways and away from Robert. He hadn't changed his demeanor since his arrival.

Robert struggled with the spindly man's apparent dismissal of his omnipotence. Robert was Hollywood royalty. Who was this little piss-ant to him? He shrugged, unsure if the spindly man was listening or not. No matter, he was determined now. No one ignored Robert for long. More of a pride thing, not vanity. Robert needed people to accept and like him. He always had. That's why he was a fan favorite. He truly loved people, especially his fans.

Robert continued talking to the spindly man, "First tip, don't ever drink the milk in here. It's always too warm, and it will give you gas." He glanced at Matthew to see if he bit on his tip. *No? Oh, well.* "Second, you need to always make good eye contact. Eye contact is the key when you're talking to—you understand what I'm saying, kid?"

The spindly man abruptly stopped rocking, seemingly irritated by the comment. He lifted his head to face Robert and began to speak. *Great googly moogly.* That voice, with its monotone inflection, sent chills up Robert's spine. Was he conversing with an android? A vision of the robot from *Lost in Space* skipped across his mind. *Beware, Will Robinson!*

"You were born on January 5th, 1931, in San Diego, California. You attended a small college in Illinois, called Principia, where you majored in drama. You have starred in one hundred and forty movies, have won only one Oscar and fifty-two other, less important awards. You are married to your second wife, Sharon, and you live on a horse ranch in Mooresville, North Carolina, in the vicinity of several famous race car drivers."

Matthew turned around and then resumed rocking, quietly humming to himself.

Robert shifted uncomfortably on the too-soft couch, gently biting his lower lip and smiling. He nervously glanced at the room to see if anyone else had heard the spindly man's recitation. *Well, if that ain't the damndest thing…Kid's a frickin' genius. I'm not sure whether to be upset or find somewhere else to sit.* "You some kinda encyclopedia? Are we on a hidden camera back here?" Scouring the room again, he looked for a camera crew, expecting Ida Winthrop to suddenly burst in, but nobody came.

Robert was stuck between a sense of admiration and disbelief. He took his hand and tried to wipe the expression from his face and clear his thoughts. His mouth gaped open with his tongue pressed behind his teeth like a convulsing epileptic.

The spindly man went back to ignoring Robert and began to rock harder, almost popping the front feet of the leather chair off the floor, humming louder than ever. His back smacked the leather upright with a hard thud.

Robert shook his head, finding no way to relate to the boy. He was exasperated and now demanded some answers. By damn, he was entitled to some answers. "Matthew, what are you here for? On the show, that is. Are you even in the show, or are you just lost?"

Matthew abruptly stopped rocking, turned his head slowly but without perceptible aggression towards Robert, and with no change in expression, he said, "I am here to entertain the audience."

Robert guffawed, like the braying of a jackass, spewing spittle all over the seating area. Then, wiping his chin with the back of his hand, he adjusted his posture in the soft cushions and said, "Now, we're getting somewhere. So, you're an entertainer. You will definitely scare the bejeebers out of them, if nothing else. What kind of act do you do?"

The spindly man replied as if nothing had transpired over the last ten minutes, no bond had been struck. "It is not an act. I am a neurodivergent Savant."

Well, damn, Robert thought, almost saying it aloud. Crashing around in his brain like waves on a cliff wall, it occurred to him that he had seen this kid before. Looking down at the end table between them, he couldn't believe his eyes. Matthew was on the cover of *Time Magazine*. There it was, lying right there on the table. He hadn't noticed it before, but that was definitely the spindly man.

Robert adjusted his position enthusiastically, leaning in towards Matthew with his arms resting on his knees.

"I know you. You're that whiz kid who can memorize names instantly, read books with one eye like a lizard, scanning each page in minutes, and do math problems in your head. What do they call you? Oh, yeah. *The Human Computer*," he said, snapping his fingers and pointing at him.

Matthew was just about to start rocking again when he stopped and said, "You know me? I don't think so. I would have remembered meeting you."

Robert burst out laughing again, pointing his crooked finger at him. "I bet you would. I know *of* you. I mean, I've seen you on late-night TV and on those entertainment news shows. Hey, I really hate to trouble you, Matthew—but can I get your autograph? It's not for me, really; it's for my grandkids."

Robert reached into his inside coat pocket and pulled out a nice leather-bound autograph book. Opening it, he turned to the next available page, passing over some huge Hollywood elites as he handed it to Matthew upside down.

Matthew took the book and the pen without rotating it. He began to sign it in the wrong direction.

Robert started to object, but decided not to rock the boat, worrying that he might have signed it upside down. Matthew seemed to be a person who didn't like to be corrected, so he held his peace and waited.

When Mathew handed the book back, Robert looked at it with awe, seeing his signature. He signed his name Matthew Le'Dain in cursive, with an eighteenth-century flair, even though the book was facing the wrong direction.

How in the hell did he do that? The kid was more talented than anyone he had ever met. Robert reflected on his earlier thoughts. He was such an old fool. How he'd underestimated the spindly man—Matthew, he meant. Every time he thought he knew, he found he did not. It must be tough for him to survive in this world of sharks, wolves, and buzzards. He

11

had to admit he was an old buzzard himself. He'd mistaken a brilliant mind for a troubled one, as they say. He should know better. If he had been judged the way he judged Matthew, he probably wouldn't be here today. Matthew 7:1 *Judge not, that ye be not judged.* How fitting that he should recall that scripture. He was no man to judge anyone—bald mostly, stout, and not particularly good-looking. Put him on a stage or behind a camera, and his lights turned on. He was in his element. Matthew must share that trait. Certain questions and topics lit him up, but like a refrigerator light, they would go off when the door was closed. How many have chosen to keep the door closed on this young man over his brief years?

A young female producer entered the room, abruptly invading Robert's thoughts. "Mr. Duvet, welcome. We're so glad you could make it back again. I see you've already introduced yourself to Mr. Le'Dain. Silver Dollar will be along in the next few minutes, I hope. You know these hip-hop rap acts. Here today, gone tomorrow."

She was standing there in her high-heels and mini-skirt, all commanding five-foot-two of her height, he guessed, with no shoes—five-seven with. She was looking down at her *E-pad*. For all he knew, she was playing bubble pop or slots on it.

Robert smiled and nodded his head while Matthew continued to rock back and forth, humming to himself.

The woman threw a curious glance at Matthew and squinted at Robert. "Is he okay?"

"Yeah, he's been rocking ever since I got here."

"All right. If you guys need anything, I'm just down the hall on the right. The bathroom is through that door," she said, pointing to the other side of the room. "The show starts in about an hour, so make yourselves comfortable."

The young woman threw one last glare at Matthew, rolled her eyes, and slightly shook her head as she left the room. She mumbled something under her breath. Robert thought she said something like "*It takes all kinds.*" Not a particularly flattering remark for someone in her position, but Robert was old enough to see how the world had changed, how people had changed. Manners, being polite, and not interrupting others were considered old-school virtues.

Robert shifted on the too-soft cushion again. "Huhhhhh!" he grunted, trying to lift himself out of the hole on the sofa. His bones ached, and his hip popped and cracked as he slowly rose like an arm on a backhoe that had been sitting idle for some time. He was thinking greedily after feeling the pangs of age rise once again: *I wonder if I can get him up out of my chair somehow.*

"Matthew, do you want some juice? A sandwich or something?"

"No." Rock, rock, rock. Hum, hum, hum.

Seeing he had no nibble on that line, Robert decided to change his bait. He perused the food bar for a while, grimacing as he eyeballed the complimentary food. "The digs used to be halfway decent around here. I remember when they had bacon, eggs, and gravy & biscuits—not all this feel-good-about-yourself-healthy crap. You know, I would take bacon over chocolate anytime."

Mathew kept rocking, seemingly ignoring Robert's jibes at the modern health craze being pushed by the network.

"Matthew, tell me where you're from. Where did you grow up? When did you know you were a genius?"

He abruptly stopped rocking. His personality—what little there was—appeared again, just like the refrigerator light Robert had imagined before.

Matthew answered in a very mechanical tone. "I was born in Florida on December 3rd, 1988, at Gainesville Memorial Hospital. I was delivered by C-section. My mother labored too hard, and I lost blood to my umbilical cord for just an instant before they removed me from her womb.

Robert thought sadly to himself, *That must be what the hell is wrong with him.* He topped off his plate with food, looking around for a better seat. No such luck.

Like some of the hardened characters he had played in the movies, Robert decided to lean on Matthew to see if he would budge. "Matthew, you mind if I sit there. I need to set my food on the coffee table so I can eat."

He stopped rocking, got up, and walked around the room as Robert sat down and made himself comfortable, finally settling into *his* familiar throne. Robert looked up, and Matthew was walking around the room, sitting in each chair, sampling each one in a very meticulous fashion. He seemed rather befuddled for a genius. Then Robert thought, maybe he was eliminating all the bad choices, one by one. Robert knew he would come to the same conclusion—that the high-backed chair in which he now rested was the best. It was the only conclusion you could make. He finally sat down in a flower-covered cloth chair and then stood back up, mumbling to himself. He tried a large couch in three spots, choosing not to stay on it.

Seeing him struggle with the problem, Robert said, "Here, Matthew. Come sit by me." He smacked his hand on the arm of the supple sofa.

Matthew came over and stood in front of the love seat where Robert had been. He turned and slid down onto the overly soft cushion, sinking in so far that his knees were higher than his waist.

"Not comfortable," he mumbled, "not comfortable at all, not comfortable."

"Sorry, young fella. But that sofa was killing my old senior-citizen hips. I'll probably have to visit my chiropractor now."

Matthew began to rock, but his movements were shorter and less accentuated on the plush sofa. No leather rustled, and no squeaking springs sang with angst at the continuous movements the spindly man had made earlier in the hour.

"See, you're settling in just fine. This chair is the bomb. I try to get it every time I come here. See, even the genius knows comfort. You were born in Florida, is that right? Tell me some more about your parents."

Matthew stopped rocking and looked at Robert for just a second, then looked down and began to speak, gently rocking back and forth, swaying in a much slower rhythm. The spindly man, to the award-winning actor, Robert Duvet, was now transforming into Matthew Le'Dain. Matthew probably had this effect on other people if they would only take the time to get to know him. Time is elusive and very valuable to most for selfish reasons, thought Robert.

"My father is French, and my mother is Floridian." His expression didn't waver, solemn and meticulous. "My parents found it hard to relate to me."

Robert's thoughts got away from him for just a moment. *Hell, he'd been having a hard time relating; he could only imagine how hard it was for them.*

"We moved three times before we made it to the Children's Hospital, living in Kentucky, Massachusetts, and Connecticut. My mother is a homemaker, and my father is a Political Strategist."

Robert's bushy eyebrow rose—he'd read somewhere that Matthew's father had been a liberal Democrat who had transformed into a diehard Reagan conservative.

An older woman entered and began straightening the food table, setting out more napkins and other items. She never made eye contact with either of them, probably following strict orders not to disturb the celebrities. The plump woman opened a closet door and took out an upright sweeper, walked over, and plugged it in. She grasped the handle and turned it on to begin sweeping—Matthew screeched and the woman dropped the sweeper, with her hand over her heart.

Matthew's demeanor had changed rapidly. He put his hands to his ears and rocked. Screaming loudly, he yelled out, "TURN IT OFF! TURN IT OFF! TURN IT OFF!" repeatedly until she shut it down.

Matthew was breathing in heavy pants, and his face had turned red. He rocked more forcefully, banging the back of the sofa so hard it moved several inches.

The cleaning lady shuddered and began to wail, speaking rapidly in Spanish that was most likely full of expletives and prayers all rolled together. Her hands were flying up and down. She covered her face and then threw them in the air like she had seen a monster. Robert jumped to his feet, attending to Matthew. The young staffer who had checked on them earlier came bounding into the room, having heard the screams.

"What in Heaven's name is going on in here?"

"I am sorry, Mees. Flores. I turned on the vacuum to sweep, and the boy started screaming at me."

"He is autistic, Lidia. The loud noise probably frightened him."

"I am so sorry, everyone," Lidia replied, trying to catch her breath and hold her chest as she continued to babble in Spanish.

The young producer continued her admonishment of Lidia, not caring to check on her emotional state. "Lidia, you know we have a policy about sweeping in this room with guests present or in occupied offices."

Then Robert took control, seeing the young woman becoming angry with the cleaning lady. "Rosie. It is Rosie, right?" Robert said in a grandfatherly tone, trying to draw her attention from Lidia. "I think Matthew will be just fine. She didn't know, and besides, we came earlier than normal."

Rosie removed her hands from her hips, abandoning her offensive posture, but then she regained her footing and started again. "Lidia, let's concentrate on other areas of the station. I can't have the guests upset before they go on stage."

Rosie and Lidia left the room, her arm around the upset maid when she'd begun to cry. Matthew paid no attention to the crying woman at all, continuing his rocking, but he began to slow his pace based on the distance the woman was away from him.

Matthew just sat there, seemingly unaffected by the encounter now. If anyone had walked in and seen him, they would never have known something had just gone down. That is, unless they looked at Robert, who was a wreck. His chest was pounding, his cheeks were flushed, and he was working his tongue behind his teeth. This was a nervous habit, a coping mechanism like Matthew's rocking, only less noticeable and more socially acceptable.

"You nearly gave me a heart attack. You need to watch that. I thought something serious was happening." Robert had been put off by the outburst, but he instinctively knew Matthew couldn't help it. He tried to ease the situation by talking with him. "Go on with your story, Matthew." Robert pushed the plate of half-eaten food away, having lost his appetite.

Rosie returned to the room a few seconds later. Commanding their attention with her posture, she said, "Mr. Duvet, you're up first, in ten," she said while looking down at her pad. Turning to leave the room, she mumbled to herself, "Silver Dollar will probably show up seconds before he's supposed to go on."

Robert looked at Matthew, shaking his head as he watched him rock. He took a drink of orange juice. "Tart, very tart," he said, smacking his lips together. "Continue on, Matthew."

Matthew gently rocked and continued with his story. "My father worked for Yale University. My mother has always cared for me. Then, the doctors made us move into an apartment at the Children's Hospital long-term care facility."

Robert took another sip of his juice and tried to talk, but nearly choked. "Uhhooo, Uhhooo!" clearing his throat, he looked over at Matthew, who was not paying attention to his coughing.

For the first time, Matthew spoke without being prompted, "That coughing is caused by the acid in the orange juice dissolving the mucus lining in your throat that triggers your gag reflex. You would be better off drinking milk, but you stated earlier that it causes you to have gas—an indication you could be lactose intolerant."

Robert smiled, rubbing his chin and trying to stay focused. "Go on with the Hospital. I'd like to know why you're not there still." Robert's tiny habit of interjecting sarcasm peeked out again. In most situations, he kept it in check, but after the choking episode, he was having some trouble keeping it down his throat.

Matthew completely missed the sarcasm in Robert's reply and continued talking. "My mother noticed a talent I had with colors and shapes when I was about seven. I used them to perform mathematical calculations. A few weeks later, we met Dr. Gottfried Dimment and Dr. Lawrence Meacham, both from Germany. She calls this *the time of illumination*."

Robert leaned forward, showing interest. "Why did she call it that?"

"Because she finally realized I was neurodivergent. My mother had kept every drawing, doodle, and picture I had ever drawn in a box under the bed. One day, while helping me with homework, she finally understood why I was different."

Robert was thinking to himself—*his parents didn't know he was autistic? Come on!* But the reality was that many high-functioning autistic children go undiagnosed, he'd heard somewhere. He didn't know much about it, but had seen shows about it on television and had read about it in magazines. He'd seen movies about people with it, too. *Rainman*—with Dustin Hoffman and Tom Cruise. That was a good one. Robert considered studying up on the subject when he got a chance. Hell, he had plenty of time between movies to do what he wanted. Thinking deeper, he realized that even in his eighties, autism and its symptoms were not widely known to the public, so he just took it for what it was worth, trying not to be too judgmental.

Robert sat back, adjusting himself comfortably in *his* chair. "Did you attend public school?" Robert hoped the answer was no. He suddenly remembered how tough it was for him, a Midwest boy, to be in a farming community that liked to act, not farm. He was marked as an outcast from the start. There were no "Future Farmers of America" awards waiting in his future at the annual county fairgrounds.

"Yes, I did not like it very much. The teachers never helped me. They placed me in the corner so my rocking and humming would not disturb the other students, or sometimes in a room by myself. Once, a teacher created a small timeout room out of a cardboard carton that had been used to pack a freezer. The class decorated it, and we cut a door and a window into it. The window on it faced the teacher. She made me sit in it most of the time."

Robert recalled his primary school years, remembering how rough certain teachers were with the students. He asked, "How did that make you feel?"

"Feel? What do you mean by *feel*?"

"I meant, did you like the teacher doing that?" Robert restated his question.

"Yes, I liked the solitude, but the school board didn't. They placed her on leave for a week. When she returned, she simply ignored me the rest of the time."

Robert raised his bushy eyebrows, feeling sympathetic. He imagined how tough it would be for a special boy like Matthew in public school. This began to eat at him, and he knew a rant would be forthcoming on the waste and inefficiency of government-run systems. He quickly changed his thoughts, still intrigued by the math. Robert recalled that he had once seen Matthew do some tricks with it on a late-night talk show.

"Show me how you do math with shapes and colors," Robert requested. Looking around, he found a small, white notepad lying on the end table with the network's logo. He handed them to Matthew, along with a pen he found lying next to it. "Take six million times seventeen and a half percent."

Robert watched intently as Matthew quickly drew three shapes on the paper. He wrote red, blue, and purple inside, along with the numbers and the answer. The two outer shapes represented the numbers, and the inner one was the answer, displayed in purple.

Robert picked up the notepad and studied it closely. His face tightened, his teeth began to clinch, and deep lines formed on his forehead. With a contorted face, he said, "I knew that leech overcharged me his commission rate on that film." Throwing it down on the table between them, it landed with a smack. Matthew paid little attention to the show of emotion.

"Almost a hundred thousand dollars difference," Robert ranted. "I'm sorry, Matthew. I hope your agent treats you better than mine. He is a cheating, lying, good-for-nothing leech!"

"My mother is my agent, and Lea Stewart is my publicist," Matthew said.

The room fell quiet, and the two sat there for a long time in silence. Robert worked his tongue on the back of his front teeth, and Matthew rocked and hummed to some unknown tune in his head.

Robert, trying to get his mind off his agent, prompted Matthew, "What did you do while you were at Children's Hospital?"

"I learned how to communicate better using my methods to teach the doctors and the staff a new language."

Robert was interested in Matthew more than ever now. He leaned towards Matthew so he could hear better, but not too close, "Explain this new language to me. I'm a little fuzzy on what you mean?"

"I see numbers and letters as shapes, colors, and symbols of all different sizes. That is why math comes easily to me. I see them three-dimensionally in my head, and I measure their volumes to come up with the answer."

Robert sat back, slapping his knee, "By golly, you are a frickin' enigma. I bet you do your own taxes, too. This Hospital, did they help you, Matthew? It sounds like you were teaching them."

"Yes, I earned a PhD in Physics before I left the University Hospital at nineteen."

"Damn, that is amazing! A PhD by the time most people have just graduated from high school. I barely got a bachelor's degree—in drama, no less. Hell, I just took acting because it was easy for me."

Matthew had quit humming but continued to gently rock. More signs that he was finally getting comfortable with Robert.

"Matthew, these doctors, were they good to you? I mean, did they treat you like a person or a lab animal?"

20

Matthew stopped rocking and turned to face Robert as if he did not understand or was annoyed at the question.

"They treated me like a person. I was very much the center of attention. Every intern in the social sciences department worked with me. There were lots of girls around me all the time."

"Heh, heh, heh, ha, ha, I bet there were. Did you like all those pretty girls around you?"

"Not always."

"Why was that?" Robert asked with a grin on his face.

"I do not like people feeling pity for me. I like them to treat me normally."

Robert sat back in his chair and sighed, contemplating his next few words carefully. When he finally had the words right, he leaned forward like a concerned father.

"Matthew, being normal is overrated and a cliché, to boot. Hey, I never felt like I fit in when I was your age. I was always doing voices, singing to myself, or acting out parts with the girls. I got picked on for being different. Those same people now write me letters begging for money or autographs, claiming they knew me way back when. There is nothing normal about you in the least, and that is a good thing. Don't ever let anyone tell you differently."

Robert sat back in his chair, thinking about his adolescence. He began working his tongue behind his teeth once more. Matthew went back to rocking, peacefully humming a familiar tune to himself.

"Matthew, were there a lot of messed-up kids at this Hospital? I mean, ones that can't talk? A lot of autistic children are not as lucky as you are."

"There were several; I mainly stayed with the doctors, interns, or my mother. I had two friends there. James, the janitor, and Marilyn Stephan Vanats."

Robert's interest in the conversation peaked once again, his appetite for information restored. Leaning forward, he pulled a piece of pineapple from his plate and began to eat it. "Sluuurrrrp," his lips smacked, trying to keep the juice from landing on his pants. He began to look around for a napkin, jumping up to find one while keeping one eye on his chair. The hallway now buzzed with people walking by the door.

Robert sat back down, wiping his face and hands with the napkin. "Who was Marilyn Vansats or whatever, Matthew? Was she a girlfriend?"

Matthew completely stopped rocking and turned to face Robert, looking him very seriously in the eye. "Her name is Marilyn Stephan Vanats. She is a girl, and she is my friend."

Robert knew he had struck a chord, so he pushed for more information.

"This friend who was a girl, was she like you?"

"Yes, she is a mute autistic," Matthew replied.

"I bet you guys had some interesting conversations. I mean that in a good way."

"I taught Marilyn the symbols and shapes, and we are able to communicate very well."

Robert looked down at his watch to check the time. It was getting very close to show time.

Rosie entered the room looking for something. "Did Silver dollar show yet?" Her demeanor was serious but flustered, all at once.

Robert shrugged his shoulders as if to say, "It isn't my day to watch for him."

Matthew did not pay attention to Rosie at all.

She continued, "If he isn't here by the start of the show, Mr. Duvet, you will have to stretch your time out. Matthew, we will bring you out at half past instead of the last fifteen minutes."

Matthew continued rocking and humming, ignoring Rosie.

"He is listening, right?" She turned to Robert with a look of near panic.

"Oh, he can hear you just fine. He memorizes everything. Watch this. Matthew, can you recall what Ms. Flores is wearing without looking at her?"

Matthew continued rocking, looking down and away from her. "She has on a pink cashmere cardigan sweater with a white silk shell underneath; a pink, blue, grey, and white plaid Boho mini-skirt; and black patent leather five-inch Manolo Blahnik pumps. She is also wearing a one-carat diamond solitaire engagement ring, cultured pearl earrings, a pearl choker, and a fourteen-karat-gold crucifix chain. She has a tattoo of something I cannot make out in the small of her back. There is also another tattoo of the word "Froy" on her right ankle."

Robert slapped his leg, laughing aloud and smiling ear to ear. "Amazing, isn't he? That's the damndest thing ever. Mathew, what type of underwear does she have on?" he said, being sarcastic.

Matthew answered, not understanding the sarcasm. "Considering her approximate age of twenty-five, her matching outfit, and the type of jewelry, she most likely has matching undergarments. My guess is pink from Veronica's Closet or Victoria's Secret. I would guess a thong and a push-up bra."

Rosie looked at Robert rocking back and forth in the chair, laughing, almost passing out. She seemed a little perturbed at him for encouraging Matthew. "They have navy blue trim," she answered, turning and storming out.

Matthew spoke up, "I only gave the predominant colors, not the trim."

"You are frickin' amazing, Matthew—amazing! I hope you do something like that when you go on stage."

Matthew sat there. Rock, rock, rock. Hmm, hmm, hmm. The tears dried from Robert's eyes as a somber mood fell upon the room once again. Robert knew he had pissed Rosie off, but she was young and would learn to get over it. *Not much she can do. I am a star, not a staffer for Ida. She gets paid to put up with personalities.*

"Getting back to our conversation, do you still see this girl, Marilyn?"

"No, she moved to New York when the doctors left."

Robert felt bad for asking.

"What about James. He was a close friend, you say. Tell me more about him."

"He was the janitor. We played poker at night with the cleaning staff. I also taught James some of the basic symbols. He was like me in many ways and could understand me. He suddenly died one day. We all die, eventually."

"Hey, kid, I am sorry about that. It hurts losing friends. I'm old and I've lost a lot over my years."

Silence came over the room for a few minutes. The conversation was winding down. Robert got up to go to the bathroom while Matthew sat on the sofa, rocking and humming. A loud roar could be heard echoing down the halls. The show was now on the air. Robert emerged from the bathroom, drying his hands with a paper towel.

Every few seconds, a roar of laughter and clapping, sighs, and an occasional "I love you, Ida" would erupt. Ida was daytime talk show royalty. There was none better at this type of entertainment. Even men would admit to watching her show and liking it. Her humble beginnings as a field weather reporter and a token game show model were long behind her. Mogul was a word most often associated with her now.

Rosie came back into the room. "Looks like Silver Dollar is a no-show. Mr. Duvet, you will be on an extra five. Matthew, I will come get you a few minutes before 9:30. Okay?"

Robert started to leave and then stopped, turning to face Matthew. "It's been a real pleasure, kid. Knock 'em dead. Remember, eye contact and no milk. Just be yourself, they'll love you. You can have the chair back now."

***

Rosie and Robert left the room. Matthew stood up, looked around the room, unsure of his situation, and moved over in front of the firm, black high-backed leather chair. Looking right and left for people several times, he sat back down. He began to rock back and forth, enjoying the solitude offered in such a busy studio. The familiar rustling of the leather and low hum of a content, spindly man continued.

A few minutes later, a roaring crowd echoed down the hallway, welcoming a box office legend. It ignored everything in its path, rushing through like a tsunami. The spindly man, like so many other things in his life, ignored the crashing sound waves, only concentrating on his sheltered world. He sat alone again, rocking by himself and waiting.

Rock, rock, rock. Hmm, hmm, hmm.

2 A STAR IS BORN

The audience was electrified. Every person in the crowd received a free copy of Time Magazine featuring Matthew Le'Dain on the cover. Several lesser-known Savants from around the world filled the background behind him. Robert had the crowd excited after showing his latest western-style movie clip. He moved over one seat during the break to let Matthew sit next to Ida.

The camera light turned on, the audience was prompted to applaud, and Ida turned her head to face the millions of viewers around the world. The audience burst into applause and catcalls. Ida was excited to have a different kind of guest for a change. A veteran of daytime TV, she had acted in several movies, playing minor roles and appearing as herself on various sitcoms.

Our next guest is truly one of a kind. He has traveled to every continent and over a hundred countries to entertain audiences with his intelligence. His name is Matthew Le'Dain, and he is an autistic Savant. His photographic memory enables him to read books in minutes, perform complex mental calculations, and simultaneously read two separate pages of a book.

Ida turned to Robert and asked, "Have you seen him do that weird lizard thing with his eyes yet?"

Robert shook his head no. He answered, but his microphone was not initially on, so he sounded like an echo in the room.

"Sound, can we get Robert's mic back on?"

He replied, finally, "No, Ida, I haven't."

Ida continued, "You were in the Green Room with him for some time this morning. What was your impression?"

Robert shifted uncomfortably in his chair. "Well, he is a very bright, intelligent young man. He's hard to talk to, but the way his mind works…he is quite amazing."

Ida, smiling as always with a soft, motherly expression, pressed for more information. "Robert, give us an example of something he did that was amazing?'

"He figured out in two seconds that my accountant and agent can't do simple math, even with a calculator."

The audience and Ida started laughing.

Ida held up the *Time Magazine* and showed it to the audience at home. "There are amazing people all around us. Often, we overlook individuals who are not mainstream and dismiss them. As we will see, I hope you will be more cautious about doing so after meeting our next guest. MATHEW LE'DAIN!—come on out!"

Matthew was led out by Rosie Flores. He kept his head down, not looking at the audience. When he sat down in the sculpted chair that wrapped around his body like a glove, he did not seem very happy. The chair made it impossible for him to rock. He focused on a point on the corner of Ida's desk, not making eye contact. Not being able to rock, he fidgeted about in his chair.

"Matthew, are you comfortable, sweetie?" Ida spoke in a motherly tone.

He replied with a quick, low tone, "Yes."

Satisfied he was okay, she continued, "Matthew, it says in the *Time* article you learned how to speak Norwegian in less than a day. Evidently, the Prime Minister and a wealthy businessman challenged you to do just that. They offered a $100,000 prize if you could pull it off. So how did he do, audience? Let's take a look."

The lights on stage dimmed, and a news clip began to play:

Speaking in Norwegian, Matthew was interviewed on a news show. Captions ran across the bottom of the screen for the audience and viewers at home to follow.

He and the reporter stood on a hill, its surface draped in a green carpet of lichen-encrusted rocks. Everyone was bundled up from head to toe, like an Eskimo.

"Mr. Le'Dain, how do you like Norway?"

Matthew answered in Norwegian, *"Det er veldig kaldt og blåser."*—It is very cold and windy—was translated across the bottom of the screen. His breath created several large clouds that were swept away by the chilly breeze.

"Oooh, ahhh," Ida's studio audience cooed at his answer.

"Do you like to ski, and is that anything you would ever consider doing, Mr. Le'Dain?"

"Nei, jeg liker ikke kulde, jeg er redd for høyder, og jeg har ingen ønske om å lære å gå på ski—No, I don't like the cold, I am afraid of heights, and I have no desire to learn to ski.— Matthew's accent even sounded Norwegian, but in a more even-toned inflection.

The audience clapped loudly. Clap, clap, clap.

Ida threw her hand up to quiet them down. "This is where they test him. I want you to pay close attention to how brilliantly his mind works."

"Matthew, can you demonstrate your extraordinary mathematical abilities or do any tricks to convince the audience further of your abilities?"

Matthew replied, continuing in their native tongue while the translation scrolled across the bottom of the screen. "Yes. I can determine your age using math."

The reporter replied in his thick Norwegian accent, "Yes, then let's proceed."

Matthew told the reporter, "Write down your age on a card and show it to the camera, but do not let me see it."

The reporter wrote down his age as forty-nine for the audience to see on a card. He looked over his shoulder at Matthew, who was looking down and slightly rocking. "Now, what next, Mr. Computer?" he said in a sarcastic tone.

Matthew replied, "Multiply the first number of your age by five, then add three. After you have done that, then double the number."

The reporter had some difficulty doing the math in his head, so he wrote it down. The calculations came up to forty-six.

The reporter replied to Matthew with the answer and said, "This is not my age." He smirked at the camera, thinking he had caught Matthew in a mistake, but Matthew wasn't finished yet.

Ida, making fun of the man's haste, said, "Watch now, audience, as Matthew shuts him up."

Matthew continued as if he hadn't heard the reporter's jibes. "Now, add the second digit of your age to that number and then subtract six from the total."

The reporter's eyes grew wide, his face in disbelief. "Forty-nine!" he exclaimed. "This is a trick, a child's number game! This proves nothing!"

Ida was twitching in her seat with a huge smile, as was the audience. "Give it back to him, Matthew," she said, reaching over and lightly grabbing Matthew's arm in support.

Next, Matthew hit him hard with his follow-up. "It is 1:23 p.m. here. What day and time were you born?"

The reporter hesitated and then said, "September 19, 1963, at approximately noon, and today is September 16th."

Matthew's eyes changed right in front of the camera, becoming glassy and distant, taking only a split second in real time. If the camera could have peered inside his mind, it would have seen: *Matthew's mind slows as if he were taking picture frames with a high-speed camera. When played back, he can see, with perfect clarity, a bullet ripping through a playing card or a horse running while all four legs are off the ground at the same time.*

Images immediately enter his mind: a long, white corkscrew shape representing time on a calendar that stretches out like a spring in his mind; and then the spring quickly contracts and bursts into a yellow, misshapen three-dimensional bubble that has both mass and volume. Synaptic impulses surge around the shape, measuring it down to the nearest second until numbers are drawn and sent back to his conscious mind.

Without hesitation, Matthew said, "You have been alive 18,258 days, thirteen hours, twenty-three minutes, and sixteen seconds or 1,577,539,396 seconds, as of right…now." Matthew was pointing at his atomic watch.

The reporter turned, smiling in amazement, and said, "I am convinced." Then the camera turned to a man off-camera who had a calculator that showed the exact number, down to the second.

Ida clapped loudly, and the audience erupted with amazement and intrigue, clapping and hooting at the stage.

Matthew covered his ears to shield the loud noise and muffle the audience near the end of the clip. The noise, stress, and attention were forcing him to employ some of his coping mechanisms.

Robert looked as if he was preparing for another outburst from Matthew, but luckily, it never came. Ida breathed a sigh of relief.

"Matthew even added leap years in his calculation," Ida chirped. "Wow. Was that something else or what? When we come back after the break, we will select an audience member to challenge Matthew to a reading contest. Stay tuned. We'll be right back."

Music from offstage cued, and the camera lights on the stage were switched off. One camera caught the audience waving and saying "Hi" as the camera panned the crowd. A few held up the *Time Magazine* showing Matthew.

Ida consoled Matthew during the break, trying to calm him while Robert sat quietly with a half-smile on his face, obviously enjoying the show, reaching down to take a sip of water.

"Matthew, are you all right, honey? Is something bothering you?" asked Ida, speaking softly.

"Too noisy, too noisy," he replied, fidgeting, moving his knees up and down, drumming his fingers on the chair.

Ida motioned for the stage manager. "Can you quiet the audience? Some of the noise is a little too loud for Matthew."

The sound guy quickly ran back to the control room, posting a message on the monitors for the audience to refrain from clapping and to refrain from catcalls during the break.

Then Ida's camera light cued, and she turned to face the camera. "During the break, I was chatting with Matthew," she said, reaching over to softly touch his arm. "The noise in the audience was a bit too loud last segment for Matthew's comfort. So, the audience at home may recognize it is a little quieter than normal here, and I wanted you to know why."

The camera zoomed in on Matthew, who had settled down.

"Matthew has thrown down the gauntlet and will challenge an audience member to a reading comprehension contest. I have seen this before, and it is, in a word, amazing. The game on his tour is called *Total Recall*. Basically, we will hand Matthew a book, and he will have two minutes to read one chapter. We will ask a question, and if he gets it right, he wins, and if he gets it wrong, you win. What do we have for him today, Bob?"

A moderator's voice came over a loudspeaker. "Today, the lucky member will win an e-reader tablet from *iRead, along with a one-year paid subscription to iRead Books*."

The audience began to clap and hoot, but Ida quickly threw her hand up to quiet them down.

"Matthew, have you ever read this book before?" She handed him a Sci-Fi thriller entitled *Exoskeleton* by Jeff Scott."

"No," Matthew replied after reviewing the cover of the book.

"Camera two, I want you to get a good close-up of Matthew's eyes as he reads. This is simply astounding," said Ida, and then explained what was about to happen. "Each of his eyes will focus on a single page independently. It looks almost like the way a sand lizard's eyes work."

During the previous break, a woman named Patrice Sanchez from Avondale, Arizona, had been selected for the challenge. The camera zoomed in on her for just a moment.

"Okay, Matthew, Patrice chose chapter seven. You have two minutes, starting now."

A clock displayed on a stage monitor counted down the seconds from one hundred twenty towards zero.

Camera Two zoomed in on Mathew's eyes. Each eye moved independently, one from the other, in different directions, reading its own page. Every eight seconds or so, Matthew flipped a page in the book. Chapter Seven was about seventeen pages long, but the first and last pages were only half a page. With three seconds left, Matthew closed the book and sat waiting.

The audience had started to chant the last ten-second countdown, but Ida quickly quieted the crowd by shushing them.

Rosie was standing on the steps with a microphone in her hand. Next to her was Patrice.

Ida looked up at them and asked, "Patrice, have you finished reading Chapter Seven?"

The middle-aged woman leaned into the microphone and said, "Most of it."

Ida smiled. "How long did it take you?"

The woman fidgeted and replied, "Counting the break and what time we have been back, about eight minutes."

"How far did you get in that time period?" Ida said, knowing that she had probably read about ten pages.

"I read through about ten pages or so," she said, acting a little embarrassed.

Ida laughed, saying, "That's about average. I just wanted to show the audience at home this is no gimmick and about how long the average person takes to read a page. Most people, on a book like this, read about a minute a page."

Robert was watching the audience's reaction while Matthew rocked as best he could, appearing to pay no attention to them at all.

"How much do you think you retained during that time, Patrice?"

"Not very much," she replied, still embarrassed.

Ida could tell she was feeling awkward, and she tried to console her.

"Before the show, Bob, Rosie, and I tried this, and we averaged about a minute a page, but only retained the general idea of the chapter, with very few details. When we come back from the break, I will have Patrice ask Matthew to recite a single line from the book."

The audience groaned, having to go to another commercial break. Ida did this to heighten the anticipation and, as always, to pay the bills. The camera lights switched off once again.

Ida put her hand gently on Matthew's arm, stroking it. "Matthew, sweetie, are you still doing all right?"

Fidget, fidget. Hmm, hmm, hmm. "Yes, I'm fine."

Robert smiled, looked back at Ida, and shrugged his shoulders before saying, "He squirmed around like this the entire time backstage. He's fine."

But Ida was worried about him. She coddled him as much as she could to keep him calm.

Okay, I just want to make sure the audience at home knows that Matthew hasn't seen the book since he read it nearly five minutes ago. Robert Duvet has been keeping me straight here and will confirm the truth, as will my audience here. Okay, Patrice, will you ask Matthew to recite any line in Chapter Seven? Counting down the page, line by line, please pick the first complete sentence you come to.

Patrice cleared her voice, speaking with a slight southwest accent, and said, "Matthew, page eighty-three, line seven. Could you read this back to me?"

Without hesitation, Matthew stopped rocking. He spoke in his methodical, robotic monotone and recited the sentence word for word back to her. "*I took a cab down to Delucca's for breakfast, the food there is great and you can't beat the service.*"

Patrice's eyes grew two sizes larger. She developed a look of amazement and remained silent for a few seconds. Glaring at her copy of *Exoskeleton*, she said, "That's it exactly. Word for word, that's it. Amazing."

The audience clapped, and Ida gestured towards Matthew with her hands, as if to yield to him the glory of the moment.

Rock, rock, rock. Hmm, hmm, hmm.

"Patrice, we already knew you would not win this game, so to be fair, you get to keep the autographed, hardback copy of *Exoskeleton* by JS Stone. Mr. Stone, can you wave at the audience?" The author was sitting towards the front-center and stood up to wave. "He is an amazing Sci-fi/Thriller writer. Also, you get the *iReader* and the subscription to *iRead Books*."

Patrice hopped up and down and clapped.

"When we come back from the commercial break, you will meet one of the hottest Rap Artists today—the one and only—Silver Dollar. Evidently, he made it here after all, and he has a new song he will share when we return. Stay Tuned."

Robert stood up and moved down to the last chair. Ida helped Matthew up and moved him down one more seat.

Patrice sat down and showed her young daughter the new *iReader* she had won.

Rosie went backstage and waited for her next cue.

"Matthew, are you doing okay?" Ida asked, to be sure.

Matthew replied, "Yes." Rock, rock, rock. Hmm, hmm, hmm.

The show was almost over, and to save time, Ida brought Silver Dollar out. He was dressed in a $60,000 pair of sterling silver Air Jordans, untied with the laces dragging on the floor, baggy jeans that revealed the black waistband of his white Versace briefs, no shirt, and an L.A. Buccaneers team logo hat with the bill turned around sideways. His ebony skin was covered in tats, he had silver-capped teeth, and he had at least a dozen silver chains around his neck. His fingernails were even capped with pure silver.

The camera light switched on, and Ida perked up. She held up a new CD on the corner of her desk so the camera could zoom in on it. It showed Silver Dollar with a wheelbarrow full of silver dollars spilling off the sides.

"Welcome back, everyone. Our next guest is top-selling Rap Artist, Steven White, but you all know him as Silver Dollar."

The younger audience members started to scream, but Ida quickly quieted them down.

"Silver, we are running short on time. You said you met Matthew backstage and you guys had prepared a little song for us."

"Yeh, you know…he is a real interestin' dude. Caught one of his shows when I's in Vegas. He is the real deal. This cat is the smartest man in the world; I kid you not. We mixed up somethin' for y'all backstage. He's got great rhythm, so we wanted to show y'all what he could do. Check this out!"

Mathew was rocking and humming in a constant, melodic beat.

Silver Dollar looked at Matthew and said, "Come on, Matthew. Let's bust this out. Can you pick it up a little?"

Matthew rocked harder and hummed as loud as he could, slamming his back against the hard chair and making a funny burst of sound as if he were beating the air from his body.

Silver Dollar stood up and began to rap, with Matthew supplying the beat: *"I am Matt Le'Dain…I have dis thang…I can 'member almos' everythang….Since I was three…I was slappin' my knee…wowing all da people wit my magic brain."*

***

From somewhere out in TV land, a man who was miles away sat watching the rapping duo. When they finished, he lifted the remote and turned off the television. The room he was in was dark, lit only by a small lamp in the corner. He tossed the remote onto the desk and sat back, resting his elbows on the arms of his red leather, high-backed chair, fingertips touching. He opened his mouth slightly to speak but never did. Bouncing his index fingers across his mouth, he stood up and walked out of the room. His white lab coat billowed as he hurried out.

3 ILLUMINATION

Matthew's mother sat holding the phone, trying to talk to her inattentive husband—an almost daily ritual. She could tell by the way he grunted that he wasn't truly listening. She knew when the oblivious man on the other end, with his slight French-American accent, put the phone on speaker and went about his business. She could hear all the noises in the room and the faint sensation of talking through the bottom of a well. She didn't know why she even bothered anymore. He cared more about his business, neglecting and ignoring his wife, who bore the heavy responsibility of caring for a son with obvious social and developmental issues.

If you added them up, it was clear to see that these issues were mounting. Pressure was building, and something had to give soon.

***

The man scanned the list in his mind, trying to be more supportive: *four before he was potty trained; slow-developing speech skills; slow to walk. More obvious were the constant and sometimes annoying rocking and humming.* He felt guilty for even thinking a thought like this, but even for the oblivious man, something was eating at him, and something had to give.

He had no time for this, but he knew ignoring the issue would only make it worse. The oblivious man had no time for anything else in his life, let alone a god. His god was work, and his work made him complete. It made him feel normal. This trait was welcomed at his place of employment, but scorned and despised where he rested his head at night.

The oblivious man began to think hard about the positive spin. After all, his job and training led him to spin things in his favor or that of his political candidate. He entertained this for a few seconds, but the droning voice over the phone made him relinquish his selfish thoughts.

"Are you listening to me?" she barked.

"Yes, dear." The oblivious man replied disdainfully.

Spin. The oblivious man began to add up the positives: *He is creative, a great artist, and seems to be an intellectual. Besides, I have my own bad habits. I like my solitude wherever I can get it. Everyone has issues. Why are we making such a fuss about it? It's not as if he's hurting anyone.*

The oblivious man found that rationalizing his thoughts helped to ease the pain of reality.

She broke through his defenses again in another wave of attacks. "Have you ever counted Matthew's emotions? He only has about five or six real emotions. He is completely fine staring at the television or playing video games for hours on end. He at least smiles and grunts out a laugh occasionally."

The oblivious man heard that loud and clear. "What do you think we should do about it?"

She sounded more exasperated than ever. "I have been trying to tell you. He needs help, a psychiatrist, a psychologist, a child development expert—I don't really know. You know your son could fail first grade? Fail first grade! Who fails first grade?"

***

The boy for whom so much concern and ignorance had been placed got up from his rocking spot and turned off the television. He walked to the kitchen table, where his homework was sitting. His mother was still talking nonstop, glancing at him now and then to make sure he wasn't doing anything wrong, continuing to puke out her concern, hopelessness, and frustration to the oblivious man.

The young boy selected three crayons, specifically yellow, blue, and green. He looked at the basic math worksheet. He studied it with his left eye while his right eye was looking for a blank sheet of paper. The lesson was on the point method, and his mother had spent all day trying to get him to understand it.

He took a blank sheet of paper, drew two small shapes on the outside and one large shape in the middle. Occasionally, one eye was looking at something completely different than the other. His mother had noticed this oddity before, but he hadn't heard her mention it again. He'd heard the doctors say they had tested his vision every year and found no cause for alarm.

When he finished his latest doodle, the three shapes were all touching, just like before. He had carefully colored them in, staying inside the lines and highlighting the edges with a darker shade of the inner color. Yellow was labeled with the number four for the first time. The blue had the number five, and the green, in the middle, had a nine.

The boy had been repeating this ritual all day, but without the numbers. This was a noticeable change. His mother had scolded him several times earlier, but he remained unemotional and ignored her.

***

She was watching him from the other room. She saw the picture, becoming aggravated and dismayed. She ranted at the oblivious man, placing the blame squarely on him or his lack of action. "See, he did it again. The pictures—all day long with those damn doodles."

The oblivious man retorted, "Well, take away the crayons, then. What do you want me to do about it from work?

***

The oblivious man's thoughts wandered wildly now. When he was under stress, his mind would race out of control. He turned to look out the window onto the campus. Several students were walking and talking; a group on the lawn was discussing something and laughing loudly; a young woman he thought he recognized was jogging by in tight shorts and a runner's half-top, her brown ponytail flipping back and forth in stride with her bobbing head.

"I am going to go now! You're obviously not listening, anyway." She hung up before the oblivious man could say goodbye.

He pulled his eyes back into his head, breaking the suction from the jogging ass he'd been watching. He lunged for the phone and grabbed the receiver, but it was too late. She was gone. Looking around to make sure no one saw his embarrassment, he replaced the earpiece on its mount and leaned back in his chair, letting out a long sigh. A typical day returning to devour his mind. He would probably get at least four more calls today, he thought.

***

Seething with fury, she took a deep breath and then walked around the counter, trying to get back to her sweet, trademark demeanor. "Matthew, go get your book bag for mommy, please. I laid it in the entryway."

The boy got up without a word and left, not looking back. His little legs chopped methodically, but he never ran at a steady pace.

She began grabbing papers and separating them into three stacks: garbage, assignments, and doodles. Even though she despised the doodles, something in the dark recesses of her infantile mind spoke to her: *save them*. She wasn't sure why, but they held meaning for her. They were a part of him and a part of her. The two could not be separated. The artwork was modern and abstract at the same time. One by one, she laid them down until she came to the last one.

She gazed at it very closely. It was different than before. There were numbers in the colors, a new feature. She picked up the doodle and held it out in the distance. Behind the doodle, along the wall, sat a baker's rack. Arranged on the top shelf were three ceramic jars. They were different colors and different sizes, but they were the same shape. Just the day before, she had been dusting them and had set them in a different order, just to mix it up. To the left was a smaller, yellow one, to the right a medium-sized blue jar, and in the middle a larger green jar. There was a very large red jar to the far right, but she ignored it.

Moving the doodle in front of her view of the jars, and then down, she noticed something. She turned towards the living room coffee table.

Sitting on top of it were wooden colored building blocks. There were several groups of three blocks set up in the same fashion. Something began to stir in her mind. A pain very nearly the strength of an aneurysm beat from her heart to the back of her head.

Something new, something miraculous, something divine. Her face started to contort. A tear slipped from her eye and landed on her cheek involuntarily. Her body tensed and then relaxed. She felt sick and overjoyed at the same time. She tried to speak, but her throat was clamped shut. She struggled to breathe, and her cheeks flushed with blood. Her chest pounded so loudly she could hear each beat. More tears fell, and she lost her ability to stand.

She fell to her knees trying to thank God. She was so strangled with emotion that intelligible words escaped her. A strange tongue spoke to the heavens above, but she clearly understood what she was saying and knew that the master of all living things did, as well.

She began to think more clearly. *How could I have missed this the entire time? I am a horrible mother.* She knew he had the answer right here, *but I missed it.*

She regained her footing and raced to the bedroom. Thudding on the floor, she landed on her knees, ignoring the pain of the hardwood floor and reaching for the secret box. The plastic container she had once looked at with shame. Sliding it out, she tore the lid off and began to sift through the mounds of doodles. Some she remembered as associations with math and others with letters. They were clues. They were mysteries solved. They were glorious signs from above. They were emancipation.

The young boy walked to the bedroom door and stopped just inside. He watched with no apparent emotion as his mother threw his artwork into the air and rolled around in it as if it were a hundred-dollar bill she'd just won at a casino.

She noticed the young boy named Matthew, her son, for the very first time. A boy, a much different boy, had been living here before, but now it was Matthew's house for the first time.

Matthew asked, "Mommy, is something wrong?"

She still couldn't speak very clearly, still choked by emotion, but managed to say, "Nothing is wrong, sweetie, everything is going to be much better now, for all of us."

She raised herself up, took Matthew by the hand, and led him back to the kitchen table. "Matthew, can you show mommy the answer to this problem?"

Matthew tried to start answering it the traditional way. "No…no…sweetie, like this one, the drawing you made a few seconds ago."

Without hesitation, Matthew did it again, then again, then again.

Then, she had him do subtraction as well. She was ecstatic, frightened, surprised, and crushed, all at the same time.

She grabbed the phone and called the unaware man. He was teaching a class. Usually, he would say whatever he needed to in order to end the call. But this time, he didn't. He listened to her. Somehow, it finally clicked.

***

The oblivious man turned to face his class with his jaw sagging to the floor and mumbled, "*I have to leave now. Class is dismissed.*"

A few of the young, mini-skirted women in the front row saw his new expression but decided to leave without questioning the free day off.

***

A few days later, Matthew and his mother arrived at the Children's Hospital complex. A sign on the office door said: *Dr. Gottfried Dimment and Dr. Lawrence Meacham*. She had finally defeated the ignorance of the oblivious man.

4 *SIDE SHOW FREAK*

Lea Tootchie was a publicist, a ladder climber, and a vixen. Like Matthew, she'd had to overcome humble beginnings. Some people struggled their entire lives. Some with a leg up struggled to overcome the doubts of others. Lea was an amalgam of the two, having to break free of the chains of her mind and also the underestimation of her talents by others. Normally, she was on her game. But lately, apartment shopping and her boyfriend, Vincent, have distracted her.

Lea was supposed to protect Matthew from the media wolves. The punishment for failing to do so was facing Mamma Bear's wrath, and she was well aware of it—Penthea Le'Dain, or Penny to her friends. Lea knew that Penthea watched over Matthew like a shepherd guarding his flock.

Born in Brooklyn, Lea always dreamed of getting into New York show business. But those dreams were shattered when her father, a transit driver, was shot and killed after taking a wrong turn and ending up on the wrong side of town, after dark, in Queens. The gang responsible for his death was after a load of vacuum cleaners—the police report said nothing was taken from the truck except the driver's wallet and a wedding band.

After her father's death, Lea and her mother moved away from family and friends to escape the pain of reality, settling in Cambridge. It's not exactly a hub for entertainment types. But through perseverance and circumstance, Lea's mother was hired for a position in the university's registration office, which gave her daughter the opportunity to attend Harvard. With grants and donations from her family, she graduated—near the bottom of her class, but she did graduate anyway.

A degree in business marketing from such a respected institution was nothing to dismiss, she constantly reminded herself. Once she was in the real world, all employers would see was the degree. Without rankings on a degree, Lea's diploma was just as valuable as that of the President of a Fortune 500 company or a college Dean. Combining Brooklyn street smarts with a formal education made her a powerful mix. Lea was always chasing the BBD—the Bigger Better Deal. That's what Penny admired about her.

Vincent, on the other hand, was nothing but baggage, a tool she would take out and use when she needed coital amusement. Lea knew in her heart he would be replaced by someone better—*sooner rather than later*. He was affecting her work now, and that was simply not acceptable. When she applied for the job, it was like a symphony. When she lost focus, as she did today, disastrous things would befall everyone around her.

Penny is going to come in here bitchin' and moanin' about her precious little boy any minute now. All he is to her is a cash cow. If he were underage, she would have called child services on her. Lea did not really believe it, but lying to herself made her feel better. *She spends every minute of every day wiping his ass—literally, I'll bet. I wonder if he goes to the bathroom by himself. Of course he does. I forgot, he obsessively goes to the bathroom: washing his hands on the plane, using sanitizer in the cab, washing them in the studio, and using sanitizer after shaking someone's hand—surprised he doesn't insist on doing the Howie Mandell knuckle bump. He can probably see microscopic bacteria with his lizard eyes. He is one screwed-up dude, but for now, he is my little screwed-up paycheck.*

Appearing on a music television show in New York was a huge risk. Lea knew Penny was against it at first, but for once, she allowed her guard to drop. She was going to be so pissed.

Oh, well. No pain, no gain. He needs to be accepted by a wider audience, or in a few years, he'll be a has-been. Just another clown who can remember two hundred names in the audience. The blue sports coat with the equations, calculator, and computer looks nice. Just not on him. He is a sideshow freak. Brantley was right.

Matthew was sitting in the large conference room with Lea on the fifth floor of a studio overlooking a partial view of Times Square. His back was to the window, ignoring the beautiful cityscape just over his shoulder as he amused himself. Rock, rock, rock, Hmm, hmm, hmm.

Still waiting for Penny to storm into the room like a hurricane, Lea gawked at Matthew sitting by the window overlooking Times Square, doing what he did best. Crossing her arms and leaning on one foot, she rocked her right foot side-to-side, nervously waiting for Mamma Bear to crash into the party. Tapping and rocking her foot had always eased her anxiety. *I wonder what that little nub is thinking about. Girls? Sex? Cars? Not a fucking chance! He's gyrating on taking π to infinity, or else creating a new programming language. It wasn't fair that a screwed up, no-life, brain fart like him gets the lion's share of brains. The rest of us have to spend half our lives learning ten percent of what he accomplishes in a year. What a freakin' waste of talent!*

Click, click, click, click, the heels of Penny's shoes stabbed the marble flooring of the Network hallway. They were growing louder; the looming confrontation sounded like a bell at a prizefight.

Lea prepared herself, tensing up and getting ready to respond. Penny was a seasoned pro and could handle herself against anyone. Lea briefly thought highly of her: she really is a great agent. Snapping out of her thoughts, she remembered why Penny was there.

Penny entered the room, heading directly for Matthew and deliberately ignoring Lea. Seeing that he was in his spot, she walked over with clear contempt and stopped just three feet from Lea. She was barely within Lea's personal space, enough to show she meant business but far enough to avoid a physical confrontation—after all, they were not enemies.

At the far end of the massive mahogany conference table from Matthew, the two women mentally fought each other. But a cheetah can't compete with a mother bear defending her cub.

Lea, do I need to remind you that your top priority is to protect Matthew? You should have vetted the show more thoroughly. Just because it's the most popular show on the network doesn't mean it's suitable for Matthew. The host is a British reject. Just look at him, he's upset now.

Lea and Penny turned to look at Matthew, who was rocking and humming. Aside from the age difference, they mirrored each other's body language, their arms crossed and their feet tapping. Lea longed to blurt out what she dared not say: *How can you tell? That's all he does. He rocks and hums. How am I supposed to sell that to a younger crowd? Just once, I'd like a real client. No! I always get stuck with Rainman.*

"Penny, I know my job. Don't tell me how to do it. He needs to be marketable to a diverse audience to have staying power. Just entertaining blue hairs and late-night crowds is not going to make for a long career."

Penny whispered softly, making sure Matthew didn't hear her, "Do you know that little prick called him a Side Show Freak! Are you going to put that on his resume? Is that good press for the National Autism Foundation? Does that make for a lasting career?"

Seeing no way for her to win this debate, Lea quickly conceded. "I am sorry. I'll do a better job vetting next time. Even the Network admitted this guy is a douche-bag. He's a loose cannon and very controversial. But he's what's in right now. The in-your-face attitude is what younger people thrive on. He's a Brit. What do you expect from a foreigner?"

The lines around Penny's eyes grew more defined when she was upset, and Lea could count every single one right now. Her nostrils flared, almost pointing up. "I expect you to do your job. If there *is* a next time, there won't *be* a next time. Understood?"

The words hung over Lea's head like a dark cloud. She seemingly ignored them at first, looking off to the side of Penny, not making eye contact.

Penny kept her eyes locked on Lea like a missile defense system target. "*Understood?*"

"Understood," Lea spat, then turned, stiffening her body and making a fist with her left hand while squeezing her phone with her right until it powered on. Then, she jumped up and marched toward the door, angrily poking at the cell phone's screen. She stormed down the hallway, trying to pull up her missed text messages from Vincent. The damned thing had vibrated at least a dozen times in the last five minutes. He probably needs money, a ride, or food.

Lea hurried down the hallway with determination. She passed several doors, noticing Brantley, the host, staring smugly back at her from one of the offices along her escape route.

What a little prick, she thought as she smirked at him. Her eyes were so squinted she could barely see where she was going. I know exactly what to do with little pricks. Vincent was unaware of what was coming, but he was about to get the best sex of his short life and then be kicked to the curb like a used beer can.

Lea would usually have called a limousine, but in New York, they weren't worth the time or money because everyone used them. She liked to use them when they would be noticed. At 2:07 p.m. on a Wednesday, no one would care. She was only going about twenty blocks, and a cab would be the fastest way.

Vincent lived in a modest, rent-controlled building downtown. The street outside was littered with trash and was populated by human urchins wandering about. The deli, bar, and coffee house were the best things about his neighborhood.

Lea tipped the cabby, and he drove off, flipping his sign to pick up the next client. The street was almost deserted. Nearly stumbling over a man digging in the trash, she trotted to the top of the steps.

Standing there, Lea felt like she was being watched. A cold shiver ran from the base of her neck all the way to her tailbone. She buzzed the apartment. Looking back at the empty street, she noticed the creepy trash can man looking at her like he was raping her with his mind. She smirked at him with her best Brooklyn attitude to let him know: *Don't F-ing' mess with me, bitch, I am in no mood for it today.*

The trash can man smiled at her, showing his missing front teeth, as if to say, *wanna come out and play?* Most likely a meth addict, the city was full of them. He dropped an empty bottle, after shaking it several times, back into the trash can. The man wiped his hands on his dirty overcoat and turned towards Lea.

She buzzed again, hitting the button several times, as if it would miraculously make the door come open. Lea stared through the empty hallway behind the glass door, praying someone would be leaving the building in a few seconds. A strange feeling of sadness overtook her. It felt just like the day she overheard the police officer telling her mother that Daddy would not be coming home that night. A small spark flared deep inside her gut, but an even stronger feeling of helplessness was dousing it out.

The man began to climb the steps. Lea panicked, fumbling with her purse as she reached inside, groping with her fingers, keeping her eyes on the bum. Feeling around for the pepper spray, her heart sank when she remembered that she had decided not to take it so she could carry the smaller handbag today. "Dammit," she barked at the purse.

When he was halfway up the stoop, he began to grunt at her. "You sure are one fine lookin' bitch. I bet you taste as sweet as a Georgia peach," he mumbled.

Lea knew she was in real trouble. Instinctively, she began formulating a defense strategy in her mind.

He was chanting like a demon out loud, but not really to her, as he ascended up the steps, clopping his worn-out shoes down hard on the concrete steps. "I ain't had no peaches in a long time, that is sure enough true." The deranged bum talked schizophrenically to himself, not expecting any replies. "Peach pudding, peach pie, peach tea for me to try. Going to the country, gonna eat a lot of peaches. Peaches and cream, I sure am hungry for me some peaches and cream."

Women are raped in broad daylight on the street all the time, Lea thought in full-out panic. She looked around and thought, *in a city of millions, how can this be the only street where no one else was outside? The only street where no cars were passing by.* In the distance, on the main thoroughfare, she could see hundreds of cars, but none here.

Her eyes had completely focused on the bum, still mumbling vulgar comments to himself as he slowly eased up the steps, topping the stairs while hanging onto the handrail. Something suddenly welled up inside her, and the spark became a flame. She reconciled in her mind that she was not going down without a fight to the death. *This prick is going to know he was in a fight*, she thought to herself, not knowing if she said it aloud or not.

After he had reached the landing she was standing on, she could smell his piss-stained pants mixed with body odor so strong her eyes burned from the ammonia. He reached out to touch her hair, and she smacked his arm away.

He smiled again, once more displaying his missing front teeth. The ones that were left had a black and yellow buildup. A rotten, decayed odor poured from his gums like a waterfall of rotting bodies. "Listen, you little smug bitch, I am gonna pump you, dead or alive. You may as well enjoy it too."

The bum lunged, grabbing her shoulders, trying to pull her to the ground. Lea's skills from the defense class kicked in. She knead him in the groin. As he winced and fell to his knees, she kicked him square in the chest, breaking her heel off from her favorite shoes. *Expensive ones, the asshole!* The bum tumbled down the steps to the bottom, landing at Vincent's feet.

Lea's heart jumped. She hadn't even seen him jog up. Vincent grabbed the bum by his jacket collar and shoved him down the sidewalk. The bum staggered to his feet, grabbing the wrought iron railing. Turning back to Lea and Vincent, he spat out, "Screw you, screw you both! Stupid bitch! Your peaches are probably rotten anyway!"

Vincent yelled back in his best Italian accent, "Git outta here, ya bum!"

He had been out jogging and was covered in salty sweat mixed with *Nior* cologne. Running up the steps, he hugged Lea, trying to reassure her.

Lea was not as frightened by the event as she thought she would be. Adrenaline was still pulsing through her body. She felt empowered; she felt vindicated. She did not feel like a victim, but an aggressor. She felt warm and excited.

She pulled back from Vincent, looking at his sweaty body with complete lust. Pulling up his T-shirt, she ran her hands across his six-pack, sliding her hand down into his jogging shorts and squeezing his manhood in broad daylight. "Let's go upstairs. I have something for you," she said, smiling with hunger in her lips.

Vincent started to say something, but Lea reached out and put her index finger over his mouth to shush him. She leaned up on her toes and kissed his lips lightly. Before pulling away, however, she suddenly bit his bottom lip hard, causing it to bleed.

"Ow," Vincent cried, clutching his mouth in his hand. He looked down at his finger and saw a small dot of blood. "What did you do that for?"

She felt excited by his shocked look, knowing it was rare for her to be so dominant. She took his hand, noticing the building key ready to unlock the door. Guiding him like a lost puppy to his mother's teat, she helped him slide the key into the lock. The door opened, and they stumbled inside, their bodies so close they could have been mistaken for conjoined twins.

Kissing and groping each other, they traveled as one moving body slowly up the stairs. Vincent's shirt hit the floor in the hallway. At the top of the step, Lea kicked off the broken heeled shoe first and then the good one. One of them bounced down the steps, banging and echoing with each drop. She shoved Vincent into the wall, grinding herself on his pelvis and kissing his bruised lips. His arousal was clearly visible now through his tight jogging shorts. Reaching under her mini skirt, she slipped off her panties, dropping them to the floor and then kicking them away with her foot.

Lea knew that after this, she would be gone. She wanted to leave him with something to remember her by, just in case she needed him down the road. Always leave them wanting more.

An Asian woman opened the door next to his apartment. Sticking her head out, she angrily barked at them. "Take that shit inside. No one wants to see your skinny white asses dry humping in the hallway."

Laughing together, Vincent tried to find the keyhole to the door. He probably couldn't see because Lea's arms were still wrapped around him, and her hands were clawing at his head and body. She reached down again and helped Vincent find the lock. He slid the key in, and the door opened with one quick thrust to the right.

Still conjoined, they fell through the door. Lea smirked at the Asian woman who was standing in the hallway with her hands on her hips. Then, Vincent kicked the door shut.

5 *GRAVITY*

Penny turned to look at her son. The one for whom she had dedicated her life, sacrificed her career.

Rock, rock, rock, Hmm, hmm, hmm. The black leather chair rustled in rhythm to the city beat outside.

She wondered, after every upsetting event, whether she was doing the right thing. Matthew needed to survive in the world. He needed enough income to live comfortably without them for the rest of his life. She reminded herself of this during quiet meditation. She knew of no other career for him to earn such good money for doing so little work. Matthew could not handle the anxiety and stress that came with working with others in a confined office environment. Manual labor was out of the question, and working in the field of science required communication skills. Matthew was not a master of any of these things.

Matthew had gradually become more social during his travels. He was now much more likely to engage with others, even strangers. His mother's careful, situational mentoring had helped Matthew develop some social skills, but it was as slow as watching grass grow. However, she saw this as a good thing. Her main concern was that his progress was so slow she didn't want him to ever reach a point where she wasn't needed. With Matthew Senior always away, she needed to feel this way. Dr. Meachum and Dr. Dimment had encouraged her to help Matthew get more involved with people. She knew that they, too, were wolves—just right, in the same sense.

In her meditative gaze, she did not at first notice that Matthew had stopped rocking. She watched, still not fully aware, as he stood up, picked up his briefcase, and walked towards her. He placed the case on the end of the table and opened it. *Click,* went the hasp with a metallic twang, jarring her full attention. Inside the case was a clutter of electronics: handheld games, a laptop, a notebook, as well as writing and coloring tools. Reaching into a pocket of the briefcase, Matthew retrieved a magazine. On the front of the *Insider's Medical Journal*, Drs.

Meachum and Dimment graced the cover. The headline read: NEW LANGUAGE, NEW ALPHABET, NEW HOPE FOR AUTISM PATIENTS.

Penny turned away, briefly collecting her thoughts, and then turned back to face Matthew, knowing what was about to come. His show of affection was minimal at best, most of the time; with Marilyn, it was almost visible.

Penny blurted out a somewhat jealous reply. "I don't think seeing Marilyn will be such a good idea," she exclaimed without waiting for the question. Penny tried to head off the inevitable fact that Matthew might be growing up in ways she never thought possible.

Matthew swayed in his stance, head turned down and away, gently rocking to and fro. "I want to see her. She is my friend."

Since leaving the Children's Hospital almost four years ago, Matthew had not seen Marilyn Vanats or the doctors. She didn't want to return to the clinical lifestyle and definitely did not want Matthew living in that world again. A world behind glass with people tapping their fingers at you like a fish in a tank. Matthew is now an adult. She doesn't have guardianship rights over him, only power of attorney for his finances. Her reason for this was to let him live independently and start building a life for himself, preparing for the time she's no longer there. But as long as she lives, she will always be there for him.

No. No way. This was not the time or the place. He is just starting to become a household name. Not that girl again—the mute harlot.

Matthew turned to look up at her with a soulful, pleading expression, something she knew he had learned to do, as all children do to get their way. He looked into her eyes the same way he had done on rare occasions when he was a child. It was enough to let her know he was in there. He was in there, and he was alive. He was not a lizard, but a boy; he was not a zombie, but a human being. That look was enough to make her press on many times when she wanted to quit and move on. She could have been a professor and left Matthew to the institutions. She shuddered at the thought, beating herself up mentally, and the thought left her as quickly as it had come.

Matthew crooked a smile, one of his limited emotions. "I want to visit Marilyn, and I am going, even if you say no."

Defiance. That was a new emotion for him. He had just developed a new feeling. With that, she knew he was serious. He was, after all, a young man now, in his early twenties, but he still only had the social skills of a very young child.

Penny turned to leave the conference room. She paused at the door, then looked back at her son. "Matthew, I have to take care of some business with the Network. We'll discuss Marilyn later. No one treats my son the way Brantley did and gets away with it. Once I bring up our attorney, I'm sure I can get them to see reason. Just wait here, and I'll be right back."

Tears fell from Penthea Le'Dain's eyes. She quickly wiped them away as she stormed down the hall toward Brantley, who was about to get a spanking for his earlier comments. Mamma Bear was protecting her cub. Penny stopped at the entrance of Brantley's office. He was sitting at his desk, messing with his phone, playing bubble pop, and talking on the speakerphone.

Brantley eyed Penny, his expression smug. "Have to go, Mum. I have a visitor."

The voice on the other end sounded desperate. "Brantley, your father is having bypass surgery tomorrow. I could really use your help right now."

Penny bent over and tapped the corner of his desk with one long, blood red talon on her index finger.

Brantley sat up and put the phone down. "Mum, I have to go now. I'll call you back."

Penny hung up the phone for him. Reaching back with her foot, she slammed the door and began to tear him apart. She did not need any help taking care of an up-and-coming squint like Brantley Mars.

53

***

Outside the closed door, a passerby heard a loud woman's voice and a weak, pathetic English stutter. The man laughed aloud and then moved on.

6 SENSORY OVERLOAD

Penny's heels clicked loudly on the polished tile as she left the conference room, triggering a solemn memory in Matthew of the melodic sound of war drums from a distant Indian tribe ready to do battle. Matthew was not interested in any of the endeavors Lea and his mother embraced, but he did not interfere, just the same. The heels, those clicking heels, meant much more to Matthew. He took mental notes of everything in his world. His senses were perfectly balanced. He did not rely on any one sense more than the other, like most people who use their eyes and have poor memory. Matthew was perfect in every way imaginable when you considered his sensory perceptions.

The wiring inside Matthew's mind was connected to all his senses. Sight, sound, taste, smell, and touch all worked together within his body to create perfect, three-dimensional memories. When he thought about something, he experienced it again in his mind exactly as it had happened. Matthew had looked at scans of his brain from tests at the Children's Hospital when the doctor was out of the room. His brain used nearly half of its capacity, unlike the average person who uses only about twenty-five percent.

Matthew opened the magazine he had shown to his mother and turned to a page he had marked. In one of the photo backgrounds was Marilyn, painting on a canvas, but her body was blocking the view of the picture. He caressed the picture as if it were a soft, cuddly kitten.

Then Matthew's mind began to wander. He remembered the last time he tried to see Marilyn, recalling the memory as if it were a movie, capturing every detail—the specific sights, sounds, smells, temperature, and his exact feelings at that moment. Matthew watched the clip in his head like a movie on the big screen.

Penny and Dr. Dimment are arguing in the hallway. Penny walks toward Matthew, clicking her heels on the tile, just like she had a few seconds ago when leaving the room. The sound, Matthew surmises, is a combination of several factors. It is a unique walk, unlike her normal one. It is a walk of determination, defiance, and dedication. It is also the sound of territorial protection and posturing to fend off adversaries. It is a distinct walk with finality.

Penny takes Matthew by the hand and leaves the halls of the Children's Hospital that day, never intending to return. Looking back over his shoulder, he sees Marilyn, Dr. Meachum, and Dr. Dimment turn and walk away.

A year later, near her birthday, Matthew recalls convincing his mother to visit Marilyn. Penny stands at the administration desk discussing the unplanned visit with a former acquaintance. Marilyn had been discharged a week earlier, departing for New York with several others when Dr. Dimment moved his practice.

Matthew feels something, but is not sure what it is. Many would describe it as adoration. Matthew wanders down the hall to the old activities room and stops by an empty table that overlooks the street below. He and Marilyn had spent a lot of time at this table. A young kid is sitting at the next table, humming and mumbling the same thing repeatedly. He has a white, crusty buildup all around his mouth from his drool. His shirt is wet and stained.

A girl stands silently against the wall, staring blankly, and a teenage boy is standing nearby, hitting himself in the forehead with his fist. There are a few kids sitting at a table, talking and playing board games. Matthew does not recognize any of them. The place has moved on without him. It has changed, and his time has passed. He won't want to come here again.

Matthew stands there holding a card and a gaily-wrapped present intended for Marilyn—but she isn't here anymore. He feels sad, and he begins to sway and rock very gingerly, but not hard *enough to help him cope with an overwhelming anxiety that is quickly spreading. It soothes him and reminds him of how he felt when he lived here—with Marilyn.*

A girl wanders by chewing on her hair. She stops in front of Matthew, smiling at him in a coy, seductive way. The girl has on a hospital gown that is drooping down on her shoulder, exposing the light brown areola of her oversized breast. Matthew pays no attention to her nakedness. The girl gestures for the box with her finger.

Matthew hands the gift to her just as his mother walks in behind him. He knows Marilyn is no longer here. She moved on, just as he did a year earlier. The girl with the present walks away, her clinical white panties showing, and her back completely exposed by the poorly tied gown. She sits down on a couch by the TV and clutches the pretty box tightly. She is smiling.

Matthew stands there, feeling melancholy. The room filled with teens and young adults has changed too much. His life is elsewhere now. These patients seem so much worse off than when Matthew was here. The hospital has moved on without him as well. Marilyn and the doctors moved on without him. The world has moved on without him, and Mathew knows it is time for him to move on, as well.

Matthew stood up, closed his briefcase, and walked down the hallway towards the elevator. Standing and waiting, he could hear his mother's and Brantley's ranting echoing down the long hallway. He pushed the elevator button, covering his finger with his jacket cuff so he wouldn't have to touch it. A few seconds later, the door opened to an empty car. Matthew boarded and pressed L. The door closed, and he went to the lobby.

He didn't like the music playing in the elevator. The electronic dance music thumped and twanged, an irritating noise. He hummed to block out the sound.

When the door opened, the light was so bright that Matthew wished he had some sunglasses. Knowing he had none, he left the building squinting. A taxi roared to a stop right in front of him. A man opened the cab door, still deep in conversation with a woman on the sidewalk. Matthew, accustomed to people opening the door for him in the limousine, stepped inside and took a seat.

The man threw his arms up in exasperation and surprise at what Matthew had done. Not recognizing his anger, Matthew shut the door, mumbling a thank you.

Looking in the rearview mirror instead of turning around, the cabbie asked. "Where to, son?"

Matthew replied, "New York Psychiatric Hospital."

The cabbie rolled his eyes and took a second look at Matthew, rocking and humming. The man outside was beating his fist on the window as they drove away.

7 THE SECRET KEY

Dr. Lawrence Meachum paced nervously, his hands shoved into the pockets of his white lab coat, his lip curled in disdain. He was standing in Dr. Gottfried Dimment's office at D&M Research in Central New York Psychiatric Center, and he didn't like being there. The serious nature of their issue forced both of them to stand, like members of the British Parliament debating social law, both men standing at odds with each other yet again. Not their first disagreement and certainly not their last.

Dr. Meachum, the stronger personality with a more youthful appearance, clearly had the upper hand. He smiled with self-satisfaction as he stared at his opponent. Dr. Dimment's body was in need of much repair. His obesity caused him to walk with an almost sideways limp. Looking closely, his special shoe heel revealed an obvious defect: one leg was half an inch longer than the other. Dimment's teeth were yellow and not particularly straight, and his pointed eyeteeth left an impression that he was untrustworthy. A man with overactive hormones, he would have had to shave three times a day to maintain a clean-shaven appearance. His peppered hair was thin all over, with oversized bunches of bushy hair hanging like slabs of meat almost the full length of each cheek. Disgusting.

Dr. Meachum was not usually bothered by Dimment's lack of appeal. After all, they were working partners, not lovers. But he always hated to see how Dimment's facial skin glistened with sweat, like a polished bowling ball. The oils from his head and neck left stains around the collars of his smock and white dress shirts. The yellow ring around his collar was also quite distracting—he couldn't help thinking: you are so loathsome, ever heard of soap?

Dimment also had an almost permanent white crust in the corners of his mouth. His overactive saliva glands pooled and dried in the creases of his jowls like a St. Bernard's, and flakes of skin fell like snow from his scalp and face. Nothing was particularly appealing about him to most purveyors.

Dr. Meacham, however, was his complete opposite with the looks of a Hollywood movie star. Brash, well spoken, like a shiny, newly minted penny. He preened just a little as he admired himself in a small mirror hanging on the wall behind Dr. Dimment, shaking his head occasionally as his partner babbled on. Close in age, they had lived very different lives, as evidenced by their appearance. Dr. Meacham was the spokesperson that made the team work, and Dr. Dimment was the mule that pulled the wagon.

The two men continued debating strategy, trying to resolve their obvious dilemma. Dimment was speaking to Dr. Meachum with very strong accusations, pointing at his finger and waving his hands in the air. "He is the key we need to complete this, Lawrence. You're the influential one. It's your job to lure him back in. That half-cocked paper you published on our behalf only buys us time. Research funding is dwindling; private donations are also drying up. We need money and a face, a poster child. No one knows who Marilyn is or even cares."

Meachum smiled and listened until Dimment finished talking and gave up the floor. Most of the time, he just blew smoke out of his ass to release pressure, but this time he was right, and Meachum knew it.

In a kind and well-placed tone, Meachum answered his concern. "Gottfried, remember when you came to the States? Your visa application had been revoked several times due to some minor indiscretions involving stem cell harvesting."

Meachum kept smiling as he talked, subtly moving around behind Dimment's desk before sitting in Dimment's chair. This was typical of him. Smiling to ease the tension but sitting behind Dimment's desk as if he owned it—showing his dominance in a quiet, socially acceptable way. Putting his feet on the corner of the desk and leaning back with his fingers intertwined in his lap, Meachum tried to settle the room's mood.

Dimment took his hand and brushed his hair back in frustration and defiance. Then he slammed it down hard on the desk, causing a pencil holder, paper clips, and a stapler to jump as he barked loudly, "What does that have to do with this?"

Meachum continued, "Everything. Again, you mistrust me, again you doubt me. It pains me deeply." He placed his hand over his heart to signal his hurt feelings mentally, even though Dimment probably knew it was all just bullshit. According to Dimment, Meachum was full of it, and Dimment made sure he knew every chance he got.

Meachum pointed his finger at Dimment, still leaning over the desk. "I can reach anyone: the President; the Queen; the Chancellor. I have people everywhere."

Dimment slammed his hand down again, but not quite as forcefully as before. This time, he was smiling a bit and almost chuckling. "You are zo full of zhit, Lawrence. Vhat are you? the Geztapo?" Dimment's German accent was almost gone, but when he felt stressed, it resurfaced, making sharp, distinct breaks and long S sounds like a Z.

Dimment turned his back on Meachum, placing his hands on both hips.

Meachum pressed on, "Your past. Your colorful past. Your sister and her needs. Does any of that ring a bell?"

Dimment turned suddenly and slammed both fists down on the desk, knocking over the pencils and sending paperclips flying everywhere. "You leave my sister out of this conversation."

"Calm yourself, Gottfried, calm yourself. The point I am trying to make is that I took care of it. I have always taken care of it, and I always will."

Meachum pulled a copy of the *Medical Journal* out of his pocket and flipped it out on the desk towards Dimment. The front cover touted their work.

Dimment fired back, "It means nothing." He waved his hand in a condescending motion, dismissing the idea. "The boy probably doesn't even read that rag."

"Mr. Le'Dain just so happens to be in town for several weeks, my sources tell me. Your star pupil *does* read the journal. I made sure he has a copy. His publicist, Lea, is a slut. She would hump a porcupine if she thought that would get her ahead in life. Besides, I know he likes that girl." His finger pointed at a picture of the two doctors and Marilyn as it toppled over onto Dimment's desk.

"He is not capable of love. You know this yourself," Dimment retorted.

Meachum grinned wildly, pulling his feet from the desk and standing. He walked halfway between the desk and the door, then stopped.

"Yes, I do know the clinical definition of love. I also know that the human body is capable of things we can only imagine." Meachum pointed his index finger at his head. "Did you know your little robot wonder boy brought a birthday present for her a few months after Marilyn left with us?"

Dimment stammered, trying to speak, but nothing would come out. "N-n-n—"

Meachum continued, "He did. That proves that he has some type of attachment to the girl. It may not be love, but there is something there. Perhaps it is a brother-sister thing or some kindred spirit that draws them together, but a bond exists. I can feel it."

Dimment walked over and stood directly in front of Meachum. "You can feel it? Here you go again with that pzycho-babble-rap about telepathy and reading mindz zhit again. You're rizking our careerz and our reputationz on the fact that the lizard boy will zee the article and come running. You are a fool!"

Meachum headed for the door, placing his hand on the knob. He stopped, turning back to Dimment, who was frantically rubbing what was left of his hair out with both hands.

Meachum gave Dimment his trademark, sociopathic grin. A grin that said: *I could kill you right now, but I won't because I need you—you little fat meat sack.* "I have always been a better judge of character and emotion than you, and I always will be."

Dimment leaped at Meachum, pointing his finger as he went, ignoring his serpent-like grin. "You better be. She is no good without him. He is the key, and she is the lock. No one can understand that bitch's doodles but him."

Meachum smiled one last time in a more congenial manner, exiting the office whistling,

pausing briefly before closing the door to say, "Have a nice day, Dr. Dimment. It's been a pleasure chatting with you."

8 SURREAL LIFE

Penny remembered the previous night as she left the studio restroom, wiping tears after her confrontation with Brantley. She needed to think of something to distract herself from that pompous jerk. Walking down the hall to the conference room where she had left Matthew, she thought about how last night had been so perfect. She smiled, recalling the billboards in the hotel lobby: ONE NIGHT ONLY, TRIUMPH PLAZA HOTEL and CASINO, MATTHEW LE'DAIN the HUMAN COMPUTER.

Dan Triumph hosted a dinner party once a month whenever his schedule permitted, inviting many interesting and popular people. Matthew's parents had attended the prom for adults with Matthew and Lea—a headline act like Matthew was always given an invitation to the ball. Dan never allowed anyone on the stage at his hotel without personally reviewing their acts, so this was a significant honor for Matthew, and Lea and Penny recognized it.

The hotel ballroom brought to mind the old days when an invitation to the right party was worth more than money. Dan Triumph was a modern, self-made billionaire, entrepreneur, celebrity, politician, and talent scout. His name was on everything, and his influence was in every business in New York. Despite all the fanfare, he was disliked by elitists who called him a Capitalist. Didn't Capitalism and America go hand in hand like picnics and apple pie? Dan was determined to ensure his view of what made America great stayed unchanged. The ballroom party showcased his wealth and influence. The decorations, gowns, tuxedos, ice champagne sculptures, and five-star foods were clear signs of his success.

Matthew, dressed in a tuxedo and holding a glass of cranberry juice to blend in, stood with his parents. Lea hurried off to practice her trade, searching for important people for Matthew to meet. Penny could almost read her mind. She was probably thinking: This is how royal people live. This is how I want to live.

It only took a few minutes before Lea caught a whale. Penny could see Lea's smile well before she noticed Dan Triumph. Now, Penny smiled. This is why I keep her around.

Penny couldn't contain her excitement that Dan wanted to meet Matthew, but that was the kind of person Dan was. He was an investor in people. Dan had many famous quotes, and one of his most well-known was: "Invest in people, and you invest in yourself." People never expected him to be so hands-on, but he had a way of taking sixty seconds and stretching it in a space and time continuum or something, making it feel more like five minutes.

Lea gave brief introductions, trying to hide Dan from Matthew's father, who rolled his eyes while taking a drink to hide his disdain for the poster child of capitalism.

Mr. Le'Dain, liberal elitist, meet Mr. Triumph, conservative capitalist, Penny thought, almost chuckling at the funny she had made. True introductions would have been made this way, but in real life, everyone plays their respective roles. After all, there was a love-hate relationship with Matthew's father and capitalism. He covets their donations and then fights to find ways to take their money for the government. A cat-and-mouse game that made no sense at all.

But this night was about Matthew. If he knows what's good for him, Mr. Le'Dain will be no problem, unless he wants Penthea down his throat.

Penny sighed as she looked at Dan Triumph up close. He had a way of making everyone he met feel special; the twinkle in his eye, his intense stare, or sometimes even his brutal honesty could make a person feel like he had always known them.

Making no small talk, Dan told Matthew he had seen a taping of one of his shows.

"Mathew," Dan began, "you have a gift, a fabulous act, and I know you are going to put on a marvelous show tomorrow night." Dan gently rubbed Matthew's back like a father would for a son.

Matthew did not like to be touched by strangers, but Dan was like a magician. He made everyone feel comfortable from the first moment they met him, and Matthew responded to Dan's charisma. *He draws people to him like flies to honey*, Penny thought as Dan worked his magic.

Matthew rocked very slightly back and forth, clutching his juice with both hands. He even managed a faint smile. "I will do my best, Mr. Triumph," he replied.

"I am sure you will do great, Matthew. Have you ever thought about becoming a tax accountant? I think you would make a wonderful auditor." It was common knowledge that the current administration was always setting the IRS on Mr. Triumph. Dan made a joke about his taxes, but Penny knew there was always some truth in every joke.

Matthew smiled and rocked, shaking his head to indicate no.

Mr. Triumph grinned and then hurried to make a perfect escape. "Folks, have a wonderful evening. Matthew, it was a pleasure to finally meet you. Ms. Tootchie, have you ever thought about joining the Triumph team? I manage beauty pageants, and some of the girls could use a good publicist. A few years ago, I had some issues with a winner from Kentucky. Let me tell you, she was as wild as a feral hog." Their voices drifted away as they walked off.

Lea and Dan quickly disappeared into the sea of tuxedos and gowns. Penny knew Mr. Triumph had a sweet tooth for young women. It was probably his only fault, but having an adult daughter now, he had somewhat curtailed his appetite for forbidden fruit. This was a trait that Penny despised with a passion, hating any sense of entitlement. This placed her at odds with her husband on several political issues, but it did give them something to talk about at dinner.

Lea was again doing what she did best: seeking out the BBD. (bigger, better deal)

Penny was proud of Matthew, especially on this night. He had arrived and was now sure to be a rock star in the world of science and stand-up entertainment. If you purchased a ticket to one of his shows, Matthew would amaze you for about an hour. Penny thought about how

Matthew changed when he was on stage—a light would seem to click on. Well-coached, he played the role of entertainer like a virtuoso on a violin.

Penny clapped as the opening act, a comedian named Jim Brewer, took the stage. Most of his audience was rowdy and filled with spirits, but not in the Triumph Plaza ballroom. Jim immediately launched into his famous AC/DC routine, and to Penny's dismay, the polished crowd loved it. There must have been more forty-something hair-band groupies in the crowd than she had initially thought.

"Mrs. Le'Dain, we are ready for Matthew," a young man said between the noise of the show.

"Matthew, it's time for you to get ready. Do you need me to go with you?" Penny smiled as she adjusted Matthew's bow tie and brushed his shoulders. She leaned in and kissed his forehead.

Matthew answered without looking directly at her. "Mom, no kissing. Someone might see you. Besides, I am a seasoned entertainer now."

Penny chuckled. "You made a joke. That's good, now save it for the audience."

"Knock 'em dead, son," Mr. Le'Dain replied.

Penny knew Matthew read and learned everything he could about a subject to understand it. Comedy was all about timing, properly placed words, and a willing audience. Matthew was a quick study and had watched hours of tape from Bob Hope to Gallagher. He would master stand-up comedy in no time.

***

Matthew felt uneasy watching Mr. Brewer walk toward him as he left the stage. He wore sound-dampening earplugs that lowered noise levels, with one side containing a transmitter in case of issues or if he froze. His mother had thought of everything, even though Matthew had never frozen. His quick thinking often worked in his favor. There were no books to help with every social situation, and that was where Matthew struggled the most.

Jim had strange eyes, and his intense stare made people uncomfortable. Matthew felt as though his gaze pierced his personal space as he approached. Usually, Matthew avoided eye contact, but the lights had been turned on. Having read several books on male dominance and prison life, Matthew understood this was a male territorial ritual he needed to learn. He also had a peculiar way of looking at people, with his head cocked like an owl, which others said was unsettling. He tried it on Jim, vying for dominance, like male cockatoos during mating season trying to compete for a female.

The standoff came to a head, and then the tension deflated like a balloon that had popped. Matthew was surprised by Jim's reaction, and he paused as he spoke, his voice loud and expressive. Matthew had read all the psychology books, and he knew that Jim's behavior fit a certain profile, most likely that of an adult with attention-deficit hyperactivity disorder.

"Caught your show in Vegas a few months ago. Great show, man! I thought they were going to eat you alive at first, then I had to follow you up after that great act." Jim laughed as they were announcing Matthew in the background.

Matthew realized he was being polite. "Thank you, Mr. Brewer. Your show was very funny," Matthew replied in a deliberate tone.

"Yeah, thanks. You're coming up, man! A few months ago, you opened it for me, and now I'm opening it for you. I'm going to have to fire my agent."

He looked back at his manager, who was standing there, but he did not smile at him. There was something hidden in his expression. Matthew studied his facial cues and listened carefully to Jim's tone of voice, watching his body language for clues on how to reply. He guessed it was a joke, but unsure, he responded, "My mother's available."

Jim guffawed at the joke. "I just may call her. What does she look like?" Jim lightly slapped his manager on the chest with the back of his hand.

Jim's last comment made Matthew pause for thought. Not understanding the joke, he simply smiled and didn't answer, looking down and away.

"Well, later, man. Your turn." Jim walked off into the darkness.

Matthew was completely at ease performing his act, having done it hundreds of times. Even though it was called an act, all the elements were real—things Matthew did every day. Repetition and routine always kept Matthew feeling calm. Although anything was possible with a live audience, he knew he had full control.

Surveying the crowd, Matthew quickly got to work earning his money. "I need a volunteer from the audience, please. You…no, you with the pink shirt, come on up."

The man scurried through the crowd like a mouse in a maze. He was out of breath when he made it on stage.

Matthew immediately noticed the man was wearing a pink shirt with his black tuxedo. A key rule in stand-up comedy is to find something unique to discuss with the audience. The man ran up the steps to the stage and extended his hand for a handshake. Matthew politely nodded in response, ignoring his hand.

"You have a lovely pink shirt on, sir. Would you tell the audience your name?"

The deep, monotone voice echoed through the room. The groups of socialites chatting nearby immediately took notice and fell silent. Matthew had such an unusually commanding voice that it often surprised the crowd. He made the slight sway in his stance part of the act, timing his fake smile to appear more personable than he really was. Lea was just as responsible for helping him with his stage presence as Penny was for his significant social improvements.

"My name is Trevor…and my shirt… It's salmon colored, not pink," the man replied, taking several deep breaths and then coughing to clear his throat.

Trevor, about your pink shirt. I did some quick calculations in my head when I saw you earlier tonight. There are approximately 500 people here tonight. So, there's a one in five hundred chance that someone would be wearing a pink shirt if you consider this a typical sample of the crowd. The average person makes about 225 decisions a day, but I'd say there's only a one-in-a-billion chance that anyone would pick that specific shirt.

The audience erupted in laughter again. Matthew knew it was always important to get a strong response right at the start of a show.

Trevor was smiling, but there was a slightly offended look on his face. Penny knew that Matthew's ability to read facial expressions was poor, so she watched helplessly, hoping he could bring Trevor back. She was not disappointed.

"That makes you unique, just like me. We have commonality."

The smile and excitement quickly reappeared on Trevor's face.

The audience was in the moment with them and cooed at the kind response from Matthew.

"Trevor, I am going to let you pick a game to play. How does that sound?"

Trevor shook his head in agreement.

"Okay, here are your options: the Name Game, Ciphering with Jeffro, or Picture Perfect." Matthew swayed back and forth, maintaining a steady rhythm while talking.

In The Name Game, a group of people would be selected, and Matthew would have to recall their first and last names to the audience. The popular Name Game song from the '60s, with the lyrics that used the words *banana fanna,* would be played in the background for a few minutes while the contestants shuffled around, trying to confuse Matthew's memory. In a theatre venue, an entire row would be selected. To win the game, Matthew would have to miss only one person— Matthew had never lost. The contestant would have to remember at least five first and last names for a bonus. Statistically, a normal person must hear a name three to seven times before they memorize it. Matthew had a photographic memory, so remembering names and faces came naturally to him.

Ciphering with Jeffro involved solving three math problems that used addition, subtraction, multiplication, or division. One of the numbers could not be more than seven, and the other three could be any value. It was meant to entertain the audience, not bore them. Matthew had sixty seconds to answer all three correctly. On stage, a large calculator mounted on rollers served as a prop, which the contestant used to input the problem, and then the correct answer appeared on a giant screen. Sometimes, Matthew would wear hillbilly teeth and be assisted by a mystery helper. Lea would dress up in Daisy Dukes, a red and white checkered shirt, and a straw hat to help him.

Picture Perfect was a perception game that Matthew loved. He and the contestant would look at two pictures that Lea would pull from a box. The box contained about a thousand postcard-sized photographs. Even though Matthew could have memorized them all, he was not cheating, and he saw no need to make up a lie. Lea assured the audience that he had never seen them, and they usually believed him. The used ones were discarded during each show by giving them to the contestant.

To play, a picture would be projected onto a big screen, and within seconds, two pictures would be shown. One would be the original, and the other would be altered to have added the missing items. This kind of game often appeared in magazines as a "find the difference" puzzle. Matthew had worked thousands of them in his institutional days. The contestant and Matthew had three minutes to find ten differences. Matthew usually completed it in under a minute. The contestants never won, ever. Offering $1,000 if they could beat him amused the audience. Every contestant earned a hundred-dollar bill for playing. Many times, if Matthew was promoting a product, free samples were given to the winner and also as door prizes.

Trevor selected Picture Perfect and lost. The show then began moving very rapidly, proceeding to a brief bio of Matthew.

"I am a recovering autistic-savant. You probably couldn't tell by my monotone voice, lack of eye contact, or my constant rocking…"

The audience always capitulated with laughter, but the facts were soberingly true. The crowd almost always became solemn during his address. Matthew always took the time to remember those who had helped him so much with time, money, and research information. He handed out brochures with charitable contact information for *Autism Speaks*.

The show then quickly shifted back to a more upbeat game as Matthew played twenty questions with a woman contestant, an audience favorite. The contestant would pick an object from her purse, and Matthew usually guessed it in fewer than seven questions.

Matthew was too engrossed in his showstopper, Total Recall, to notice most of the audience. The lighting was too bright, and there were too many people to get facial recognition with them all, but for a brief second, he thought he recognized someone standing in the back of the room—someone from his past. However, he couldn't be sure, so he turned his attention back to the game. Then the show ended, and Matthew exited stage left with Lea.

Dan Triumph had apparently been waiting off stage. "Congratulations, Matthew. That was a terrific show."

Lea, now in a naughty librarian's attire, captured Dan's eyes. She batted her eyes at him. Matthew noticed, but he didn't acknowledge them, looking down and away. Females did interest him, but not in a sexual way. They were quite different creatures, and Matthew liked to study them as if they were ants under glass.

Penny and Matthew, Sr. approached. Seeing an exit time, Dan excused himself, and Lea followed, waving and winking at the Le'Dains as they approached.

***

That lucky rich prick, thought Matthew Sr.

***

That dirty old man, thought Penny.

***

Dr. Lawrence Meachum watched Matthew's performance from the rear of the room with great interest. He had left a copy of his most recent exploits in the medical field for Matthew at the front desk—and then he was gone.

***

Standing in the ballroom after the show, Matthew watched his mother and father dance. A strange feeling washed over him—loneliness. Something he had only felt once before, after he stopped seeing Marilyn every day. That feeling had only lasted a short time then, probably caused by wandering adolescent thoughts, but now it was back. Matthew did not welcome the feeling, instead trying to dismiss it immediately, like foreign bacteria attacked by a group of white blood cells.

Then Matthew felt another emotion taking over him, as if she was desperately calling for him. He could almost hear her voice in his mind, but then it faded away.

Even though Matthew was unsure what real love felt like, he thought maybe he could enjoy a life of companionship with her. This was a new idea for him. Definitely a new emotion he needed in his toolbox. How would his current lifestyle fit into this need for companionship or his desire for isolation?

Matthew often thought and spoke in a language similar to that of the Founding Fathers of the United States. His mind jumped back and forth between the proper English of the past and today's casual slang. In his mind, he aimed to be proper and even eloquently correct. However, the constant stream of poor grammar and word choices he encountered daily reminded him that he was different—very different from everyone else.

As his parents twirled to a waltz, Matthew reflected. *I must remember to adopt a more provincial style of language to fit in, even though fitting in is not in my nature. Regarding relationships, isolationism would not be conducive to a long and lasting partnership. Its obvious contradictions to the idea of being simpatico are an abomination to the institutions that support their nuptials. This is not an endeavor to take lightly, nor is it a house I am willing to live in at this time. Far be it from me to upset the ebb and flow of matrimony. Besides, I am at best too young to enter into an agreement. Marriage today requires preparation. There is college, failed relationships, building a nest egg, and travel. Yes, I have done them all except for the failed relationships. However, never failing is not my fault.*

Matthew continued to ponder his feelings about a relationship with Marilyn, using a scientific approach to weigh the pros and cons, which left him feeling confused and disappointed. The confusion stirred up a rarely entertained, angry emotion within him. Venting seemed to be what he needed to clear his mind. Yes, the wolves—those wolves that had tried to hunt him down and hurt him in his youth. He had kept the neighborhood pre-teen wolf pack at bay, silencing their taunts and cruel physical behavior. They had thrown rocks, spat on him, and called him names. The memory of the torment howled through his mind until he became furious. He had spoken proper English before, and it only brought trouble. Now, because of thoughts of Marilyn, they long to be free, no longer bound by his mind's ropes.

I must reconcile the fact that provincial, modern language littered with grammatical errors and cursing is a more socially acceptable means of communication, Matthew conjectured. *I must practice the provincial style of language in order to fit in, but with Marilyn, I could be myself with no filters about my mind. I prefer to piss on my own tree and dare any other wolf to hike its leg there. The symbolism of marking territory may seem comical, but if you observe men in a conversational group, you'll notice that the alpha males always compete to become the pack leader. It does not matter if it is a locker room full of jocks or a comic bookstore full of nerds. Yes, even amongst the weaker physical members, speaking in an odd language in an unpredictable manner will garner unwanted attention. With this, language plays a large part in your perception of others. Being well read, even in these packs, does not assure the alpha male can tread above the tall grass without suffering some abrasions to his nether regions.*

Matthew's thoughts, for now, had bested his mind. Normally in complete control of his emotions, the thought of Marilyn had unleashed something new, and he had to have more. He was like an addict needing a fix. Marilyn made him feel something different, but what? Why was he breaking into a dreamy world that had moved on with a language that sounded so proud, yet prejudiced at the same time?

A memory suddenly popped into his head. It had been locked away but had broken free. He could see it just as it happened. *Pride and Prejudice*, Marilyn's favorite book. He had read the entire thing to her in a single day. At the Children's Hospital, by the window, overlooking the courtyard. Marilyn had hung on every word as they watched the people come and go outside. Matthew yearned for that closeness once again.

9 REUNION

This part of town looks very unforgiving, Matthew thought.

Texting Lea on his cell phone to inform someone of his destination, just in case there were any unfortunate incidents, Matthew fought off nausea from the cab ride. Lea argued with him and threatened to call his mother, but Matthew was resolute. After reminding her about the music television incident, Lea quickly changed her mind about Matthew.

Lea had plenty to keep her busy. Matthew knew that babysitting him was becoming less of a priority each day. Landing a two-week show on Broadway, thanks to Mr. Triumph's contacts and Lea's sharp business skills, made Matthew realize he had time to explore other options for his life. Moving temporarily to New York satisfied Matthew's desire to explore his world and gave Lea a career opportunity.

The Plaza Hotel was luxurious, but it could only comfort him for so long. The cab stopped in front of a very plain, clinical-looking series of buildings, none of which were more than five stories high. A small, barely noticeable sign read *D&M Research*. Matthew looked down at his phone to ensure his GPS Navigator App had directed him to the correct location. Yes, this was the place—the Central New York Psychiatric Center. *This was a perfect place to gain an endless supply of research candidates for Dimment and Meacham*, Matthew pondered. The city was full of lunatics. You could pull a thousand of them off the streets today, and odds are that no one would even notice.

Matthew tried to imagine whether Marilyn would look the same or different. What would she be like? Would she even remember him?

I need to turn off my location tracker, or my mother will surely see it. Matthew toggled the locator off with one touch, then paid the cab driver, tipping him a dollar.

Insulted by the gesture, the seasoned cabbie scolded Matthew. "You can forget me coming back for your sorry ass," he said and then sped off in the broken-down Impala.

The car groaned and huffed like a steam engine as it sped away out of sight. Drips of oil marked the pavement where it had been parked, and the smell of alcohol-infused fuel burned Matthew's eyes and nose from the exhaust. He waved his hand, trying to brush it away.

Picking up his briefcase, he turned and went inside through the only entrance he saw. The front of the huge building looked like a giant face grimacing at him with its barred windows. Inside, a woman at the reception greeted him.

"My name is Matthew Le'Dain. I have come to visit Marilyn Vanats," he said to her, looking down and away.

The woman was heavy-built and not particularly pleasant-looking. Matthew ignored her physical appearance and rough demeanor. He stood waiting, surprised when she called for Dr. Meacham instead of Marilyn Vanats, as he had requested.

Matthew tried to get her attention to object, but she put her hand in front of his face like a condescending crossing guard and waved him off to shush him. His rocking became more pronounced due to the agitation from his obvious rejection, and he mumbled his thoughts aloud, repeatedly.

"Marilyn Vanats. I asked for Marilyn Vanats, not Lawrence Meacham. Marilyn Vanats, not Meachum. Marilyn…"

***

Dr. Meacham grew excited when the receptionist described the Spindly Man. He asked her if he was alone, and when she said yes, he shouted while looking at the lobby camera from his computer, "It's him, Gottfried. He's here. I told you." Then, turning back to the receptionist, he said, "Keep him busy. I'll be right there. Don't let him go anywhere, or it's your job."

***

The woman wiped the annoyed look from her painted face as she hung up the phone, then looked up and forced a smile. Matthew looked back at her, still rocking and mumbling, all the while thinking: too much blue makeup. She had half-inch tall eye shadow and drawn-on eyebrows. She looked like a rodeo clown or the Mimi character on the old sitcom, The Drew Carey Show. Matthew was more concerned with her than the harsh street outside the building.

***

Dr. Meacham hurried down the hallways like a run-walker. Frustrated by the double-door locking system in the hospital wing, he could not get there fast enough. One set of double-doors had to fully close and lock before the next would open. The government-paid guards were never in a hurry to move things along, and seeing Dr. Meacham in such a rush provided some much-deserved entertainment. To further annoy him, they asked that he show his ID at each checkpoint by holding it to the camera and then joking about not being able to read it. By the time they had reached the last set of doors, he was furious. When they finally began to open and he could see freedom, he decided to correct them.

"You two scants remember who helps fund this place. I will have your jobs yet."

***

The two guards sat back in the chairs, laughing. "Did you see his face?" Guard One asked.

Guard Two replied, "You could almost see the red in the black-and-white screen—and who walks like that?" He stood up and mimicked his walk-run style, squeezing his butt cheeks together and flapping his arms in quick, sharp motions. This was the highlight of their boring day watching cameras. The only other excitement was spying on the naked women who occasionally strolled up to a camera in the psychiatric ward. Well, what do you expect from a minimum wage job?

***

Dr. Meacham met Matthew in the lobby. He watched as the handsome man got off the elevator, walking toward him with his hand out, a huge smile on his face, acting as if he were his long-lost son or something.

Matthew did not offer his hand, so Dr. Meacham reached down and took it. His grip was so strong that Matthew's hand went numb once it was released. Then, he patted Matthew on the back as if they were old friends from college. Too much affectionate behavior for Matthew, so he jerked away violently.

"I'm sorry, Matthew. I didn't mean to invade your personal space. Why don't we go up to my office?" said Dr. Meacham. "You know, I've been trying to contact you and your mother for a long time. I heard you were in town, and I even TIVO'd your SNL skit. Very good… very good. You've made some real progress, I see. Being out in public has broadened your horizons. I'm really surprised."

Matthew could barely keep up with Dr. Meacham's hyperactive chatter. He was speaking as if he'd been drinking coffee all day. He didn't recall Dr. Meacham ever being this excited about anything. He practically pushed Matthew into the elevator, making him feel trapped, like a fish in a barrel.

The security in this complex seemed to be built like Fort Knox. Matthew started to feel nervous as they moved from one door to another. *I've never seen so many locked doors, Matthew thought. The Children's Hospital was nothing like this, but then again, everyone wore GPS wristbands or ankle bands. There's no decor on the walls. It smells like a mix of bleach, alcohol, and a mildewed mop*, Matthew kept thinking, taking it all in. That's exactly how the Children's Hospital smelled.

Walking down the corridors, Matthew could see inside some of the tiny windows on the doors. The people inside looked horrific. These people were severely mentally ill. Matthew moved closer alongside Dr. Meacham as they went.

Dr. Meacham's voice echoed down the empty halls as he kept talking nonstop. Matthew saw this as nervous talking. His rants went on and on about his research, grants, awards, and all the progress they had made since leaving Children's Hospital. It focused on him and what he had accomplished, mentioning Dr. Dimment only once during the entire conversation.

Matthew was relieved when they finally entered a more pleasing area of the Hospital that actually had some windows. Taking mental snapshots, Matthew noticed the various types of artwork on the walls. It was like being in the hallway of a kindergarten school. In fact, as he studied them more closely, he found that they were not artwork at all. They were handmade paintings and drawings, all blown up on canvas prints, from the patients.

Matthew finally broke the silence. "Dr. Meacham, why are all these letters and numbers on the walls?"

Dr. Meacham didn't respond immediately, giving a second look at a bunch of doodles and scribbles. Then he said, "Oh, those… of course, Matthew—that's why we need you to help us out. We're not sure what some of these are. Marilyn has been teaching the others and learning from them what she can—but even she is stumped by some of the artwork's meanings."

Matthew noticed Marilyn's name on several of the prints. He couldn't read all of them just by glancing, but they all held significance. They appeared much more complex than the simple shapes the two had used to communicate in earlier years.

Matthew turned and said, "Dr. Meacham, is Marilyn here?"

"Of course, Matthew…of course. I wanted to give you a tour of our research facilities before you got sidetracked. Matthew, we have been working with her, and I think you will see some miraculous changes. I don't want to spoil Dr. Dimment's surprise, but I think you will even approve."

Turning the corner to a very pleasant and colorful area, the new corridor looked more like a school building than a hospital. The ceilings were much higher, and the walls were painted in color. Continuing to move forward, they ran into Dr. Dimment.

Matthew realized he hadn't changed much at all. He had more age spots on his face and neck, but he was as creepy as ever. Dr. Dimment was just as eager to see Matthew. Showing more affection than Matthew had ever seen, it seemed grandiose, Matthew thought.

Dr. Meacham and Dr. Dimment exchanged several facial expressions like encoded monkey language. They didn't think Matthew noticed, but inside he was gathering and analyzing all of it.

They whispered to each other just behind his back as he studied his surroundings.

Matthew's mind started to realize they wanted something from him. Distracted from his thoughts, Matthew's pants pocket began to buzz and shake. He pulled out his phone. It was Lea. Matthew ignored her call. Just as he was about to put it back in his pocket, it buzzed again, and this time it was his mother. With every fiber of his being, Matthew fought to send the call to his voicemail. Lea must have caved quickly, knowing his mother was paying her salary.

Dr. Dimment broke Matthew's concerned concentration with a crackled voice, "How have you been, Matthew?"

Matthew answered with a one-word reply, "Fine."

Dr. Dimment had always made Matthew feel uncomfortable, so he kept his conversation short. Matthew had always thought his creepy smile was unnerving.

Dr. Dimment assumed command by offering a plan, "Lez show Matthew all the wonderful work we have been doing. Thiz iz our language arz room. Here, we have nearly maztered a universal communication zystem with our moderate-to-high functioning neurodivergent patienz. Along the wall, you may see some familiar zhapez."

Matthew looked along the wall; many of the shapes and drawings that Marilyn and he had developed were there. The doctors had apparently refined them to create a remedial pictograph. The entire setup seemed illogical to Matthew. It looked like a complete diorama of a bunch of numbers and letters, not even in order. The order made no sense at all. Numbers were mixed with letters and math symbols.

Dr. Dimment looked as proud as punch, asking, "Matthew, what do you think?"

Matthew paused, looked around at all the patients and their aides. They were sitting there, either making new shapes or holding up flashcards and working with them. It was a menagerie of complete chaos.

"Dr. Meacham—" Matthew started to say.

Replying, he said, "Call me Lawrence. We're friends, Matthew." He started to pat Matthew on the back and put his arm around him, but Matthew flinched away.

Matthew, not really burdened by cultural politeness, blurted out, "This is complete chaos. They're being taught random bits and pieces of information. Nothing is complete and nothing is in any kind of logical order."

Matthew, not fully understanding some cultural norms, had just hit them with hard facts. Not trying to be rude, it simply happened that way. Matthew noticed Dr. Meachum seemed surprised and hurt. Dr. Dimment appeared more pleased that he was right about something. He wondered if they were somehow using this as a form of manipulation against Matthew. "So, would you like to help us out? You know, be a... a consultant, of sorts? In case I am not making myself clear, how would you like to come and work here? Organize this menagerie of complete chaos, as you see fit."

They had stopped exactly where Dr. Meacham had intended—in front of what looked like an activities room. Matthew saw several patients painting and drawing, and several more playing games. It reminded him of the Children's Hospital.

Several people were watching television or working on the computer. Something in the room caught his eye. A woman, a familiar woman, was painting, but her back was to Matthew. Dropping his briefcase on the floor like a sack of potatoes, he realized who it was.

Marilyn.

Matthew ran up to the tinted glass window and put his face and hands against it like a kid in a candy store. She turned to clean a paintbrush off and glanced up. Matthew waved with his right hand, frantically trying to get her attention, and then he pecked on the glass.

She laid the brush down, wiped paint from her hands slowly with a towel, and walked toward the glass wall.

Matthew suddenly froze. He couldn't move a muscle. That strange feeling, an unknown, emotional angst, swept over him again. Matthew felt an enormous explosion of joy and happiness. Some tears leaked from the corners of his eyes, but he ignored them.

Dr. Dimment and Dr. Meacham seemed ecstatic. They could not have expected a more welcome response. Dr. Meacham hit Dr. Dimment in the arm with the back of his hand as if to say, *I told you so*.

Marilyn walked toward Matthew, pushed open the door, and said, "Matthew. Matthew Le'Dain."

Matthew turned. He could not speak, but his mind was racing ninety miles an hour. Finally, something broke through to his lips. With utter surprise, he said, "You can speak now."

10 *DROPPING ANCHOR*

Marilyn studied Matthew for several moments, observing his masculine features. He no longer had the baby face she remembered. Although he was taller and slightly more muscular now, he still appeared as slender as ever. Matthew's chiseled jaw, prominent cheekbones, defined eyebrows, and short haircut did not match his slim frame. In fact, his face didn't seem suited to the body it was attached to. It looked designed for a more debonair man—one of strength, of leadership.

He was breathing in shallow pants, trying to catch his breath. She knew his anxiety must have been off the charts. She figured any nearby seismographs were probably registering movement because he was breathing so hard. She watched as Dr. Meachum and Dr. Dimment moved out of the way, looking at each other with Cheshire Cat grins—Meachum had a grin of confirmation and arrogance, while Dimment showed relief with a slight glow of arousal.

Matthew spoke her pet name, "Mare." He had called her by this as far back as she could remember, but only in her presence. In the company of others, Matthew normally spoke her proper name out of professional courtesy.

"I have missed you so much," Marilyn replied. She lunged at him joyfully, wrapping her arms around him like a hippie hugging the last tree on earth. She noticed that Matthew, normally not one for physical contact, did not get overly excited, but he also did not push her away.

He finally patted her on the back and then moved her off his body gently by taking a step back. She noticed that he almost smiled at her, which was a rare emotional occurrence for Matthew. He never laughed aloud, as she recalled, but he would smile.

***

Mathew's consciousness finally reconnects with his body. *This is the most amazing thing I could have ever imagined. Mare is there now—she actually said words. She embraced me, and I just stood there like a statue or a robot. What is wrong with me?*

***

Dr. Dimment spoke up, obviously overcome with excitement and anticipation. "Zhe iz not zeh young vomen you remember, iz zhe, Matt-u? Juzz think if you vere here vith uz you could be vith her every day," said Dimment, falling back on his German accent.

Dr. Meachum shot Dimment a wicked grimace—flames blazing in his eyes. Dimment stepped back and cleared his throat, sniveling—looking away like a submissive pup bowing to the pack leader.

Marilyn knew Matthew was not trying to be rude; he probably just wanted to see her face. She noticed he seemed barely able to concentrate, something that Matthew normally never struggled with. But now, he was at a loss for words, and the moment felt surreal, like being a character in a Monet painting on a summer day—something Marilyn could have only imagined a few minutes earlier. Suddenly, she became aware of her own sense of security, something that must have been missing; otherwise, she wouldn't have noticed it at all. The feeling of loneliness had vanished; her work and mentorship had replaced the emotions she felt as a woman.

Without warning, it happened—just for a moment—anxiety, fear, a sense of betrayal. Although she had no reason to feel this way about Matthew, she felt it nonetheless. It stemmed from feelings of intimacy with men in general. Secrets she kept locked away. Marilyn despised these feelings and pushed them out of her mind.

Then Dr. Dimment dampened their moment, saying, "Matthew, why don't you take Marilyn down the hall. We can show you the way. It's lunch time, and you two can reconnect in the lounge."

Traveling down the corridor past several learning centers, they turned left into a small dining area. One wall was partially opened a few feet. Inside, a conveyor belt carried old food trays toward the kitchen. Torsos and arms could be seen through a small window removing dishes and trays. Glasses were roughly stacked together in one basket, plates in another, and utensils in the last basket. A quick spray of scalding hot water was used to knock off larger chunks of leftover food. The man inside pushed the baskets into a dark hole in the wall, where they soon disappeared.

Marilyn watched as Matthew's eyes snapped back to reality while they passed the noisy dish return. He had been standing there, motionless, as if his mind was rebooting. His expression changed to that of a concussed fish floating on the water's surface after a redneck dynamite fishing trip. Weird. It was as if he hadn't been inside his own skin for the last few minutes as they walked down the hall.

But the longer Marilyn was with him, the happier she became. She felt a sudden glow spread through her body. A piece of her soul had returned—something she hadn't realized had been missing until today. She wondered if Matthew felt the same—or if he felt anything at all. His sudden absence and then return gave her cause to reflect. Sometimes, she noticed that Matthew showed only the most basic of emotions: a smile, a grunt of laughter, a grimace when he was displeased. But she had never seen him check out like he did a few moments ago. It made her feel, for once, that Matthew was actually human.

Dr. Meacham and Dr. Dimment excused themselves with the usual pleasantries before heading off together like two schoolboys skipping class. They chatted like two women at a beauty salon as they walked down the hallway.

"Is this okay with you, Matthew?" Marilyn pointed to a table in the farthest corner of the room. It was a table mostly used by Dr. Dimment. Dr. Meacham usually ate in his office.

Matthew nodded slightly, so Marilyn took that as a yes. Just as she was about to sit down, Matthew quickly moved behind her and grabbed the chair from her hands. He waited for her to sit and then gently pushed the chair in.

"Thank you, Matthew," she said, smiling at him.

Again, she thought he almost had a full smile, but he quickly retracted it before it became too obvious.

As they sat chatting, Marilyn struggled to keep Matthew involved in the conversation. He responded with the simplest answers, not bothering with any follow-up. She noticed he was engaged, but not as full as a typical person would be. Unsure if he was concentrating on her words or just trying to come up with a way to connect, she hoped for the best.

Marilyn listened and smiled as Matthew shared stories about the places he had visited and the things he had done. He was a very different person now than the shy boy who used to sketch pictures and shapes in hopes of getting a response from her. They had both come a long way.

Contemplating whether to share any deep secrets with Matthew, Marilyn decided to show him the sacrifices she had made to learn to speak. She reached up and pulled the hair above her ear aside. Several scars ran along her head from front to back. You could still see the faint lines where the sutures had pulled her delicate skin together through several experimental surgeries. She also had participated in several controversial stem cell therapies from donors abroad, arranged by Dr. Dimment. The surgeries, along with medications and treatment, had awakened her, she explained.

Matthew, Dr. Dimment has given me something I couldn't even imagine a few years ago. The ability to communicate and function as a normal person was completely beyond my capabilities. Yet, here I am now, talking with you.

Matthew hesitantly reached out, looking at Marilyn for approval. Using his index finger, he gently stroked the scars on the side of her head. "Are there any side effects?"

Pausing to choose her words carefully, she answered, "I get severe migraine headaches and have to be quarantined, at times for several days, in a sound- and lightproof room. Dr. Dimment has constructed a special, climate-controlled facility for when I have these episodes."

The expression on Matthew's face changed, and his lips tightened. Marilyn knew he felt something, but what?

Continuing on, she explained, "The facility was designed to pump additional oxygen to speed up the healing process. I also have had rare but occasional seizures. They started occurring shortly after I began the experimental medication Dr. Dimment developed just for my condition. Matthew, please promise me you won't tell anyone. Dr. Meacham doesn't even know about some of the treatments I receive and…well…he said he would discontinue it if I told anyone. Mathew, I am trusting you with a secret."

Marilyn looked at his face for understanding, searching for a sign he comprehended. He nodded his head in agreement, and she responded with a confirming smile.

"Well, enough about me, Matthew," she said, laughing affectionately. Then, she reached down to grab Matthew's forearm in a loving gesture, but he pulled it away, continuing to smile. Inside, she was crushed. Maybe she had overplayed her hand.

"Matthew, can I trust you with another secret?" She looked him in the eyes and tried to hold his attention. Sending signals of concern, want, and helpless need, she shared something very personal with him. Something she thought he might get upset about, but he had to know. *He had to know everything in order to make the right decision, didn't he? He has come so far, and he is now in my reach. I need this. I need this to work. For us to be together like we used to be all the time. Together.*

A long silence filled the room. Marilyn drifted into a trance, lost in her thoughts. All those years of listening without speaking, years of seeing without truly feeling. Matthew and she shared many similarities, yet there were so many differences. Especially now, as both had been awakened.

"Mathew, I need your help. I need you to stay with me. I've lost my ability to decipher the pictographs and drawings from the patients. I mean, I know all the old ones, especially the ones you showed me, but I am at a loss with the new ones. Dr. Dimment thinks he's developed a pattern to decode them, but I know he's wrong."

Matthew sat there expressionless. He was processing what she said, or so she thought.

"Dr. Dimment and Dr. Meacham have been using me to work with the other patients as a gatekeeper to study and develop a new language. I became stagnant about a year ago and was unable to move forward. Dr. Dimment was very upset with me over this. Matthew, what if he stops treating me? I could go back to being mute… go back to being isolated from the living world." Marilyn looked deep into his eyes. She looked so deeply she could almost see the red of his retinal veins.

***

Matthew came into his own mind. Reality had a way of doing that for everyone. *She just asked me to help her, to stay with her. I think she wants me to be with her. Mother won't stand for it...she won't allow it...she will not let me help. But I want to help Mare. She is my friend.*

The defiance his mother despised had reared its ugly head again. Twice in one week. *I will tell her that I have to; she needs my help. I can help other people.*

***

"Matthew, did you hear what I said?"

Marilyn waved her hand in front of Matthew's face. He was so lost in thought that it took a few seconds for him to react and move. She watched as he rubbed his hands up and down his pants legs to wipe away his nervous sweat.

Look, I know this is a lot to ask. We haven't seen each other in years, but I hope you understand the good you could do if you set your mind to it. We could uncover the secrets of autism. We might even unlock your mind, Matthew. Please... I know your mother will tell you no, but you're a man now. Capable of making your own decisions.

Matthew abruptly stood up. He walked away and began to pace, humming loudly to himself. Marilyn noticed that he had not made any such tics the entire time they'd been talking. All signs of his autism had evaporated while he was with her, but now they were back, and he had become increasingly agitated.

She stood, looking back at Matthew. He stopped pacing and stared back at her.

11 *TIES THAT BIND*

Penthea held her baby boy as they sat on the end of the hotel bed. He rested his head on her shoulder, and his bags sat on the floor by the hotel door. She grimaced at them while she stroked his head in a calming motion. "Matthew, you could never disappoint me with anything you do. I will love you no matter what. Listen very closely to Mommy, I mean me."

Matthew sat up and turned to look at her.

To her, he was still the little boy who sat on the sofa rocking back and forth so hard the couch would scoot across the floor. His cowboy footy pajamas and loud humming had left a permanent image burned in her mind. How far he had come—and the journey that remains.

Penthea brushed away her tears, her heart swirling with a flood of emotions—joy, sadness, pride. Her boy had become his own person, and though the ache of letting go was heavy, a mother's love is unshaken. No matter where life took him, she was just a phone call away, a constant in his world. No harlot, no doctor, no vast distance could break that unbreakable bond. Her voice trembled as she whispered, "Promise me you'll call? If you ever face trouble, promise you'll let me help."

Matthew nodded in agreement.

A knock at the door broke the moment. Matthew stood up, walked over, and opened it. A young man in a suit entered and collected the bags. Matthew followed him through the door and then stopped. Turning back, he looked at Penthea and smiled. Finally turning away, Matthew walked down the hall and out of her sight.

12 *NEW BEGINNINGS*

Matthew sat stone-faced in the back of the limousine as the driver transported him to his new residence at the New York State Psychiatric Hospital. He would not be a patient but a highly paid research consultant.

The driver glanced in the mirror as he drove, slightly turning his head from side to side in a disapproving manner. Matthew paid no attention to his subtle taunts. He had bigger things to worry about now.

He developed significant human behavioral traits by observing his parents over the years. Their occupational therapy-style parenting equipped him with essential skills for dealing with others, even if he didn't understand or feel what they did. Knowing they were staunch liberals, he knew Penthea would agree with his decision to participate in research that helped develop language and communication skills for neurodivergent patients. They had to agree or face the consequences of appearing hypocritical to their elitist friends. After all, he could have said he was willing to sleep in a cardboard box for a week to understand the plight of the homeless, but then complain when real homeless people crashed the party—that would be hypocritical.

Matthew reasoned with himself aloud. However, his life was becoming more complicated, and each day it seemed to get worse. He knew he needed to meditate daily. It was a calming practice, like rocking or humming. His compulsions drive him to stick to a routine. Not every personality trait is magically cured.

One: Humming—humming will be confined to my room or office. I can't allow it in front of the patients. They may take it the wrong way.

Two: I'm glad Mom, I mean Penthea, dealt with Lea. Dan Triumph picked her up for his team. She'll be just fine...she has street smarts, as she calls it.

Three: As for Mare, I will need to start reading up on relationships between men and women as they relate to business professionals and friendship boundaries.

Four: Dr. Dimment: I will need to pay close attention and guard myself and my thoughts around him. He is very peculiar, and I really don't think he deserves to be trusted. He has given me no reason to mistrust him. However, neither has Dr. Meachum, but I will have to pick one of them to trust. Mare can help me decide later.

The limousine came to a sudden stop, jolting Matthew from thought. Then, looking outside his window, he saw it. It looked different this time. It looked exciting, Matthew thought, not sure if that was the right word.

D&M Research. Matthew stared at the sign. The driver opened the door, and he stepped out onto the dirty sidewalk. A black man approached them, and as he passed, he muttered an odd statement.

"Welcome to hell, cracker boy!" The man chuckled aloud as he continued on his way.

Matthew was unsure how to interpret the strange remark. He stood there with his head tilted to one side, trying to understand the slang used by the man. He remembered a lesson he was taught early on—just smile and a quick flick of the hand. Sometimes fitting in requires you to mimic the behaviors of others. Keeping quiet masks any deficiencies.

The driver caught sight of him out of the corner of his eye while rummaging through the trunk for Matthew's bags, and he shook his head again with a smirk on his face. As the driver walked past Matthew, lightly tapping him on the shoulder with a suitcase, Matthew dropped his arm and stopped waving.

Matthew entered the building, and the once rude receptionist acted like a professional kiss-up. "Mr. Le'Dain, welcome. We are so glad to have you. Leave the bags here, driver. I'll have them taken from this point forward."

The driver pursed his lips in a smug fashion, turned, and left the building.

Matthew heard the elevator door open. Turning around, he saw Mare come to greet him. Time seemed to slow as she walked toward him.

He just stood there with a blank look on his face, unmoving, not even blinking, until she was almost right in front of him.

"Matthew… Matthew…this way," she said, gesturing toward the elevator.

Dr. Meachum held the door, waiting for them with a huge crocodile grin on his face.

Matthew could sense the rubbing alcohol tingling his nose hair. It was a familiar smell, a comforting smell, one he had grown to love as a boy. He was comforted by its stinging bite, providing the comfort of a germ-free feeling. He felt at home. As the elevator doors closed, Matthew felt a sensation like something great was going to happen.

13 *ROSETTA'S STONE*

Matthew was extremely proud of his new office, which was outfitted just the way he liked it. He preferred the indirect lighting provided by soft white lamps to the harsh glow of fluorescent lights, and although his workspace would be considered immense for a person of normal psychological tendencies, it was just right for Matthew because, with the many demands of a genius, tabletop space was quickly used up. Mare had tried to decorate the workspace with large canvas prints of her best drawings and easy-care potted plants, but she would have been better served to just concentrate on work, in Matthew's eyes.

A large standing table in the center of the space was made of stacked cubbies, which Matthew used to organize and store papers he had collected. The nice desk in the corner was mainly just a place for items like lunch, mail, or other nonessential things.

"Mare, will you please bring me the most recent pictographs you collected from the test group?" Matthew didn't realize that his clinical tone was neither very flattering nor pleasant. He had no idea that he came across as demanding and unappreciative, with the mechanical side of his personality always showing, even if it wasn't intentional. The expression on Mare's face shot back at him, which went unnoticed, and said it all. He was simply immersed in his work.

With the blinds closed and the overhead lights off, Matthew sifted through the piles of pictographs, scribbles, and rubbish. What would normally take months, Matthew could memorize in just days. To help organize the data, Matthew scanned stack after stack of the hand-drawn images into a computer database. He needed every bit of space in his mind for interpretation—not for storing useless images.

Placing two large monitors side by side on a table, Matthew's scans were easily visible. They were consumed by the computer's endless appetite for data, and Matthew's self-taught programming skills helped him create a macro to categorize images as they were stored.

Steadfast in his habits, Matthew nearly took over the research once led by several less-capable individuals and interns. One thing he knew for sure was to trust no one but Mare. A pragmatic leader, he didn't realize he was alienating her in the process. His ability to express his feelings to her was, at best, lacking. He hadn't spoken to her as a person since he arrived three days earlier. In fact, they hadn't conversed about much of anything, not even lunch. He truly had a one-track mind.

Dutifully, Mare brought back the last box of pictographs and placed it directly in his path. He looked up at her with irritation but didn't speak. Since these pictographs were more basic than all the previous sets, Matthew huffed as he examined them, sorting them into seven piles, with the largest designated as "trash."

"Matthew, why don't we go out for lunch today?" asked Mare. "Somewhere nice. I know a place—"

Can't, Mare. Once I get this last batch in the system, I want to start analyzing them right away. I have them categorized in my head, but I want to start working on a new computer program to detect pattern associations.

Matthew could feel Mare glaring at him, but he was too busy, much too busy to be bothered by figuring out why she was angry. For a moment, he wondered why she was angry, then he filed the thought away for later. Too busy right now. *I need to organize these, not only by symbol groupings, but by a hierarchy of difficulty. There are way too many, and I am still finding duplicates.*

Matthew looked up, sensing a cold stare coming from Marilyn. She'd been standing there for a long time with her arms crossed, looking almost despondent. He didn't recognize the look, so he interpreted it as sad.

"Mare, you look sad. What's wrong?"

She didn't answer for a very long time, just stood there staring into outer space, so he looked down and continued working after giving her a few polite moments of recognition. He had no time for silliness, and he refused to guess. He had seen his father in similar circumstances to Penthea, but just like his father, he was at a loss on how to address it.

This will just have to wait. If she is not going to tell me, then I may as well keep working.

She finally broke the silence. "Matthew, I thought we would be working more closely together… as partners."

He looked up for just a second, puzzled. "We are partners… You collect the data…and I analyze it."

Mare kept explaining. "I have no idea what we are doing or where we are going with this." She moved from the doorway toward him.

Matthew stood up with a quizzical look on his face. She reached down, took the papers from his hands after some initial resistance, and then set them down on the table.

Finding his voice, Matthew explained, "I am developing an alphabet of symbols. I equate this to many of the same pre-development steps that went into creating sign language or Braille. You have already spent an enormous amount of time sitting with patients, collecting the information we need. I thought it was understood that I would be developing the rest of this on my own."

Matthew began to gently rock while he stood there, waiting for her response. Surely, Mare would see his nervousness and understand that he wasn't purposely ignoring her. It was about the work... it was all about the work. But instead of the understanding reassurance he expected, she just looked at him as if she couldn't believe what she was seeing.

Okay, he would try another tactic. He would appeal to her logic. "Mare, you and Dr. Dimment traveled to some of the most premier research facilities, both here and abroad. There is a year's worth of work here. I was just trying to get it cataloged and organized."

Mare circled around the cubby table toward Matthew. She didn't look happy at all. In fact, she looked like she was about to cry.

"I just want to be a small part of your world, Matthew, and if you keep shutting me out, I can't help…I can't contribute…I can't...well...get to really know you." Her eyes suddenly filled, and tears ran down her cheeks.

Matthew's face became hot and flushed. He was completely bewildered by what she expected of him. He was feeling quite uncomfortable. Choosing to dive right into his research, he had not read any books on human relationships, as he had planned. Standing there dazed and confused, Matthew imagined fishing in a barrel, how easy they were to catch in a net. Feeling more than confused, he reacted the only way he knew how.

"I am going to create a map of symbols to develop a visual, three-dimensional language for neurodivergents... like me... and you, Mare," he said, gesturing with his hands as he swayed in his stance. "It may not seem reasonable, but with a few thousand words, you can communicate with others in nearly any language. Autism is a language of silence. Severely autistic children cannot focus, nor do they have the mental capacity to understand language. So, I'm focusing on the mild-to-high-functioning group. We will need to conduct clinical trials to determine where the line is drawn. It will take time, and I am not convinced that even moderately autistic children will be able to learn enough symbols to communicate clearly."

Matthew cocked his head to one side, wondering at the girl in front of him. Mare was smiling from ear to ear. He couldn't understand why she would be smiling while he told her of the struggles they would be facing in the coming months—but she smiled, nonetheless.

"This is wonderful, Matthew...we can work out all these issues...you just need to remember to communicate with me...after all, no one can read minds," said Mare.

Matthew noticed Dr. Dimment standing by the door, looking in while Mare was talking, and a sudden pain pierced his forehead. He rubbed it in a circular motion, trying to alleviate the pain. Mare grabbed his shoulders when she saw him wincing, and the pain disappeared as quickly as it had come. When Matthew looked up again, Dr. Dimment was leaving, with Dr. Meachum close behind. Dr. Meachum gave them both a quick wink and nodded his head with a gentle smile.

***

The next few months were crucial in determining whether a common thread existed. Through clinical trials, Matthew and Mare built a strong working relationship. The first major challenge was to develop an alphabet with a numbering system. By building on much of the work already done, Matthew successfully filled in the missing pieces.

The alphabet and numbering system consisted entirely of odd-colored shapes. Mathew recognized all the shapes and had added many of the more advanced ones. The shapes were arranged in order, starting with numbers one through ten, then the alphabet, and finally whole-word pictographs. The pictographs ranged from three-letter words to five-letter words. Matthew stopped at this point, having nearly five hundred symbols in total.

Representing many symbols in two dimensions on paper was very difficult. Mare got a modeling program from a company that specialized in automated drafting using lasers and gelled plastic to create shapes. All Matthew had to do was draw it, press a rasterization button, and the laser would harden the gelled plastic into the rough shape. He could also select from thirty-two different colors. It wasn't perfect, but it was better than carving them from wood or clay.

With the first edition of language sets completed, they started working with several promising autistic patients. Some of these fortunate few were children of athletes and celebrities.

Matthew called a meeting with Dr. Dimment, Dr. Meachum, and Marilyn to demonstrate the practicality of his newly developed language. Marilyn scheduled the meeting in the main conference room. Lying across the conference table from one end to the other, organized much like a periodic table of elements, were seven months' worth of work.

On the day of the meeting, Matthew nervously rocked back and forth, waiting for Marilyn to escort them in. He was dressed in slacks, a nice shirt and tie, a sweater vest, and a white laboratory coat buttoned down the front. He had carefully chosen a laser red tie for the occasion.

When Dimment and Meachum arrived, with their scowling faces, they looked like they could be members of a major corporation's board of directors on the verge of bankruptcy. Dr. Dimment sat down first, then Dr. Meachum. Mare offered each of them a glass of water, but they both refused. She then handed a glass to Matthew, who drank it in one quick gulp, as if he were extremely thirsty and it might be the last glass of water he would ever have.

Mare smiled at Matthew and gestured with her hands for him to begin.

"Thank you for coming, Dr. Meachum, Dr. Dimment," he nodded at the two men. "As you know, Marilyn and I have been working on a new language for autistics, and we're ready to share our progress with you. This is how it works. As you know, the average person is a three-dimensional thinker, but neurodivergent people see things in four dimensions—"

Dr. Dimment interrupted and smirked, "I would wager differently."

Dr. Meachum shot him a cold look.

Mare grimaced at him for interrupting and for being rude.

Matthew waited patiently and then continued, "You can look at three dimensions like this: length, width, height." Matthew held up a child's wooden block with the letters "ABC" stamped on it.

In the depths of a mind unlike any other, the senses are amplified beyond normal perception. This unique thought process sets neurodivergents and savants apart from the rest—perceiving in four dimensions, feeling in four, seeing in four, all at once. The shapes and colors in their pictographs and numbering systems hold secrets that only a select few can comprehend on a larger scale. The line between autism and savantism is merely a matter of communication—an elusive skill that allows individuals to speak in ways others cannot. To unlock these mysteries, training must be adapted, carefully tailored to their extraordinary minds.

Matthew looked at Dimment and Meachum. He found their facial expressions hard to read. Matthew's lack of skill with human behavior made it hard for him to tell if his opening statements were well received or not.

"What you see on the table in front of you is a new language. We have already been vetting this with a couple of promising mute neurodivergents. Mare has gotten them to count to ten, and they almost know the basic alphabet."

Matthew picked up an object shaped like an odd orange kidney bean. He passed it to Dr. Dimment, who looked unimpressed.

Matthew continued. "This is a three."

Dr. Dimment and Dr. Meachum studied the object and then looked back at Matthew. Dr. Dimment seemed sterner than ever. However, Dr. Meachum almost cracked a smile, as if he understood.

Taking Dr. Meachum's expression as a sign of acknowledgment, Matthew plowed forward. "I feel that a fifth dimension of reality is possible, but I have no intention of pursuing it at this time. These would include extrasensory perception, known commonly as ESP. When I refer to ESP, I mean gravitational manipulation, as one example, and reading thoughts, as another. There are several others, and possibly some that have not been discovered yet. If the mind could sense, feel, and manipulate gravity, a whole new sub-atomic level of reality could be achieved—including trans-temporal cognitive abilities."

Dr. Dimment leaped out of his chair and threw the bean down on the table, scattering the ordered mass of shapes. As pieces fell to the floor, Matthew stepped back and stared, frightened by the doctor's furious expression.

"So, this is what we have wasted our money and time on? A set of tinker toys! And that stupid mind manipulation bullshit that Lawrence dreams about," shouted Dr. Dimment, his eyes flashing. He turned and pointed at Dr. Meachum, his voice full of venom. "He is just as crazy as you are. Good luck, you two deserve each other."

Dr. Meachum, Mare, and Matthew watched with open mouths as Dr. Dimment stormed out of the room, slamming the door behind him.

Matthew sighed. At least Dr. Meacham supported his theory that the human brain could be developed and converted from three-dimensional to four-dimensional thinking. He would just have to forge ahead with the help of only one of the doctors.

Dr. Meachum apologized for Dr. Dimment. "I am sorry, Matthew. He's under a lot of stress right now, and he doesn't understand the amazing work you two have done here." Walking around to Matthew with a smile on his face, he looked him in the eyes as if he were looking into Matthew's soul. "I think it's time for us to take this research to the medical community and start gaining some support. You've done well. I believe you really have something here."

"Thank you, Dr. Meachum," Matthew replied.

"Yes, thank you," Mare added.

Dr. Meachum squatted down and picked up a piece from the floor. It was a squiggly shape in bright yellow. Studying it for a few moments, he looked at Matthew and said, "Times." He handed the piece to Matthew and smiled.

Matthew replied, "Yes, that's right. Times." His face lit up with excitement, thrilled that Dr. Meachum had *gotten* the concept, the symbol having been one Matthew had used on many occasions to perform multiplication of numbers.

Before Dr. Meachum left, he turned and said, "You really think it's possible for humans to have trans-temporal cognitive abilities?"

Matthew looked at Mare and then back at Dr. Dimment, who was smiling broadly and said, "Yes, I think autism may be the evolution of man into many different worlds we have yet to imagine."

Dr. Meachum grinned and began to whistle as he turned and left the room.

***
ONE YEAR LATER

Matthew and Marilyn's innovation and hard work finally paid off. Dr. Dimment, Dr. Meacham, Marilyn Vanats, and Matthew Le'Dain were awarded the *Nobel Prize for Psychology and Medicine* for their research on "The Trans-Lit Project: Unlocking the Mysteries of the neurodivergent Mind."

14 *ARDUOUS ENDEAVORS*

Marilyn was worried because the recent success of the Trans-Lit Project Pictograph Dictionary for those on the spectrum was fleeting. She had read somewhere that success always comes with a price. The Federal government had demanded that D&M Research leave the New York Psychiatric Hospital and relocate near Washington, D.C., if they wanted to secure funding to continue their work. When research captures the world's attention by winning a Nobel Prize, it must be guided and regulated along its path. She sighed. No good deed goes unpunished, and no good idea escapes the control of those in power. Their growth would be severely restricted and much more costly, all in the name of protecting the public.

The once-coveted Nobel Prize they had earned was now little more than a political folly, considering many of its most recent recipients. Prizes are awarded to individuals who may do something that attracts media attention, rather than being based on hard work. Still, those who successfully weathered public scrutiny and made it through the tough way could be proud of their achievements. But Mare couldn't care less about any of her lifelong dreams that were about to come true.

Government funding, an endless source of unmanaged capital, was about to help her bring her dream to life. Public scrutiny was at an all-time high in Washington. Wasting money on those who could not fight the good fight would not sit well with the public right now. Pretending to closely monitor the research and its public funds would require Dr. Meachum's special talents—a role he relished and a feat he was eager to accomplish.

Mare knew she was the hidden creative drive behind their success. Dr. Meachum urged her to use this creativity to design a learning center for the general public, all at taxpayers' expense, of course. Her dream had always been to develop a public education center for autism, one that would also serve as an educational and training facility for educators and researchers.

Matthew, much too busy setting up his own laboratory, did not spend much time with Mare in developing her dream world. Again, she felt separated from him, but this time by both distance and lack of communication.

"I would like the centerpiece of the main hall to be an octagonal-shaped stone, rough and ancient-looking, like the Rosetta Stone. It will have to be grand enough to include over five thousand pictographs and word symbols," Mare explained to an artist, seemingly annoyed by the level of detail she was providing. She shaped the stone in the air with her hands, trying to describe her vision.

The relatively unknown Virginian sculptor had his own vision and was not inclined to listen further. His unkempt hair, rough beard, and barely tolerable clothing choices actually made her feel confident that he lived for his work, a trait many observers would dismiss if they were not keen enough to notice. Worn tennis shoes with stains of paint, plaster, and dirt provided her with additional confidence in his abilities.

Mare had seen some of his work at the Museum of Modern Art, and she liked what she'd seen—but there were other things about him that gave her the creeps. *Like Tibert. It was such a peculiar name. And why did he stroke his beard so much? And those bushy sideburns, ughhh! She couldn't imagine...no, she wouldn't want to know if he washes that thing.*

Shaking his head in agreement to clarify his timeline with Mare, he turned and headed for his car. She shrugged to herself as she watched him stalk away. Even though Tibert had some hygiene issues, she was enjoying every second of the planning—her dreams, about to become reality!

This moment... her moment...her ideas coming alive...she knew how Matthew had felt during the pictograph development. It was as intoxicating as a drug. The feeling was not adrenaline, but something else. Like a chemical release, she felt as euphoric as being in love for the first time. Still, something was lacking. The feeling was whole, yet empty. Hard to describe, but it was there.

It must be her maternal clock or something. No, it was more than that.

She suddenly had an overwhelming feeling that consumed her entire being, taking hold like a disease; it began to possess her, control her. Emptiness...the abyss...darkness. She felt a sudden wave of nausea. Something new, a womanly feeling of detachment. All she could think of in her most proud moment was...Matthew.

What is he doing right now? Has he eaten today? What are his plans for later? Why has he not called? Why can't she stop thinking about him suddenly? Is he alone, scared, does he need her? Is he even capable of loving her back? Did she just think that? She was going nuts! Was she going crazy? Work...concentrate...work is the cure, for now. He needs his space, that's all, just a little space.

Mare suddenly realized she had literally checked out. She was standing in the center of an abandoned plot of land littered with trash, weeds, and scraps of building debris scattered about. Even worse, a well-dressed young woman and two men, one older and distinguished, the other younger and similar in face, were standing there looking at her.

The young woman was trying not to laugh out loud, but she was failing badly. The younger man elbowed her, attempting to establish professional order.

The distinguished man looked her over from head to toe twice. Mare figured he must have seen something he liked or, worse, he was thinking with the wrong organ. Those types can be very unnerving, with their long, lingering stare. What she didn't need right now was a tool.

Extending his hand and stepping towards her, almost tripping on a scrap of old metal fence post, he introduced himself. "Good day, Marilyn Vanats, I take it," he said, smiling with his best behavior in check. "We are the architects. Dr. Meachum said we could find you here."

Mare nodded but did not speak. It was time to be an astute businesswoman.

"Weimer, Weimer and Weimer," he continued. "This is my son, Jessup, my daughter, Jenn, and I am Roland."

Mare decided to return the favor. She looked at each one from head to toe, cataloguing their attire, odor, and facial features to store away in her memory. Not quite as savvy as Matthew, she was still highly gifted in the art of memorization, as well. The young man she nick-named *Drakkar*, the girl, *Eternity*, and the distinguished man, *Old Spice*. Old Spice was a dead giveaway; in his own mind, he thought of himself as a player.

Seeing all three dressed in suits, Mare replied, "I'm not sure I'm dressed appropriately for the occasion. We are just missing Mrs. Weimer."

Mare was not trying to be insulting; she was just breaking the ice. However, she had apparently tapped into a nerve. Like so many offhanded comments not meant to sting, she found that her foot was almost completely inside her mouth, with no room for words to recant her statements.

The distinguished man smiled, but then tried to use it to his advantage. He stepped forward, turning to stand next to Mare, gently tugging her by the elbow towards the construction trailer that had been placed on what later would be a parking lot.

Mare glanced around one last time, seeing the city in the background, a single electric pole with a meter, and an old, dented trailer. It would be her office and home for several months.

"Actually, Mrs. Vanats—" he replied before being cut off by Mare.

"It's *Miss* Vanats. I am not married."

A dubious grin emerged on his face as he continued to lay the track for a future proposition outside of work. "Miss Vanats, it is, then. To answer your question, there is no Mrs. Weimer. We parted ways about a year ago. Divorce is a nasty thing. I wouldn't wish it on my worst enemy."

Mare thought to herself as he yammered away. *Let's see...Mrs. Weimer caught Mr. Weimer with lil' Weimer in something that he was not supposed to be in. Mr. Weimer lied, denied, then spied to keep his kingdom intact. A painful divorce ensued, and Mr. Weimer and the kids blamed her for everything. Mrs. Weimer was left with broken dreams, a little money, and failing looks. Piecing her life back together now is nearly impossible, so she now lives with her aging mother, caring for her every need, just like she did for these three ungrateful bastards.*

With a start, Mare realized she had done it again. Checking out of reality seemed to be the theme of late, and it was getting worse. Still, she was grateful to Dr. Dimment for making sure she'd had no seizures or migraines in quite some time.

"So, if you will allow us to spend a few minutes with you asking some basic questions, I think we can have conceptual models in a week or so," Mr. Weimer finished.

Not hearing most of what he said, Mare decided to be frank. "I'm sorry, but I did not hire you; Dr. Meachum did. He controls the budget. Now, if you can impress me as you said you would with some unique ideas, then you're hired; otherwise, I am inclined to look for other options."

Within a few short weeks, Weimer architects had completed two three-dimensional computer-generated model concepts. The first was a multi-storied dark tower theme. Mare and Dr. Meachum both agreed this would not work at all. The second theme was more than they could have imagined, and the private opening scheduled for mid-September would never be the same once the dream was turned into reality.

During the spring and summer months, Mare had coveted the monthly meetings at D&C research, now located in a military research complex about an hour away in Restin. She did not like the secured fencing, the military police, or the dungeon-like qualities of the facility. However, she saw that Matthew loved the regimented lifestyle it offered. Consistency and regularity were cornerstones of his make-up, and she also knew he was safe there.

Matthew had been learning to drive during these months, something Mare had never thought he would do. He had made some remarkable social improvements during his time away from her, and she noticed that he would ask her how she was doing and other normal questions.

Today, however, was very special, and she could not wait to share it with Matthew. Working around the clock, six days a week for over five months, the Education Center was nearly completed. Mare would give her last update to the team and invite them all to the grand opening on September 23rd.

Anxiety-ridden and full of anticipation, Mare parked her car just outside the research facility. Fumbling through her purse, she found her badge and clipped it on her shirt. Looking in the rearview mirror, she saw Dr. Dimment arrive in his older, dented Beemer and Dr. Meachum in his shiny new Mercedes. One last drag of her eyeliner, and the face she had been waiting to show off was complete.

Exiting her car, Mare exchanged pleasantries with both doctors. Interrupting their greetings, she heard a deep, groaning hum, as loud as a Chinese minibus. Out of the corner of her eye, she saw an all-terrain camouflage vehicle approaching. It was a four-seater with a short cargo bed and no doors. Mare did a double-take when she saw the driver—it was Matthew!

Dr. Meachum winked and smiled at Mare, standing with her mouth hanging open. "I've been teaching our Matthew how to drive. First with golf carts, now larger vehicles. I think he's ready to start practicing with a car. Perhaps Dr. Dimment would offer his gently used Beemer?" He chuckled at his own joke.

Dr. Dimment made a huffing sound and threw up his hand in response to the comment, trying to rebuke it. "Ah, rubbish."

Feeling both happy and worried at the same time, Mare threw up her own hand to wave at Matthew. Doing the same, he walked over to the turnstile gate awaiting their clearance to enter. She stared at him for a few moments, steadily rocking to and fro slowly, like a leaf caught in a gentle summer breeze. He was so handsome, so well defined, and he had even filled out a little more than the last time she'd seen him. He wasn't spindly anymore.

Dr. Meachum continued, "Our young Matthew has been studying martial arts. He is very astute, and he's adapted to it remarkably well. What level have you reached, Matthew?"

"Blue belt," Matthew responded.

"That's right, blue belt," said Dr. Meachum. "He practices every morning and afternoon, before and after work."

Mare almost walked into the turnstile bar when her card missed the proximity reader. "I can tell he's filled out very well," she replied. Her tone was of interest and intrigue. "He has muscles now."

Dr. Meachum and Dr. Dimment smiled at each other, and Mare blushed. She knew that Dr. Dimment wanted to create a child with the potential to be a super savant, and he hoped she and Matthew would be the parents. She felt both excited and disturbed by the idea. There was a strong chance the child could be normal, or it might even be born with serious birth defects. She quickly pushed the negative thought out of her mind. After all, she and Matthew were just friends—though sometimes she imagined herself truly in love with him. But the chance of Matthew ever having a romantic relationship was unlikely right now. She suddenly felt less hopeful. And she really wanted a baby—if she ever had one, Dr. Dimment would never get his filthy hands on it.

She restrained the strong urge to run over and hug Matthew. Looking around and waiting for Dr. Dimment to get through security, she enjoyed the sunny day. It was still very warm, but a gentle breeze provided some relief from the sun's intense rays. It was one of those days when you felt like you could fall asleep if the temperature were just a few degrees cooler. With bright smiles, they looked at Matthew, apparently lost in thought. But even though it was hot, Mare was just glad to be near Matthew.

Driving up to the doors of Building Six, Mare admired how clean and pristine the military base always looked. No trash, no cups, plastic bags, or cigarette butts littering the ground. The landscape matched the sky—clear and beautiful. Mare's thoughts grifted to the unkempt lot they started with at the Education Center compared to how it is now. Dr.

Meachum was the only other person who had seen inside the new facility, so Matthew and Dr. Dimment would be seeing it with fresh eyes.

When it finally came her turn on the meeting's agenda, Mare quickly outlined the upcoming schedule of events for the Education Center's grand opening. Reviewing the attire, schedules, and attendee list, she informed Matthew that she had already arranged a tuxedo rental for him. It would soon be just a matter of playing the role of a courteous host to politicians and government officials.

The real fun was about to begin.

15 *BLACK TIE AFFAIR*

A ribbon cutting kicked off the grand affair. Excitement and anticipation had consumed Mare's inner core for the better part of the day. Tonight, everyone, including Matthew, would see what her hidden talents really were. Reluctant to gloat, she didn't want to appear vain, but waiting to get the evening started was nerve-wracking.

One last dab of mascara and a quick swipe would do it. Turning her head to the right, then to the left, she inspected her handiwork, raising her chin slightly. Then, picking up a pair of tweezers, she plucked away an unwelcome free-range white hair from her chin.

I remember when I could throw on a touch of foundation and pinch my cheeks a little. Now, it's twenty minutes just for make-up. My mother's age spots are starting to appear.

Mare opened the makeup stand drawer, pulling out an old photograph of a woman very similar to herself, yet different. Her hand shook and her skin became cold as she laid it down on the table. Taking both hands, she pulled her cheeks up a little to match the young woman's high cheekbones. It was no use; her face must have matched her father's more. Yet she had no picture of him in the drawer. Picking up the picture, she flipped it over and read the faded-ink writing on the back. *"Merritt Rene Stewart, Class of 1964."*

In a few months, Mare would be thirty…thirty…unwed…no prospects…and childless. She quickly stuffed the picture back in its safe place, almost smashing her fingers in the process. Then she removed a more recent photograph from her mirror. It was creased in the middle, only catching a small bit of a man's shoulder. On the right half, a smiling Matthew was dressed in a black Tuxedo, holding an envelope in one hand and a trophy in the other. To the right of him, Mare looked enchanting in a dazzling blue dress with a conservative sprinkle of sequins and a matching scarf. Unfolding the picture, she felt her skin prickle as she revealed Dr. Meachum and his million-dollar smile, along with Dr.

Dimment with his menacing cold stare and unkempt appearance. The team.

Knock...knock...knock!

The loud rapping at the door startled her. She jumped up, grabbed a sweater and her handbag, and darted for the door. Tonight, they would ride to the affair in style. A black Lincoln Town Car, courtesy of the military research branch, was there to pick Mare and the others up and deliver them safely to the event. Opening the front door, a very dapper Marine Sergeant decked out in dress blues, stood facing her.

"Ma'am," was all he said while offering her a courtesy bow.

Looking him over, Mare took in his shiny black shoes, his blue pants with the blood red stripe, his trimmed, dark blue coat with gold buttons, and his white hat. An explosion of brightly colored awards and medals decorated his chest, including a Purple Heart and a Bronze Star. The young Marine offered her an arm, revealing his white gloved hands to escort her out to the car. His sword clanked once as he abruptly turned to make room for her to step into the hallway.

The ride to the facility was quick, Mare thought. However, she poked at her phone the entire time, catching up on social media. One thing she wanted was to convince Mathew to allow her to track him by phone and vice versa. But since they were not dating, she was hesitant to engage in such close personal contact.

The D&M research crew had arrived an hour early to make final preparations for the event. Dr. Dimment was already on his third drink by the time Mare arrived. Developing a strong affection for Kentucky Bourbon, his mistress sometimes became unmanageable when Meachum was not around. Mare just hoped he could keep him under control tonight.

This event also served as a fundraiser for the facility's operations. To ease public scrutiny, Meachum had floated the plan to try and support as much of the facility's operations as possible with public donations. The rest would come from grants. Mare secretly resented the salaries paid to all four of them. She would have done this for free, but having to bring in over half a million dollars just to pay the salaries of the four people seemed excessive. Of course, the two doctors were each paid twice as much as she and Matthew combined. Meachum would joke about it, saying, "People gotta eat." And why Dimment was on the payroll was a mystery to her. He did almost nothing to support the facility, and he had gruffed and grumbled for a year about its creation. But regardless, Mare was still proud of her accomplishments, regardless of Dimment or not.

The last of the "Fantastic Four" to arrive was Matthew. Mare had waited impatiently for him, pacing at the entrance of the red carpet. As the limousine door opened, Matthew stepped out, and she noticed he didn't look much different in body build than the Marine he was standing next to. A couple of inches under six feet, he stood like a shining knight in his black tuxedo. Nothing like the boy she knew at the Children's Hospital.

Matthew walked towards Mare, glancing at her and then looking down awkwardly. She thought it was cute that, after all the time they had known each other, he was still bashful around her. Suddenly stopping, Matthew bent down on one knee. He took his finger and traced out some of the symbols in the stamped concrete entryway, having immediately noticed the words she had placed in one section: "Time to listen."

When he stood up, he looked at Mare and smiled. Matthew had wanted those words as the foundation of his work. Dimment and Meachum had decided to go with something different. She was not surprised he would notice her insubordinate contribution. The doctors had stepped right over it, not even giving a second look at the symbols representing those words.

"Good evening, Mare. You look very nice," Matthew addressed her with no fanfare whatsoever. Monotone as always, but his emotionless demeanor seemed somehow less abrasive than usual. He seemed more comfortable with her.

"Mr. Le'Dain, you look absolutely debonair in your tuxedo and black tie," she responded, giving him her most dazzling smile.

Matthew looked around, making sure the coast was clear, and then tapped a button on the inside of his lapel. His tie lit up like a flashing, multi-colored Christmas tree. He smiled widely but didn't laugh out loud.

Mare giggled and covered her mouth to try and hide her smile from errant onlookers. She took Matthew by the hand, noticing he did not resist her advances this time. Slow, steady progress. She wanted to give him a personal tour before everyone else invaded their evening.

Having chosen the "wagon wheel concept" from Weimer Architects, she wanted to experience it with Matthew the first time he saw it to get his thoughts. The concept had seven sections separated by hallways, all coming together to form the wheel. The main entrance to the hub of the wheel was an open entryway. Earth tones, stamped concrete floors, western stucco walls, rough-cut wooden beams, and mud-stomped ceilings fully integrated the Trans-Lit system. Since the letters and numbers of Trans-Lit were three-dimensional shapes and colors, they could be hung like origami from the ceiling throughout the facility.

Tibert had lent an artsy touch to the actual symbols from their language system. Even though Mare had the most difficulty with him on schedules, his work was a monument to creativity.

The average person walking through here would probably think it was a museum of modern art. In some ways, it was. Mare knew that at some point, to advance the language and math, more human senses would have to be incorporated into the system, as Matthew had insisted on many occasions. He had always said that neurodivergents are four-dimensional thinkers, placing their sense of smell, touch, hearing, and so on, alongside their memory.

Coming out of the atrium were six other sections. They were all connected by a back hallway that led from each side of the entrance. You can either follow the seven steps of understanding autism from the main entry hall at the center hub or tour each one from beginning to end using the rear hall.

Each section was unique in what it offered the guest. One of the sections made you feel as though you were learning sideways, challenging the conventional approach of repetitive memorization. Another room made your mind think your eyes were deceiving you, placing one's mind in a four-dimensional world. Each room was designed to help visitors understand how the world appears from an autistic person's perspective. The most amazing room was the glass floor. The lighting and projectors underneath the floor actually changed. You could make people think they were falling, flying, or moving in the opposite direction. The room could transform into an ocean, a desert, or a forest. This, along with the air jets and mist sprayers, added to the effect. Cinematography and advanced computer simulation programs from the military were also utilized to create holographic images of the symbols, enabling a neurodivergent student to stand and become an integral part of the learning experience.

In the holographic room, the low lighting and looped computer program were already running. Matthew stepped into the center, seeing some familiar words pop up...happy, help, and hurt. He turned, almost with a sixth sense, and placed his hand on Mare's forehead as if taking her temperature. It was almost as if he could read her vital signs. His hand was warm and sensitive in its touch. Maybe he was remembering how tough the week had been for her?

Mare had never been prouder of herself than at this moment, but the constant workload had been taking a toll on her body. Earlier in the week, before the opening, she had collapsed in the hall with a seizure.

She hated having these episodic blackouts. She knew she was headed for one again and was powerless to stop it. To prevent a migraine, she had learned to just ride it out until it passed. There was no telling what her body was doing right now or what Matthew was thinking while she was in her catatonic state. The most peculiar thing was that her body would react to her surroundings, causing her to walk or sit. It was as if her mind had separated the part of thought from the parts of reality. Nothing like schizophrenia. She was completely aware of her body and her surroundings, but without control.

Matthew had been sitting on a chair in the corner of her room one day, reading books on neurology, angiography, and epilepsy. There were literally thousands of books on the subject. Matthew was so dedicated that he read books on the subject for the entire week to be able to discuss Mare's condition intelligently with Dr. Dimment. She remembered Matthew saying something wasn't adding up, but Dimment refused to let Matthew help.

Mare felt herself regress a little more with every seizure. However, It had been over a year since the last one. Dr. Dimment assured her that it was nothing to worry about.

Matthew had made claims that during her episodes, she really didn't appear to have had a seizure. He had told her it seemed more like a form of catatonia. She would just stop talking and stare into space. Mare had thought the same thing, but could not really remember anything about the event. Matthew described how it was very similar to how she was at the Children's Hospital years ago. He had said it was as if her battery had suddenly gone dead.

Mare knew Matthew had been worried she might not wake up in time to enjoy the opening of the Trans-Lit Education Center. She had a vague recollection of Matthew staying with her every minute, only leaving long enough to reload on books. In particular, she remembered Matthew having a deep discussion with Dr. Dimment about why he had kept her at his research facility and not at a regular hospital. She recalled the details of the discussion as if it were a movie starting, with Dimment administering some drugs to her through an IV.

"Mare's condition, what is the cause of her seizures, Dr. Dimment?" Matthew asked.

Dimment replied very defensively, "It's all perfectly normal. She just needs her medication, nothing more!"

But Matthew was suspicious and he continued to pry deeper. "If that's all she needs then why not send her to a regular hospital for care and let them administer her anti-seizure medication?"

Mare could hear Dimment's voice growing louder and more pronounced, but she was a prisoner in her own body and could offer Matthew no aid. Dimment stammered and stuttered. If Matthew could only see…recognize he was being misled. And then he took her by the arm and led her to a nearby chair.

"I haven't the time for these accusations," Dimment barked, but Matthew didn't back down.

Matthew was accustomed to ignoring emotion, and he therefore continued debating with Dr. Dimment.

Anguish for Matthew replaced Mare's thoughts of her own despair. She was more worried about him than her own safety, but unfortunately, she was the one incapacitated at the moment.

Matthew replied to Dr. Dimment, as calm and direct as ever, "I haven't made any accusations. I simply asked a logical question about her condition."

Dimment was now livid, and he replied defiantly, "I told you…you little busy body…she needs her medication. It is experimental…you can't simply fill a prescription at the local pharmacy. It is very expensive, and it takes months to develop and harvest only a small amount. What do you care? You were never worried about it before?"

With a loud "Humph," Dimment bumped Matthew with his shoulder—no apology—on his way out the door. Mare could hear the rude doctor huffing and puffing like an old steam engine.

She was worried that Matthew was beginning to suspect something. Even though, in a perfect world, discovering the truth would allow Matthew to rescue her from Dimment's clutches. But she knew that there was no way possible for her to share her secret with him, so it was better for Matthew to remain clueless.

And then she heard a kindly voice calling her name. The mind skip she had been experiencing had seemed so real. Somehow, Mare was aware that she was reliving an old memory, but it was being played out in her mind as if it were occurring now. Mare's eyes were wide open and she had not blinked for several minutes. Finally, she saw an image of Matthew's face looking down on her in a bed, but also straight ahead as she sat up. At that very moment, she was in two places in her mind, and she knew she was waking up.

"Mare," the kindly voice called out.

She began to blink normally as her mind settled back into her body.

"Where am I?" Hearing her own confused voice was startling. Snapping completely into real time, she awoke fully and found that she was standing up.

"Mare, you're in the Education Center. You had an episode, and you blanked out. I don't think it was a seizure, though," Matthew pointed out.

"I don't feel like I had a seizure, either. The last thing I remember was showing you around the Education Center. Maybe the flashing lights in the holographic room triggered it."

Matthew looked upset. "I'm sure it's not a seizure. If you would like to, I could study more on this and try to find out what is really wrong."

Mare knew what was wrong; she just couldn't share it with Matthew right now. She hated being in that dark place and didn't want to go back. As much as she disliked Dimment, he did save her from being a prisoner of her own mind.

"Matthew, please don't tell Dr. Dimment about this, promise me?" She squeezed Matthew's hand to reinforce the message.

"Okay, Mare, but you will need help if this continues."

Taking a deep breath and then picking up where she'd left off, Mare took Matthew to her favorite room at the Education Center. Walking along the hallway, she felt accepted by Matthew. No longer an outsider. He showed concern for her. Was he really developing social skills? And were they real or scripted? At the moment, she didn't care. She just needed a friend.

"The Learning Room is the best room. This is where you can find all the teacher resources. I have plans to bring every special needs and gifted learning teacher in the country through here. This is where the most impact will be gained. Our life's work is in this center, Matthew."

He nodded in agreement, as if he were a business associate, but she let it pass. It was good enough for now. Not wanting to waste the opportunity at hand, however, she decided to take a shot in the dark and confide her feelings to him.

"Matthew, none of us knows how much time we have on this earth. If we did, we would establish a schedule and strive to accomplish as much as possible. Right?"

"I suppose so."

She took a deep breath and made the plunge. "This also applies to you and me. I really care about you, Matthew. Why can't we be together all the time?"

Matthew paused, as if he were thinking on the question, trying to read her body language. Then he began to shift uncomfortably, looking down and away. Rocking in his stance, he replied, "Mare, we are together all the time."

Smiling, Mare corrected him, "No, Matthew. I mean in daytime *and* nighttime." *For a guy who has almost an incalculable IQ, he is oblivious to what I am saying. Are all guys this way?*

Matthew continued to rock, no longer looking at her.

Is he doing this as a defense mechanism, or does he understand what I'm saying and refuses to deal with it? "Just think about it, Matthew. I know you can do that, and the answer will come to you."

Seeing that the conversation was at an impasse, Mare felt it was time to return to her guests, so she left Matthew to his thoughts. Having been sidetracked by Matthew's private tour, she had said what she had wanted to say for some time. With conflicting thoughts of togetherness and separation shifting inside her head, she tried to focus on what was important at the moment.

The philanthropy and volunteer room was filled with hired young women and men there to schmooze and collect checks from the wealthy. Mare spent the next hour hosting the hordes of visitors. Touring through the entire facility more than once, she noticed Matthew had not rejoined them. Thinking hard about where he could be, she decided to go looking for him. Knowing he would retreat to a quiet place, Mare headed for the administration bathrooms.

***

The restrooms near the administration offices were posh—nothing like the public facilities. The doors on the stalls went all the way to the floor. You couldn't tell if anyone was in them or not, and the only opening was above the stall doors. Too high for even an NBA star to look over and see Matthew tucked away in the very last stall, reading a copy of Popular Science.

When two men entered the restroom, continuing with an argument as they burst through the door, Matthew recognized them right away—Dr. Meachum and Dr. Dimment. And because they were so loud, he decided to stay in the stall until they left. He knew that loud voices often meant trouble. Not being a covert operative, his instincts told him to stay put and be quiet.

"You're going to have to be more discreet, Gottfried. Otherwise, the whole European Union will be down our throats."

"Listen here, Lawrence, you have to crack a few eggs…you know exactly what I am referring to."

"I know, but you cannot let her go comatose and keep blacking out. People will start to notice… *He* may notice. And furthermore, you cannot forget that we need the boy, Gottfried. If that girl dies, we have nothing."

"I'm not worried about him. I have this under control. I'll smooth this over with the local officials in Berlin. They have the stomach for it there…*Lawrence!*"

"All I'm saying is if this gets out in the States, we're done for! We're finished! Who knows…if these two get together and mate, we may have an *ultra-savant* to play with."

"Now, who is being sick, Lawrence?"

The two men chuckled loudly and then proceeded to do their business at the urinals. Matthew wasn't sure what to make of the conversation, but his instincts told him to remain as still as a mouse. Who were they discussing and why?

"Look…I know you've been hiding your little research projects across the pond for years. I've overlooked it because I know you can't do research like that without live donors. But I'm warning you. You had better be less conspicuous. Not every parent will stay away for nine months. Besides, at some point, someone always finds out."

"Bah! Like you don't have your own little secrets, Lawrence."

"I took care of your other little problem in New York, Gottfried. Luckily for us, that nurse had some mental problems already on file."

"Please! Give me a little credit for hiring her."

"Well…nevertheless, we dodged a bullet. Our little problem is now locked away in a room, with a little white strait jacket and padded walls."

The two men laughed and then left the room. The urinals were still flushing when Matthew stepped out of the stall. Not knowing what to make of the conversation, he made a mental note and filed it away in his brain.

The conversation between the two doctors Matthew had overheard bothered him. He knew Dr. Dimment spent a lot of time away overseas, but he had never had a reason to be concerned before. Now, however, he found himself consumed by curiosity. Thinking of only one person he could turn to, he decided to see if Mare could help him piece it together.

Trying to find Mare in an immense facility like this would be impossible, so Matthew decided to retreat to a safe place—her office. He knew that eventually she would either go looking for him or come back here to retrieve her purse.

Sitting down in her office chair, he glanced around at the items that she looked at each day. From studying books on social behaviors, he knew that a person's desk was a showcase of what was important to them in their personal life at work. Looking around the mostly empty landscape, the only photograph was a picture of himself.

He picked it up and studied it, trying to recall when it had been taken. Oh, yes. At the Triumph Hotel. It was his last show, and he recalled it very vividly. *Performing a live show and managing personal interactions was one thing; entertaining politicians and wealthy donors was another.*

Hanging on the wall was a familiar picture drawn with colored pencils. Matthew recognized the math problem. It was the very first one he had ever done with Mare. The colors were striking. On the outside were two spatial numbers, and on the inside was the larger.

Matthew thought long and hard about how far they had both progressed since the institutional days. Taking a deep breath, he looked around the room. The smell of fresh paint, formaldehyde, and glue burned his nostrils. Mare's scented candles did little to mask the new building's stench.

Hearing footsteps, Matthew looked up, waiting to see who it was…the clicking sound of a woman's heels. He concentrated harder, listening to the density of the vibrations. Yes, it was a lighter person…the rhythm of the steps was familiar. Mare.

"Well, hello, Matthew. I thought I would find you hiding in here. Are you Okay?"

"Yes, I wanted to be alone. Away from all the noise."

"Well, come on, let's get out of here. We've done our saintly duty for this afternoon, and it's getting late."

Matthew had been thinking, in the back of his mind, about the question Mare asked earlier. Feeling a mutual kinship, he thought it would be nice to have a roommate. However, Matthew had misinterpreted what Mare had really intended, and he was just about to ask Mare an important question when Dr. Meachum burst in.

"There you two are! It was a success! A complete success! We could not have pulled all this off without you two."

He attempted a half-hearted hug on both of them at the same time. The attempt was awkward, however, and Matthew jerked away, feeling threatened by Dr. Meachum's invasion of his personal space. The noise of the wine glasses he held in one hand, clanging together, caused Matthew discomfort; feeling a cold bottle of champagne resting on his shoulder blade completely sealed his discomfort.

"Where is Gottfried…I mean, Dr. Dimment," Matthew inquired.

"Well, young lad… he had to take off, important business abroad."

Matthew, not being a person gifted with tact, remarked, "In Germany?"

"Yes, I believe that was where he was going. Nothing to worry about. Just a part of doing business." He filled three champagne glasses, offering one each to Mare and Matthew.

"Now that the Education Center is completed, what else is there for Dr. Dimment to do?" Matthew asked, causing an awkward silence.

"What do you mean?"

"Mare and I have discussed our next step. We can continue to expand the language sets, but we are at a place of diminishing returns based on the level of the students."

Mare spoke up, "The Federal Education Administration has asked me to serve on a committee to develop implementation plans to incorporate our system into the public schools."

Dr. Meachum glanced at Mare, and she looked back at him. He seemed to dislike her statement, but Matthew wanted to know what was next.

"Before we continue talking business, how about a toast? To the health and prosperity of the program and of our future."

The glasses chinked together, Matthew took a very small sip, and almost spit it out. Dr. Meachum and Mare chuckled. Reaching out and taking his glass, Mare set it down on the desk.

Dr. Meachum turned and set his glass down on a lamp table. Looking first at Mare and then at Matthew, he smiled while pausing to take a deep breath. "Matthew, you're a very brilliant young man. I am confident that you understand the fundamental concepts of business and economics. Along with the business aspects of any endeavor are the residuals that must be met. In this case, the residuals happen to be favors or requests."

He glanced at Mare again and then back at Matthew, providing a professional pause. Struggling to find the words to explain whatever it was he was trying to say without really saying it, he continued.

"Because we take money from government resources along with the private donations, we must also entertain other, more profitable pursuits. I'm not saying Mare can't embark on an adventure or two, or that we can't continue what we've started."

Mare looked startled, and Matthew was lost for a moment.

"What are you trying to say then?" asked Mare.

Pausing again, Dr. Meachum sighed and then continued. "We've been working on other programs far beyond what we've done here. Now, what we have done here is remarkable. You are a Nobel Prize recipient because of it, for God's sake. I would like you to consider using your talents to embark on a new adventure, a new journey. One of the discoveries. With your intellect, the sky is the limit."

Matthew looked at Mare and then back at the doctor. "What are you asking, Dr. Meachum?"

The doctor continued, "Matthew, we have a rare opportunity to branch out into several other areas. These endeavors are research in nature and highly classified. We're talking pharmaceutical, medical, and military."

Matthew began to fidget in his chair, feeling uncomfortable. However, his curiosity started to awaken. "Military? How could the military possibly tie in with autism?"

Dr. Meachum leaned forward, excited that Matthew had finally nibbled on the bait. "It is very complex, Matthew, and we can get into all that later. Let's just say this is not the first time the military has used savants. Most of the codes we deciphered and broke during World War II were cracked by a genius. He was a master cryptologist. What I am saying is that we have the opportunity to surpass codebreaking. We can unlock, no...*unleash* the human mind to do what it was always meant to do. Think!" He gestured wildly with his hands in the air, framing the picture of his conversation.

"By doing what?" asked Mare.

Dr. Meachum made a funny face at her question. It would be interpreted by a normal person as irritation, but Matthew didn't catch on.

"Using the aforementioned areas of science, Gottfried and I believe we can develop a brain trust."

Matthew replied, "A brain trust?"

The doctor forged ahead. "Yes, using gifted volunteers who are already four-dimensional in their thinking, we can build a brain trust. A pool of the most brilliant minds to predict and forecast events, crack computer viruses, and even new science we have never dared to dream of."

"What you're saying, Dr. Meachum, is you want to create a human-driven computer," said Matthew.

Replying with hesitation, Dr. Meachum answered, "In a way, yes. You know, yourself, what miraculous results come from using just a small percentage more of the human mind. With help, we plan to expand the human mind to its full potential. That's where you come in. You are the key, Matthew; you have always been the key with the Trans-Lit work. None of this would have been possible without you."

Mare shifted in her chair, seemingly hurt by what Dr. Meachum had said. Matthew knew what sadness looked like, and Mare had it on her face.

Mare spoke up, "This is a lot to consider, even for Matthew."

Matthew replied, "The science of the concept is very intriguing. I would like to push my mind further. I also want to help people. People like me. I know there is a fifth dimension of reality. I think I could prove it."

Dr. Meachum's eyebrows rose. Then, standing up, he had a smile that could not be wiped clean, for any reason. Matthew did not sense the danger, and so he proceeded on without considering any of Mare's objections.

"Dr. Meachum, I am interested in this notion. What is the next step?"

He leaned towards Matthew with a smirky smile and said, "Matthew, I am giving you a chance to go forward with almost no limits. All you have to do is say yes."

He looked at Mare and then at Dr. Meachum, "It must be used for the advancement of the human condition. I want to continue to look for a link to awaken and possibly cure autistic persons."

Dr. Meachum wrapped his arm around Matthew's shoulder and said, "It will be like the space program. There's no telling what discoveries we will find along the way. A cure for Alzheimer's, cancer, dementia, and possibly expansion of the brain's capabilities. To advance the human condition, as you say."

***

Mare was frightened for Matthew as well as for herself. She knew what Dr. Dimment was capable of doing, but she wasn't sure about Dr. Meachum. The prospect of dealing with him sent chills up and down her body. She always had an uneasy feeling around him, but his charm effectively balanced his peculiar personality, so it was quickly masked. Somehow, though, she felt that Matthew had unknowingly made a deal with the devil.

She watched with trepidation as Dr. Meachum let go of Matthew, feeling him pull away, and said, "Okay, my boy. Then it's settled. Tomorrow morning, Matthew, you will be the next McClintock. Matthew, this is what you were born to do."

16 *FANDANGLORIOUS*

Men of scholarly drive and great achievement never reflect much about their extraordinary lives. Matthew was no different. Accomplishing more than most people could hope to aspire to in a single lifetime and barely in his mid-twenties, Matthew's scientific life had given life to the world. Celebrating successes was an irrelevant human emotion he neither possessed nor endeavored to embrace. Never meaning to seek out fame, his pursuits of knowledge and perfection in thought fueled his drive for results. Now was his time to surge forward and strike before the enthusiasm and energy of youth passed by.

A drop in the bucket... a second in the sands of time... I need to focus... focus.

Matthew rocked the new leather, high-backed, lumbar-supported office chair to the limits of its mechanical integrity as he contemplated his path forward. The rhythm and timing of each forward and backwards rock was as accurate as a metronome.

The cheap battery-operated clock ticked so loudly it invaded his thoughts. Tick... tick... tick. Matthew had requisitioned an atomic digital clock that automatically adjusted itself to be precisely on Greenwich Mean Time for the Eastern United States Time Zone. Small things like this could get under Matthew's seemingly thick skin, but larger things like complete chaos and the world on fire would not faze him in the least. He squinted his eyes together as he rocked and covered his ears to block the noise. With no luck, he finally broke down and inserted a pair of mushroom-capped industrial earplugs from his top desk drawer.

Matthew could think of many a narrative to describe his ever-growing intellectual accomplishments. The opportunity afforded him by Dr. Meachum to explore them freely opened a vast chasm in which to bury his constant need to expand the boundaries of the mind.

His comfortable high-backed leather chair barely made a sound as he rocked back and forth in a socially acceptable manner. Matthew's office looked out into the laboratory on one side and the testing room on the other. With a simple touch of a button on his computer or a voice command, he could black out the windows completely or just prevent wandering eyes from looking in on him with a one-way tint. Matthew paid little attention to technical gadgets but admired them just the same. The water cooler, on the other hand, with its programmable flavors, energy, and vitamins additives, was his favorite gadget of all.

Deep in thought, Matthew found himself distracted at a time when distractions were a nuisance. Matthew still carried a heavy burden from the black-tie event. He never reflected on his work much; he just continued to move on. But now he had a personal life, out of nowhere it came, taking excessive amounts of time... time for which he felt lost without accomplishment to show.

His social skills were, at best, rudimentary. A cumbersome burden at hand was trying to find time for Mare. Though he had never considered having such a close companion, their compatibility from an intellectual view did make sense. Instead of parsing his mind to manage new scientific endeavors, he was in deep thought about improving his social life. Something he definitely had never imagined just a few years earlier. Mare had made him think about something other than work. Matthew, thinking earnestly, compiled a list of pros and cons of his situation.

There is a distance separation between our workplaces, which is very bothersome. My one-room residence is also an issue that needs to be addressed. Then there are my routines... my need for order... they may not run parallel to Mare's. In fact, we could experience significant deviations to the point where conflicts could arise.

Then there is her insistence on living together, which also made sense. We are best friends... she is my only friend. The distance separation would then become a pro instead of a con. Our working base's would allow separation to concentrate on work during the day and cohabitation activities after working hours.

A fearful thought suddenly entered his mind, a terrifying thought in fact. Matthew dwelled on it, trying to resolve it in his mind. His face contorted in an odd manner as if he were on the bathroom throne, struggling to resolve an intestinal issue. Matthew often battled with his mind. At times, it was as if there were two or three free-range Socrates trying to gain control.

I have barely considered the alternate reality that Mare did not want to be just roommates or just friends. In addition to all the other things, I need to find time to study the boundaries of male and female relationships. I just need to know the basics, nothing elaborate. Finding time to read right now would be difficult, but I will just have to make the time. After all... how difficult can heterosexual relationships be?

Physiologically, my body had changed. Taking martial arts training, as suggested by Dr. Meachum, has vastly improved my physical well-being. Clumsiness, balance, and strength had all improved as a result of the training. Internally, I could sense other parts of my body changing. There is the occasional burning in my groin, with the intense pain it causes. Paired with the overt aching pain in my testicles that came and went without notification. I know what my private possessions are meant for from a reproduction perspective, but that type of coital cohabitation is nothing I have endeavored to pursue. The thought of it is fear-provoking and, most of all, an outlandish consideration. I have never seen nor expect to see Mare in that manner. I would expect the luminosity of her thoughts to coincide. Integration on that level is too much to consider now.

Matthew struggled with his thoughts, volleying back and forth between different scenarios. A relationship was time-consuming, nearly mind-controlling. Wondering how his parents had been together for almost thirty years now seemed to be a major accomplishment, of which he had never given proper credit. His mind, however, began to become congested with thoughts outside of his own needs for the first time.

Books, articles, and television episodes flooded his mind like a tsunami. Waves of images and voices crashed down on him, tossing him in every direction. Matthew reviewed every relationship he had ever seen, from Captain Kirk and Edith Keeler to Clark and Lois and Rachael and Ross. He tried to reconcile his predicament as normal development, not really sure if it was or not.

The psyche and its construct show all of this as normal development according to Dr. Young's research. I know I am different… according to experts in the field of neurological sciences, but I am just me. I am Matthew, born of Panthea and Edouard Le'Dain. Social skills are my Achilles heel, and emotions… real emotions born of love and affection are adrift on a boat that may never reach shore.

Matthew's chair popped off the floor, startling him from his trance. Standing up to stretch his body and his mind, he walked into the research area to the water machine. He began hitting the touch screen. A pleasing affirmative electronic beep sounded each time he made his selections. When he hit the final selection button, the cooler played a catchy jingle in electronic format, matching a television commercial he had seen for Gold Water Springs, a subsidiary of a large soda company. In a few seconds, his vanilla-flavored water laced with multi-vitamins was firmly in his grip. He held the cup under his nose for just a few seconds. The smell of vanilla was strong, but just under it, he detected the more pungent odor of vitamins. Satisfied, his water smelled the same as the last time he had made the trip, and he took several sips. Matthew returned to his thoughts as he walked back into the office and took a seat.

Emotions require the correct chemical stimuli to be released in the brain, as well as pathways that are typically developed in adolescence, which I may not possess. Does the human brain create new neurological pathways in adulthood?

Matthew briefly pondered his new theory.

Conventional science says no, but I know I have felt changes. Have I created any new synaptic pathways, or have I just been able to memorize enough information to replicate real emotions?

This was a question he refused to answer for the time being. There were too many experiences left to be lived and too many opportunities not yet taken.

The struggles of life were finally catching up to him. Having avoided living a real life for so long, isolated in the comfortable solitude of his mind, Matthew had a major breakthrough. One he never even recognized. The mere fact that he was contemplating relationships, thinking about his future, and dealing with his feelings was akin to storming the beaches of Normandy in his small world. Matthew was thinking of someone besides himself.

Spending hours inside his mind meditating over the meticulous details of cohabitation with another person, Matthew had convinced himself that much research on the subject would need to be completed first. Besides, his only experience with cohabitation with others was his parents and Lea Tootchie and her man-child, Vincent. Socially, Matthew had been withdrawn, never noticing he was so different from the mainstream of relational society. Matthew's first recollection of being different was his time on the road with Lea. Her under-breath comments and loud phone conversations pointed out everyone's faults but her own.

Matthew's constant need for seclusion conflicted with these new thoughts and feelings he had recently been experiencing. This paradox had bested his mind for the moment.

Matthew shifted his thoughts back to work, deciding that too much time had already been devoted to non-work issues.

Dr. Meachum had moved Matthew's office to the underground 3rd level of the military research base. The two above-ground floors were for the less important research groups. Your importance ranking was largely determined by the number of floors you could access in the complex; everyone knew that. Security tightened with each floor you went down. In fact, only a few people knew the extent of the complex's depth. Embedded in Virginia limestone, the lower levels could withstand a near direct hit without sustaining much damage. Specially designed seals allowed the station to be secured level by level. Generators, emergency food supplies, and water could sustain the assigned personnel on each floor for months, maybe longer.

Matthew never worried too much about ever needing the safety features, but they were part of his training and security plan.

To compensate for Matthew's advanced ability to read independently with each eye, Dr. Meachum had his office space equipped to accommodate his special talents. Matthew's security access level was bumped accordingly as well. If warranted, Matthew had access to a limited number of satellites and most governmental databases.

Having spent an entire workday thinking about personnel matters, Matthew swore to be more productive in the coming days and weeks.

Matthew studied social relationships in the evening, as he had promised himself, and worked on his research. He spent the first three weeks reading research papers on what had already been completed, adopting a broad-spectrum approach. Reading everything from real science to science fiction on the subjects of genetics, pathology, neuroanatomy, neuroanthropology, neuroscience, and cybernetics. Matthew concentrated primarily on the connections between working, episodic, and semantic memory.

He knew firsthand that for savants in particular, episodic memories were stored in the hippocampus area of the brain. With the ability to access this area to a much higher degree, Savants could converge the four dimensions of reality and memory here.

Savants and gifted neurodivergents remember events just as if they were recorded on film. The major exception was their amazing ability to bind the five senses of touch, taste, smell, hearing, and sight to form four-dimensional memories in the mind. A difficult subject to grasp for laymen, true long-term memories are most often tied to a person's senses or feelings. The body senses the chemicals released in the brain, such as dopamine, which evoke the euphoric feelings of love and associate them with a memory. Memories such as a first kiss, a first love, or a happy moment. When the memory is recalled, those same chemicals are released in lower levels, making you feel the same. Now, add the senses of smell, touch, or taste. When you recall a savant's memory, you actually relive the moment in every detail. A gentle warm breeze on your cheek and the smell of chlorinated water in the air may be tied to fond adolescent memories at the local pool.

For Matthew to advance far beyond the known conventions of the day, he knew he had to reach a fifth dimension. He would have to establish a sensorial link between Gravitoreception, Electroreception, and Magnetoreception and the memory receptors in the brain. There may be other links that have never been explored as well. To become fully enlightened, Matthew sought a way to tap into parts of the mind that had never been accessible to human use. The details of getting there had left him at an impasse for now. His mind was getting ahead of itself as usual.

Baby steps... I have to take baby steps... map out a plan. If Mare were here, it would have already happened, but she isn't here to hold my hand and keep me on the straight and narrow.

Matthew knew he had to not only prove his theory was possible but also obtain repeatable results. To allow others to experience and develop the capacity to replicate what happened in his own mind could change the world. Normal conventions of learning and memory would be transformed.

Matthew had often thought of his predicament as either a curse or, at times, a blessing in disguise. What if the evolution of the human mind were emotionless, focused solely on logical thinking? Gene Roddenberry's envisioned race of Vulcans was the closest example Matthew could find as a model. Yet, even within the structure of Vulcan development, there were constraints. Crossbreeding caused conflicts, and with the apparent dilution of human DNA, the chances of breeding or maintaining a superintelligent race were very unlikely. That was not Matthew's goal anyway; his aim was human development toward a state where emotions took a backseat to creativity and logical thought. Perhaps autism, as we know it, is an evolutionary change in human development that is not yet fully perfected. Moving from emotionally guided thought to logical, clinical, and rational thinking could be the ultimate goal of human progress. The pinnacle of existence.

Memories created within the fifth dimension of the mind would essentially be relived exactly how they happened. Sensing déjà vu or surreal moments in time are as close as a normal person could ever come to scratching the surface of what Matthew aspired to achieve. Doubts arose; however, he was not even sure it was possible. Nevertheless, if that level of awareness could be reached, body experiences would not only be possible but also controllable. Reading someone's mind would be old hat. Seeing the world around you from a five-dimensional view would be... it would be fandanglorious.

Not one for frivolity, the endless possibilities excited Matthew in a way he had never seen. Feeling excitement over an accomplishment was also not a trait he normally embraced, either, but he was changing internally... mentally... neurologically, to be precise.

Matthew's aspirations were broad, but they opened up the possibility that memories could be shared, traded, and stored just like information in a computer file or book. It was not outside the realm of possibilities that telekinesis and telekinetic powers would be achievable as well.

There was a saying Matthew had remembered seeing in Popular Science magazine, "Today's science fiction is tomorrow's reality." De Vinci's flying machine sketches became the Wright Brothers' reality. The world continually moves on, the players may change, but imagination has no limits. It charges forward... sometimes painfully... tearing down walls... but forward nonetheless. Matthew was a firm believer in imagination and no limits on the human mind's capabilities. He dreamed of a new world where computers would become extinct. One in which the human mind made them obsolete.

Shifting his thoughts to his new laboratory and research area, Matthew concentrated on the work at hand. Matthew opened his well-stocked mini-fridge and grabbed a yogurt. He never left the laboratory except to use the restroom. There was no need to. He came to work in the morning and left in the evening like a ghost.

Matthew tinkered with the computer monitors and keyboard. Setting up his voice recognition signature, he was almost completely settled, having made all but final adjustments over the last few days. Compensating for his often manic research blitzes, he set up a four-screen computer monitor system. Using newly accessible NASA mainframe computers, the speed of his computer processing time was enhanced tenfold. Abandoning his old two-screen system, the two-by-two stack of screens was much more attuned to his abilities.

Frustrated with a normal keyboard, the boys at NASA sent Matthew a prototype. Originally designed to utilize natural finger movements and prevent carpal tunnel disease, the natural keyboard, as it was called, was installed. It was equipped with conjoined thumb and acceptance pad features for either hand. Combined with the right and left hand index finger keys inside an envelope, key stroke and entry times were also reduced. Matthew rarely used it anyway. Voice recognition was his favorite electronic vice.

With Mare a permanent part of his life and his access to military security, Matthew hacked into Mare's work security system and her personal computer's camera. This allowed him to observe her habits and demeanor, gaining a clear understanding of who she was.

Mare, unaware that her computer camera could be activated, was oblivious. In fact, Matthew had stumbled onto a well-kept military secret that allowed any cell phone with a camera to be activated. This type of technology in the wrong hands was terrifying, but Matthew was a responsible and respectful hacker. With his clearance and the Patriot Act behind him, he kept her in the lower right corner of one of his vision in a three-by-four window.

His monitors were so revolutionary that he could pull work from them with a Dipolar glove and place them on the holodome monitor in the center of the room. More advanced equipment from the NASA team. The Dipolar glove was another experimental perk of working in the government system. Dr. Henry Hanover, a renowned computer development specialist, had developed it for NASA while doing research with his small Positronics company. Matthew had never met him, but Dr. Meacham was in with many people Matthew had never met.

Matthew created a complex matrix of his theory, based on priority, risk, and need, to map out a plan to tackle major issues one at a time. The plan was encrypted so that only he had access. On the holodome, it displayed as a holographic diorama or map. The holodome was a very capable piece of hardware that made tracking progress on his neurological research effortless. The research block was tackled first. Being the easiest, it was also the number one priority, like a roadmap; you cannot pick a direction to move forward until you know where you came from.

The mind is a considerable variable to tackle. Even with the Rosetta Project's language, varying degrees of autism, along with the patient's age, further complicates finding consistency in research data, Matthew discovered.

Between the ages of three and nine, the brain develops at an astonishing rate. Neuropathways grow and branch out like crabgrass in these early developmental stages of life. For these patients, a pharmacological cure to open their minds was a possibility. However, gaining permission and access to do human trials was very risky, and the returns could be very inconsistent.

For ages ten through seventeen, the rate of synoptical development slows to a more predictable pace. Modeling this age range would make it easier to tap into their cognitive abilities. Research could be divided into two areas: pharmaceuticals for high-functioning patients and surgical modifications for those with moderate to severe autism. Once again, collecting a test group would require guardianship permissions. No longer accessible to patients as they had been in New York, Matthew decided to focus on a select volunteer group.

The eighteen to twenty-five age group was chosen because it would be easier to find volunteers. Advertisements were specifically placed looking for individuals diagnosed with broad-spectrum disorders related to autism who have high-functioning speech abilities and decent motor skills. In fact, the characteristics most closely matched those diagnosed with Asperger's syndrome. The listing never mentioned anything about disorders. Behavioral and ritualistic traits like isolation, tics such as rocking, tapping, or humming, high IQ scores, photographic memories, inability to make and keep friends, obsessive or unusual hobbies or interests, etc. Matthew was amazed to see from the applications how many people believe that because they can memorize every episode of Star Trek or build a computer at home, they think they are geniuses. Sadly, many of these applicants went home feeling sad and dejected.

After several long weeks and hundreds of applicants, hoping to earn substantial monetary compensation for the year-long trial, plus free room and board, he settled on twelve volunteers. This test group would first undergo several detailed tests to discover any hidden talents and the degree of their natural intellect. One week after the selection of the twelve, he was down to nine volunteers, then seven.

Matthew intended to keep the group small, but not this small. Within this group, he ended up with five borderline savants and two broad-spectrum autistic mutes. None of the test groups had suffered any major head trauma or known birth defects according to MRI scans. Advanced cognitive neurological mapping resulted in dissimilar brain scans. Comparing them against one another, stimulated areas of the brain varied. This is exactly what Matthew had hoped for. With historical research completed weeks ago and a viable group to work with, Matthew was ready to move forward with the real work at hand.

Matthew began to study surgical implant designs. His goal was to create one similar to that of a Turret's patient that emits electrical impulses to stimulate and promote neurological growth in the areas of communication and speech. All of his research so far had been computer simulated, but the goal was to design one that breaks down the proteins blocking natural signals. He also hoped it would stimulate new growth. He had read that damaged areas of the brain can repair themselves, but it was very rare, and a healthy brain might not respond to that kind of radical treatment.

17 GROWING PANGS

Although Seclusion was Matthew's shield and his mind was his sword, he struggled to master the politics of professional life. Without Mare to lead and guide him through many routine everyday work issues, Dr. Dimment had come to his aid.

Matthew began to focus as much on the discussions and presentation of his work as he did on the research. Matthew was aware that Dr. Dimment was not only jealous, a concept Matthew found intellectually disturbing and juvenile, but also very displeased with the test group.

Dr. Dimment and Dr. Meacham had started dropping by during the testing phase. They reviewed Matthew's progress based on his research logs and observations from the room above his workspace. Matthew was aware that they answered to a team of military and government bureaucrats. What they were looking to gain from his research was unclear. Matthew's goals were very clear. Unlock the secrets of the Savant mind and awaken the Neurodivergent mind to communication and possibly emotional contact.

Dr. Dimment had disagreed with Matthew's test group and tried to force Matthew to use moderately functioning neurodivergent patients, most of whom could not communicate except through Rosetta's methodology. Dimment's goals were to continue promoting and building on past accomplishments. Ride the success of a great invention and be a one-off. This was not Matthew's or Dr. Meachum's style. This is one trait they shared. However, for now, Dr. Meachum supported Matthew.

Separating his mind briefly from the growing pangs of professional life, Matthew watched as Mare entered the room. Like clockwork, she sat down at her desk. Her cup of herbal orange spiced tea steamed just in front of her. Looking at her computer, Matthew leaned in to enlarge the viewing screen.

Matthew's interest in watching Mare at work had been growing over the last few months. He studied every detail of her face, memorizing every imperfection, no matter how slight. There was an almost unnoticeable mole the size of a pinhead under her right eye. A tiny scar from childhood above her left eye from stitches. There were no real deep age lines around her eyes, but being at least in her early thirties, tiny creases had begun to form when she laughed, winced, or had the sun grins.

Their conversations had been relegated to the monthly staff meeting and a weekly dinner on Thursday evening at Leo's Greek diner. Mare had not pressed Matthew since the black tie event, but somehow, he was receiving the subtle dissatisfaction in her conversations and looks.

Matthew was mechanical and predictable in his behavior around her. They were learned behaviors, not innate. For instance, his greeting was a compliment to her appearance. Not really being tied to her actual appearance, but a need to be proper and courteous. Women's magazine articles seemed to provide Matthew with the most help, but still, it was an act, a rehearsed line, or an unnatural gesture. He could tell Mare picked up on it. She would grin or smile just enough to let him know, but not so much as to be rude. He thought she at least applauded his efforts.

Seeing Dr. Dimment peering into his office through the testing window with his hands cupped to the glass, Matthew quickly shrank the screen down to hide it. Fortunately, Matthew had set the observation window for one-way. She could see out but not in. With a one-word command, he said, "black." The window went dark, and Dr. Dimment's greasy face disappeared from his view.

There was a sudden banging and pecking on the window. Matthew exited his office to compensate for Dr. Dimment's complete lack of patients.

Dr. Meachum greeted Matthew with a million-dollar smile.
"How are you today, my young man?"
"Fine," Matthew replied.
"A man of few words as always."

Dr. Meachum had thought about slapping Matthew on the back like an old chum, but remembered who he was with and placed his arm down awkwardly in mid swing.

"I guess you know Dr. Dimment is on the war path."

Matthew surmised this was an analogy, not a fact.

Matthew nodded to signal he had heard him.

"The test group, Matthew, he just needs some assurances that you made the right decision. Well, we all do."

Dr. Meachum gestured to the observation room one floor up, looking over the laboratory and test area. The high ceilings in the work area gave way to observation decks, which were enclosed behind glass and walls. It was designed to allow anyone with clearance to monitor and observe the work at any time. Matthew paid no attention to it, and most of the time, they were empty.

Dr. Meachum escorted Matthew up to the observation room. They both scanned their credentials in front of the proximity reader. The door slid open, allowing them to exit. Down a concrete-walled hallway to a set of steel and concrete stairs through a second sealed door that required a scan, they went.

Entering the observation room, Matthew was met with a sea of stern faces. Not being a person of emotion, he ignored the cold, clinical look that would have made others quake in their boots.

In front of the review team composed of high-ranking military officials, scientists, and bureaucrats, Matthew began to state his case.

Matthew picked up a remote and turned on the projection screen. From his phone, Matthew sent the slides to the projector. A series of colored slides of the brain's response maps from the cognitive testing of each team member was revealed.

"This series of slides is the result of the brain scans during cognitive testing."

Pausing, Matthew looked around the room… no one moved… no one spoke. They appeared not to even blink or breathe. They sat there quietly like a series of decaying Roman statues. Dr. Dimment fidgeted and twisted, waving his hands in the air, trying to gain their attention. Still, they stared intently without judgment or emotion.

Once the team of seven had displayed their work, Dr. Dimment struck without warning.

"None of them is the same. They are a random group. There is no way to gauge progress or compare results. See what I am saying?"

The group broke their motionless trance and looked around at each other, but still did not reply.

Dr. Meachum threw a bone out hoping Matthew could bite on it.

"Matthew, I am sure you have a logical reason for your choice. Why don't you go through it?"

Matthew touched his phone, showing a combined slide of the synaptic responses; about sixty percent of the brain was covered. Matthew paused, and he saw some of the members lean forward to make sure their eyes were not deceived. To complete the synaptic map, Matthew added his own response diagram, which nearly completed eighty percent of the puzzle.

A low murmur of conversation erupted from the group. Dr. Meachum smiled wildly as Dr. Dimment stormed out of the room, embarrassed.

Dr. Meachum spoke up again.

"Matthew, to be clear, could you describe what you are doing here?"

"My purpose for selecting this particular group was to try and provide a glimpse as to what it would look like to have a single individual be able to utilize one hundred percent of their brain's capacity to think, feel, memorize, and learn. Since no one has that ability, it would take a group of people to accomplish this."

The room was full of smiles and nodding heads.

"Go on, Matthew," one of the military Generals responded.

"By studying our differences, I am hoping to discover how each person has developed to use a particular part of the brain that another has not. Once known, I will move my research into developing a method via chemical, surgery, or other methods to try and expand a single person to reach this level."

"It's not possible," a woman barked.

"We are wasting time and money here," another person proclaimed.

Dr. Meachum held up his hands as he stood trying to hush them.

"Wait... wait... wait... ladies and gentlemen. I think what Matthew is saying is that the ultimate goal is to reach this level or capacity. However, since we normally only utilize ten percent of our brain, increasing it to fifteen or even twenty would be an astronomical leap."

Dr. Meachum walked around the room, capturing their attention and looking each member in the eye.

"If this is possible... and I believe it is... what Matthew is proposing has immense possibilities. Look at what mankind has accomplished with one arm... no, both arms tied behind his back. No, imagine what creativity would be unlocked, doubling the mind's capacity to think... dream... create... memorize... cure."

The General stood up, followed by the others, and spoke for them all.

"I think we have seen enough to continue forward. I suggest that your team work as a team."

Matthew had no intentions of discrediting Dr. Dimment, but each day after that meeting, he seemed to grow more envious and hostile towards Matthew. Matthew had heard a rumor from a fellow researcher that Dimment once tested himself to see if he was of a savant's level of intelligence, but fell well short of the criteria.

Six months had passed since Matthew had moved into his new home. Working long days and even sleeping nights at the base had taken a toll on his body. Mare had suggested he... they needed to take a break. Agreeing, Matthew arranged a trip for Mare and him. It was a regular spot his mother and father went to every year on their wedding anniversary.

Mare had been seizure-free for some months now and seemed to be healthy enough for travel. Dr. Dimment was very opposed to Mare being very far away. Matthew never questioned his intent behind it, assuming that he acted as a surrogate father to her.

Mare never discussed her parents. Matthew only knew they had died in a car crash, and she nearly perished with them. From a very young age, the only people she has ever really known closely are Dr. Dimment and Dr. Meachum.

18 *CALAMITY FALLS*

Mare looked at Matthew funny as they exited the plane in Buffalo. After claiming their baggage and hailing a taxi, they headed towards the falls.

"Matthew, why did you want to come here? We could have gone anywhere."

Matthew, staring out the window, not really looking at Mare, replied, "My mother and father always came here… it has scenic views."

Matthew turned to look at Mare, sensing she was unsure. "Do you not want to be here?"

Thinking she may have been too harsh, she replied, "Yes… I wanted to go on vacation… this is just a peculiar place to bring a girl."

Matthew developed a confused look on his face. "I really don't know what you mean."

"Matthew, I want to ask you something, and I want you to be completely honest with me. How long have you been watching me when I am at work?"

Turning to look Mare in the eyes, he moved from confused to a new feeling. One he had never experienced. It was odd and uncomfortable. His palms became sweaty, and the air in the car suddenly felt stuffy. Feeling his mind was battling a war of good and evil, he phrased his thoughts in his mind first. He struggled to be honest, but an even stronger voice was echoing a call of deception.

Several awkward moments passed, and Matthew finally stammered a reply. In his usual deep matter-of-fact voice, he replied. "For several months, as soon as I obtained level two clearance."

Watching Mare's face, Matthew decided she seemed relieved by his answer.

"But why do you want to do that secretly? Why not just ask me? We could have been video chatting all this time. You know… getting to know one another."

Matthew hastily replied, "But I have been getting to know you by watching you work. I just want to know you're safe."

"Safe! That's an odd answer."

"Odd…, Matthew replied, turning his head sideways as he thought about the implications of her statement. "Why is that odd?"

"Well, let's just say it was not the answer I was looking for. I guess you do the best you can."

A long pause passed between them, then complete silence as they turned away from each other, staring out the window in opposite directions. The wheels of the cab beat methodically along the concrete highway as they passed the time, locked in their own separate world of thought. Thump… thump… thump… thump… over every seam in the concrete the cab went. Matthew mentally timed the instant the cab wheels hit each seam to pass the time. He calculated the length of each section based on the cab's speed and the time elapsed between the sounds. They were averaging seventy feet per section, with some being much shorter due to road repairs. He would have the distance between exits they had traveled down to the nearest foot by the end of the trip.

The cab reeked of a musty, cheap air freshener and dank, mildewed carpet. As Matthew ticked away the seconds in his mind, he looked at the floor of the cab. It was not particularly clean. There was a chocolate smudge on the back of one of the seats. The floor was composed of tiny granules of rock, sand, and soil. Old chewing gum marks blended with the black carpeting, having been soiled by hundreds of dirty shoes. A broken corn chip was stuck beside a seat bracket on the floor. It looked particularly fresh, Matthew thought.

Silence dominated the ride up to the falls, but Matthew had been too observant of trivial pursuits to pass the time to notice Mare.

The female driver, after asking for a destination, had not spoken another word except to request her fare when they arrived at the hotel. Wearing a ball cap and an oversized hoodie, she concealed her particularly pleasant looks.

"What do you want me to do with these bags, sir?" she asked as they exited the car.

Mare replied, seeing the hotel staff arrive immediately with a cart, "he will take them."

Matthew walked around the cab to meet Mare. The sun offered them both a pleasant warmth, neither too hot nor too cool. Bird chirps twirled through the air and mingled with the scent of water. A constant loud thunderous roar echoed in the background, consuming much of their ability to hear one another. Tuning into its origin, Matthew escorted Mare towards the fall lookout as the luggage scurried off on a cart in a different direction behind them. Matthew had been there several times before with a nanny while his parents honeymooned in a separate suite. The nannies liked the falls Matthew recalled.

The closer they came to the far-removed lookout, the more Mare's face began to brighten. She had been glum the last half-hour of the trip, Matthew thought. Looking down into the gorge from several thousand feet away, you could spot tiny taxi boats bobbing up and down at the base of the falls.

The enormity of the falls was spectacular. The angle of the sun created a rainbow in the mist, which was visible from several spots from their vantage point. The roaring sound of millions of gallons of water pouring over the cliff and crashing on the stones below deafened the sounds of the seagulls passing overhead. Matthew felt small looking at the falls, but not as frightened as he was as a child. He recalled briefly throwing a tantrum as a child, not wanting to ride the taxi boat near the base. In his mind, the falls were a huge gaping, slobbering mouth of a Saint Bernard waiting to swallow him whole. He had always viewed them from a distance, not wanting to be very close. Still, how could anyone look at them and not be amazed?

Mare was quickly bored with the view, to Matthew's surprise. Almost every person, at first glance, stared at their majesty for hours, lost in deep admiration. Matthew finally sensed something was eating at her as she turned and began to walk back towards the hotel.

Matthew had brought her there to simply show he cared, to strengthen their friendship. He did not really know how to be around her. He would have to use any and all rehearsed scenes from movies, television, and his parents to survive the trip with their friendship intact. Giving his best effort, Matthew caught up to Mare and reached out to take her hand. This simple gesture was normally carried out by Mare. She looked down when he touched it and clinched with a light grip. It was not the way she normally held his hand. It was limp and lifeless. Matthew hoped that dinner would go better.

***

They headed back to the hotel to check in and freshen up. Mare waited on a velvet-cushioned oversized chair while Matthew checked them in. It was next to a water fountain adorned with cherubs shooting arrows. Flowers, plants, and lilies inside the fountain completed the picturesque view. Mare watched the comings and goings of all the patrons. Couples, couples, couples in all directions. There was a uniform mixture of ages amongst them, she noticed. They were from nineteen to ninety.

Her heart felt heavy. She watched Matthew from behind. From her vantage point, he looked and acted normally. Deep down, she knew he was not normal, not in the traditional sense. He was talented, handsome, and gifted, but not with the commonly associated emotional traits she so desired him to have.

Would I trade all our success and accomplishments just to live a normal life with him?

Not entirely sure of the answer, her heart said yes… yet her mind, her considerate mind, said there was still much to do. Matthew had not reached his full potential and may never. He had so much to offer the world, and what right would she have to deny the world of him? The language system they had developed, the Autism Awareness Center… where would those on the spectrum go in their absence? A revolution had begun, and now even the government's educational system was fully on board, gaining ground with the public.

Martial arts... in a million years, she never dreamed Matthew would have become a black belt. Every day at four o'clock, Matthew took private lessons at the complex gym in the racquetball room. He had filled out so well that the spindly man he once was... was now a faded memory.

Mare noticed Matthew walking towards her. She reached down towards the floor and retrieved her handbag, stood, and smiled to let him know she was proud of him. Proud of him for just trying, yet the smile was thin, and she knew it.

***

"I have the room key, Mare. They gave me two."

Matthew extended his hand, reaching the card to her.

"Did you say room or rooms?"

"Room. It has two separate bedrooms with locking doors."

Mare's face changed from a thin smile to the glum look she had in the car instantly.

Matthew knew he had said something aloof but failed to pinpoint what it could have been.

He made his best attempt at a smile. Looking like a chimpanzee instead of a human smile Mare giggled affectionately. If nothing else, Matthew had changed her mood, he thought.

Mare laughed saying, "We wouldn't want anyone to talk about us would we?"

Matthew went from smiling to his confused look, "Talk about us....why would they do that?

"What did you have in mind, Matthew?"

Failing to understand the sudden change in her expression, it reminded him of the girl who had taken Mare's present at the Children's Hospital. She twirled her hair with her fingers and walked around half-naked. Matthew did not understand her demeanor any more than the look

Mare gave him. All he knew it was one she had never expressed to him before.

His palms turned sweaty, and he could feel an uncomfortable wetness develop under his arms. His temperature elevated, and Matthew swore he could smell something in the air. It was not her cologne but something else in it. He felt a little woozy, and his heart began to beat faster. Mare took her hand, gently rubbed her finger down her face, still looking at him the same way.

Matthew's comfort level was shattered, but he could not pull away. It was intoxicating, even though Matthew had only tasted alcohol once by accident, he immediately felt that same tingly sensation it provided. This feeling, though, was multiplied by a hundred.

"You're blushing, Matthew."

He said nothing, trying to fight an unrecognizable sensation overtaking him. His pants felt tight, but he was too embarrassed to adjust them. It began to hurt down below, and it was uncontrolled and uncomfortable.

As quickly as it started, Mare changed her demeanor and the conversation, letting Matthew off the hook for now. "Well, what's the plan? We can't stand here all night."

Matthew finally came to when a small yipper barked at him; it was a Yorkie. Matthew was terrified of dogs, and it caused him to jump sideways. He fell into a luggage cart, almost flipping it over.

Mare reached out a hand to help steady him, giggling as she came to his aid.

"Are you Ok, Matthew?"

"Yes, I'm fine. Dogs don't like me."

"That's nonsense." Mare straightened his shirt, brushing her hands down each shoulder to reassure him.

"You're as cute as a button and as sweet as candy. What's not to love? So what's the plan, Mr. Le'Dain?"

"Freshen up… dinner… then maybe we will discuss our work."

"You're so cute when you answer," she said, laughing as they walked towards the elevator.

"So, what's our room number?"

"Three-forty."

Mare turned towards the elevator. Matthew took a few steps and jumped again as the littler yipper barked at him. He was acting like Jerry Lewis in "The Nutty Professor."

When Matthew opened the door to their suite, it was like entering a luxury home. He had rented the Presidential suite.

Mare's face brightened again, he noticed.

"The room is huge, Matthew. You didn't have to be so extravagant, but I love it."

"Taking into consideration supply, demand, and basic economic factors, the most expensive room had to be their best room. It was the only one available with two bedrooms."

Mare laughed from another room.

"Matthew, can I take this room? It has a bathroom attached to it." She was standing just inside a set of double doors to a white and gold decorated room.

Matthew, standing in a similar room with its own bathroom, did not quite understand the difference but agreed. He was generally a trusting and very agreeable person.

Walking back into the kitchen, he looked through the fully stocked refrigerator and cabinets. They had anything you could want. The cabinets had cereal, rice, caviar, and several other food amenities. He turned and headed back to the main living area to sit down.

Matthew, surveying the space, noticed Mare's door opened well enough to see in easily. She was undressing out of his view. A blouse dropped to the floor. A few seconds later, her skirt drifted down in front of the gap.

Mare belted out, not really knowing Matthew was right next to her door.

"I am going to take a bath and get rid of that cab smell if you don't mind."

"No...I don't mind."

Mare shifted her position, and he could now see just a small sliver of her entire right side. Matthew noticed some small scars and marks on her legs and back. He thought they must have been from her childhood car accident. Nevertheless, she still looked magnificent to him. She looked like a statue of a goddess. Matthew was fixated on her, something he found to be intriguing. He did not see her in a sexual way but more as a cherished friend.

Passing by the crack in the door towards her bathroom, he noticed her braless breast. Still wearing her underwear, she disappeared into the bathroom, leaving the door cracked halfway open. Matthew could see through the ajar door better now than before. The thought of moving had never crossed his mind. He studied her movements just as he had done at work. His thoughts were born of innocence, naivety, and a curious mind. She was now fully exposed to him from her waist up in the bath mirror. She leaned out of view to turn on the water in the bath, then returned. She slipped out of her bottoms. For a few moments, he watched as she washed her face with warm water, soap, and a washcloth at the sink.

Turning, she went out of view, sliding down into the water. Only seeing part of her head now, Matthew watched intently. He had never seen anything like it ever... especially not in person and so close up. He had seen a woman's body in medical pictures but had never looked at them in the manner he now did. The mirror began to fog up, masking his view.

As the water stopped flowing, she reached out, closing the curtain. Silence fell in the room, and Matthew began to look around to see what else was in their richly decorated suite. Matthew turned back towards the crack in the door, hearing loud sloshes of water. When he looked up, he noticed Mare looking back at him, nude, reaching for a towel to wrap around her head. Exchanging eye contact, Mare sat back down in the bath, paying little attention to Matthew's voyeuristic curiosity.

He could not pull his eyes away from her. It was like studying a beautiful butterfly in the wild and trying your best not to startle it away.

Suddenly, there was a loud banging on the door. Matthew nearly jumped out of his skin. He could hear her low giggle as he went to the door.

"Champagne, sir," a man offered. Matthew peered back at the man like a statue. He handed Matthew a card just as he was about to ask who it was from. Looking down, he saw it had Mare's name on it. Matthew took the liberty of opening it anyway, reading it to himself. "Marilyn, we all hope things go well for you on your trip with Matthew. You're friends at the Education Center."

Matthew, having studied many languages and, above all, human nature, recently thought the note was cryptic in nature.

The man cleared his throat to regain Matthew's attention.

Matthew moved aside, opening the door for him to enter.

The waiter took the cart inside. He grunted again, having pulled the cover from an array of strawberries and cheese. A bottle was nestled snug in a silver ice bowl wrapped neatly in a towel. Condensate beaded on the exterior and ran down the side to the tablecloth.

"Will this do, Sir?" he replied.

"Yes, thank you."

The man held out his hand, and Matthew, not really understanding the custom, reached back and shook it oddly.

The man sneered and turned to leave.

Something came over Matthew. A thought, one that had not occurred to him, but it was unclear. It involved Mare and himself, but he needed to figure it out. He needed to take a walk to clear his head. There were too many odd things happening, way too fast.

"Mare?"

"Yes, Matthew!"

"I am going to go downstairs."

"Ok, don't stay gone too long. Oh…and make sure the door locks. I know this is the Presidential suite, but you never know. There are wacko's everywhere nowadays."

"I will."

Matthew went down the hall to the elevator and waited for a moment. When the doors opened, a newlywed couple was inside. They broke from their embrace when the door opened, but just barely. Matthew nodded politely, and they smiled back.

Trying not to stare, he couldn't help but notice the man had lipstick smeared over his entire face. The young lady's neck was covered with red and purple suction marks. They smelled of spirits and seemed overly joyful.

Matthew had always viewed reproduction from a scientific stance as a means to continue a gene pool, species, or family line. He had never been a believer that reproduction for the sake of repeated mating was a necessary part of life. In fact, Matthew had hypothesized more than once that some humans should be forbidden from reproducing. That was the very reason why the overall intelligence of society as a whole was falling. That and the fact that most adults behave as children themselves.

Not realizing he was staring too long, the man was giving Matthew a steely-eyed stare, so he moved his eyes to look at the wall just to the right of them. It was covered with advertisements for wedding chapels and honeymoon specials. Knowing capitalism makes the world go round, Matthew paid little attention to them.

When the doors opened, Matthew let the couple out first, then he exited. He heard them whispering loudly as they walked away. "What a strange guy. Did you see the way he looked at us?"

Matthew clearly heard them but ignored them as usual. He walked through the lobby towards the gift shop. The hotel's shopping area offered tuxedo rentals, wedding dress rentals, and a jewelry store. He glided by, oblivious to the signs flashing in front of him.

The door to the gift shop jingled as he opened it. Matthew's senses were immediately pummeled with various candle scents, Irish wedding music, and lighting so bright you could have seen it from space.

Matthew squinted for a few moments, trying to recover from the assault on his. Having adjusted his eyes to the light, he looked around. Scouring the shelves and counter space, new to the front of the shop, looking past the knick-knacks and sundries, he found himself at a loss. Gum, mints, and candy were typically located right at the cash register, allowing children to pester their parents for impulse purchases. It took several minutes of pacing before a young shop girl appeared out of nowhere.

"Can I help you find something?"

"Yes… gum… I am looking for gum."

She learned towards Matthew, chewing her own gum like a cow chewing cud, and pointed behind him with a smarmy look on her face. Her entire body was swaying to the side to the rhythm of her iPod music. She twisted her butt back and forth as if trying to attract a mating partner. It was oddly out of place paired with the music blaring in the shop. She must wear them to drown out the sound. Her hair was two-toned, a mix of black and white. She also had several piercings, missing jewelry in her ears, nose, and lip, where tiny holes showed like a penny on a sidewalk in the summer sun. The hotel policy must forbid her from wearing too many piercings at work, Matthew surmised.

Picking out two flavors of gum, he headed to the counter still in deep thought.

Why do gift shops always smell like cinnamon?

Matthew caught himself almost saying it aloud. He had talked to himself before in public by accident, but realized quickly that it was a social rule you do not break.

Waiting to pay, he turned to look out into the hallway as couple after couple strolled by. "I noticed there are not many children here. Are there?"

The girl smirked again, huffing out a sarcastic reply, "It's hard to have a good time with extra baggage."

The colloquium puzzled Matthew, but street slang often did.

"I mean, like a third wheel, Sherlock."

Matthew's face contorted, and his head tilted sideways.

"Let me spell it out, sweetie. Across the hall is a Tuxedo and gown rental shop, next door a jewelry store, and down the hall two wedding chapels that run twenty-four seven. Upstairs are the rooms where the kids get made. Well... nine months later they show up, anyway, four-seventy-nine dear."

Matthew reached into his wallet and handed her a fiver. Then it hit him. The counter seemed to move away at light speed. He began to sweat, and he felt lightheaded. Although he was not really moving at all, the gravity of his emotions struck like a kick in the chest, making him feel as though he was floating.

Something had happened. Another new emotion he had never had before. What was going on? That was two new emotions in the same day.

"She thinks I want to marry her." Not realizing it, he had said it aloud for the shop girl to hear.

"I sure hope so. If a guy brought me here and did not propose, I would drop him like a bad habit. Well... unless he was really good in the sack. No... I would drop him."

Looking at her nails and thinking deeply, she continued to debate with herself. Matthew was in no state of mind to judge her right now and would not anyway, having committed the same social indiscretion in private on a daily basis.

He moved away from the counter after buying the gum and inched toward the door. He could hear her mumbling the entire way. She continued debating with herself long after the door closed.

He staggered down the hallway and out the main door to get some fresh air. Before he realized it, he was back at the fall lookout again. Collecting his thoughts, he tried to calm himself to a point where he could think more clearly. The falls were roaring and seemed to be louder at night. Matthew knew he could not stay long, or Mare would get worried. Finally, composing himself, he decided to do the only thing he could.

He took out his cell phone and canceled dinner reservations at the formal French Restaurant he had intended. Matthew made a call to a small, local Polish restaurant, not exactly in the best part of the area his parents had visited. The food was good, but it had been several years since he had been there. Matthew tried to make a reservation, but they said they were not required.

Matthew returned to the room, never mentioning the change to Mare. His head still churning away on what to do next.

When the cab pulled in front of the place, the cabby inquired, "Do you want me to leave or stay out here and wait?"

Matthew replied, "Wait, we should not be long."

"Ok, pal, it's your dollar."

Mare looked worried and somewhat disappointed. "I thought we were going to a nice place to eat."

"This is a nice place; my parents came here several times on their..."

"On their what, Matthew? You're acting strange, and your cheeks are flushed. I don't want to hurt your feelings, but you're not making me feel very comfortable at the moment. Are you getting sick?"

A sign outside proclaimed, *"The best local home-cooked Polish meals in Niagara."*

Matthew opened the cab door, ignoring her questions. He was much too deep in thought, trying to get out of this mess.

Work... relationships are harder than any work I have ever done. Biogenetics is easier than this.

In his youth, Matthew overheard two doctors discussing a fellow nurse of mating age. One told the other that he never dates at work. When asked why, he replied, "You don't shit where you eat?" Matthew never understood the slang logic until this moment.

158

Exiting the cab, they headed towards the door. A homeless person in front was peering inside with her hands cupped to the glass. Matthew politely asked her to move. She grunted and threw her hand down at him. Mare grabbed her nose as he opened the door with the woman having left a scent trail that smelled worse than cat urine.

The restaurant was not that bad inside; it was old, but very well-decorated. It seemed out of place for the neighborhood.

Seeing they were overdressed for the location, an older lady jumped up and escorted them to their table.

"Look lively, we have a set of newlyweds here," her partially toothless mouth barked at a younger, portly man behind the counter preparing food.

He made a funny face back at her, then nodded at them.

Matthew quickly corrected her, "Oh… we are not married, we are just friends."

"Well, tonight's the big night, then I get it."

She put her index finger to her lips to signal silence on the subject.

Matthew thought she was acting oddly about their presence, and he did not like it at all.

Katarina's, as it was called, had plenty of local atmosphere and hometown décor. The moose head mounted over the bar area seemed to disgust Mare, as Matthew noticed by her facial expression. The stuffed beavers gave Matthew the willies. He was not an animal lover. It was not that he did not appreciate them; it was just a trait of his spectrum mind that still remained intact. Animals had always frightened him, dead or alive. The most comical decoration was the obvious attempt to imply that there is a species of rabbit with antlers. If you like home-cooked Polish food with a side of dust and cobwebs, this was the place for you. It was like a poor man's Cracker Barrel.

The woman brought out water and menus. After informing them of the special, Matthew and Mare decided on it.

The mood was off, and the conversation matched it. Time passed slowly with little conversation between them.

Matthew noticed a tick... tick... tick... noise combined with a mechanical grinding sound that almost drove his mind insane. A cat clock hung on the wall. Its tail and eyes moved side to side, taunting him like an evil cartoon character.

Mare barely looked at him and only twiddled with her food. Matthew had eaten everything in under ten minutes and sat there, looking around with no attempt at conversation.

The dinner took an agonizingly long time to prepare, and even longer to eat. Luckily, the cab was right out front as they left.

Mared stared out the front window while Matthew looked out of the side on the way back to the hotel.

"It's so nice outside, Matthew. How about we take a stroll?"

The very thought right now petrified him to his core. Being as polite as he could, he declined. "How about tomorrow? You really cannot see anything at night anyway."

The next day, Matthew packed it full of sightseeing, shopping, and three separate tours of the fall. A hiking tour at the top, a boating tour at the base, and a helicopter tour over everything else. Matthew had covered every angle of the falls except behind them. He did not know what else to do. Marriage was not even a subject he had ever considered. The thought of it was out of the question.

In the evening, he made up an excuse to use the phone and check his email to avoid conversation with her. When he went into his room and shut the door, he had no intention of leaving his protective sanctuary.

Matthew knew that by doing this, he risked damaging their friendship now. Matthew filled the next day with more of the same, taking a speed boat ride that nearly terrified him to death.

Matthew noticed that the trip was taking a toll on her, and he could see her beginning to crack. Just one last day, and the trip was over. Matthew barely talked, and the trip to the hydroelectric plant and the history of electricity was almost unbearable even for him. Mare insisted on making dinner reservations, upsetting Matthew's plan. However, her insistence made Matthew very uncomfortable.

When they returned to their room, Mare went out onto the balcony, pulling Matthew with her.

From their vantage point, you could see a small piece of the fall and the river. The landscape was spectacular, and the garden below them was teeming with roses and other flowing plants surrounding a huge fountain.

Taking Matthew's hand, she turned to him to look at her. He was staring off in the distance, rocking in his stance, and humming to himself at a low volume.

"Matthew, I thought since this is our last night, we could actually try to be together."

Matthew did not respond.

"I made reservations for us. You have to wear a suit, so I took the liberty of renting one for you. I also selected a gown for myself."

Matthew tried to pull away and rock, but she tightened her grip on him. Matthew was very uncomfortable and acted like a rabbit that had been snared, struggling to break free.

"Are you ok? You have been so distant with me, I feel like we are moving apart, not together."

"I am fine, Mare."

Matthew still refused to look her in the eye.

"It's normal to be scared, Matthew. We all get frightened of the unknown."

With that, she said no more, and Matthew was thankful for that. Releasing his hand, he practically ran to his room, leaving a vacuum behind him.

Mare had taken them to a dinner theatre. It showcased a big band error theme with songs by Glenn Miller, Duke Ellington, and Bennie Goodman, amongst others of that era.

Matthew excused himself to go to the bathroom. There was a man at the sinks handing out towels, cologne, and combs. Matthew struggled to get his flow going, feeling uncomfortable with a man just standing in the bathroom.

Matthew walked slowly and reluctantly back to the table and sat down. Mare was shifting around in her seat and grinning ear to ear as if she were expecting something from him.

With no other options left, Matthew decided to discuss his intentions for the trip with her. He knew avoiding the subject altogether would leave a festering wound when they returned home.

"Mare, I need to talk to you about something important." She sat up, excited and grasping Matthew's hand tightly.

"Yes, what is it?"

Matthew cleared his throat and continued hesitantly, "You know we have known each other since we were children."

Interrupting him, she said, "Yes, go on."

"I have always been friends with you. I think you're wonderfully made."

Mare was almost bouncing out of her chair. Matthew had never seen her this way before. Her face and chest were flushed, and her lips seemed thicker and fuller.

Matthew began to get distracted by her cologne; he was sensing the strong pheromones mingling in the sweet aroma. She smelled so good.

"I… I am not wired like you. I am a more logical being as opposed to an emotional one."

Matthew noticed her expression began to change immediately with his words.

"Matthew, what are you trying to say?"

"I am not sure what love feels like or if I have it."

"What do you mean?"

"Love… I have been reading about love, studying it, and exploring various books and movies. I don't have it."

"Matthew… love is not something you can analyze and mimic. You either feel it or you don't. Evidentially, you don't feel it for me."

"I want to always be best friends with you. If that means we have to get married because you are a female and I am a male, then… I will."

"Matthew, is this a proposal, or are you trying to find a nice way to break up our relationship?"

Matthew noticed tears welling up in her eyes. She looked completely torn and broken inside.

"Mare, I just want you to know you are my best friend and my only friend."

Mare stood up slowly and grabbed her handbag. Her napkin fell to the floor. She looked ill. "Just take me home, Matthew. I want to go back to the room right now!"

Matthew, confused, worried, and unsure of what had just happened, was lost in his own thoughts. A wilderness of emotions that he had no way to categorize and file. They were floating about like a dandelion seed in the summer breeze.

The cab ride back was silent. The walk to the hotel and the ride on the elevator were silent. Mare went to her room, and this time she shut the door and locked it.

Matthew started to feel a small amount of sadness, but he was unsure why or what to do. He just felt uncomfortable.

Matthew went to his room, tugged at the bow tie, then pulled it off and unbuttoned the top two buttons on his shirt so he could breathe easier. Pacing to release an enormous amount of anxiety building deep within his gut, he paced back and forth at the end of the bed.

Leaving his room, he went to Mare's door and was going to knock on it, but heard sobbing inside.

Matthew Le'Dain, a man with the highest known IQ in the world, stood at the door of a sobbing woman with no answers or clues. It was a problem he could solve by reading a book or magazine for advice.

Matthew walked over and plopped himself down into the chair he had sat in before. Like a Greek statue, Matthew sat frozen, thinking as hard as he could.

He began to try and think like her, a woman. Trying to apply what research he had done, he began to think about her needs and realized that the only thing he could do was ask her.

Thinking he was doing the right thing, finally Matthew bolted out the door and down to the jewelry store in the lobby just as a man was locking the door for the night.

Matthew knocked on the door as he turned to walk away.

"Excuse me..." Knock... knock... knock. "Excuse me!"

The man slowly turned, squinting to see who it could be. "Yes, young man."

"I need to buy a ring."

"Can it wait? We are closing."

Matthew pleaded with him, "No...right now, I have to right now."

"Ok... ok... ok... settle down."

The man opened the door and stepped back, letting Matthew inside, then locking it behind him.

He was very short and with very little covering on top. He must have been a jeweler for some time, for Matthew, he looked ancient.

Leaning in, he looked closely at Matthew's face. "Don't I know you?"

"I don't think so, I would remember it."

"I mean, I saw you once. You had a traveling show. You are that smart kid, the one on Ida Winthrop. The kid who does all those numbers in his head."

"Yes, used to."

"I knew it. So, what kind of ring are you looking for?"

"The right one."

"Well, how about this one?"

He pulled a smaller ring out and showed it to Matthew.

"No, that does not look like the ones in the magazines."

"Oh... I see... A special girl, huh? How about this one?"

The man pulled out a larger two-carat ring.

"It's a little pricey, but the best one I have right now."

"How much... well, it's priced for twelve thousand, but I can let you have the celebrity discount for... let's say nine thousand."

"Do you take credit cards?"

"Of course," the man said, grinning ear to ear.

Matthew returned to the room to find Mare sitting on the sofa in a hotel robe.

Mimicking his best memory of a marriage proposal, Matthew got down on one knee and, as bold as brass, blurted it out, "Mare, will you marry me?"

His request sounded forced. There were two mar… sounds in the same sentence. It sounded like he had puked into the toilet as he had belted it out inside the silent room.

Matthew had expected the smile to return like before, but it did not. She sat there for several awkward moments.

Mare reached down and closed the open ring box. Taking her hands, she grabbed Matthew's. Trying to smile, she began to speak.

"I guess I always thought you would grow and be capable of loving someone. I thought maybe I could change you, but this is who you are. I cannot change you, no matter how much I want to. You are the way you are. Matthew, I want someone who can love me back."

Mare took another long pause.

Matthew was again at a loss for words. Nothing came to mind. Mare continued.

"I don't just want someone who will like me a lot or just cares for my safety. A woman wants to be loved. Truly, deeply, madly loved. Can you understand what I am saying?"

Matthew knew the answer to this question, or thought he did.

"In a psychological and physiological sense, I know what love is supposed to be… You are right, I am just not wired that way."

She looked sad to Matthew, but the truth was always the best. It was the only thing Matthew knew.

Mare smiled at him like his mother used to when he was very little, trying to reassure him during his silent years. "It's ok, Matthew. I do and will always love you."

Kissing him on the forehead Mare stood up and went back to her room.

Matthew flashed back to his childhood. He felt sad inside, not empathetic for Mare, but just sad and empty. He felt isolated again. Matthew thought he heard his mother's voice. "Matthew, it's Ok, mommy will always love you no matter what."

Matthew stood up and went back to his room, locking the door.

The living area was empty and silent. Only locked doors and the low, muffled sound of the falls echoed in the background.

19 *BERLIN*

Speaking in a thick German tongue, a younger, well-dressed dignitary approached Dr. Dimment. The man was accompanied by two security agents, also smartly dressed. The dimly lit hallway concealed the smug, almost gloating expression on the man's face. However, his arrogance was well-dressed in a fine pinstriped suit, a black silk scarf, an overcoat, and oil-slicked hair. Dr. Dimment was accustomed to smug faces. He had been beaten down by it many times over by his partner, Dr. Meachum. It was a face he secretly detested and only put up with out of necessity. There would be no love lost if this face or any face like it were forever removed from his mind. Dimment's tolerance for that face had grown shorter every passing year. His mind suppressed thoughts of smashing that face for now.

Dr. Dimment listened impatiently with a German ear but translated the words to English in his mind immediately due to habits he acquired back in the States.

"We have to pull the plug on your little research project and clear all of this out," he said, waving his arms about in the long hallway leading to the parking structure.

Dimment returned the smug look, holding papers in the man's face, "We have a contract. You owe me, brother. I have to complete or at least appear to have completed my research before that brat does."

"Listen, Doctor… brother… your problems are not my problems. I will not let them become mine either." His boots scuffed along the concrete floor as he swung around, looking for confirmations from his henchmen. Turning back swiftly, he rubbed his chin, slicking his hair back again, even though it was not out of place. "I can only give you a few more months."

Dr. Dimment peered at a congressional pen attached to his brother's lapel. Being a congressman had its privileges, but having a scandal erupt during an election cycle meant blood would not be thicker than water, and he knew it. The two spoke as if they were acquaintances, not blood brothers, most of the time. In a way, they were almost eleven years in separation. Dimment was never home much after he became of age. His brother had come to the United States much earlier than he had. They had lived separate lives for the most part, never forming a strong bond other than by birth mother.

Dimment needed this and was willing to fight for it. He loved being home in Berlin so much. He felt at ease exploring his research here, where condemnation was less prevalent. His dream was to return home as the celebrated research Doctor who had cured autism, Alzheimer's, turrets, and other brain-related infirmities. His reality, however, was that of a doctor in hiding from the German Government, the Russian KGB, and possibly the United States Government, if word were to get out about his latest research project.

Dimment tried half-heartedly to plead with his younger sibling, "I need at least six more months minimum. I cannot fulfill my harvest quota at that time."

"Three months and that is it... brother! I will not lose my reputation or my standing for your cockamamie ideas... even if you are my brother. Senator Moabae no longer has a desire to invest in this endeavor anymore either. We are both up for reelection... besides, he doesn't have the stomach for a stateside project like this, let alone one overseas. We cannot afford a scandal over misappropriated government funds for live human research."

"They're not alive, they are fetuses."

"That is not up to me to decide, Gottfried, that is up to God."

"Your hands are no cleaner than mine, little brother."

The congressman turned abruptly, waving his hands at the two security officers to move out of his way. Overly animated in his actions and impatient in his thoughts, the younger sibling rushed away in a hasty retreat.

Dimment watched as they strutted down the hallway like the Italian mafia, bounding through their territory, collecting protection dues. Turning a corner, they disappeared out of sight. Dimment, now livid, turned in the opposite direction, walking briskly and slamming into a set of double doors. He bumped into a gentleman passing along the wall with an IV in tow. "Out of the way," he barked, unaware that he had almost knocked him down. A nurse helped the man regain his balance, yelling out, "passen Sie es Arschloch auf (watch it ass-hole)." She scowled at Dimment as he steamed along.

He continued to storm down the hallways like a bullet monorail out of Tokyo. Stopping at a secure area, he scanned his security badge, opening a set of double doors. Taking a quick second to look around, he continued down several more hallways, finally stopping at a more advanced security reader. Dimment placed his badge in the reader, put his thumb on the pad, then leaned forward. He grunted and growled at not only the inconvenience but the compression of his gut from leaning over. A machine scanned his retina as a loud metallic pop rang out down the empty hallway, releasing the locks on the door. Pausing, Dimment looked in both directions to see if he had been followed. Pulling his card, he pushed the heavy door open and went inside the private laboratory.

The laboratory was littered with large jars and glass containers. They contained complete embryonic sacs with developing fetuses inside. Humans in nature, they would occasionally move and twitch. Bundles of wires and tubes went into and out of the containers, splicing into blood vessels and flesh mass. A machine adjacent to the area clicked and spun on a timed cycle. Akin to a dialysis machine, it was more compact. Another machine pulsed and pumped nutrition along the same tubing system to the living containers.

The laboratory had a clinical smell to it. A mixture of alcohol, ammonia, bleach, and formaldehyde scented the air like the back room of an embalmer's studio. This was no studio to preserve and protect the recently departed. The dimly lit mortuary was filled with the cries of those who cannot cry and nightmares of those who would never find the comfort of a loving mother's arms. The lives of those housed inside its blank walls were to be a short-lived hell on earth with Dimment as its dark master.

Dr. Dimment walked over to one of the containers and tapped the glass. A startled eye opened, peering back at him, kicking with its legs and arms. Taking a vial from his coat pocket, he picked up a large syringe with a small needle and filled it.

The vial contained a hormone used mainly to accelerate livestock growth. He injected 5cc's into the IVs above each of the eight containers, one by one.

After completing the injections, he stood back observing their reactions for a few moments. He took out a notebook, scribbling down a few notes until he was interrupted by one of the fetuses. Not responding well to the increased dosage, it began to kick and move violently, shaking the container and causing it to move on the countertop. It continued for a few moments as he watched without emotion until it stopped moving altogether.

A beeping alarm sounded. Dimment walked over and pushed a button on a control board to silence the noise. He turned and walked back to the container, disconnecting the wires and tubes. Opening a pipette valve, he decanted the liquid inside the container from the bottom. Suiting up in latex gloves, a mask, and goggles, Dimment removed the embryonic sack and its contents from the container and carried them over to an operating table, determined not to lose the progress he had made.

Dimment worked without emotion or care, as if the human remains were a cadaver to be dissected in a medical school class. He turned on an overhead light and pulled it close to the sack. It looked like a jellyfish. Taking a scalpel, he cut the sack to reveal a partially developed fetus. It was only four months old, but it was a tiny, deceased human figure. Taking a sterile syringe, he stabbed it into the umbilical cord, removing every drop of blood he could.

Dimment picked up the lifeless fetus, flipped it over, took another sterile syringe and rammed it into the base of the neck of the fetus, and removed more fluid. When finished, he held the syringe up to the light, satisfied he had retrieved all the precious spinal fluid containing stem cells that he could.

He took the linens off the table, wrapped them over the fetus, picked the entire thing up like a bag of trash, and walked over to a door on the wall. It was marked hazardous with an international medical symbol. Dimment struck a button on the wall with his elbow and tossed the contents inside. Taking off the latex gloves, he tossed them in along with the mask. Removing the goggles last, he tossed them onto a nearby bench top.

Dimment walked over to a locked refrigeration unit and opened it with a push-button key code. Inside, he selected two containers. One was marked spinal stem cells, the other umbilical stem cells. Dimment mumbled to himself, "At least I got something for my trouble." He shot the collected samples into the storage containers and placed the contents back inside a small cryogenic chamber deep inside the cooler.

Satisfied that everything was working well enough, he walked over to the exit door and turned off the overhead lights. The room was devoid of light except for the few monitor lights, glowing red, yellow, and blue on the countertops. Surveying the laboratory one last time as if something had been different to him, but he just could not put his finger on it, he opened the door and headed back to the parking structure.

His brother's visit had made him feel more suspicious and cautious than before. A predisposition to paranoia had been instilled in Dimment since birth by his mother, a holocaust survivor in her own time. Dimment made sure that any wayward eyes kept to themselves. Even in Berlin, this type of research still carried certain stigmas with it.

Gottfried climbed into a black Mercedes and drove several miles through the city, eventually arriving at a hotel. He handed his keys to the valet as he went inside. An attendant opened the door for him as he entered. Inside, he stomped through the lobby and into a long hallway. He went to the end, taking time to continually look behind himself several times. Dimment took a left into the hotel restaurant.

The hotel had an older, more distinguished décor reminiscent of generations past. Burgundy and gold carpets, bronze sconces and chandeliers, along with tapestry curtains and velvet seating. High ceilings with ornate plaster crown molding topped each room. Large spiral columns, intermingled inside the walls, with ornate feet, completed the structure. Old oil paintings of Barren's and royalty, long since passed from the days of Hessian mercenaries, blended in brilliantly with the surrounding style.

The air smelled of cooked cabbage, fresh bread, and ham. He walked up to the bar and ordered a beer in German. "Ein Bier, bitte?" The bartender selected a fresh stein and then filled it from the tap. The barkeep set it down in front of Dimment. "Danka," he replied out of habit. He drank the entire pint in three gulps. He cleared the foam from his facial hair using the back of his hand, then turned and went into the formal dining area.

Two men in suits were sitting at a table as he approached. They were speaking in German. When the man facing him saw Dimment, he smiled and quickly ended his conversation. The other man slid out of his side of the booth to let Dimment in, grimacing, and then left the room.

Dimment sat down with a grunt, saying, "Hallo, wie sind Sie gewesen?" The man interrupted him. In English, unless you can also speak Russian. Dimment winced, almost closing his eyes, not amused.

The man started to light a cigarette. He gestured to Dimment, politely offering a fag to him. Dimment waved his hand and shook his head no. "Nasty habit, but I can't seem to break it. I understand that you are not progressing as we had hoped. Why is that?"

Dimment answered, "The little brat went on vacation with his girlfriend. He will be coming to me very soon, I know."

"Why not just tell him and speed things along?"

"I can't, he is a saint. He wouldn't harm a fly on purpose. I have to let him come to me. Soon…very soon, he will discover he cannot progress without newborn stem cells."

The Russian blew smoke into Dimment's face and leaned forward, "What then? What if he does not come to you? What if he does not need you?"

172

"Dammit! I told you he would! He has to! I have already been down this road once before."

The Russian leaned back in his chair, smiling calmly, "and you failed. Don't get upset, facts are facts."

Dimment was visibly disturbed. His face and cheeks were flushed. His neck also began to show color. Beads of sweat formed on his oily forehead, sliding down like grease from a roasting pig.

"I have a plan. If he does not come to me in the next few weeks… I will make him see the light."

The Russian seemed interested. He leaned forward to show Dimment he approved, "What do you propose?"

After looking around the room once again, Dimment leaned in, "He does not know about his little girlfriend. She has to have the stems and the medication I provide her to stay with us. I let her go down once before to show him. The little brat did not really get the hint… she looks after him like Bo Peep. Fortunately, he has a thirst for knowledge. I may have to step her down. Then he will come to her aid once again. I have to be careful, or she could die, then we will have no way to keep him focused."

The Russian responded, "You could always bring him to Berlin. We could keep our eye on your little friend for you."

Dimment was irritated, "Like I would give you the key to the door with the gold in the next room. Do you take me for a fool?"

The Russian smiled, "Are you, Gottfried, the Joker or the King?"

Dimment became furious and started to leave. The Russian chastised him as he grabbed his hand, pushing it down into the table top to stop Dimment's retreat. "We expect results… soon, Gottfried. If not, we will get them by any means possible." The Russian snuffed out his cigarette butt into an almost full ashtray.

Dimment jerked his hand free and stood up. He turned and stormed from the restaurant without looking back.

The Russian watched as Dimment fled the room, smiling in the background.

Dimment waited out front for the valet to bring his car around. After several moments, the car finally rounded the corner and pulled up out in front of the hotel. Dimment met the valet, handed him a reward, and as he reached down to open the car door, two men in suits grabbed him from behind. He had taken his eye off the ball during his blind rage. A car skidded to a halt beside him. Grabbing Dimment by each arm, they threw him in the back seat. Once inside, he continued to resist. One of the men pulled a gun out and pointed it at him without speaking. The other took a black velvet bag and placed it over his head.

"What is this? Who are you? I am an American citizen," Dimment whaled out to deafened ears.

The car sped away. The valet counted the money he had gotten from both Dimment and the black sedan. He jumped in Dimment's Mercedes and sped off to store it for safekeeping.

The black sedan roared through the wet cobblestone streets as the driver pushed the car to its limits. Dimment was tossed back and forth, becoming nauseous from the motion. The trip seemed to take hours, but in reality, it only took about thirty minutes. The car came to an abrupt stop.

Dimment heard the driver ask someone to open the gate. "Öffnen Sie das Tor, haben Sie ich das Paket." (Open the gate, I have the package.) An iron gate of some size began to creak and moan as it opened. The car took off again, drove a few thousand feet, and stopped. The driver exited the car, then the two men in the backseat followed. Dimment was handled a little more gingerly this time as they assisted him from the rear of the car. He was helped up some steps and pulled inside. A door closed behind him. Escorted with the hood still on, Dimment was placed in a chair. Suddenly, the hood was removed to reveal a dark room with little light, except for the light coming from behind him. Dimment tried to regain focus, but the ride had left him dizzy.

He realized he was in an office. A man was sitting in the dark across from him some distance. You could not see his face at all, only the silhouette of a man. He was sitting in a large high-backed chair. A light had been pointed at Dimment's face, making it even harder to see him. He held his arm up to block the light, but it didn't help very much.

The man began to speak in English but with a German accent. "Welcome to my home."

Dimment was in the military as a young man. This was not his first rodeo with this kind of treatment. Dimment said nothing.

"You may speak, we are all friends here."

Dimment remembered his training: be friendly, gain their trust, offer them a beverage or a smoke, then talk about something with no real meaning.

"Would you like a drink? How about a cigar…No? How do you like Berlin? Silly question to ask a man who was born here?"

Dimment broke his silence, understanding the man knew much about him. The next step was some mild violence. He could sense the two thugs next to him were wanting to get started.

"Swen…Rene' leave us." The two guard dogs left the room and shut the door.

"Who are you?" Dimment asked.

"My name is not important. What is important is why you are here and what you are doing?"

"I am a research Doctor." I know everything there is to know about you, Dr. Gottfried Dimment. "Why don't you ever visit your sister? Not a very good brother, are you? Your brother Steffen visits her all the time. He is a congressional representative from the states, I hear. It must be very difficult for him to make time for her. Don't you feel a little guilty putting her there?"

Dimment's mouth quivered, trying to repress his rage. "That was a long time ago. My skills have improved. I have resources and money now."

"If it matters, your work was not a complete failure. Perhaps you used the wrong patient? Since you have been away, others have picked up your research and carried on. When I say others, I really mean me."

Dimment pushed the light out of his eyes. He still could not see the shadow's face. He felt a sudden sharp pain in the front of his skull. It felt as if an iron wedge were being forced through, separating his lobes one from the other. He took both hands and grabbed the side of his head, trying to squeeze it and block it.

"I can almost read your thoughts, Gottfried." The figure spoke to his mind briefly to demonstrate his abilities, then relinquished him.

Dimment gasped; it was very painful.

The man reached into his pocket, took a pen, and laid it on the desk where Dimment could see it very well. The pin slowly started to move in a circular motion. It continued spinning and gained speed. It spun so fast you could hardly see it.

Dimment jested with the man, "A trick, anyone could arrange that."

Bothered by the lack of respect, the pen left the table and rose up. It was levitating in the air and spinning. It slowly moved towards Dimment. Inching closer and closer, the suspense grew as it moved closer and closer until it stopped and hovered just in front of his face. Abruptly, the spinning ceased, it clicked, revealing the ink ball, then darted right at Gottfried's eye, stopping short of piercing it.

Dimment jerked his head backwards, striking the chair back with his head. The pen fell on his lap. Dimment was breathing very hard; his heart could be heard beating out of his chest.

"Still think it is a Jedi mind trick, Doctor? It is real...very real...But I agree, child's play. I have only scratched the surface. I am at an impasse, as you say."

"What do you want from me?"

The man shifted in his chair.

"I want information. In exchange for this, I will pay you very well. I have, as you say, unlimited resources. What do you say, do we have an agreement?"

Dimment challenged the man's sincerity, "What if I say no?"

"Gottfried, you have no choice in the matter. Who do you think has been putting pressure on Steffen? Who do you think looks after your sister? Who do you think provided you with the facilities and the cover you needed to harvest embryonic stem cells in Berlin? I can let you go back to extracting bone marrow from mentally ill patients and taking your chances with the US authorities."

Dimment sat back in his chair and took a few calming breaths of air. He had been running blind for years and did not even know it. Who was this man to him, and why was he just now making his presence known?

The man behind the chair scooted a drink across the desk to him.

Dimment reached out and hesitantly took it.

The dark figure proposed a toast, "To a meaningful relationship, may it prosper us both."

20 *IVORY TOWER*

"What I need for each of you to do is concentrate on the same thing. The same idea. The same object."

Matthew walked around the oval table surrounded by his volunteer research group. He glanced up at the observation deck at Meachum and Dimment, observing him almost daily now. The group was attempting to levitate a pen in the center of the table. Having no success at all, he was beginning to feel anxiety set in.

Matthew misread frustration and many other emotions as simple anxiety. His coping skills had been improving every day since leaving the confines of an overprotective mother. Although he was far from being what you would call normal, he worked to recognize his non-conforming behavior. Matthew had caught himself several times standing in place, beginning to rock to and fro, and corrected it.

Working double duty was nothing new for him. Trying to guard against his own behavioral deficits and guide a team of highly intelligent young people was more difficult than he had imagined. Something was missing with the trial group.

Until recently, Matthew had achieved little success using pharmaceutical treatments to stimulate the correct neurological regions of their mind. A few in the group had become violently ill, throwing up from the increased levels of dopamine. It had subsided after a few hours. However, Matthew was not one for emotional frailties, charged forward, stepping the dosage up until the maximum for each person's body mass was achieved.

Synoptical receptor mapping had shown growth for all seven patients over the first week, but it had only been incremental. Mathew had ruled out any surgical implants for now. His goal was to create and maintain permanent links between the synoptical areas of the mind that are not normally accessed, thereby broadening thought and memory.

Unknown to the group or Dr. Meachum, Matthew had been injecting himself along with the group. He did it not only to understand the drug's effects firsthand but also to aid his research in any way he could. Matthew had also noticed little change in his own response to the injections. Still, the best they had done as a group was to make the pen vibrate.

During recent attempts, Daniel sustained severe nosebleeds. Sara passed out, and several others had developed severe headaches and were confined to solitary rooms to recover. The migraines were impeding progress. Temporary Matthew had miscalculated how long it would take for these side effects to subside. Not one to doubt his calculations, he waited out the inconvenience. The strain on the group's minds was almost too much.

Having a terrible day, he sent everyone home early so he could concentrate. Matthew sat down in his office. He had not had Mare's camera on since they returned. He was still unsure what she would think or if she minded. No time to worry about it now, he had work to concentrate on.

What am I missing? What do I need to stimulate new growth?

Matthew stared out his office window, looking up towards the observation deck. Dimment and Meacham were debating about something. Matthew tried to read their lips but could not make them out clearly because of the glare from the overhead lights. They turned and walked out, still debating as they left. Matthew hit the remote button and blacked out his windows. Sitting back in his chair, he collected his thoughts.

Sitting for several minutes, thinking, something abnormal crossed his mind. Matthew stood up and entered the conference room to access the holographic receptor maps of his test group. Studying them intently, he compared each one with its baseline mapping. After an initial burst of growth, the synoptic paths stabilized and then stopped advancing altogether. Injecting higher dosages could cause permanent brain damage in some of the weaker patients, like Daniel and Sarah. The answer had to be here somewhere, and Matthew knew it.

He accessed his office computer from the conference room and started running through files at breakneck speed. Reading article after article and paper after paper, one thing resonated in every article. Stem cells kept popping up.

Matthew perused old research papers for patients with other types of brain abnormalities, like multiple sclerosis and Alzheimer's disease. Matthew stumbled upon a database that had created an antiquated brain receptor map. Although he had searched the keyword several times before, he had not discovered this particular file before. In fact, it wasn't available before. Recalling his photographic memory, Matthew was sure he had never seen it before. Not a suspicious person, Matthew ignored the reasoning behind why it had suddenly appeared.

Researching the web host name, he discovered it was from the University of Berlin's medical school archives. The report was buried in various patient studies from the pre-WWII era to the early 1980s.

The primary patient was Katja Dimment. Matthew began to develop an investigator's curiosity upon seeing the young woman's surname. Reading the file carefully, he began putting the pieces of the puzzle together. Katja had contracted Multiple Sclerosis in her early twenties. A young Dr. Gottfried Dimment, still in his residency, worked with other progressive doctors of the time, experimenting with stem cell therapies. Completely new and previously undiscovered in the Western World, stem cell research had not even been published in any medical journals of the day. It was an unknown Frankenscience. When the methods and requirements to harvest stems from live donors were revealed, public pressure mounted. Intervention was sought by several post-WWII nations who were reforming the new German Government, and live human research programs were abolished due to public outcry. Holocaust victims had begun telling their stories of human testing, closing the door on this type of research for decades. Dimment continued, however, with a few colleges taking the research underground.

Matthew, amazed at the level of detail in the files, continued to read on. Katja was thought to have been a savant of the time. Due to a terrible miscalculation, the stem cells used for her treatment were rejected, and she suffered permanent brain damage, also negating her advanced thought abilities as a savant. The worst of it was that the treatment accelerated the advance of her MS she suffered additional neurological degradation. Left paralyzed and mute, Dr. Dimment was forced to leave Germany discredited and disgraced.

With only a rudimentary two-dimensional receptor map, Matthew manipulated the data set from a scanned image until he developed a decent holographic display. Having made several assumptions to complete the three-dimensional version, Matthew knew it would be a close representation. The colors, however, were displayed initially in a traditional green and orange color combination. After one last reformatting, Matthew was able to display it along with the group results. Floating in the center of the room like a row of Halloween lanterns, Matthew walked around the scans, comparing and studying the synoptical differences.

Matthew put on gloves that allowed him to manipulate the holographs in mid-air. Pushing, turning, and overlapping the images like apples floating in a rain barrel, he noticed that Katja had developed white spots across her receptor landscape. This was a definite sign of advanced MS. She was clearly not a candidate for this type of treatment. Something Dimment may not have known then. Even if Dimment could have removed the protein buildups, tissue spotting would have inhibited new receptor growth. Even in areas where new growth was possible, they would have most likely succumbed to protein blocking in a short period of time. Gottfried had most likely thwarted any chance she ever had of recovering or living a normal life. She had to be in her mid-to-late sixties now, that is, if she was even still alive.

Matthew was intrigued by the case file to the extent that he memorized everything in it. It was very interesting to say the least. Not questioning why it suddenly became available, it was definitely the link he needed to push forward.

He continued reading other research papers noted in the references section of the Dimment case study. Radiological, chemical, and surgical methods had been tried with little success in mutating or accelerating the growth of her own stem cells. One comment stood out, in fact, in Matthew's creative mind. That all the stems had been harvested from normal or seemingly normal individuals. With the donors having no special talents or abilities, there was little chance of harvesting a stem that would stimulate growth in the receptor areas Matthew had hoped for.

Matthew took off the gloves and tossed them down. He went back into his office, shut the door, and dimmed the lights.

Sitting down in his chair, he regressed deep in thought, trying to piece everything together. His naïve mind never questioned the new availability of the file. It was a key file. He also never questioned why, if Dimment had such valuable research, he did not share it earlier. He only concentrated on its value and how he had skipped forward weeks, if not years, in his quest. Matthew had begun to formulate what it would take to advance the point forward. He knew the only thing he could do was break protocol.

Matthew was just about to open a new high-security file on his computer when he accidentally hit Alt-F7. It was a shortcut he had saved to access Mare's computer camera. Dormant for a couple of weeks, Mare's face popped up on the computer monitor. He had not seen or spoken to her in several weeks. Matthew started to turn her camera off, but hesitated.

Just before he hit the key, Mare walked partially out of view, and Dr. Dimment came into view.

Why would he be at her office? What could he possibly want?

Matthew, already intrigued by the sudden appearance of the file, decided to break the privacy rules he held in very high regard. A nagging feeling, not one he was normally accustomed to, came to him. Just like a new idea birthing in his mind, an impulsive moment overtook him, and Matthew reached down and tried to turn up the sound with no luck.

Impulsive behavior without forethought, acting without knowing all the residual consequences and outcomes. This was new territory to Matthew, a region of being he had never thought to find himself in. However, the world had a way of changing you, pulling you in, chewing you up, then spitting you out like unwanted phlegm on the ground. When careful, well-placed, thoughtful analysis is all you know, impulsiveness borders on anarchy at the least and total chaos with no bounds of control as the eventual outcome. Mathew found himself abandoning his instinctual nature for her.

Dimment and Mare were discussing something very important, and from the looks on their faces, they were becoming agitated with one another. Matthew tried to read lips but could not see enough from the side view to make sense of them. The camera feed was too grainy and intermittently displayed large, unfocused, multicolored pixels across the screen.

Thinking fast, Matthew accessed Mare's computer remotely, disregarding her right to privacy. There was no time to wait, and calling would most likely end their discussion. Toggling the mute on Mare's speakers and switching them from speaker to microphone, Matthew was finally able to get a rough sound. It was not very good and sounded like they were standing inside a giant metal sea-box container.

They moved out of view, but sound was the more important sense at the moment. Matthew managed to catch the tail end of their argument.

"Marilyn, be reasonable. Remember who gave you your life back. In fact, I gave you a life. You owe me."

"I know, and you're constantly reminding me every chance you get. Haven't I repaid you by now? Haven't I!"

"It's not about repayment anymore. It's about survival. No flashy sideshow freak or some broken-down, scared-up degenerative one-off is going to keep me from getting what I want. Just do it?"

Matthew heard Mare begin to cry just as she did when they were at the falls. He shut off the camera before she noticed it had been on.

Matthew, sitting back in his chair, began to feel a warm sensation. His palms were moist and his heart was racing. He felt anger with Gottfried. It was a basic emotion had always owned but almost never used. He never found the need for it. It was a slightly used emotion, still carrying the new car smell, but it was strong, much stronger than Matthew had ever recalled. Lea Tootchie had made him angry a couple of occasions, but never like this. It felt… it felt personal… it felt territorial, raw, and animalistic.

Matthew's hands were hurting. He looked down, and both hands were clutched into fists. His knuckles were white, and the backs of his hands were blood red. Matthew both loved and hated this feeling. He felt empowered yet out of control, strong yet a victim of his emotions… his circumstance and more importantly, Mare's.

He had become completely distracted from what he was doing. Against instinct, Matthew made another impulsive decision to take a trip to the Education Center and check on her. Arranging a cab to get there as quickly as he could, Matthew raced to Mare's office.

In the cab, his thoughts changed. He began to compare instinct with impulsiveness to rationalize these new behaviors. Where were they coming from, and why were they there now when before they were not? It was like a whole new person was struggling to break out, to break free. The changes were intriguing yet very troubling. Matthew realized he had had the same issues of confusion and uncertainty when it came to Mare and whether or not there was love or boyish affection like a mother figure for her.

No matter what, the feelings were not regimented, planned, or calculated. They were instinctual, and Matthew could feel his mind shifting. Was it the medication he took with the group, or just him growing and expanding as a person? Developing and breaking the stalemate of autistic development that many find themselves in with that infirmity. Growing and developing socially to a single point and never progressing beyond that... never living.

Had he been held back all these years, had the right treatment and worldly influences been withheld from him? Becoming frustrated with all the racing thoughts running through his mind, Matthew was relieved when the cab finally pulled in front of the Education Center.

Matthew bounded from the car, tossing the driver a fifty-dollar bill without even saying, "Keep the change."

The driver yelled out, "Do you want me to wait buddy? The fare is only $23.95."

Matthew paid no mind; he was on a mission and never saw the drive ogle the fifty, smiling like the owner of the ring of ultimate power in a fantasy novel.

Darting past the administrative lady whom Matthew barely knew, towards Mare's office, she tried to be cordial. Matthew threw up a hand but said nothing as he stomped by.

"Mare, what's wrong?" Matthew belted out as he barged into her office unannounced.

Mare had almost stopped crying, but her eyes were red, and her face flushed. She ran to him, embracing Matthew like a soldier returning home after a long tour of duty.

Matthew awkwardly hugged her back. Squeezing her a little too much, Mare made a funny noise as if the air were being forced from her lungs. She pulled back a bit, breaking his bear hug to a more comfortable, loving embrace. Mare continued to hold him with her head on his chest.

Feeling his chest becoming damp with tears, he was a little more than bothered by her constant sniffing. Yet... her cologne intoxicated him. Pheromones swirled through his mind like a tornado, clearing everything in its path from logical thought to lasting memories as it passed. A warm, fuzzy feeling came over him. A euphoric nirvana was forming within his body and mind. It was queer and almost mind-numbing, yet he did not want to end it. Like an enjoyable dream you do not want to wake up from, he held on to her as long as he could until she broke away from him, ending it.

Pushing Matthew back, she said, "Let me guess, you were concerned for my safety."

Matthew said nothing, trying to regain his thoughts and his composure.

Mare tried to laugh through the tears and sniffling, "It's alright. I have missed you anyway. I guess I needed some time to think and clear my head."

Matthew asked again, "What's wrong?"

"I received some bad news, that's all."

Matthew watched as she rubbed her nose and tweaked her ear. She was being deceptive, but why? Matthew knew that did not make a good basis for a friendship, let alone a relationship, but he spared her embarrassment for now.

"Are you alright now?"

She sniffled then blew her nose, "Yes, I'm fine. I will be ok now. What brings you out of your cave?"

Matthew rubbed his neck. Thinking fast, he made up something out of the blue. Impulsively and instinctually, he asked her, "Diner... you want to go and get dinner?"

This new Matthew was good, he thought. Letting him drive was making things easier, and it felt inwardly like he was becoming real... alive... normal.

Matthew worried about her safety, yet again asked Mare to move in with him at dinner, and she accepted.

Matthew lived in a condominium complex along with many high-ranking officials and military personnel. The complex was equipped with 24/7 security.

Over the next few weeks, Mare came to Matthews' laboratory more often just to be with him. Matthew never realized he had missed her assistance. They had always worked well together.

Matthew used Mare to administer the Zener card test, allowing him to observe the group members during testing. The test consisted of several basic symbols that a person with extra-sensory perception would easily be able to guess correctly. Individually, patients would receive one or possibly two cards each time they tried. As a group concentrating, they would get two or three.

With no progress, Matthew had seen Dr. Dimment's face in the observation room grow angrier and more agitated each passing day. The normally smiling Dr. Meachum had even begun to have a more concerned appearance.

The tension mounted for Matthew from the lack of results and pressure on Dr. Dimment Matthew was unaware of until they ended up in another conference room showdown. This time, Dr. Meachum was able to confine it to the three of them.

"What's wrong?" Dr. Meachum asked politely.

Before Matthew could answer, Dimment blurted out, "He's not taking any chances with his precious patients! That's the problem. He's emotionally attached to them."

Matthew objected, "That is a ridiculous remark. We are restricted on what is legally allowed to do." Trying his best to stand his ground and not look intimidated, Matthew stared Dimment down.

Bothered by Matthews' usual lack of territorial backtracking, most likely Dimment smacked the tabletop with his hand, trying to intimidate him.

"If you want an omelet, you have to crack a few eggs."

Matthew had learned how to debate and was now accustomed to Dimment's diatribes. Like Meachum, he had begun to figure out you had to put the loudmouth in his place. Impulsively and with an almost evil tone about his comment, Matthew retorted, "Yes, like Katja?"

Dimment's cheeks immediately flushed red, and his head looked like it was about to explode. "How did you find out about her, you little bastard!" Dimment lunged forward at Matthew.

Dr. Meachum stepped between them, restraining him. Matthew had moved into a defensive stance without thought, acting instinctively on his martial arts training.

After Dimment pulled back and moved away from them both, Matthew continued with his explanation. "It's true; I have hit a temporary wall. I am trying to work through it. However, it's difficult when I see you scowling down at me all the time from the observation room."

Matthew never broke eye contact with Dimment.

Dimment took his hands and stroked his hair back down. Adjusting his delivery method to an accusing tone, he replied, "We will see just how motivated you are. I think you know what the problem is, but you won't come down from your Ivory Tower long enough to see it." Dimment got up and left the room, slamming the door behind him.

Dr. Meachum sat back down and turned a chair out for Matthew.

"Sit down and talk with me for a few minutes, Matthew."

Matthew sat in the chair across from him, sliding it back so he was not too close.

"What's the problem, Matthew? Maybe if you included Dimemnt, he could help. He is under a lot of pressure."

Matthew noticed something in the way Meachum leered at him. It was unsettling, but he continued to do it. Matthew began to feel a small tingle in his forehead. For just a second, he felt like his personal space had been violated as if he was standing in front of a close talker. It quickly went away when Matthew rubbed his forehead

Chalking it up to all the tension he was feeling at the moment, Matthew tried to put it behind him. Somewhere, it occurred to him that Meacham was trying to read my mind. Knowing it was not even remotely possible, Matthew disregarded it when Mare came in the door behind them, breaking the awkward silence.

Matthew noticed that Dr. Dimment's facial expression had returned to its normal, joyful self. "How have you been, Mare? I hope you're taking good care, my boy. I heard you, too, love birds moved in together."

Matthew knew Meachum must have known it was a plutonic relationship, but wanted to pretend it wasn't. Meachum stood up and left the room. Sitting there in silence contemplating what had just happened, not only with Dimment but now Meachum Matthew stood up and left the room with Mare.

21 *GUIDEING LIGHT*

For the first time in his short life, Matthew had come to an impasse. Something he could not seem to think his way out of. Trying to break away from the strains of a stalemate research project for a while, Matthew planned a date with Mare at the Planetarium. With his government security clearance, he was granted full access and was able to secure the place for themselves.

***

Mare had never been to a Planetarium before, and just the thought of Matthew making time for her made her feel he cared more for her than just friends. Living with him was more like sharing a dorm room with another student. They had their own bedrooms and bathrooms. Neither a fan of television, they occasionally eat together but with little conversation. Matthew worked long hours, and between his hobby of martial arts and work, there was little time left except for sleep.

Still, Mare knew it was almost like a typical relationship that had become stagnant. Her feminine side wants more, so much more, but the practical part of her knows that it may never be possible. What prospects did she really have anyway? Feeling like damaged goods, she seemed to always let her past beat her down.

***

Going inside to find a place to sit down, Matthew pointed out the obvious layout of the theatre. The seats were in a circle and all the seating pointed up into the air like a pilot's chair on a space shuttle launch pad. The entire show was displayed on a domed ceiling, resembling a massive screen in color. Matthew had selected an original piece he had enjoyed as a child. The "Big Bang Theory, How the Universe was Formed." It was narrated by one of the greats, Leonard Nimoy, Matthew explained. A man came into the room, down the ramp, to the center console. He turned on a computer touchpad. After a few short moments, the movie began to play.

Mare whispered, "We should have brought popcorn?"

Just as she finished, another man came in with popcorn and drinks. Smiling, she touched Matthew's cheek affectionately. Unknown to her, Matthew had been racking his brain, reading many romance novels, women's magazines, and relationship guides, trying to learn what she required emotionally. Matthew had watched several podcasts of Ida Winthrop's relationship-building segments. He wanted to try to make her feel loved, even though he was physically incapable of feeling it deeply. Matthew had concluded that simulating the characteristics of love would help Mare feel better about herself.

The show started with a loud bang erupting out of the darkness, and the theatre lit up. Lenard's voice roared out, "The universe begins. A cataclysmic explosion followed by a wave of white light spreads across a dark, empty vacuum." Matthew sat back, munching popcorn and trying to free his mind. Lenard's voice was soothing.

Matthew did not subscribe to the theory wholly, although parts of it were very plausible. He was instilled with a creationist point of view and believed there was a master designer creating all that he knew and all he would know. Very simply, he knew you cannot create something from nothing. It was impossible. Even studying the hypothetical realm of magic, it dealt with the transformation and manipulation of things around us.

Matthew began to concentrate on the movie screen. The domed ceiling and three-dimensional glasses they wore began to form into a four-dimensional memory in his mind. The salt and buttery smell of the popcorn, combined with the sweet scent of soda, created a lasting memory. Matthew looked out into the universe above and could see everything. He felt the same as the grand designer himself must have felt.

The photographs in the film were a combination of artistic creations and real NASA telescope shots. The most interesting was a shot of the entire universe shown in one still shot. Matthew began to lose himself in a deep trance-like state. The still shot displayed overhead for a very long time. Jumping from one constellation to the next, one universe to the next, explaining when they were first discovered, and who discovered them. However, Matthew began to see them in a much different light than intended.

His mind took in the images and began connecting dots and forming patterns. A new construct started to take shape in his mind. The planets transformed into synaptic nodes, and the galaxies looked like synoptic intersections. Closing his eyes, Matthew concentrated so hard he felt himself being pulled inside his mind.

The construct gaining volume took shape. Matthew processed the information as it took shape, trying to make sense of it. The universe as he now viewed it was in the shape of a holographic brain, like the receptor maps in the lab, but without the colored sectors marking the areas of involuntary control and memory. He realized that he could move around inside it as if he were real, not an abstract image that vanished with a blink or a sneeze.

It was the most amazing thing he had ever perceived. It was filled with beauty, intrigue, and danger, stirring feelings of delight and fear within his soul. Feeling like an astronaut, Matthew looked out into the vastness that seemed to have no end. Acute colors of neon, such as blues, magenta, purple, and yellow, stood out against the dark seascape of black. Menacing black holes on the edges seemed anatomically to be located at the cerebral cortex, ears, and eyes, where they would be situated in a human being. Matthew assumed they were exits or conduits out of this place. The construct began to fill in and turn gray as the colored sections faded away in the distance. He could see small blue electrical pulses firing off at the speed of light everywhere he looked, like bullets of light.

Matthew realized he had been pulled away from the beauty by some force without his consent. His presence struggled to stay with the euphoric feelings of weightlessness, as unknown forces beckoned him to stay. Matthew realized the black hole was dragging him deeper towards its center, and there was nothing he could do to stop it. He had already been pulled into the fringes of the centripetal force field. Drifting without a body, as if he were a pair of floating eyes, Matthew was unable to control his direction using his limbs and succumbed to the pull of the spinning holes.

As he descended inward, he saw rays of light and electrical pulses stretch out and disappear into the dark, spinning void like strings of caramel stretching from a candy maker's spoon. Matthew moved helplessly forward, gaining speed until he entered the center of the dark, swirling mass. The light pulses shot past him as he descended straight down without spinning or feeling completely out of control. Picking up speed like a runaway train, he traveled down the center of the passageways like digital light through a fiber optic cable.

With a sudden moment of realization, Matthew dropped out into an ocean-shaped spherical orb. Colorless waves rippled around him like heat off a hot desert landscape in summer. The orb fluttered intermittently, moving and shaking like an earthquake. The walls of it appeared to be covered with reflective glass. Seeing his reflection or the lack thereof was frightening. There was no physical shape to him anymore, only light, an electrical pulse floating in space. He felt as if he had no mass, no defined shape, and no human features of any kind, and would never regain them. He suddenly felt paranoid, and an almost schizophrenic state of mind overwhelmed him for just a few seconds, then dissipated.

A strong, bright light flickered in front of him, almost blinding him. It felt safe, though, like a guiding light. Matthew felt himself being drawn to it. An overwhelming urge beckoned him to go towards it even though he feared what it might be. A second flicker, followed by intense light, erupted, then one last blink, and he was instantly thrust out of what felt like his own eye and back into the seat.

Mare nudged him with her elbow, saying. "Wake up, you're not supposed to sleep when you take a lady on a date."

Matthew was disoriented for a few seconds. Not really knowing what just happened, he wondered if he had been in an out-of-body experience. A glimpse of the mysteries of the universe, or was he just dreaming inside his own head? He was at a loss as to what had just occurred. Somehow, it felt miraculous. He felt like he had seen something no one else had ever seen or imagined in their life. He felt like he had visited the lands of the grand designer. It was like a drug, intoxicating, and every fiber of his being wanted to be there. He wanted to return immediately there and never leave. The feeling was overwhelming, and Matthew felt helpless to control his urge to return.

Mare nudge and prodded him several more times, but he had gone dormant and was almost speechless.

"You have been working too hard, Matthew. Let's get you home and in bed early. No reading tonight."

Matthew made a vow to himself that somehow, someway, he was going to get back there. All the way home, he kept thinking about where he had been and what he had seen.

Mare was not comfortable with the silence. "You seem very distracted?"

"Really, I don't mean to be. I just have a lot on my mind."

Matthew thought that he should have told her he had a lot on his mind. Things he wanted to see and discover.

"I am trying to get my mind off work so I can recharge and get back to work."

Mare replied, "What if tonight we try something different, something you have never done before, to try and get your mind off of work?"

Matthew hesitated; he suddenly visualized a fish in the barrel, and for some reason, he felt as if this time Mare had the gun in her hands.

In their shared apartment, Matthew realized he had been so zoned out that he never recalled the ride back from coming up the elevator to the room. The next thing he recalled was lying face down with nothing on but my boxer shorts on Mare's bed.

The mind trip had left him intoxicated and disconnected from reality for several hours. Despite the fact that he really wanted to be back there, he had lingering effects of being drunk and out of control, almost in a drugged-like state.

Mare had heated scented oil in the microwave as he lay on the bed. The feeling of the warm oil dribbling down his spine made Matthew flinch.

"Too hot," she asked.

"No, it just surprised me."

"You're tense. No wonder you can't concentrate."

Her hands felt soft and firm at the same time. It felt good to him to do something new; he did not want to shy away from it.

He slowly drifted his mind back into reality, but it was another soothing, dream-like state. Matthews' defense was completely down, and his normally protected personnel space was open.

He had never had a massage before in his life. Actually, as he enjoyed it, he began to feel at ease. Even though he was not back in whatever place he had been earlier, some of the same feelings and emotions were coming back to him. The warm glow, the euphoric mindset, and the feelings of carefree weightlessness. Not really knowing for sure what she was after, he went with it.

Mare placed warm stones on different areas of his back. Real or imagined, he actually felt better. Matthew was familiar with various massage techniques and stone therapy, but had previously dismissed their merits. Now he understood their effects and actually began to believe there was a connection to the mind.

Matthew was fully back, at least in his mind, not his body, to reality started running through the possible scenarios playing out in his mind. His first thought was that the chances of a romantic encounter increase exponentially when two people are alone and physical contact is involved. He decided to go with it, having only read about such things, he knew he would have to emulate what he had read and pray that the rest would come instinctually. Having recently tapped into instinct and impulsiveness, this seemed to be the next logical step in his social development.

Matthew decided to reciprocate the massage, which Mare was open to. Mimicking her actions and those in his memory banks, he began by gently moving Marilyn to the side. Rising up very close to her face, Matthew looked deep into her eyes. He knew this technique increased sexual tension and arousal during the lovemaking ritual. Not as frightened and timid as he thought he would be if this moment ever occurred. With the technique working better than expected, an uncontrollable adolescent friend suddenly rose up between them, trying to escape his underpants.

Without losing eye contact with her, he reached down and pulled her shirt up and over her head. Like a professional actor, Matthew leaned in slightly, his lips touching hers. Sliding them on past, he gently rested his cheek against hers. Reaching behind her, he awkwardly unfastened her last undergarment. Putting her arms down and shaking slightly, it fell between them. Matthew picked it up, keeping eye contact, and tossed it to the side. Matthew moved towards her again, and she towards him, meeting in the middle. Mare embraced him with her arms so as not to let her escape a third time, and they began to kiss.

Awkward and strange at first, Matthew realized it to be soothing and pleasing. It was as if he were sharing a secret without speaking, a precious moment without a word. Mare's tongue touched his. At first, Matthew pulled it back, and that's when he discovered a direct link between this act and sensations down below. Each time their tongues touched, a growing stiffness developed in their lower regions. It kept growing and pulsing as if the skin were ripping off the outer shell like Clark Kent ripping off his suit to reveal Superman.

Matthew noticed that when she stopped kissing and using her tongue, it retreated. He did not want it to, though, and forced her back to him strongly but with a gentle kindness as well. They lay down on the bed, still trying to kiss on the way down. Some dark, deep instinct was taking over. To Matthew, it felt tribal, almost barbaric, yet also pleasing and soft.

Continuing to writhe on the bed like snakes intertwined, Matthew felt normal. He felt better than normal in a state of almost euphoric delight. Matthew fell on top of her, now on his hands and knees, kissing, and felt her foot touch his stomach. Her toes snagged his boxer band and, with a single motion, slid them completely off, exposing him completely. Highly sensitive, he felt an ache between his legs that was damn near painful to bear. Immense pressure had built up and was in dire need of relief. Matthew squeezed his legs together to make it stop. Briefly, it subsided, but as his heartbeat built back up again, aching more than ever. Taking Mare's lead, Matthew moved away, reaching down and unzipping her skirt. Trying to save time, he pulled both her skirt and underwear off at the same time.

Matthew felt the need to kiss her knees and thighs for some odd reason as he moved back up. It was a strange move, but she did not seem to mind. Spreading her legs slightly, he wedged between her thighs with some resistance and hesitation from her. Lying on his stomach, Matthew kissed her abdomen in different places, stroking her arms and sides with his hands.

Matthew could feel intense heat on his chest just below the moist folds of her feminine region. It was hot, almost burning his chest. His body drank in the scents in the air, and he felt himself thrusting forward into the sheets, trying to stop the unbearable aching feeling between his legs. It had moved now from an enjoyable pain to an unbelievable ache he thought would never go away.

Making soft noises and moving slowly around in the bed, Matthew could feel her thrust her hips up slightly in a rhythmic motion now. Fully aware of what was going on now with the theatre experience firmly behind him, Matthew noticed a very faint scar horizontally at her waistline. It was an unmistakable mark of a C-section.

It occurred to him she must have done this before, but that was not what concerned him. What was the child she had birthed now? That would have to wait for another time; right now, the ache was no longer bearable, and relief had to come soon, or he was going to pass out.

Most likely at the same point, Matthew felt her pull him up to her face. Kissing erratically now and moving about, Matthew sensed she was more than ready. She felt very warm to the touch all over now. Moving her hips a few times, Matthew could feel a wet and warm sensation. Instinctively, he moved towards it, pushing back into her hips. Suddenly, an overwhelming moist heat completely surrounded him. The feeling was so intense he tried to pull away. Not knowing if he did or not, Mare wrapped her legs around him like a vice and thrust uncontrollably. She moaned loudly as the sensation began to take hold of her. Not sure exactly what to do, Matthew moved with her, meeting her every thrust in the middle. Matthew began to lose his mind and drift into a trance.

He began to lose himself again, and it felt just like he did in the theatre. Still feeling the aching pain and trying to push it out, he closed his eyes. Matthew concentrated so hard he could feel himself inside his mind again. The feelings of lovemaking and the euphoria of losing himself in the theatre felt almost the same, and he was confused once again as to what reality he was entering.

Seeing Mare below him one last time in complete ecstasy, he closed his eyes one last time. The construct of the universe he had seen before formed before his eyes. Concentrating, he fell deeper and deeper inside as his body was left behind working like a heaving, thrusting, pulsing machine. Inside again, Matthew took better care not to drift towards the swirling black holes on the outer edges. Taking advantage of the limited time, he moved around inside with more control.

In a strange way, in the back of his mind, he could still feel himself deep breathing harder and harder. His heartbeat boomed inside the construct, echoing off the walls. Electrical pulses are fired off at the speed of light in every direction. Previously, when Matthew was relaxed, there were fewer light pulses. Now that his body was busy in a lovemaking ritual, the lights raced past him in a firestorm and an electrical shower over the ocean.

A voice called out in the darkness. It was a deep one; he did not recognize it. "Why are you here again?"

Unsure where it emanated from, Matthew ignored it.

"What do you seek?" the voice demanded.

"Who are you?"

"Id!"

"What are you?"

"I am chaos, order, pleasure, pain, nonsense, and knowledge."

Matthew was not expecting such an incoherent answer.

A complete, euphoric feeling completely consumed him, both physically and mentally, this time. Before, only his mind enjoyed such pleasure, but now it was complete. Feeling slightly bad, he was cheating on Mare mentally; he had a sense his body was doing its job and was in control without him seeing it. He could not bring himself to leave and return to reality; the sensation was like a powerful mind-altering drug. Brought on by intellectual interaction, this trip was last spawned from intense physical interaction.

Matthew felt Id could be trusted, yet he did not know him. He felt like he was a close friend yet a stranger, and like he was all-wise yet ignorant and silly. Throwing caution to the wind, he felt a need to ask a question that had been needling him for some time.

"Why can't I feel love?"

The entity spoke almost in riddles. It was annoying, yet Matthew still understood what he meant.

"Love is an altered perception. It is not a feeling. Love is an unconscious chemical reaction made up of acts, affection, impulsiveness, and control."

A sudden pain struck on the side of Matthew's head. A flash of light bolted from the direction of the voice, even though Matthew could not see it. It felt like an entirely new neural pathway had broken open in his head. The pain was intense, like a blood vessel bursting in his mind. Like a cataclysmic birth of a new planet, a new pathway emerged.

Distracted by the creation and expansion taking place around him, Matthew had not realized it, but he had been drifting away from Id towards the edges. The pull of a black hole had been dragging him towards its center. Seeing the rays of light and electrical pulses disappear into it, he voluntarily moved forward into the passageway with more control this time. Matthew dropped into the spherical orb. The walls were shaking like an earthquake. Strong, bright light flickered in and out of view in front of him. He did not resist it this time, timing a flicker. Matthew went straight at it, and in the blink of an eye, he was thrust back into the room.

Over top of Mare, moaning uncontrollably, he felt sweat drip from his body onto hers. His body was convulsing, and he felt a release easing the ache he had been feeling for some time. Matthew cried out, "Dopamine."

Still not relieved, he thrust forward several more times until the pain and pressure below subsided. Out of breath and physically exhausted, he fell to the side of Mare. They lay beside each other on the bed, trying to catch their breath. Matthew felt a rush, as if his body had released a cocktail of chemicals and hormones into his system. Drinking it, they experienced a euphoric feeling that stuck for several minutes after they had finished. He had accomplished something that he never really imagined he would. It was wonderful, and it happened twice in one night. In turn, he had stepped forward with Mare, and they were now bound for life. A connection had been made that could not be broken.

As they lay silently, enjoying the afterglow in their own way, Matthew pondered if the answers he had been looking for were there all this time. Had he tipped the scale and reached just for a moment the fifth dimension?

Mare broke the silence laughing as she spoke, "Dopamine…dopamine, who says dopamine when they're in the throes of romance but you, Matthew."

"I apologize… it just came out."

"I see what you're thinking when you're making love for the first time."

Matthew felt bound to explain it to her, "No... Are you misunderstanding what is going on? I had an epiphany. I know what love is now, and I am capable of it."

Showing interest in hearing him, Matthew noticed she pulled the blanket up over us, then adjusted a pillow under her head. Doing the same, they lay on their backs just talking.

"Love is a neurological and chemical combination that takes place within the brain, Mare."

"Matthew, it is ok. You don't need to explain why you can't feel it again. Obviously, you felt something. My God, I hope you felt something!"

She seemed to suddenly be frightened. Matthew tried to comfort her with his words.

"Yes, I did feel something."

Mare replied in a stern tone, "I am sure you did."

Clutching a blanket, she turned away, looking hurt and angry.

"Mare, I am trying to tell you that I actually felt, not saw, a new neuroconnection birth in my mind. I had a huge release of dopamine, and I think it opened up a new emotion for me. In fact, I know it did!"

Matthew did not realize his scientific approach to every little thing put people off, but it was all he knew.

"I am happy for your discovery while we were making love."

Losing the intellectual battle, Matthew allowed instinct to take over. He reached over forcefully and turned her towards him.

She resisted at first, but then succumbed to his demand.

"Mare, I love you...I really LOVE YOU!"

Matthew looked into her eyes, watching as the information penetrated and took effect. A funny look on her face.

Mumbling in a half-garbled voice, she spoke. "You're not just saying that, are you? You can't just be saying that because you couldn't fake that emotion. I would sense it."

Matthew realized she was talking to herself as well as him at the same time, almost out of it.

"Matthew…" She stroked his head and moved her hair on his forehead, staring deeply back at him. "I love you too. I have always loved you… I always will."

Pulling him down to her, she said, "Hold me, Matthew."

Matthew lay down beside her, wrapping her in his arms. He tried to rationalize what had just happened over the last hour. It had been amazing, wonderful, a miracle. Matthew was still growing and expanding, and now, for whatever reason, it was a physical growth as well as an emotional leap of faith. Life experiences were continuing to expand his physical and mental portfolio.

Matthew had nearly lost track of how many new emotions he had developed. Ten… ten came to mind.

Realizing he was becoming more mainstream each day, he suddenly realized why in sitcoms they always showed the guy trying to escape after making love. His arm was falling asleep and began to ache. Not to mention the fact that he had a new pain. A kidney pain that could easily be addressed if he could get to the bathroom. Matthew realized he was more like a normal male than he thought. The only thing on his mind now was escaping from a warm cuddle, using the bathroom, and getting something to eat.

22 HOUSTON, WE ARE GO FOR LAUNCH

An entire weekend of making love had served to clear Matthew's mind and put him back on the path of discovery. More often now, he caught himself thinking about how his actions affected Mare. Did it really matter that making love came with a free ticket to natter on trivial topics with Id? It was more of a moral issue than a scientific one. Pursuing knowledge at this point was more important, Matthew rationalized, so he pushed away any doubts about cheating on her. Why would it hurt anyone that he could enjoy physical stimulation in reality and an intellectually stimulating conversation in another?

Matthew had discovered one thing about Id. He was never the same. Always changing and switching his opinions and thoughts from one conversation to the next, never really taking sides. A very complex being, he was also nonjudgmental, nonsensical, aloof, and a genius at the same time. Matthew, a genius in his own right, was intrigued with his newly found acquaintance. He seemed at times to be incoherent, but other times perfectly alert. He was there, but he was not. Matthew had never experienced anything like him before. An enigma, the more frustrated Matthew became with Id's personality, the more he drew him in, beckoning Matthew to learn more.

Matthew had so many questions, and a gut feeling Id may know the answer to them all. It was like having a direct link or connection to the grand designer. However, he could sense there was a dark side to Id he had not yet met. One he was fearful to discover. Matthew had not been able to sustain contact long enough to establish any kind of rapport on any particular topic, and Id never seemed to recall previous conversations. Each conversation was new and unconnected to the last. Matthew's encounters had been a few minutes at best, and Id a Wikipedia of the mind, could discuss anything you desired, you only had to ask.

Realizing Id would be an unreliable source and knowing Mare would worry, Matthew decided to confide in Dr. Meachum. His distrust of Dr. Dimment had reached an impasse. His constant scowling from the observation deck, confrontations in meetings, and deranged facial expressions when they passed in the hallways. Matthew arranged a private meeting with Dr. Meachum while Dr. Dimment was out of town.

That morning, Matthew worked to review phase I of his confidential design, waiting for Dr. Meachum to arrive on his desktop computer. Not wanting to divulge too much information about what he had envisioned as a permanent solution to providing stem cells, he quickly closed his work as Dr. Meachum entered his office.

Always the gentleman, Matthew jumped out of his chair to greet him.

"Good day, Dr. Meachum. Thank you for your time."

"Not a problem at all, Matthew. Call me Lawrence. We are professional colleges. You have earned it, Matthew."

Dr. Meachum patted Matthew on the back while shaking his hand.

"Thank you, Lawrence..."

"You're very welcome, Matthew."

Lawrence smiled with a twinkle in his eye and his trademark gleaming white smile.

***

Dr. Meachum picked up on several things that were different about Matthew immediately. He was not as timid as he had been in the past, looking down and away. He wasn't rocking or swaying in his stance at all. In fact, his posture had improved greatly, and he was standing upright and tall… full of confidence.

Whatever Matthew had secretly been working on so far, Dr. Meachum knew he must have been including himself in the experiments. A risky move, knowing he had little success with the test group, it had worked with Matthew. He must be on to something, so whatever he wanted to discuss must be important. Matthew had never requested a private meeting with him exclusively and had only had one other occasion with both of them.

***

"What's on your mind, Matthew?"

"A few weeks ago, I discovered a file that had several case studies, including a patient… Katja Dimment."

Matthew studied Lawrence's reaction to see how he responded. He looked intrigued but withheld comments for now.

"Go on."

"It was odd how it suddenly appeared unclassified, and I am sure Dr. Dimment meant for me to find it. I remembered searching that site before, and it was unavailable."

"Why is that a problem?"

"Well, he could have just shared it with me… we could have discussed it. Maybe things would not be so tense between us."

"I suppose so… maybe he was too embarrassed."

"What do you know of Katja? Is she still alive?"

"She is very much alive, Matthew. She is in a private hospital in Europe. I am not sure exactly where. Gottfried... Dr. Dimment has always been very sensitive about her, as you know... protective if you will. Also... I think he ran into a little trouble using her as an experimental test subject without consent."

Lawrence stopped himself from saying more and gave a half-spirited laugh as if he knew more.

"Water under the bridge, now that was decades ago."

Lawrence spoke with compassion and concern.

Matthew listened intently as he studied Dr. Meachum's mannerisms. He seemed sincere enough.

"Why? Why not just share?"

Lawrence ignored Matthew's question and moved on to something else. Did he not want Dimment and him to be friends or at least friendly? There was no reason to think that, so Matthew put the thought away for now and moved on.

"Did you find something useful in the files, Matthew?

Matthew brightened up immediately and almost smiled. Leaning forward, he continued to explain.

"Yes, as a matter of fact, I did. It has fast-forwarded my research years."

Matthew hesitated, developing a concerned look. He did not want to divulge too much information, but did want to slowly bring Lawrence on board. He needed an ally, and he was the only other person he knew besides Mare.

"Do tell Matthew, no need to be shy."

Lawrence leaned in intently, smiling more than usual. He was obviously blood thirsty for details. Normally, a hands-off manager of personnel, he was prying into details that Matthew was not sure he wanted to share just yet. Something about that particular smile made Matthew feel uneasy, but Lawrence had never given him cause for concern. Trust but verify, Matthew remembered the Bushism and continued to trust until he had a reason not to.

"I have come up with something in my mind. A theory, if you will, and I will need some help, possibly."

"Sure, anything you want."

"It will require an invasive medical procedure."

"Really… What kind of procedure?"

"An implant, perhaps. A stimulator for creating… for stimulating… Well, let's just leave it there for now. Step one is collecting stem cells from my body. To be exact, I need a bone marrow aspiration. I cannot operate on myself, so I just wanted to see if there was a medical facility here on site.

"Matthew, before I would participate or even allow you to experiment on yourself, I would have to know all the details. You're too valuable an asset to end up like Katja Dimment."

"I understand, and when the time comes and I am ready, I will share everything."

"Well, let's hope it is soon. Dr. Dimment is about to go off the rails of a crazy train."

"I know… he has become more agitated with me every passing day."

207

"There is no telling what he has gotten himself into now. He is always shitting were he eats. Sorry, Matthew, for the language. I mean, he is always messing where he is not supposed to."

"Then, in a few weeks, when I am ready, you can provide a facility."

"Sure, there is an empty medical laboratory a few doors down. I can get you clearance today, and when you're ready, nursing support."

"Thank you, Lawrence."

"Matthew, there are other means to obtain stem cells. Have you considered them?"

Meachum looked serious, and Matthew was hardly impressed by his question. Matthew would never consider such an inhumane request. Besides, he needed stems from a particular source, not just any common person would do.

"I have Dr. Meachum, and this is what I have chosen."

Lawrence shook Matthew's hand again. He turned to leave, then spun back around to face him.

"Oh… and Matthew… I would keep this to myself if you know what I mean."

Lawrence winked and smiled.

"I have not included Mare if that is what you're asking?"

"A brilliant young scientist, you're becoming, Matthew. Need to know… good… very good."

Many scientists and doctors had developed and performed experiments on themselves as test subjects. You had to have courage and conviction to be successful. There was no way Matthew wanted a Katja

Dimment on his conscience. Look what it had done to Dr. Meachum. Besides, the test group had only produced two near-savant candidates with the possible characteristics and receptor scans. Daniel and Sarah were the nearest match, but they were also excessively frail and too weak of constitution to survive what Matthew was proposing.

The failures of Dimment's experiments on his sister were rooted in stem cell incompatibility. To provide stem cell treatment for a savant, you must harvest it from a savant. If you wanted to create a savant, the same principle applied. At least that was Matthew's hypothesis.

Bone marrow aspiration was the only way Matthew knew of collecting a large enough sample of stem cells. Subjecting himself to a very risky and painful process was a penance for the advancement of science. Like the early inventors of X-ray, who eventually died from cancer caused by overexposure to gamma radiation, Matthew had to take a chance. He would be spared the pain due to anesthesia and painkillers. However, he had never gone under before, so it was a major concern to him. Anesthesia alone is a very risky endeavor.

A large needle would be injected into his pelvic bone, and a liquid from his marrow would be withdrawn. The volume is small, but the stem cells contained within the marrow are even less abundant, yet of very high quality. The current methods for harvesting stems are very invasive and pose a danger to adults. That is why stems are mainly sought after due to the grotesque methods of embryonic harvesting. A fetus is dominated by stem cells because they are developing very rapidly. In an adult, stem cells account for less than one-tenth of a percent and are only found in specific areas of the body.

It is plausible that if the human body could reproduce stem cells at the same rate as a fetus that it could self-repair. In other words, humans could mend injuries and wounds. The aging process would almost halt, and living to a thousand would be a very real possibility. At some point in every human stem cell growth, it slows to a rate at which you begin to age. Diseases set in. There is no evidence to suggest that the brain contains any stem cells. This is why the other effects of aging begin to take hold. Alzheimer's, dementia, and other neurological diseases develop crippling us. Our hearing and eyesight fail, then our organs, and eventually we die. Even if we had a twenty-year-old body, our brains would fail without regeneration. That is why what Matthew was on the verge of discovering in this laboratory could change mankind's existence forever.

Matthew planned a covert operation with Dr. Meachum's help. They were going to attend a conference in Canada on neurological disorders. Lawrence picked up Matthew, so there was no need for Mare to drive to the airport with him. Feeling slight guilt over his deceptive behavior, Matthew rationalized that the scientific benefits outweighed the social risks and complications it would cause with Mare.

Deception was not even a part of Matthew's conscience a year ago, but the growth hormone he had been taking and the experiences he had endured serve to make him more normal but less of a moral being. Matthew thought for a moment about it as he entered the changing room next to the laboratory, where he would be living for the next three days. Was he progressing as a human being or regressing? Not wanting to fall into a philosophical debate with himself just before a major operation, Matthew concentrated on his next task. What to do with the stems once they are collected? He did not want to endure this treatment a second time.

Matthew would be placed into a drug-induced coma. Suspended in a semiconscious state, they would be able to bring him around enough to ask questions if need be, but mostly he would lie in a peaceful suspension.

In a hospital gown surrounded by Dr. Meachum, several military nurses, and an anesthesiologist, Matthew thought about himself. Just a few years ago, someone in his personal space annoyed him. Now he was allowing complete control over his very life to other people. In large part, Dr. Meachum and Dr. Dimment had given him new life, and Mare had breathed it into him. Matthew knew it was normal for someone's life to flash before their eyes during a traumatic event. Even though this was more regulated and clinical, he still felt slightly that he may not wake up.

The anesthesiologists asked him to count backwards from one hundred. As Matthew mouthed the words, he remembered it had been months since he called his mother 99… 98… 97…

Over the next three days, bone marrow was withdrawn from Matthew in small amounts every twelve hours. The marrow was aspirated, separating the stem cells, and then reinjected back into his body. The stems were safely suspended in a frozen state immediately in a cryogenic chamber.

About every twelve hours, the anesthesiologists would come back in and bring Matthew to a barely conscious state, ask a few questions, and let him go back under. Unlike the theatre and love, making Matthew was unable to drift deep enough into his mind to reach Id.

Several times, Matthew's body fought to come to. He felt chilled and remembered the nurse placing new warm blankets over his body. The bright lights in the room, pulsing, clicking, and beeping of the instrumentation made Matthew realize he was not at home. On one such occasion, he saw Panthea standing over him, but she was wearing a mask. Her face transformed into someone he barely recognized.

Matthew hated being confined, with no control over his own fate. Several times, his anxiety over it made the heart monitor beep so fast that he was given other medication to slow it down.

Like being chained in an underground prison cell, Matthew realized he could not go through this twice. His upper thighs and hips ached even though he was given pain medication. The oxygen tube under his nose was irritating his nostrils, and his face itched nonstop with no way to scratch it.

Late on the last evening, Matthew saw Dr. Meachum, and he thought about withdrawing blood. Nothing to worry about, but he also obtained hair samples, a mouth swab, and it felt as if he took a skin sample from his scalp. He remembered that when he came to Lawrence, he spoke out.

"Don't... worry... Matthew... , just... a... few... more... hours..."

Lawrence had kept Mare busy at the education center and even sent her to the National Education Association's yearly conference in Las Vegas to speak on autism for a day. This kept her busy and mentally occupied. It was not unusual for Matthew to go several days without talking to her, but over the last few months, since they had moved in together, it seemed out of place for Matthew. He had Lawrence text her several times to keep her at bay and occupied.

Waking early morning on the last day, Matthew's hips were so sore he could barely walk after the procedure. Worst of all, Dr. Dimment had seen Matthew in the laboratory from the observation room, trying to get around with a walker. Distracted by the pain, Matthew had forgotten to black out his windows.

Making eye contact, neither of them flinched or blinked for several moments. It was like two cowboys squaring off in the desert streets of Arizona. Matthew broke the standoff when he blacked out the windows, but watched as Dimment lingered, then stormed off. He looked like a scorned child ready to tattle on their sibling.

Matthew had released everyone in the test group except for Daniel and Sarah. Having them about to assist, especially now, has worked out well. They had requested to be more involved and not wanting to discourage young talent, Matthew took them on as laboratory assistants. Sarah was about Matthew's age, and Daniel was a few years older, yet they looked up to Matthew as a mentor.

Matthew had relocated his work to a private, high-security laboratory with double-locking doors. The laboratory was equipped with facial recognition and retinal scanners for both eyes. The first door opened upon facial recognition. The second door opened after a retinal scan. The only one having access to the laboratory meant there was no fear of infringement or spying eyes from Dr. Dimment or anyone else. Matthew continued other research with Daniel and Sarah so as not to raise Dimment's suspicion further, but he knew that would be short-lived.

On day seven, Matthew returned home to Mare, walking normally and in need of rest. Rest would be far removed, as Mare had been restless and in the mood the week before her monthly feminine clock reset. Matthew struggled to be productive, but his legs and thighs ached in total pain as he went through the motions. Id was nowhere to be found, and Matthew noted that medications and extreme pain served as blockers from reaching the mental state he required to reach him. Matthew had never seen what he looked like anyway and started to wonder if he had been real or something of a coping mechanism, like an imaginary friend. Self-doubt was not something Matthew had ever dealt with, but there were a great many things he did now that he had never dealt with.

Matthew's day off was no day off at all. Even at bedtime, he struggled to rest. Leaning against the countertop in his new laboratory, he struggled to concentrate. Matthew had started a new habit that morning. Coffee… coffee with three creams and three sugars. He had tasted it before and hated it, but now it was the best-tasting drink he had ever tried, and after one cup, he was feeling better and had already started a second. Knowing caffeine was highly addictive, he continued anyway with abandon.

Finally able to concentrate clearly, his first task was to separate the stem cells from the residual marrow without damaging them.

Knowing there would be some loss of cells, Matthew kept it to a minimum. His goal was to have approximately ten thousand cells, barely enough to make enough for one treatment. Matthew separated the samples into two lots, safely preserving one lot and working with the other. To prevent a second operation, Matthew had to work quickly to develop a method to stimulate the cells to regenerate on their own. Attempting something that had never been done before never detracted Matthew from his quest. The challenge emboldened him, and he knew that if he were successful, the seed he created would have the potential to transform anyone into a savant.

Matthew named the two samples in his notes Adam and Eve. The names had a symbolic air to him, but more importantly, they allowed him to encrypt his research. Matthew had created his own encryption code, which utilized numbers and letters to mask his notes. Having a thirty-six-character alphabet and a photographic memory, Matthew wrote as fluidly in his new language as he did in English. He could read his notes just as easily. It would be very difficult, if not impossible, for his notes to be deciphered by anyone but him.

Taking Adam, he injected it into a fluid sack, almost like a placenta. The fluid inside was similar in chemical makeup to that of the first developed embryonic sack of a mother. Matthew tested several known methods of radiation and frequencies to stimulate growth. Stems by their very nature want to reproduce and regenerate. However, the rate of death far outpaced the rate of growth, especially in a foreign environment. The radiation slightly damaged the stem cells, triggering them to regenerate. His theory was that a non-ionizing radiation with the correct frequency would be strong enough to pierce the cell wall but not fatally damage or retard it.

Pure light dialed in a variable laser that Matthew had obtained from another laboratory, set to a frequency of 1017 (Hz), pulsed Adam for the first trial. Matthew watched the results using an electron microscope. He continued to hit the cells with increasing durations, allowing them time to respond until it was too late. A split... a stem regenerated, then another, then another. Matthew reviewed his data, noting that the cells split once with seven pulses, each lasting seven thousandths of a second, and waited seven seconds between each pulse. Waiting several minutes, Matthew repeated the experiment several more times until he had around fifty thousand stems. five times the original sample.

Storing the new sample at a peak reproduction temperature of 100.5 degrees, Adam was allowed to rest overnight. Matthew wanted to see how Adam would respond to normal reproductive temperatures. Eve was still tucked safely away in the cryo-freezer.

Matthew left the laboratory to return home using a cab as usual. On the way home, he decided to stop at a local market. Matthew had noticed the car as soon as they left the base. He had no recent cause to be suspicious, but the promise of what Adam and Eve could deliver had him paranoid. At first, he thought it was a coincidence, but Matthew noticed the same navy-blue car coming out of the security turnstile at work as he did exiting the cab at the supermarket. His photographic memory was now becoming a survival tool.

Leaving the market with several sacks of fruit, cereal, and milk, Matthew positioned himself in the back seat so he could look out of the passenger side view mirror of the cab. The separation glass between the front and back seats provided a brief glimpse of the car every time we passed by a streetlight as well. Matthew had never been tailed before, and he was unsettled by the entire ordeal. The car followed them just short of the gated complex. Matthew knew he was safe once inside the gate. Security at the facility had been top-notch up till now, and there was no reason to suspect it had changed.

The car following them had stopped several hundred feet short of the gate, pulled over, and turned off its lights. Matthew paid the cab driver and went inside to the elevator in the lobby.

Matthew's phone rang and vibrated in his pocket, startling him. Pulling it out, he noticed that Mare had called him several times; he had not heard the phone or felt it vibrate. The grocery store had been too noisy, and he had left his coat hanging on a rack in the laboratory earlier, forgetting to check it. He knew with that many calls, the news couldn't be good. She rarely bothered him when he was working.

Matthew had shown the night watchmen his security pass and again to another guard at the elevator. Normally, having to pass only one guard, the security level must have been raised slightly concerning Matthew. Threat levels determined the security level, and in most cases, they were precautionary, so he was not too apprehensive about it.

He rode the elevator up and went into the condo. Security had been so tight that only one person or one party could be in one of the two lobby elevators at a time. This level of security, Matthew was aware, never allowed both of them to stop on the same floor or pick up from the same floor. No one would ever notice things like this, except for Matthew or a criminal. He had often contemplated the security of the building. He knew where the weaknesses were and where not to keep the information as a mental note. Overall, the building was remarkably secure, considering it was not located within a military installation.

Inside, Matthew entered the empty apartment. Mare had been invited to another conference and had left that morning. Letting in the evening now, Matthew entered the empty condo, setting his phone on the countertop. The ringing sound of his phone echoed through the kitchen walls, bouncing off the tile and appliances. Matthew hit the speaker button, answering. Matthew could immediately hear music and loud talking in the background.

"Hello… Mare, can you hear me?"

"Hold on a minute and let me go into the hallway so I can hear you!"

The loud roar subsided to a dull groan.

"How have you been? I have missed you so much, Matthew."

"I have missed you, too."

"Have you made any progress?"

It was a little unusual for her to ask about his work. That was something they rarely ever did, especially now. The only time they ever discussed work at home was if Matthew brought it up. Matthew, now being more cautious, thought she must really miss him, or she was a spy. Now, knowing the latter was just a joking thought, he ignored it.

"Fine… It's fine. As a matter of fact, I have made a leap."

"Really…do tell."

"I will tell you when you get home. How is everything there?"

She was silent for several seconds. Too long for a normal conversational pause.

"Hold on a minute?"

Matthew could hear her moving just by the way people's voices in the background would become louder then subside. Concerned by the awkward pause, Matthew questioned her.

"What's wrong, Mare?"

"I am in the lobby now with lots of people. A man… a man has been following us all day. At first… I was not sure. Then I thought maybe I was imagining it. He was at the hotel earlier watching me, and when I left, I saw him here inside the awards banquet."

"Are you sure?"

"Well, making sure I was not being paranoid, I asked Sophia, and she told me she remembered seeing him too."

"You two need to stay close together and do not go anywhere by yourselves."

"We have been. You remember Sophia, Matthew. Is she the new director at the Education Center?"

"Yes…I remember her. You won't believe this, but I think someone has been following me, too, Mare?"

"Who was it? What do you think they want?"

"I am not sure, but I'm concerned now that Dr. Dimment is behind it somehow."

"Are you sure? How do you know?"

"I did not want to scare you before, but he has had a very colorful past before coming stateside."

"I know he is strange and not very cordial, but stalking us?"

"He has been watching me closely at work. Of late, he has been very confrontational with me. That day I came to your office, I saw him threaten you, Mare. I didn't want you to know I was eavesdropping on you."

"It's ok, Matthew, it is kinda flattering."

"I logged into your computer and listened to you two arguing. I only caught the tail end of it, though. What were you guys arguing about? It could be of importance."

"I guess I should tell you now, Matthew. I have been hiding some things from you as well. Dimment did threaten me. He said if I did not spy on you, he would… well… he said he would…" Mare began to cry. "He said he would stop treating me."

"Treating you? What do you mean by treating you?"

Matthew became very concerned, "What is he treating you for?"

"It started several years ago after you left the Children's Hospital. He…he…"

Mare began to wail, losing complete control of her emotions.

"You have to calm down. Maybe you should come home now so we can talk in person?"

Gaining her composure, she continued in a tearful voice.

"No! I need to finish this and tell you now. It's easier for me to talk over the phone."

Matthew's heart sank. In the dark recesses of his mind, hundreds of tiny circumstances and coincidental remarks and actions started to pool together in a sea of deceit. Anger towards Dimment welled up inside, and his fists were clutched together so hard his hands hurt.

"Gottfried artificially inseminated me. Shortly after he awakened me, I gave birth. I was young and really did not understand what had happened and what was going on."

Matthew felt something run down his cheek. Something warm and wet he had never felt before. Again, it happened, and several salty drops hit his lips. With the phone still lying on the countertop, he turned his body with his back against the cabinet doors and slid down until he was on the floor. He wrapped his arms around his legs and tried to rock in a fetal position to dissipate his anxiety.

"Matthew, I feel so ashamed. Are you still there?"

Matthew put away his feelings long enough to answer. Even though he strained to sound strong, his voice came out cracked and broken.

"I'm still here for you, Mare."

In his heart, this did not change a thing. He loved her more than ever, and all he wanted to do was ease her pain. His mind raced with malevolence towards Dimment. He wanted to squash him like a roach under the sole of his shoe.

"Matthew, he made me promise to never tell anyone, or he would fix me where I could never awaken again. He implanted a neurostimulator that causes me to produce the dopamine that I need to be here, conscious."

"It's ok, Mare… I am sorry you have been carrying this burden all too yourself."

"There's more."

Matthew wondered how bad it was going to be. He had been completely crushed already, and now more.

"He has also been injecting me with stem cells."

"Stem cells, where did he get stem cells?"

Matthew was crazed with anger, almost unable to think. There was only one place he could be getting stems. Those trips abroad. This was more than just him and Mare now. More than just his research, he has been working alongside and standing next to a monster... an evil monster of the worst kind humanity has to offer.

Mare was sobbing again, uncontrollably and hard to understand.

"Please don't think badly of me, Matthew. He gets them from a laboratory in Berlin. That's why he is gone a lot. They are harvested from embryos."

Matthew suddenly felt ill again.

"Mare, you knew where he was getting them from?"

Matthew felt alone and abandoned suddenly. It was one thing not to know and just go along, but she knew how he felt about that type of research, yet she went along. His mind would not let him understand.

"Matthew, I know how you must feel, but if he stops the treatment, even with the dopamine, my brain will start to degenerate and fade away. If I wait too long, he said it would kill me."

"Mare, I don't know what to think right now and who to believe anymore. Relationships are built on trust?"

"I know Matthew, and I am sorry. You have to believe me. The car crash that I suffered as a child caused brain damage. The stem cells Dimment injected repaired it. I feel so ashamed, Matthew. I feel selfish. I will understand if you hate me."

Mare broke out in a loud, tearful eruption. Matthew felt helpless to comfort her over the phone. He decided to worry about the consequences later and concentrate on her. Mare had no choice in the matter, and who could blame her for going along? Still, the lack of trust ate at him like a cancer.

"Mare, it's OK. I won't let him hurt you anymore. I think I may be able to help you, treat you myself. You just need to come home...now!"

Composing herself long enough, she finished her confessional.

"Matthew, the baby. He took my baby for his experiments. He thought it might be a savant like you and me. He told me that I had a stillbirth, but I know that was a lie. The nurse at the Psychiatric Hospital in New York confessed to me. She was there when it was born, and it left the room with him alive."

"Mare, I am so sorry."

"I confronted him and he denied it. I was persistent, and he finally admitted it. He wanted to collect stem cells from it to try to save his sister, as he did for me, he said. He pleaded, telling me he needed stems from a savant. He used another man's seed from Europe. That man is dead now. He supposedly died in a plane crash. Anyway, he said he was very sorry. He wanted a live donor who could regenerate the stems. He accidentally killed it when he placed my baby under anesthesia. He was trying to do a bone marrow aspiration on an infant… an infant, Matthew!"

Matthew felt like all he had known and the isolated world his mother had always kept him in were distant memories. Being alive, being normal, was it worth it? Was it worth this? This pain he felt inside was too much; it was too crazy.

"Mare, get home now! Do not leave Sophie's side."

"Mathew… I love you… I really love you, please don't leave me over this."

"Mare… I love you… You are my best friend."

Matthew stood up, reached down, and ended the call. He immediately called Dr. Meachum and let him know both he and Mare

222

were being followed. Special agents were contacted and provided security until they returned home. The man following Mare was never identified. Using still shots from security cameras and facial recognition, they were still not able to identify him.

The next day, Matthew left without saying goodbye to Mare. She was still in bed, and he kissed her on the forehead, trying not to wake her. He felt tired having been awakened early as she arrived on a private plane in the early morning hours. Matthew heard her enter the room and felt her kiss his head, but he pretended to sleep, not wanting to discuss anything further until he gathered his thoughts.

With coffee brewing, Matthew stepped into the private laboratory to check on Adam. Shocked, he adjusted the microscope to make sure his eyes were not deceiving him. Down to less than half of where he had left him, Matthew was horrified to discover what was going on.

The monitor showed the stems breaking down slowly, then dissolving. Matthew racked his brain to try to figure out what was going on. Radiating the sample again using the seven, seven, seven method from before, he was able to recover much of the loss.

Matthew sat down, reading through his notes and staring off into space. If only he could talk with Id, if only he could talk with anyone. Knowing the answer was no, Matthew separated a portion of the sample and injected it into a new sack in a separate radiation-proof chamber. Once set up, he obtained a single low-grade radiated atom and injected it into the sample. Figuring a slow-decaying atom would not be harmful to normal cell development. The movement of any radioactive materials inside the complex was accompanied by a manifest. Matthew would have to obtain one even for such a minute amount. Lawrence would question it, and he would have to divulge his secrets at that point. Something he could not do at this point. He needed something that produced a low-level amount of radiation as it decayed.

Matthew began to recall any and all the information he had ever read in his mind. Just like he had done when he was a side show freak, he began to slip into a trance. Coming back on command, Matthew recalled image after image and word after word of anything and everything in his memory about stem cells, radiation, its effects, and the creation of life. His mind worked like a random picture generator. Totally immobilized for however long it took, he kept his eyes closed, remembering. Vulnerable just as much as he had been, having the stems harvested, he was safe inside the confines of the high-security laboratory.

Years since he went this deep, searching his memory, his eyes flickered, resembling someone in REM sleep. Waves of information passed by his vision. Differing versions of the periodic table of elements zoomed past. The symbol K kept repeating itself, Potassium. When potassium decays, small amounts of radium are released. The wavelength and frequency may be close enough to stimulate the stems to reproduce. He would need to construct a porous vessel about the size of a small aspirin to store the potassium. The porous vessel would need to be placed inside another small porous sphere containing the stems of Adam. There would need to be just enough microscopic openings to allow the timed release of stems after the capsule reached maximum volumetric capacity.

Matthew recovered from his trance, exhausted mentally. His head began to throb slightly. He made a cup of coffee, then sat down to scribe the information in his notebook. Within a few minutes, he locked it in a safe located below the laboratory floor.

Leaving the security of his laboratory, Matthew moved from one laboratory to another and searched for any laboratory to which his access allowed him entry. The genetics wing of the research facility had benefits, as well as a high security level. Finding suitable material to house both the potassium and the seeds of Adam in the genetics lab, Matthew left a note for the users.

He borrowed several items he did not need to mask the fact that he was taking some implant devices from the biomechanics laboratory without asking. Implants had been developed and studied inside the facility for years, and Matthew was just contributing to a long line of scientists who had come before him. Except this time, he had come up with something he knew had great potential, but he never imagined where it would take him.

Matthew completed Adam, then repeated the process with Eve, working late into the evening. He had created two viable stem regenerators. For the first time, there was a possibility that brain cells could reproduce. Know that Mare would no longer be under the care of a maniacal miscreant, he was doing for Mare.

Nothing like this has ever been done before, and there is the possibility that it may not work at all. His thoughts of failure were tempered by the chance, a slim but plausible one, that this would be the greatest gift to the human condition that had ever been accomplished. Matthew thought this must have been how NASA control felt after they put the first man on the moon, or a race car driver felt after winning his first race.

Assuring himself one last time that they were working properly and sustainable on their own, Matthew placed them inside a fluid-filled container before placing them in the safe. The container was equipped with a small heating and cooling system on opposing ends to regulate the internal temperature to that of the average human fetus.

Matthew had captured a few still shots on the monitor before storing his creation. It showed the stems floating out of the sphere at a steady rate. Of course, without a home, they would eventually dissipate and dissolve, becoming nutrients for the surviving stems.

Leaving the laboratory exhausted, sore, mentally taxed beyond what Matthew would not wish on his worst enemy, he only thought of

Mare. What he would say, what he would do, what would happen now. Matthew had secrets of his own to share about Id, but they paled in comparison to what had already been revealed, and he did not want to add to her misery right now.

Lawrence greeted Matthew in the hall as he exited the elevator on the ground level. He walked with him as he headed out.

"Matthew, because of Mare, I arranged a security escort for you as well. They will stay with you everywhere you go. Have you cracked the proverbial egg yet?"

Matthew tried not to show any emotion. With a lifetime of emotionless living, he found it nearly impossible to hide his excitement. To cover, he filled his mind with all of the things Mare had told him last night, then replied.

"Not yet, but I am very close."

"I knew you would… I told you before, Matthew, you are the key."

"Thank you, sir."

"Lawrence, remember."

"Certainly, I apologize."

"I don't know if you have been told, but Dr. Dimment has disappeared."

"Really… any Idea where to?"

"Probably in Germany by now. We have notified the authorities, and they are currently searching for him. He is crafty and has military experience, so he will be hard to catch. This is not his first time going into hiding… but you already know that, don't you?"

Matthew looked at him without replying and went out the door.

23 REVOLVING WHEEL

In the early morning hours, a control station at Tegel Airport, Northwest of Berlin, blanketed in a pink-orange sky of daybreak, yielded to a private charter plane taxiing on the runway to dock. Beacons on the plane's body flashed like warning signs to the unaware inhabitants of the awakening city that darkness had arrived. With the air-stairs in position, a plump figure descended with his oily skin and half-shaven face concealed by the darkness that remained. The lone passenger quickly scurried like a rat to an awaiting black sedan being loaded with a single bag and a briefcase.

Dimment entered the driver's side door of the sedan, speeding off towards a chain link gate, allowing his escape. His passport credentials, not yet revoked, had just been updated, having beaten an email sent hours before. Still awaiting discovery in the inbox of the Berlin State Department Building, as it was springing to life to be read.

***

Sitting down with her steaming cup of hot tea, an administrative assistant began poring through a list of fifty or so emails. Although marked urgent, she took her time as she scanned through junk mail, social media updates, and routine business mail. Arriving at the email stating that Dr. Gottfried Dimment was wanted by the United States Government for unspecified reasons to be questioned, she quickly read it.

Making a copy, she hustled to a confidential printer to retrieve the bulletin that should have been sent directly to the security office and the Berlin Police Department. This email was different. Although urgent, it was also marked private and confidential for the Ambassador's eyes only. She quickly took it into his office unannounced. Laying the document on his desk in front of him, she nodded to him, and the Ambassador nodded back at her with no further verbal remarks. This was an internal investigation that required discretion.

***

By the time the email had reached the Ambassador, Dimment had already driven from the airport to the Berlin Psychiatric Hospital. He rummaged quickly through his laboratory, collecting documents and papers. Having few to deal with anyway, he disconnected the embryonic chambers one by one and flushed the fluids from them all. Taking a blue tube, he emptied the contents of each one into it and pushed the cart over to the biological waste chute, disposing of the still-living fetuses. Without antagonism or remorse, he turned off the machines that once breathed what brief life into the unborn.

Unlocking the secured refrigeration storage door, Dimment retrieved a small thermos-sized stainless steel container and opened it. He twisted the bottom of it and pushed up. It hissed, and fog began seeping from it. Dimment opened the cryofreezer and removed all his stem vials, loading them into a container, sealing it, and then tossing it into his briefcase. Slamming the case shut, he picked it up and headed for the door. Suddenly forgetting something, he stopped. Turning back inside the room, he went over to a set of locking drawers. Unlocking the set at the top with a Steelcase key, he opened it up. Inside was a thirty-two-caliber nickel-plated revolver with cheap, black hand grips. He picked the gun up and placed it inside the front of his trousers, concealing it with his shirt. Going back to the door, he exited without bothering to lock the door or turn off the lights.

***

The Ambassador to Germany had just hung up the phone. He had detailed a plan to retrieve Dimment to a couple of unknown agents from an unnamed intelligence organization. Not ready to even begin a manhunt, they went back to their computers, pulling up a photograph of Dr. Dimment's passport picture and the whereabouts from the last thirty-six hours. Retrieving satellite images, airport security shots, and a

Seven–Eleven security camera, they pieced together information quickly, preparing a covert extraction operation.

***

Dimment climbed into his Mercedes and sped from the hospital. Immediately, a car began following him. Accelerating, he darted up narrow streets and alleys. Dimment's mind worked better than his hands and arms arm the steering. The faster he went, the closer the other car would get to him. He was wasting too much effort looking in the mirror and over his shoulder, but was too stubborn to change.

His lack of skill finally caught up to him. He banged hard into some trash cans, overcorrecting, and struck a light post, throwing an array of orange metal sparks into the air. Turning up a narrow alley, barely missing the brick corner, he noticed a truck backing up the main street. It was the break he had been looking for. Dimment darted around the rear of the vehicle, barely catching the huge steel bumper, kicking orange into the sky once more. The truck continued to back up slowly, reacting to the collision, blocking the path of the pursuing car.

Free for now, Dimment sped to the hotel where he had met the Russian once before. Slamming on the brakes as he pulled in front of the building, he jumped out of his car, leaving the door open for the valet. Remembering the prize in his briefcase, he rushed inside with the case in hand. The Russian was sitting alone at the same table. Dimment, out of breath and huffing like an overweight man taking the stairs for the first time, slid into the booth.

The Russian finished lighting a cigarette and watched Dimment breathing heavily. Exhaling a long plume of blue-white smoke across the table into the distressed face of Dimment, he spoke finally.

"What's wrong with you, comrade? You look as if you have been running a marathon." Smiling, he continued as Dimment regained his composure. "I hope you have something for me? My people are growing extremely impatient."

Dimment discreetly pulled the briefcase into the seat next to him. He looked around the room, scanning for prying eyes. A couple of patrons sat at the bar with their backs to each other on opposite ends. The restaurant no longer served breakfast in the main dining area, so the rest of the room was empty. Chairs were tucked neatly away, and all of the tables had been set, awaiting the lunch crowd later that day. The bar, open twenty-four seven, had the only action this morning.

Dimment was satisfied that the place was secure and opened the briefcase's latch. He took out the metallic container containing the stems and slid it across the table. The size and shape resembled a drink mixer.

"Excellent... excellent," the Russian said with an evil tone. He began to reach inside his coat to retrieve something.

Countering, hastily reaching inside his trousers with some difficulty, Dimment pulled the pistol out where the Russian could see it, then concealed it under a cloth napkin. The gun had been gouging his abdomen, and he mainly pulled it to relieve the pain. He also wanted the Russian to know he was not stupid.

"Easy... Easy comrade! There is no need for that. I don't even have carry weapons on my person." The Russian padded the breast of his coat, sat back, and then raised his arms to signal surrender.

"Take out whatever it is you were reaching for very slowly." The Russian moved more slowly and pulled out a thin white envelope. He set it on the tabletop and slid it across to him.

Dimment looked down at it. "What is it?"

The Russian snuffed out his cigarette and leaned forward. "This is the dissolution of our relationship. Inside this envelope is an account number accompanied by a passcode for a bank in Switzerland. I know it is cliché, but as we discussed, the money you requested will be there when you want to access it."

He smiled, sitting back, waiting for a response from Dimment that would not come. Impatient, he continued. "Gottfried... I am a businessman. We are the new Soviet Union. We are capitalists now. It's all about the Ruble. Besides, I have no stomach for violence anymore.

We do not kill people. It draws too much attention. Please... put away your weapon?"

Dimment pulled the gun down carefully and placed it inside the briefcase, and closed it. Smiling Dimment offered a surrender of his own, "Well then, let's have a drink."

He motioned to the bartender. The man laid down his towel, making a face, as he was interrupted from his morning routine. They sat silently waiting until he arrived.

"Two Kentucky Bourbons on ice, please." The Russian nodded approvingly. Dimment kept looking around the mostly empty room, trying to memorize faces for future reference.

The waiter returned quickly with two Bourbons on ice.

The Russian held it high in the air, looking through the caramel liquid with pleasure. "I like your style, Gottfried. Kentucky Bourbon," he said as he swirled the contents of the glass and sniffed its aroma. They hit their glasses together and drank.

Dimment slammed the glass down empty in seconds. "It's time for me to go."

"What's your hurry? The day is young."

Dimment retrieved the envelope and his briefcase.

"By the way, asshole, I ditched your thugs on the way here."

The Russian's smile disappeared; he was not amused. "I have no clue what you are referring to, but have a nice day just the same."

The Russian looked around the room, clearly unnerved by Dimment's comments. Dimment looked at him as if he were not telling the truth, but he had funds, so he was no longer concerned with him. As far as he was concerned, his business in Berlin was done.

As he left the lounge, he bumped into a man but did not see his face. The man had his collar pulled up and a scarf nearly covering his face. His hat covered most of his hair. Dimment replied politely, "entschuldigen Sie mich." (Excuse me). The man said nothing and continued on. Dimment looked at him from behind for a second, but seeing no cause for alarm, he hastily left the hotel.

***

The man who bumped into Dimment walked over behind the Russian and dropped his hat on the table. The Russian was startled by it and looked up as he was removing his scarf. The man sat down and said, "You have something that belongs to me?"

The Russian smiled, lit a cigarette, and exhaled the smoke. "Yes…and what is that?" Two men approached the table, one of them saying. "I think you'd best come with us, comrade."

The Russian had placed the container inside his trench coat pocket just before the man entered, concealing it. He started to resist, but the two men showed him concealed weapons. He snuffed out his cigarette after taking one last drag from it, standing up. The four men, led by the man with the hat, went to the elevator in the hotel lobby and rode it up to the Russians' room.

The Russian was placed in a chair. One of the two men turned on the television. The other one turned the volume high with the remote control, then tossed it on the bed. The man in the hat sat in a lounge chair across from him.

"Where is it?"

"As I stated before, I don't know what you're talking about."

He motioned to the two other men. They went to the door, opened it, and waited outside. The man stared at the Russian. The Russian stared back and smiled, pursing his lips and placing his fingertips together, bouncing them impatiently.

"What are you reading my mind?" The Russian laughed before the smile jumped from his face. His expression suddenly appeared like he was having a heart attack.

The man in the hat smiled menacingly, "I am now."

The Russian fell to the floor with his hands grasping his head. He was trying to scream, but the immense pain prevented it, and he only gasped and moaned. He reached towards the man, pushing his hand down on the glass coffee table. Trying to stand, the glass shattered beneath his hand. A shard ripped through his palm, and it began bleeding profusely through the cut. He was of a strong constitution, but the man with the hat relented not until he had the information he wanted.

The Russian stood upright, clutching his hands to each side of his head again. Falling back down in the chair, blood now stained his face and clothing. He garbled out a response, "It's…in…my…coat…pock…et!"

Suddenly, the pain stopped. The Russian, still reeling from the immense pain inside his head, tried to regain his mind.

The man with the hat spoke again, saying, "I already knew where the container was. I just wanted to know if you knew anything else." Standing back up, the man with the hat pulled a cover from the bed and tossed it to the Russian. He then went over, took the container from inside his coat. Sitting back down, he leered at him with a gleaming smile and a sparkle in his eye.

"What are you?"

"Don't you mean Who am I?"

"No…what kind of abomination are you?" he asked, trying to stop the bleeding from his hand.

The man did not care for the comment. He refocused on the Russian and intensified his trance. Inside the Russian's head, the blood vessels began to pulse. The veins on his head and neck swelled like an oversized bun in the oven, turning from grey to blue, then bright red.

The Russian could not yell and was not even strong enough to raise his arms. The vessels began to burst one by one. After the first one popped, his eyes rolled back into his head, and as the others released, he convulsed in the chair violently until his entire body stiffened.

The man with the hat released him. The Russian fell limp, never to move again. Blood oozed from his ears, nose, mouth, skin, and eyes. The whites of the Russians' eyes were now colored red. He lay there, eyes open and lifeless. The man with the hat stood up, looking at the container, and threw it up in the air a few inches, then caught it in his hands. He whistled as he walked to the door. Taking one last look around the room, he exited the door, leaving it ajar.

***

Slow to react, the intelligence agency set up a task force room and began to brief a group of agents on Dr. Dimment's history. Handing out photographs and detailed information, they planned for a raid late in the afternoon at the earliest.

***

Dimment returned to his home in the Western part of Berlin, watching for tails as he drove cautiously there. Pulling into the garage, the door closed automatically behind him. Once secure, he stepped out of the newly dented Mercedes, looking it over. Irritated, he grabbed the briefcase with a forceful grip, clasping and wrenching the leather handle in his palm. Thinking about the damage, he grumbled to himself. "Damn Russians."

Walking to the door of the house, he typed in his pass code, deactivating the alarm. Inside, he locked it, securing the house once again, and then turned on the alarm with his key fob.

The house was rough and neglected. Piles of open mail and old newspapers decorated the kitchen and dining areas. Empty food containers and dishes sat molding in the sink. Flies buzzed around it, circling like buzzards over a rotting carcass. Dimment began thinking as he set the briefcase on the kitchen table. Tossing his coat down, he kicked off his shoes, loosened his belt, dropping his trousers and shirt on the dining room floor. He removed his socks, tossing them into the kitchen towards two open doors with laundry machines inside, stacked high with unwashed clothing.

In a T-shirt and boxer shorts, Dimment teetered into the living room, taking the briefcase as he went. Sitting down in an oversized recliner, he turned on the television, setting the briefcase in his lap. Opening it, he removed the pistol and laid it on the table beside him. He pulled the envelope out, closed the briefcase, and tossed it to the floor. Sliding his index finger in the corner, he slid his finger down the edge, cutting it as he went.

Grunting in pain, Dimment shoved his wounded finger into his mouth, sucking on it, continuing to mentally curse the envelope. His nostrils were flooded with the odor of fresh blood. Dimment struggled to finish opening the letter with one hand but ended up using the other to steady it. Inside, there were two inscriptions. An account number and a pass code, GENESIS-1:27.

"At least those stem cells will be mine someday." They were just ordinary stems, but the quality made them very valuable. The Russian, a former KGB agent, had required the stems of a Savant but instead was cheated with ordinary stems, still difficult to obtain. The particular type harvested from Dimment's embryos was more active, lived longer, and was more substantial in reproducing than ordinary stems. They were the building blocks of life in their infancy.

Parched with a dry alcoholic's mouth, Dimment opened the bourbon bottle sitting on the lamp table next to him. Picking up a dirty glass, he filled it halfway. Turning it up to his lips, he drank it all in one gulp.

Flipping on the television, Dimment blindly stared at a news station. The newscast in German was annoying him, so he switched it to an English Channel on the BBC. A rerun of Top something was on, and he recognized the three men. It was a car show. He heard the man on the show say, "The revolving wheel causes the car to appear to be in motion when it's not." They were discussing new rims for a sports car. He relaxed as soon as the alcohol began to take effect and fell asleep with the television on, sitting upright, exhausted and jetlagged.

24 *BINDINGS*

Mare at home safe… Matthew committed time to tidy the laboratory. In an attempt to shroud any traces he may have left behind. Unaware of happenings outside of his own world, Matthew had a strange sense that all was not right with the world.

His days of rocking, humming, and sitting quietly in a comfortable chair thinking about whatever he wanted seemed so far removed from the here and now. Those soothing, methodical strokes through his hair that his mother used to calm his soul as a child felt so distant, almost unattainable now.

His mind now filled with fear for Mare's wellbeing, protecting his dreams… their dreams, and complete mistrust of almost everyone around them. The penance paid to be normal… it felt too costly now… dirty and stained. There was no returning to the days of old, and he could feel it. Matthew knew exactly what the phrase, "You can't go home," meant, now. His mind was telling him that things would never be the same and would most definitely be worse before they got better.

Sweeping the laboratory floor, placing glassware in the dishwasher, dusting, and organizing had replaced rocking and humming. The menial task of a janitor, James the janitor. His diligence shows how something so mundane can calm the mind. Although that weightless feeling rocking provides is in the past… it called to him like bourbon to a recovering alcoholic. How simple it would be to just rock all the troubles away. Watch television and dream.

Cleaning allowed Matthew to think with clarity. Matthew spent a lot of time with Mare before returning to work. He had continued to ponder their conversation as he tidied up his world and set it straight. She had made one wonderful suggestion. Take my handwritten notes and place them along with Adam in a bank safety deposit box, and leave Eve in the safe at work. Separating them would provide so much added protection. If need be, he could sacrifice one or the other to protect himself and, most importantly, Mare.

Seeing Matthew so disconnected, lost, and out of sorts, Lawrence made a mandatory request that he spend a few more days at home with Mare.

Hoping to catch up on his sleep as well, Matthew realized how secure he felt next to Mare. She would sometimes stroke his hair when he was lying next to her, just like when he was a child. A cliché, you marry the woman who was most influential in your life during your formative years. Mare did possess many of Panthea's traits.

Matthew lay in bed, deep in REM sleep, unaware of the room around him. He drifted effortlessly as he floated just feet above a grassy meadow. He was naked but felt clothed, flying but felt still, and secure, yet he felt as if he were being spied on. A strong feeling that ID was near came about him. In the distance, he saw a lone tree on a mound and began to drift towards it. The more he tried to move closer, the wider the distance between him and the tree grew.

Daisies dotted the landscape, breaking up a sea of green rolling meadows. The air smelled like ocean air, but there was no ocean in sight. Matthew felt no wind on his face nor temperature on his skin. There was light with no sun, and sky with no clouds. A manufactured paradox was all that existed.

Struggling to gain ground, he forced his bare feet to hit the grass. As he stood there looking at the tree in the distance, the grass turned from a lush green to a dead brown. It then shriveled, turning grey, disintegrating around his feet like ash. Daises burst into ash like a puff of powder drifting towards the ground. As the ash turned to sand, Matthew felt his feet begin to sink. Trying not to be sucked down into the sand, Matthew walked at first, but then began to run. To keep from sinking.

Sweat poured from his body as he tried to reach the tree, reach Id. He could not see him, but he felt his presence was near.

Suddenly, a buzzard of immense size cawed in the distance. Matthew saw it descend, landing in the tree's branches. Matthew, undaunted by the bird, continued to run for the only living thing left in the world he now found himself in.

A crack of lightning struck the tree, splitting it in two. The upper half turned one side dead, and the other side was left unharmed. The leaves on the dying side transformed from green to ash, floating away. The bird had leaped from its branches, cawing. Flying high into the air, Matthew continued to run towards the tree, finally able to gain ground on it. The bird circled, now joined by five more.

Matthew was less than fifty yards from the tree when one of the buzzards dove at him, cawing. Ducking out of the way, he kept moving. A second bird dove at him, nicking his bare sunburnt shoulder with its talons as he dodged it. In a swarm, all six birds dove surrounding him, cawing louder and louder, scratching at his arms, and pecking. The noise kept growing louder until his body heaved in a massive jerk, awakening him in a cold sweat.

The noise did not go away. Lying in bed, breathing heavy, Matthew heard a weird cawing noise inside the room, startling him. He looked over for Mare, and she was gone. Matthew leapt from the bed and ran towards a light shining from the bathroom. It sounded like someone was dry heaving inside. As Matthew entered, he saw that Mare was bent over the toilet, vomiting.

"Are you Ok, Mare?"

Wiping her mouth with a wet cloth, she replied, "Yes, I think I've caught something."

Matthew went over and placed his hand on her head.

"You're not running a fever."

"Well, I feel like crap, and I am nauseated."

Doing his best to act concerned, his mind had already gone into diagnosis mode, void of feeling. He asked Mare several questions, trying to diagnose her symptoms. Mare replied combatively and was uncooperative.

"I will go see a doctor if it persists."

"I am just trying to diagnose what is wrong with you, Mare."

"I know, but you're not really a doctor… doctor."

Matthew was hurt by the comment, letting her know it was the illness talking.

Why is it that your girlfriend will always seek the advice of someone else first before taking their partner's? A relationship axiom he did not understand, Matthew did his best to help her feel comfortable.

Managing to help her into a robe, they went into the living room and sat. Matthew heated some water in the microwave to make her favorite tea. Sitting there, rough-looking and pasty, she sipped it, trying to recover her dignity.

"How are you feeling now, Mare?"

"Much better. It was probably just sinus drainage or something."

"How long has this been going on?"

"Not long, just a few times the last few morning's but mostly it is nausea. This is the first time I have actually gotten sick from it. Usually, after I blow my nose, it subsides."

"Maybe you are having severe allergies?"

"That's probably all it is."

Matthew finished making his coffee. He stood in the kitchen, drinking it, looking at Mare. Her color had returned, and she was starting to resemble her young self again.

"Mare, I need to talk to you?"

Looking back at him with concern, she did not reply.

Matthew took another sip of coffee and set it down. "I was not planning on using Adam and Eve on our research patients, but I feel it is too risky. So, I was planning instead to test Adam on me."

Sipping tea, she spilled it down the front of her robe, burning her lips and tongue before spitting it out. Taking her robe sleeve, she wiped her mouth off quickly. "You will do no such thing! We will get an ape or something first!"

"Like Dr. Dimment." Matthew made an untimely joke. Something had never been done before; it just felt right to say it. Personally amused by it, Mare didn't laugh.

"Why would you want to subject yourself to your own experiments, Matthew?"

"All of the great ones do it."

"So this is a male Ego thing, then."

"No, they do it to make sure it works, to make sure they won't harm anyone. Do you think Louis Pasteur let his kids drink the first batch of milk he pasteurized? No… he did… and probably vomited all over the place a few hours later."

"Well, I don't want you to!"

Matthew walked around the counter from the kitchen into the living room, where Mare was sitting. "It's the only way, Mare."

Unable to negotiate on an intellectual level, Matthew watched as she started to cry. Knowing it was a woman's shortcut to manipulation, he also knew she deeply cared for him. "What if something goes wrong, and you become a vegetable. What if you are disfigured…paralyzed, or God forbid, die?"

Sitting down in the living room, Matthew stared out the window, thinking. *Of all people, I thought she would understand me the most. Instead, she is my worst enemy when I need support most.*

Mare went to him, sitting on her knees on the floor in front of him. She put her head in his lap, reached up around his waist, and hugged him tightly.

"Remember when you first saw me, Matthew?"

He nodded his head slightly up and down. Mare peered up at him with teary, swollen eyes.

"I was asleep to you. I could not talk and could barely communicate. Inside… inside I was alive. I could hear every word spoken. I could hear what people said about me. Inside… I would cry. I could not defend myself or strike back. I was in prison."

Without sobbing, tears fell from the corners of her eyes as Matthew looked down on her with concern.

"Some of the doctors did things to me, horrible things. I had to lie there and suffer every needle, drug, electroshock, or other even more sinister treatment they tried. I heard every word, though, and felt the pain of their treatments."

"I am so sorry, Mare."

"When Dr. Gottfried and Meacham found me, my life began to change for the better. Then you came along. During those first couple of years, even though I still could not speak, I was in love with you."

Mare turned her head away and removed her hands from his waist. "Then… then you went away. Dr. Gottfried moved us to New York, and shortly after we arrived, he became more malevolent when Dr. Meacham was away. The baby he took from me was not the worst thing I can imagine right now that would hurt me. It's you, Matthew… you."

"Mare… I…" Matthew could not find a reply.

"When we made love, something inside of me changed, and I know it did in you also. You told me that something deep inside you changed and came alive. That your mind… your emotions grew by leaps. Matthew, I know I am good for you, and you are good for me. Please for me… for us… Don't do it? I don't want to be alone again."

Matthew looked down at Mare, her head returned to his lap, softly sobbing again. He stroked her hair to try and comfort her. Knowing she was right, he thought about her words carefully, considering them. She had had a strong positive influence on his life. He wasn't bouncing around from city to city. He had applied his talents to a cause and made a genuine connection with his mother for the first time because of it. With their Rosetta Project, they had changed lives. Matthew did not want to do anything that would hurt her.

Mathew left Mare asleep in the room, heading to the laboratory with full intentions of placing Eve in the bank safety deposit box with Eve. Sliding in and out of the laboratory without being seen by Lawrence was the key, and Matthew, learning to move with stealth, was able to do so without much notice. Not being noticed for much of his life by the outside world seemed to be of no help either. Moving in and out of the high-security complex, Matthew felt as if every eye was on him.

Matthew returned to the cab and headed to the bank. Checking into the vault with little opposition, Matthew waited until the attendant left the secure room with his box. Matthew opened the box, and it was empty. After passing the brief moment of panic, he tilted the box slightly, and his notebook, along with Adam, slid to the front of the box. Matthew had purchased a black leather cigar case a few days earlier at a gas station. Taking Adam and Eve, he placed the containers inside, checking the readout on the side to ensure the temperature and cell counts were still functioning properly. He placed them back into the box and had the attendant relock it. Matthew watched until the box was secure and then left the bank.

Being more aware of his surroundings, he looked around the area to ensure there were no unusual cars parked or following them home. Once in the cab, he told the driver to head home. Looking out the back window and the side mirrors to make sure no one was following him, the cab driver stared at him like he was crazy.

Matthew's cell rang, startling both him and the driver. It was security at his building, something to do with Mare. She had collapsed in the hallway while retrieving the mail and was rushed to the hospital. Matthew quickly redirected the driver to the hospital.

Fearing the worst, Matthew was sure she needed stem treatment, but he had no idea how to treat her now that Mare had shot down any plans of using Adam and Eve. Her last treatment from Dr. Dimment was several months ago. Having been able to go longer periods of time between treatments was a sign she had been improving, and her brain had been able to repair damage. The other drug that Dr. Dimment had been administering to her was a mystery. Most likely a synthetic form of Dopamine, Matthew had never found out for sure what it was, but he had his suspicions. Assuming she would not need another treatment for several months, he doubted himself now.

Was he doing right by Mare? Could he treat her as well as Dr. Dimment had? Or had he just written her a one-way ticket to an internal prison of the mind? Not knowing what to do, Matthew considered finding a test surrogate to prove the method was safe. Was it right to use Eve on an unknowing stranger to save Mare? Was he now being selfish?

Arriving at the hospital, he raced through the emergency room. Finding the admitting desk, the nurse informed him that she was in station 4-D. She was very busy and would not provide any other information. Frustrated and anxious, Matthew walked briskly passing the rows, A… B… C… then finally D. Counting the slots as he went, he flung open the curtain.

Inside, he had surprised a nurse and Mare in the bed. The nurse turned, smiling oddly. Mare smiled in the same manner. It was as if the females of the species were sharing some sort of bond he was unaware of. Matthew had often wondered about nonverbal communications taking place through scents and chemical releases. Trees and plants are thought to communicate in that manner. He had wanted to study if humans did as well. Endorphins and pheromones were thought to be released by humans to attract one another, but an epiphany on the topic could wait for another day. Now was not the time; Matthew needed to concentrate on Mare. He had been relieved to see that she was not in a compromised state.

Sitting upright, Mare sipped some juice from a small box. The nurse spoke to Mare, ignoring Matthew for the time being. "Is this the lucky guy?" The young woman chuckled oddly as she left the room and closed the curtain. Matthew was surprised when the young lady winked at him as she closed the curtain behind her.

Matthew turned his attentions to Mare, shucking her odd behavior off, not realizing the hidden communications. "Mare, what's wrong? Are you OK?"

Smiling at Matthew, he noticed a glow about her face. He had not seen it before. Her face had been either upset or pasty-looking the last few days, but now it looked different. It was unsettling for some unknown reason.

"I am fine, I just fainted. Matthew, you may want to sit down?"

No sooner than those words had left her lips, than Matthew's mind went into a trance. Traveling through his mind like a tunnel, the room faded away from him. Suddenly, every second of every moment with Mare replayed in fast forward in his mind. From their first time making love to her being sick in the bathroom several mornings, ending in the image of an egg and sperm uniting. The forward progression of a human developing from mitosis to a baby crying rang out loud and clear in his mind, all too real.

Seating himself without realizing it, a baby cried over and over in his mind. The noise grew louder and louder. Mare broke through in waves, barely making contact with Matthew's ears over the crying, until it registered with an echoing sound.

"Matthew… I'm pregnant… Isn't that wonderful?"

The words came out in slow motion and much deeper than Mare's own voice in his mind, continuing to resonate. "I'm pregnant… pregnant… pregnant. Isn't that wonderful… wonderful… wonderful."

"Are you OK? You kinda look pale?" Still processing it in his mind, he could barely hear her. Mare reached over, ruffling Matthew's hair. The baby crying finally registered with Matthew. It was coming from the room beside them.

"You're going to be a father, Matthew."

In a sudden burst, Matthew leapt from his trance back into reality. Everything sped up, then came to a screeching halt in his mind. Feeling woozy and almost nauseated himself Matthew finally acknowledged her. "That's wonderful, Mare. Isn't it?"

"Yes, Matthew, that is wonderful. After Dr. Dimment... I... I wasn't sure if I could get pregnant again. Looks like your boys can swim." Mare laughed.

Matthew could only concentrate on one thing. A father... he was going to be a father. He was going to be a dad. He was going to have to read a lot of books on parenting now.

The nurse came back in, handing Mare some enormous bottles. "These are prenatal vitamins. You need to take these and drink plenty of orange juice. No alcohol... no cigarettes... no heavy lifting... no undue stress..."

"She doesn't smoke," Matthew announced, interrupting her speech.

The nurse looked sternly back at him, continuing until she was finished. Most likely noticing that Mare did not have a ring on her hand, she threw an obvious hint at Matthew. "You know, this is the tie that binds a relationship together." Smiling, she winked at Mare, then, wincing her eyes at him, she left the room, drawing the curtain to.

Why do women herd together like that? They are like packs of wolves, sometimes smelling fresh meat, they go in for the kill.

Matthew's new experimentation with Adam was now entirely out of the realm of possibilities. He had more than just Mare and himself to consider; he would have to be more careful now.

Enjoying a nice, quiet evening at home with Mare, Matthew was already busy reading everything he could on parenting. His touchpad was too slow to keep up with the speed at which Matthew read and comprehended the text. Monotonous, each article was just like the last.

Finding more value, he concentrated on nonprofessional webpages written by real mothers. They seemed to be the most helpful, using real-life experiences to explain occupational and social dilemmas in a common-sense format.

Matthew's peaceful solace was by a song playing out of nowhere. Hearing a familiar buzzing, Matthew also saw Mare's cell phone ringing in the kitchen. Noticing she was in the bedroom room Matthew answered. As he picked it up, he noticed a headshot of Sophie, her friend from work.

"Hello… No, she's in the next room... Ok… allow me to get her for you."

"Matthew, who was that on the phone?"

Matthew covered the phone to muffle his voice. "It's Sophie."

Walking into the room to meet him halfway, Mare took the phone and walked off. She was only on it for a second while trying to walk around the house and pick up at the same time. Matthew had been doing most of the cleaning now that Mare was with child, especially if it involved cleaning products. Stubborn, she insisted on doing everything herself.

"I have to go to the Education Center."

Matthew shook his head no.

"It's just for an hour. We have VIP's coming from Germany, and Sophie needs some help."

"Let me go with you."

"No… I need you to run to the Market, finish picking up, and dust. The laundry needs to go to the cleaners, also." For a moment, Matthew thought she sounded more like his mother than a girlfriend.

248

Tanking time to primp and put on makeup, she finally made it out the door after about half an hour. Matthew had already done everything but the market shopping. Matthew stood in a trance, visualizing Mare walking down the hall and getting on the elevator. His mind was becoming more dynamic every day. Like an internal time clock, he could visualize Mare's gate and stride as she walked in his mind. To test how accurate he was becoming with this newfound tool, he went over to the window, expecting to see her walk out of the building at the exact instant he expected. Accurate to the second, he watched her climb into her car and drive out of sight.

Matthew had begun shopping organically as soon as they found out Mare was pregnant. At the Market, he perused all of the endless selections, sticking to the shopping list Mare provided him. Even though money was not an issue, Matthew could not believe a box of organic cereal cost seven dollars. Free-range, organic milk was nearly $8. Eating healthy would be expensive, but worth it to Mare and the baby.

Matthew wondered why so many lower-income people were unhealthy and overweight. It costs them too much to eat a healthy organic diet.

Waking him out of his thoughts, he felt a buzz in his pocket. Matthew was torn, as he couldn't reach it in time because he was checking out. There was a sign hanging near the register asking people not to text or use their phones in the checkout line.

Matthew, a slave to habit and order, obeyed signs religiously. Finishing up, he paid while a young boy took his groceries and put them in a compact hybrid SUV that Mare had purchased to encourage Matthew to drive instead of taking cabs everywhere. Before starting the car, he checked his phone. It was Mare who had called.

Matthew returned her call, noticing that she had not answered on the first ring, as she normally did. Matthew allowed it to continue to ring until it went to voicemail. Matthew paused, considering whether this was cause for alarm or not.

Knowing Dr. Dimment was out of the country, he decided to drop off the laundry and return to the apartment. Matthew unloaded the groceries, then put away the laundry he had picked up to keep his mind occupied. It wasn't working. The fact that she had not answered the phone as she had promised began to alarm him.

Matthew decided to call Sophie's phone after Mare did not answer the second attempt. *She probably just set her phone down where she couldn't hear it.*

Sophie's phone rang a couple of times, and a man answered. "Hello, Sophie's phone." "This is Matthew Le'Dain, Mare's…I mean Marilyn's husband… I mean boyfriend. Marilyn is Sophie's supervisor at the Education Center. Anyway, is Sophie there?"

The man chuckled sarcastically, Matthew thought, saying, "This is Steve, Sophie's Husband, you know Marilyn's employee's spouse. No…she is taking a bath right now and can't come to the phone."

"I am sorry to bother you, but I was trying to call Mare, and she did not answer her phone. I thought maybe she was with her."

"How is that Sophie's problem…"

"Who's on the phone, Steve?" a woman's voice in the background said.

"It's Matthew Le'Dain, Mare's husband… no boyfriend… your boss's other half or something."

"Give me the phone and go take care of the kids!"

Kids ran by screaming near the man's phone. After several moments of rustling and wrangling on the other end of the line, like someone whisper-fighting, she answered.

"Matthew…sorry about that. Steve can be a real jerk when he wants to be. He's mad at me because I am going to work on a Sunday. Mare called, but she hung up in mid-sentence. She told me not to come in, but I decided to go on in anyway."

"I assumed you called from work earlier?"

"No… am I supposed to be?"

"Mare said you called and asked her to come in."

"No, I never called her. She called me."

"Sophie, do me a favor and call Dr. Lawrence Meacham. Have him meet me at the Education Center. You stay home, do not go there."

"Matthew, what's wrong? You're starting to worry me. Is Mare in danger? You don't think that Creepy stalker guy is after her, do you?"

"I'm not sure, but something is not right. Please call Meacham as soon as I hang up."

Matthew raced over to the Education Center. It was as close to speeding as he had ever come. His mind raced as well, thinking of scenarios and a proper countermeasure to combat it. Using the voice command feature in the car, Matthew tried to call once again, and this time her phone went directly to voicemail. Knowing she must have used her phone at some point since the first call, he tried to calm his anxiety.

Pulling into the parking lot at the center, he noticed two vehicles, Mares and Dr. Meacham's. Thinking Sophie had reached him, he was much relieved.

Matthew scanned his card, but the door remained locked. Scanning it a second time, the door unlocked. Breathing heavily from the stress, his senses were all trying to work at once, canceling each other out.

Moving directly to Mare's office, Matthew found her comfortably sitting at her desk, with Meacham sitting in a guest chair.

"Matthew, what are you doing here?"

"I couldn't get a hold of you, and your phone started going to voicemail."

"I must have left it in the learning room."

"She's fine, Matthew. I am with her. You shouldn't let your pregnant girlfriend go off by herself, you know."

"I know it won't happen again."

Mare looked flattered and annoyed at the same time by all the attention Matthew was giving her.

Matthew walked around her desk and leaned down to whisper to her.

"Mare. Sophie said she didn't call you."

The smile she had left her face, and she acted concerned.

"Either that or she is a good liar. What's going on?"

"Matthew, I am not sure what you're talking about. Let's talk about this in private. We're being rude to Dr. Meachum." Mare looked at Matthew like a scolding mother. He knew the look well and stood up, turning to face Dr. Meachum.

"Well...Matthew," Lawrence interjected.

"Maybe it was Gottfried's people. He also has access to gifted people. Some of them, I've heard, can mimic anyone's voice identically just by hearing it once. They most likely called Sophie, heard her voice, and then called Mare. Gottfried would be the only one besides you two who has all those phone numbers."

"And you, Doctor?"

"Yes, and me, Matthew. Are you implying…"

"No… Sir… I was just pointing out the obvious. I apologize; I am just a little nervous with his whereabouts still unknown."

"You have a right to be… he is a very dangerous man. A Russian gentleman, a few weeks back, was found dead in the same hotel where Gottfried had met with him."

Mare's face was astonished. Mathew did not want her to be upset, especially by this news. What else did Dr. Meachum know that he was not sharing with them?

"Did they find out what his business was with him?"

"They think the man had a massive stroke. My sources told me it was like nothing they had ever seen. There was nothing in the toxicology report other than a low amount of alcohol. All of his blood vessels had just exploded inside his head. There was also a cut on his hand, but the report implied it must have been done during the stroke."

Matthew and Mare looked at each other, amazed but concerned. It sounded like it was straight out of a spy novel.

"Nothing was taken from his room, and there was no evidence of forced entry either. He was actually a businessman. He worked for a huge medical and pharmaceutical company in Europe. The hotel is old, so the only security cameras are on the exterior of the building."

Matthew immediately knew Dr. Dimment must have been working with stems somehow. He must have been testing them on Mare without her knowledge. Rage welled up inside him, and the more he thought about the man whom he thought had once saved Mare, the more he detested him. He was nothing more to Matthew now but an inhumane thug for profit.

Matthew, angered, belted out, "What about Dimment? Where is he?"

"The authorities raided his house the next day but found nothing. Someone had been there recently. They set up a stakeout, but he never returned. They think he must have seen the news about the Russians' death."

Matthew and Mare exchanged angry looks as they listened.

"Gottfried is well-connected in Europe. He has many well-to-do friends. If I had to guess, he is in a country where extradition is unlikely. He is probably in Norway. Some of his old college chums practice medicine and teach at the University of Oslo."

Two security guards walked in, interrupting the conversation. "Ma'am, we have checked the entire building. There is no one here. We now have six additional guards patrolling. We will stay until you leave, then lock the place down tight."

The guard turned to face Dr. Meachum. "I suggest we up the security level for a few days?" Lawrence nodded in agreement, and the guards left.

"Well, Matthew, this is more than enough excitement for a pregnant woman in a day. Why don't you take her home yourself? I will have security drop her car off later."

"Thank you, Dr. Meachum, you're a good friend."

Lawrence smiled and winked just like always.

Mare interrupted, saying, "I am ready to go home, boys. My stomach says Chinese food sounds really good right now. Dr. Meacham, would you like to join us?"

"No...I have other plans." Meacham walked over to shake Matthews' hand. He stared intently at Matthew for several seconds. His eyes looked different, and for a moment, he thought he saw clouds behind his pupils.

Matthew broke his gaze as soon as Dr. Meachum spoke.

"You need to take better care of this little lady now. She is eating for two. Who knows, you may have a brainchild even smarter than the two of you combined. Wouldn't that be magnificent? Remember, children are the tie that binds?"

Matthew looked back at Mare, saying, "Yes, I have heard that somewhere before."

Mare called for curbside and, only stopping briefly, he returned her home to the security of the complex. Sitting in bed, they ate out of the boxes with forks.

Something gnawed at Matthew, but he had grown used to his new feelings of instinct and impulse. They had served him well so far, and he was not sure how he had lived without them for so long. "Mare."

"Yes, Matthew."

"Was Meacham there when you got to the Education Center?"

"No, why?"

"When did he arrive?"

"He got there just a few minutes after I did, I guess."

"When was that?"

"That was around 12:30 or so."

Matthew's mind went into data recovery mode for a brief moment. He flashed back to his phone. Recalling the exact times when he called Sophie. The phone flashed at 12:49.

"Are you sure that's what time it was? What's wrong, Matthew? You're acting weird." "It's probably nothing. Can I see your phone?"

She handed her phone to Matthew. He studied the call log. All the numbers were right. Sophie's number was there, he was there several times, but not Meacham's.

"Mare, who is 782-3000?"

Grabbing the phone, she looked at it. "Am I under investigation now? That is security. I called them on the way there just to be sure Sophie and I were going to be safe there alone."

"Are you sure it was 12:30?"

"Not exactly, but it was close. Why?"

"I had Sophie call Meacham, but I did not get off the phone with her until 12:49. It would have been ten till by the time she called him. He would have had to have been close by."

"He said he saw my car in the lot, so he decided to check on me. What's wrong with you? You're acting very paranoid. Meacham has always been our friend."

"You're right, I am just being silly. No more separate ways. We need to stick together."

Over the next few weeks, Matthew and Mare worked from home, only leaving to buy food. Matthew worked to find a surrogate test subject but had no luck. He joked with himself, thinking the only way to get one was to clone himself. Self-testing is the only other option off the table.

Meacham had traveled heavily promoting a new book he had authored with Dr. Dimment on gene therapy. It discussed techniques similar to those Matthew had used to harvest cells, but their theory involved the extraction of genetically manufactured stems, stimulating their reproduction, and re-injecting them into the problem areas. He had no test data, so it was largely based on conjecture and theory.

The first four months passed quickly with no signs of Dr. Meachum. Mare's next treatment was approaching, and Matthew grew increasingly concerned, having no solution.

25 *OSLO*

Leaving Mare alone after everything that had happened was not an option. Matthew needed someone he could trust completely, someone who could protect her and the baby. His usual go-to people were all out of the question. Sophie, Mare's assistant, had a family of her own. Dr. Meachum's constant travel schedule made him too unreliable, and besides, Matthew had a mounting unease about him. He couldn't pinpoint the cause, but his instincts were screaming at him to keep his distance. Panthea, Matthew's mother, was out of the question as well, living several states away and not knowing about the pregnancy.

There was only one person he knew he could rely on: Mrs. Anna Werner, the kind-eyed, vanilla-scented widow from across the hall. He had befriended her when he first moved in, and she and Mare had bonded a few months prior. Matthew didn't know her connection to the government, but he assumed her late husband had worked for them, which was why she was permitted to stay in the complex. Matthew decided not to dwell on it. There was no time to worry about a harmless elderly woman, and she was more than eager to feel wanted again.

Mrs. Werner was the perfect retired American poster child. She teetered around, talking to herself and smelling baby powder. She was the grandmother everyone dreamed of, full of good advice delivered with a gentle tongue. Her parables, born from both the Bible and a life of experience, made you feel warm and welcome even when things were completely off kilter. Matthew and Mare had both lost their grandparents, so it was a perfect situation for all of them: a surrogate grandmother for the young couple and grandkids for the elderly woman across the hall.

Mrs. Werner often regaled them with stories of Europe during the war. She had become a nurse after moving to the United States, having escaped Berlin with her family after her father testified at the Nuremberg Trials. He was considered an American hero, but an enemy in Germany. Mrs. Werner's father reluctantly testified, having once believed in Hitler's misguided dreams, but chose to save his family. Matthew had never heard her maiden name, Kaiser, ring a bell, but he took no pause for thought. Most trivial facts were cast aside as unconnected bits of information in his complex memory system, dumped into unmanaged areas of his mind like a hoarder's treasure pile, slowing his thought process.

Matthew recalled Mrs. Werner's apartment décor as he pondered if he was doing the right thing. It was a time capsule of an earlier age, featuring a floor-model TV from the 1980s, hand-crocheted doilies, ornate lamps, and a China hutch filled with German antique dishware and beer steins. Her real hobby, he recounted, appeared to be bell collecting. She had numerous bells made from brass, China, silver, and even gold scattered throughout her living space.

She was also a passionate cook. Not having anyone to cook for in a while, she had prepared several German dishes for Matthew and Mare, sharing her love for a country she hadn't seen in decades but still remembered with the imagination of a child. Mrs. Werner had jumped at the opportunity to play mother on a short-term basis while Matthew took a long trip. Having Mare taken care of put his mind at ease, allowing him to focus on the things that mattered.

Matthew arranged a meeting with Dr. Meachum to discuss his work. He had still not divulged his creation of Adam and Eve and was not planning on sharing that part yet. Still untested, Matthew did not want to risk his reputation on an unproven theory. He felt obligated to share his feelings about Dimment with Dr. Meachum. It seemed very odd that the government could find Bin Laden but not Dimment.

"Lawrence, I've been investigating Dimment."

"Whatever for?"

"I was thinking I may be able to apply my skills to locate Dr. Dimment."

"I wouldn't worry about him anymore, Matthew. He is never coming back here."

"How do you know? He has many friends, you said. He could still try and harm Mare."

"That's just silly. Why would he do that?"

"I am worried about our baby. He had always wanted a super savant, and there is a strong possibility that our child could be one."

"He prizes his freedom and research over anything else. He would not jeopardize either to come back to the states."

"Dr. Meachum… I mean, Lawrence… I need to know how he was treating Mare's medical condition. Something was not right with his treatment, and I have not been able to figure it out. Mare said he had implanted an electro-stimulator, but she thought he had also been doing stem cell therapy."

Lawrence sat back, rubbing his chin with his left hand as if he were surprised by this news.

"I see. I wasn't aware of this. The Feds searched his office, home, and files here, but did not find anything of value, Matthew. I'm sorry, I don't have access to any personal notes he may have had. He kept handwritten notes, but he most likely destroyed any evidence of her treatments."

Matthew looked away, thinking, and stood up, walking around the room like a detective.

"What doesn't make sense is that she is overdue for a treatment and is doing just fine. In fact, she seems to be getting sharper mentally each day, not regressing as you would expect."

"Whatever could Gottfried help you with that your brilliant mind cannot figure out on your own? I think it is a bad idea to pursue this anymore. He is a very dangerous man."

"I know, but my instincts are telling me I can find out more about his past in Berlin. The records here are very sketchy, and most of what is available there is still in print. They do not have very many digital records, especially on anything prior to 1985."

"Where will you start... what do you expect to find and who will look after Mare?" Lawrence asked the questions coming in rapid succession.

"I will start in Berlin. He has a sister there, and she is still alive."

Lawrence's eyes widened. "How did you know about her?" he demanded, taking a step toward Matthew.

"When I was doing some background on Gottfried, I ran across his time as an intern. I know he was trying to help her, but something went terribly wrong. I thought she was deceased, but you confirmed she was still alive."

Lawrence stood at the side of the conference table, within arm's reach of Matthew. "Matthew, you would be well served to stay here, with Mare and look after her. That's your number one priority. Secondly, you need to finish your research here. You can find a cure for her right here… not gallivanting all over Europe. What if something happens to you? Who will look after Mare then… and your son?"

Lawrence's logic was sound, but something even greater pulled at Matthew from deep inside. Like a sailor drawn to the sea, Matthew had his own storms to weather now.

"How did you know we were having a son? We never told anyone that!"

"I just guessed, but I know now," Lawrence chuckled. "Matthew… I am not your father, but I have always tried to give you good advice. Your place is here. Your life is here, and your future is here." He grabbed Matthew's wrist gently, squeezing it as he leaned in.

Matthew was drawn to his eyes. He had been drawn to them ever since he met Dr. Meachum. There had always been something beautiful but dangerous about them, deep blue like an ocean sky. Matthew thought he had seen something in them on more than one occasion. Storm clouds rushed by like an impending storm behind his iris. This could have been discounted as a reflection except they were several stories below ground. It gave him an unsettling feeling knowing this. He had experienced it several times over the years, but after the discovery of Id, it went from a feeling to seeing as well. Beckoning him to stare, they called to him to gaze in a trance, as if he were one of Dracula's concubines. Confusing his senses, Matthew felt Id's presence when Meachum was around, something he had not realized until now.

"I can only ask that you take my advice. If you open Pandora's Box, you can't put her back inside." Meachum smiled like a Cheshire cat, knowing the answers but refusing to share.

Matthew pulled his arm away, walking to the door of the conference room. "Let me ask you something, Dr. Meacham. If you had someone you cared for and they were ill, wouldn't you do anything in the world to make them better?"

Dr. Meachum looked away, then back at Matthew, sighing, "I suppose so."

Matthew looked back at Dr. Meachum with a determined look. "Me too."

After leaving the laboratory, Matthew drove to the bank to check on Adam and Eve. He had been checking on them at least a couple of times a week since their creation, systematically running tests to make sure they were both reproducing accurately. He was concerned about the rate of phosphorus breakdown and the heightened radiation levels, needing to stay below 10 millirems to be confident that he was not destroying the stems faster than they could reproduce.

Inside the vault, where there were no cameras, a lone guard stood watch. Just as Matthew was about to place the pair back inside the safety deposit box, something came over him, as if Id were speaking to him in his mind. *Take it with you, for safekeeping.* The urge to take the cigar case with Adam and Eve was strong, and Matthew followed his will without thinking. Not knowing if the strange feeling was his own instinct, he listened just the same.

Matthew carefully removed Adam and Eve from the cigar case. Opening each container, he removed both seeds with a syringe, placing them in what appeared to be refill cartridges for a ballpoint pen. Adam is in the top half; Eve is in the bottom. The pen worked, so if anyone ever tried to write with it, they would not know that inside the temperature-controlled casing were the secrets to solving the infirmities of the mind. He placed the pen in his pocket, then threw the cigar case back into the safety deposit box with his notes.

The little voice inside Matthew's head had grown a little stronger every day since he had injected himself with the growth hormone to stimulate receptor growth. Even though he had discontinued its use after ending the failed test group, he still tracked his receptor mapping to ensure there were no degenerative effects. His scans were far more reaching than an average person to begin with, but he still dreamed of a day when his entire mind would be accessible. He thought about what Adam and Eve could bring all the way home as he contemplated how he was going to break the news to Mare that he was going to find Dr. Dimment on his own.

Id was calling him, guiding him, directing him to seek out Dimment. There was no specific reason or question to answer, only that he needed to find him. The fear of Dimment had subsided some time ago. Matthew knew if he could only get back into his mind, he might be able to question Id, but for now, with Mare's health in question, her mood swings, and lack of desire, Matthew would have to seek out other methods to reach him. He had considered deep meditation but had no time for it currently. Pulling into the complex, Matthew parked, staring up at the front window of their home. He saw Mrs. Werner pass by, breaking his trance. Matthew gathered his thoughts and his courage and went inside.

With a tearful initial reception, Matthew negotiated with Mare. "Mare, this is no longer about just you and me. Complications with your health can also affect the baby. You can't afford to have surgery or worse, go into a coma. You could... You could lose the baby."

"Matthew, don't you think I have thought about that a thousand times. I can't think of anything worse than losing you right now."

Matthew walked over and reached out to hold Mare's hands. "We are together and will always be. I promise everything will be fine. Something is telling me Dr. Dimment has the answers I need... that we need."

"I can see this is not just an ego thing with you, Matthew, and I can't deny the fact that my health affects the baby's health. I just don't want to lose you. Please promise you will be careful?"

Matthew never replied out loud. He nodded his head, hugging her tightly. Matthew stared out the front window again at the clouds moving by in the distance. The sky was darkening as a storm approached from the West.

After providing Mrs. Werner with detailed instructions, Matthew departed for Berlin. It had been some time since he flew in a plane. Long enough to forget how much he disliked it. The first class was a nice touch; Meachum spared no expense in assisting Matthew, even expediting a passport through his State Department connections.

Of all the people in the world, Matthew ran into Jim Brewer on the hop from Washington, D.C. to New York. Jim, an energetic guy, talked nonstop. Matthew liked him, but forty-five minutes was all he could handle at a time. "You still touring the circuit, man?"

"No... I am a research scientist at D&M Research."

"Wow, that's cool. Do you do human testing... use apes or something?"

"No... we do have voluntary research trials, but no animal testing."

"You don't want PETA up your ass, I dig it, man." Jim continued, "You ever see that chick that paints herself like panthers and cheetahs. I hear she chases the circus around protesting. Totally nude except for body paint. She looks pretty hot if you ask me."

"I can't say I have ever heard of her."

"So... what's new with you? Married... kids?" Jim asked in a sarcastic tone, not really expecting an answer. The surprise on his face said it all when Matthew replied.

"I have a girlfriend, and she is almost five months pregnant."

"Geez, man. I... I never pictured you that way. In fact, you seem different, a lot different. You've been working out or something."

"I have been practicing martial arts. I have a second-degree black belt."

"Wow... that's awesome, man."

"I do a lot of twelve-ounce curls."

Matthew was puzzled by the remark, so he smiled politely. Relieved when the plane landed, Matthew finally relaxed, having felt as anxious as Jim appeared to be.

"Good luck, Mr. Brewer."

"Hey, you too, man. Don't be too stiff with the kid. Be loose and carefree. Kids are a trip; you can learn a lot from them."

Matthew endured a more peaceful flight across the pond, taking time to plan out a strategy in his head. The first place he wanted to go was to the Psychiatric Hospital, where Gottfried's sister, Katja Dimment, was living. But first, he had to check into a hotel. Meachum had booked a room for Matthew at the Excelsior Hotel in Berlin. This was the same hotel where the Russian had been found dead. Matthew was unaware that Dimment's acquaintance had died there. Still naive in many aspects, his intellect always seemed to find a way to outwit any circumstance.

Matthew had learned to speak Dutch many years before. Having many similarities to the German dialect, he had reviewed common terminology during the flight. Still rusty, he felt confident he would be able to communicate clearly enough to get by. Not a fan of planes, Matthew had flown into Paris first, then hopped a train from Paris to Berlin. The extra time had afforded him an opportunity to practice his linguistic skills.

Taking care of his husbandries, Matthew called Mare to let her know he had arrived and was doing well. Finding Mrs. Werner was treating her very well, as expected, Matthew was more convinced he had done the right thing. Security escorts were common at the complex where they lived, as they were home to many dignitaries. Mare had no trouble shopping safely without Matthew around to protect her. When it came to safety, Matthew's thoughts were to throw common sense out of the window. Paying for peace of mind was well worth it.

Making sure he was not being followed, Matthew operated as if he were undercover. Lawrence had provided a telephone number to call in case of an emergency. Feeling like James Bond, Matthew had rented a BMW to drive from the train station. Having no contacts in a strange land, Matthew trusted no one. Strong advice from Dr. Meachum, Matthew followed it religiously.

Matthew drove from the train station to the Excelsior, the sounds of profanity and honking horns filling the streets of Berlin. The rental agency had preset his navigation device, making the female voice the only pleasant one on his journey. Matthew was a very careful driver, obeying all traffic signs and speed limits. In a city full of cameras, the locals did not seem to care about "Big Brother" at all. Driving like every day was Sunday, Matthew managed to arrive safely. His uncanny ability to block out distractions made the locals even more agitated. Even then, Matthew was privileged to witness several instances of universal sign language that he found to be most undeserving.

Dropping the car with the valet, Matthew finally rested his head in a room very similar to the one the Russian had frequented. He tried to sleep, finding it difficult without Mare. He lay in bed with the television on, drifting between sleep and awareness, but his mind was overloaded. He longed for a big dose of Id's illogical logic, but the noise in his head was too great.

He reached over to the empty area where Mare usually rested. He missed her stroking his hair, her snuggles, and the way she rubbed his back at the end of the day. But he realized he missed something more than knowledge, accomplishment, or discovery. It wasn't the physical touch, but the certainty that it would always be there. It wasn't the slow, rocking motion of making love, but the internal connection it provided —the feeling that their thoughts were one.

He tried desperately to reconnect with his inner psyche, finally succumbing to exhaustion. With the time change, he had forgotten to reset his alarm. He would have slept through most of the day if not for the sound of a vacuum cleaner. Matthew awoke in a panic, disoriented and lost. The room was foreign; a hazy film covered his eyes. He quickly realized he was no longer in Kansas.

Frustration overcame him. This mission had separated him from Mare, and the weight of it pressed down on him like the depths of the ocean. He felt disconnected from her and from Id, who had become nothing more than a hazy dream. He started to doubt if Id had ever been real, a logical defense against the terrifying possibility that his past experiences were just a family mental disorder, a schizophrenic episode that required the right diet and exercise to keep at bay. But he was more logical than that. He righted his mind, concentrating on the fact that the freethinking he once owned had been replaced by worry and doubt. He wished for the days when his life was simple and filled with discovery.

Wanting to prove to himself he was not going insane, Matthew recounted each meeting with Id, trying to piece together a profile. With very little to go on, he knew Id was logic, but also a renegade, with a potential for darkness. Reflecting on one of the most interesting experiences of his short life, Matthew lost track of time, causing a brief moment of panic.

He bolted out of bed, dressed, and headed for the lobby. After grabbing a coffee and a banana, he set the GPS in the Beamer for the Berlin Psychiatric Hospital. As he drove through the busy streets, he remembered Mrs. Werner's stories of the war, the air raid sirens, and the thunderous booms that shook the ground. Looking around, he saw hardly any signs that a war had ever happened.

The hospital was located in a less desirable part of town. The navigation system overlooked several one-way situations, routing him through alleys and road construction. His innate sense of direction brought him to the hospital parking facility, several floors below ground. Matthew felt strange and unnerved. The echoes of conversations in a foreign tongue reminded him he was a stranger, and the scuffing of shoes and clicks of high-heeled shoes added to his unease. The smell of diesel from the European engines burned his eyes.

Matthew made it inside, riding the elevator up with a couple who stared at him. It was as if they could smell the foreign on his body and the fear in his mind. He felt the judgment of the city's "wolves," a sense of being sized up and judged without a trial.

Arriving at the front desk, Matthew inquired about Katja Dimment, using his best German accent. Grimacing, the attendant rustled through a ledger before standing up. The nurse told him to wait, returning much later to say that no visitors were allowed. Thinking on his feet, Matthew reintroduced himself as a Doctor of Linguistics. After several minutes of convincing her, the nurse, who was familiar with his work on the Rosetta Project because it had helped her nephew, agreed to his request. Smiling, she left again, returning with one of Katja's doctors.

The man, Dr. Hans Gedlhoff, met him with a congenial nod and led him to his office. Seated in a less adversarial manner, Dr. Gedlhoff quickly inquired about his business with Mrs. Dimment. "What is your business with Katja?"

Matthew explained without revealing his life story. "I am working on a confidential project based on the original work from Dr. Gottfried Dimment." He studied the man's face, which showed neither invitation nor dismissal, leaving Matthew with little to interpret. "We believe we may be close to developing a treatment for patients like Katja. I just want to examine her to see if there's any chance of awakening her."

Dr. Gedlhoff, responding in English to show his own prowess, countered, "She has been in this condition for far too many years. I see no chance at all for a recovery. She only uses about fifteen percent of her brain, and it has been rapidly declining. You're wasting your time here."

"If there is a chance, wouldn't it be worth exploring for her sake?" Matthew pressed.

"Look, we know of your professional affiliation with Dr. Dimment. Steffen warned us you may visit."

"Steffen?" Matthew replied, surprised.

"Steffen Dimment, or Congressman Steffen Dimment. He is Katja and Gottfried's much younger brother. I see from your expression that you had no idea."

"No, I was not aware there was a brother."

"Perhaps there are more things you are not aware of with the Dimment family. I am not sure this is a place for you."

"I see… so there is no way you will let me see her?"

"Well, Steffen and Gottfried are very different people. Gottfried would not allow it in the least. However, Steffen is more liberal, as you say. With Gottfried's legal issues, Steffen has become her legal guardian."

"So, I can see her?"

"Both care for their sister dearly. I am not sure what the connection with her is, but they both visit often, or did. I have not seen either of them in a few months. I feel Steffen would not object to my allowing you some time with her. I think they both still believe there is a slim chance she could be saved. At least if I allow you to examine her, we can put his question to rest once and for all."

Dr. Gedlhoff put his head down, then looked away. "It is strange how even the smartest people in the world can have faith in what they cannot see."

"Faith, Dr. Gedlhoff, is what we need more of in this world, faith and prayer."

Dr. Gedlhoff did not reply verbally but nodded his head in acknowledgment. Standing up, he led Matthew down the hallways to Katja's room. It was depressing, void of any interesting decorations, and clinically white. The nurse had gotten her up and sat her at a small table in front of a television.

"She has movement and can eat on her own?" Matthew was surprised, fearing she was bedridden and in a vegetative state.

"The Dimment's spare no expense for her care here. It may interest you to know that we have been working with her for over a year, trying to teach her the Rosetta techniques. We have had no response from her, I am afraid."

Perhaps you haven't been asking the right questions, Matthew thought.

He took a piece of paper and a pencil from the dresser top, sketching letters in color and shape to say hello. With a box of crayons and paper in front of her, Katja never moved. Recalling Mare's advice, Matthew spoke the word "hello" as well. He held out hope, thinking she might be like Mare once was, with the ability to hear but not respond. Still no response.

Matthew continued to ask questions and talk to her. Taking a light pen, he tested her eyes, and her pupils opened and closed as any normal person would, but much slower. Thinking, Matthew wrote the name Gottfried down in the Rosetta alphabet. "Gottfried, your brother. Has he been to see you lately?" Like an animatronic robot just booting up, Katja slowly and methodically turned her head sideways with her head cocked like a bird. It was unnerving, and nothing like Matthew had ever seen before. The robotic mannerisms sent a chill up and down his body. It was like looking at an amalgamation of Mare and himself.

Picking up a red crayon, she made two nearly complete Rosetta shapes. Studying them closely, they appeared to be an N and an O. "Your brother, he loves you dearly?" Matthew tried to draw out the letters to the question, but Katja began writing at the same time. It took a few minutes, but she finished before Matthew did. The word symbols were sketchy, but she had written the symbols for yes.

"Do you love him as well, Katja?" She colored out yes one more time before turning to stare off in the distance, not focusing on any particular thing.

How could someone in the shape she was in, by a man Matthew believed to be so evil, be this complacent? It boggled his mind. It didn't make sense at all. She must not understand why she is the way she is. It is because of him, and she does not have the mental faculties to know any better.

This settled it right then and there. Matthew would have to seek out Gottfried's whereabouts. Even though Lawrence and Mare were both opposed to it, he knew the answers would lie with him. It could take months or years to get anything out of Katja.

Having thanked Dr. Gedlhoff, Matthew bought some time. Giving an immediate diagnosis would be of no benefit to him at this point. Matthew had learned by watching Dr. Meachum to build suspense and make people want to hear what you have to say by always leaving them wanting more. He let him know he would be getting back with him after he had carefully considered her case. Leaving this door open was important, as showing progress to Gedlhoff had seemed to leave a positive first impression.

On the way home, Matthew stopped to purchase a train ticket from Berlin to Denmark, then a water taxi from Denmark to Oslo on a hovercraft. These seemed to be the most direct routes available without chartering a private plane.

That evening, Matthew made his domestic calls, having briefly chatted with Mare. His calls to Dr. Meachum went unanswered. Matthew made sure to highlight only the pertinent information about Mare to Katja. Of course, she wanted to fly over immediately to work with her, but in her condition, it was out of the question.

Matthew fell asleep rather quickly that night. Exhaustion had caught up with him. He slept through the night, only recalling one dream in particular. He had remembered hearing the sound of forties music. No song in particular, but perhaps the trumpet playing of Harry James stood out the most.

Matthew recalled a dream in which he was a private detective, dressed in a suit, tie, and loafers. Hired by a man whose face he did not see, he searched for an unnamed woman, all while staying one step ahead of a stalker. The dream, which was in black and white, made no sense, but he was the only one in it who had a face. Sitting in a dark, seedy bar, the only peace he found was in the waiting. The low, melodic sound of a trumpet playing '40s music soothed him, and he felt as if he belonged to that time, that place, not the here and now. He had often felt he was from another era, another reality. He never spoke of it with anyone, not even Mare, but he felt it strongly. He felt comfortable in his own skin for a change. Just as things started to get interesting, his alarm went off.

He knew dreams were sometimes apparitions, veiled representations of reality. However, he had no time to contemplate it right now; there was still too much to be done.

Arriving in Oslo, Matthew noticed a man he had seen on the train from Berlin and the hovercraft. While it was a well-traveled euro-business route, it seemed too coincidental. As he waited in line to secure a car, the man ended up right behind him. The man attempted to engage in small talk. "Gutentag." Matthew nodded.

"Do you speak English?" the man asked.

"Yes, why do you ask?"

"Sven's the name. Dr. Meacham asked me to keep an eye on you if you decided to leave Germany."

Matthew's internal alarms blared. "How do you know Dr. Meacham?"

"We have been acquaintances for some time."

"Professionally or socially?"

"Professionally mainly."

"Are you a Doctor?"

He laughed. "Goodness, no, security. I also looked after Dr. Dimment when he was here." Matthew thought to himself that it would make sense; the man was brawny and in very good shape. He had a very discerning smile. Matthew didn't like it very much.

"Well, I won't be in your way. The number that Meacham gave you, call it if you need me." He held up a cell phone, then put it back in his front shirt pocket. Matthew nodded without replying. The man smiled, pointing forward at the long gap in the line. Matthew moved forward with his bag.

Matthew was unsure whether he should be worried or not. It was comforting to know that Dr. Meachum was still looking out for him, but it was also a little strange that he knew exactly where he was and what he was doing. It dawned on him that he was accessing the tracking on his smartphone. It was the only way he would have known. Surely, Meachum wasn't spying on him.

Matthew finished renting a car and called ahead for a hotel as well. He took a room at a local establishment, a small place with no television and a single unisex bathroom at the end of the hall. It had a sign on the door that read "fifteen minutes." He had to shave and brush his teeth in his room at the dresser, where he could see toothpaste stains on the carpeted rug and watermarks all over the wooden dresser. There were two pitchers for holding water and a chamber pot under the bed, which he would not touch. Mare would laugh at him, he thought; she knew he was a germaphobe. Speaking of Mare, he called her but did not let her know where he was. "Why do you have your GPS location turned off?" she asked. He had to think fast. "I do not want any of Gottfried's thugs to be able to use my phone to track me." This seemed to satisfy her. He only knew of one place to look for Gottfried: The University of Oslo Medical School.

***

The campus was nice and historic-looking, much nicer than the surrounding buildings. You could tell when you entered the campus that most of the local money probably flowed into and from the University. Matthew was very impressed as he walked through the medical college halls. He was heading for the Dean's office when a wall full of old photographs caught his eye. They were graduating classes from the late 1800s to today. He scanned them, finding Gottfried in a photograph from the time he was an intern in Berlin. He had been correct; when they banned him from completing his medical apprenticeship, he had come to Oslo. He studied the photograph closely, moving through the classes for several more years.

There was another man in a photograph that caught his eye, though. He graduated several years after Gottfried. He swore it looked

273

like Meacham. He looked at the name, and it said **Erik Hoffmier**. Matthew took a picture with his cell phone, trying to zoom in on his face. The black-and-white photograph had yellowed over time, making it difficult to see. This particular photograph was a panoramic shot, taken on the front lawn. There were two young men on the left and right sides of the picture who looked identical. Either they were twins or he ran behind the class to get to the other side before it finished. Since it lists the same name twice, Matthew assumed the faculty had simply gone with it.

He heard footsteps coming down another hallway, getting louder as they went. At the university, there weren't many people around. The noise entered the hall he was in, but he turned away. He could see his back and decided to follow him. He walked to the end of the hall and turned left. The place was like a maze of rectangular hallways all connected together. There were three sets of double doors on the right. He walked down the hall to the second set and went inside.

Being careful, Matthew inched closer to the doors. A low, muffled sound emanated from inside. He reached the first set of double doors and tried to crack them open, but they were locked. He slid to the second set, cracked the door, and all he could see was a wall—a wall with more pictures. He opened it and went inside. There were steps that led up to another level that ran the length of the entryway. He went up, and there were more doors, but they were all open. He looked inside, and the entire school and faculty were inside, having a lecture or demonstration. "Komm og sett seg, er forelesningen om å begynne," a student motioned to him. (Come and sit down, the lecture is about to begin.) He went over and sat down.

The lights dimmed, and a man came out, and everyone clapped. It was Dr. Gottfried Dimment himself. They say you can't keep a good man down; evidently, you can't keep an evil one down either. He was speaking Norwegian, and Matthew, having recently learned the basics, could not understand everything he was saying. What little he could understand was on stem cell research and development. He spoke for about 45 minutes, concluding with the latest advancements and achievements. Like a good professor, he left them with a question, prompting them to seek more. They clapped, and he left the stage. He did not go back and sit down; instead, he left through another exit. Matthew decided to follow him.

He quickly went down the side row of seats to the front of the stage and out the door, Gottfried went. He wondered if he had seen him sitting in the audience. If he did, he was very good at concealing it. Matthew passed a bathroom and heard a familiar throat-clearing sound. He waited a few seconds and hid inside a recessed door opening to a lecture room. The door opened, and Gottfried walked out. He did not come back towards Matthew and the Auditorium. Instead, he continued on down the hall and took a right. Matthew followed him, and he went across a breezeway into another building. Matthew had to wait until he was almost out of sight. He walked as fast as he could. When he got to the end, he looked left and saw nothing. He turned right, hearing a noise, and just saw his back turning left. He continued following him.

When he made it to the end of the hallway, he peeked around the corner. He saw a door closing. He went over and looked through a small windowpane. He could smell alcohol, formaldehyde, and other laboratory chemicals in the air. It was a laboratory. Curious that it did not have security like the one in Berlin, he opened the door and went inside. This must be the student laboratory. He saw an office to the side with a light on. He walked over as bold as brass and went in. Gottfried was sitting with his back towards him. "Dr. Dimment."

Matthew startled him. He spun around in his chair, almost falling out. "Matthew, you should not have come here. What do you want?"

"I came to ask you a few questions."

He sat back in his chair, relaxed, and said, "Why would you need to ask an old man like me anything? You're the Savant." He smirked, threw his arms up, and shrugged his shoulders. He sounded bitter, very bitter.

"I wanted to ask you about Katja." He looked funny and replied, "Katja? Don't you mean Marilyn? I figured you were here to beg me to tell you how to save her, or have you figured it out already?"

"Marilyn is fine, she is doing well. I wanted to know about Katja?"

A very serious look came across Gottfried's face. "Katja was born special. She was the one we all looked after. My mother loved her to death, and my father tried to find a way to awaken her before the war. When Hitler's regime took over, he did not allow my father to continue his work. He made him work on other projects. He vested his time just before and during the war, working on chemical weapons."

Matthew sat back and tried to listen. Gottfried opened a desk drawer and left it open after retrieving a butterscotch and putting it into his mouth. "My father barely survived the war. He emotionally died when Hitler was defeated. My mother had been taking my sister, brother, and me to the shelters by herself. We stayed almost three months during the last push. We sat in our own filth. Many people began to get ill and die from the living conditions. Finally, the war ended. The Americans saved us, as they claim, and we escaped. We went back home to nothing. My father had sent some money and jewelry to Switzerland, and that is all that saved us from complete poverty. My father was sequestered for years during the trials. We rented an apartment, and my mother went back to work. My brother and I watched Katja and went to school when we could. My mother put me through medical school. When I became an apprentice after graduating at the top of my class, she gave me my father's research notes. The Americans moved us as promised to the States, but my father died shortly after arriving. I pleaded with my mother to move Katja back to Berlin."

Matthew sat there in amazement. He had it all wrong this entire time. Dr. Gottfried was not an evil person, just blindly driven by passion. "Dr. Gottfried, I had no idea. If you had told me…"

"Told you what? Then you would have just given up a miracle, your life's work, to save my sister. That's preposterous." Using the mental filters in his mind, it probably was preposterous to think someone could be so kind.

"Dr. Gottfried, if you could save your sister still, would you?"

"What kind of idiotic question is that? Of course, I would. I have congestive heart failure, sugar problems, and hardening of the arteries. I am a ticking time bomb."

Students started pouring into the laboratory. "I have a class to lecture," he said, then took a pen and paper, wrote down an address, and handed it to Matthew. "Meet me here at six o'clock and we can finish our conversation."

"One last question, Doctor. Do you know Erik Hoffmier? He was several classes behind you."

"No... why do you want to know?"

"He looks very familiar. I saw him in the class photographs. He would be in his mid-fifties now."

"I have access to all the historical data files. I will take a quick look to see if it is that important to you."

"Please, it may answer a very important question for us both. I will see you at six." Matthew picked up the card and left the office. All of the young people stared at him as he waded past them.

Matthew went back to his room and called Mare. "How are you feeling?"

"Fine, I am just really tired and drained all the time. Since Mrs. Werner has been coming over and taking care of everything, all I want to do is sleep."

"Well, you need your rest, and so does the baby. I have been thinking a lot, Mare, and I need to talk to you about something very important when I return."

"What is it, Matthew? You're scaring me."

"Nothing bad, it's good... I promise you."

"Okay, hurry home. I really miss you and I need you right now."

"Okay, I love you too, bye." Matthew felt like a dog when he got off the phone. He tried to call Meacham, but he did not answer. The GPS indicated that he was in Washington, D.C.

***

At about five-thirty, Matthew drove to the address Gottfried had given him. He went inside an old and noisy apartment building, not the kind of place he would imagine Gottfried would stay. He guessed he wanted to keep a low profile. He went up the stairs to room 5D. When he got to the top, he noticed the door was open. He knocked. He could hear a man breathing heavily and making noises. Then he heard the sound of metal clinking, like someone running down metal steps. Matthew ran inside and found Gottfried on the floor, clutching his chest. He saw an open window to the alley, ran over to look, and saw a man almost at the bottom. He was too far away to see, but Matthew could make out that he was not a young man but still in good shape. He had a hat, coat, and scarf on as he ran off.

Matthew went back over and helped Gottfried into a chair. He was in a great deal of pain. "Matthew, I told you, you should not have come here."

"Meacham is not his real name. It's Kaiser... Erik Lawrence Kaiser. Hoffmier is an assumed name he took after the war to protect his identity. Kaiser," he yelled out in pain and clutched his chest. "Mare is in danger. You have to go to her now. Please, if you can... save my sister. Promise me!" He was squeezing Matthew's hand so hard that it had lost all feeling. When he let go, he left a note in his hand. "Meacham... he's some kind of super savant. He did something to my heart with his mind. He's evil. He read my mind somehow... and the pain! He knows everything." Gottfried moaned again. "Matthew, there is no way you can stop him. He resembles the kind of superhuman that Hitler's Doctors were trying to create. His father was one of those Doctors. Matthew... I know I have done some horrible things in the name of love, but I am not a bad person. Please don't think badly of me?"

Gottfried grasped his chest again and began to spit up blood. He was dying. "You will have to be some kind of superhuman to stop him..." His voice was garbled and trailed off. He groaned one last time, then lay still. Matthew heard a woman coming down the hall, her voice frantic. He thought he had told her that Gottfried had a heart attack. He left quickly. Someone had called the authorities. He had to return to Berlin.

He called Mare on the way. Mrs. Werner answered the phone. "Mrs. Werner… where is Mare?"

"Matthew, she is fine. She is sleeping now."

"Mrs. Werner, don't let anyone in the house… I mean, no one."

"Okay, Matthew… Lawrence will be by tomorrow."

"No! Don't let him in, Mrs. Werner. I can't explain now. Just don't let him in."

"Well… I'll try, dear, but Lawrence is my brother."

It hit him hard, like a freight train… Kaiser. Lawrence was Mrs. Werner's little brother. It all made sense now. He had to get home to Mare. He had to stop in Berlin first. He checked his cell phone. He had Lawrence's number. He checked it on the GPS one more time. Meacham was still showing in Washington, D.C. Something was not right. Maybe he left his phone with someone there. He had not turned off his location, or maybe he wanted him to see it. Matthew felt helpless. He knew what he had to do.

26 ENLIGHTENMENT

Matthew returned to the Psychiatric Hospital in Berlin. He met with Katja's doctors and handed them a letter signed by both Steffen and Gottfried. Gottfried must have known he would come for him; he was smarter than Matthew had given him credit for. The letter allowed Matthew to perform the stem cell implant on Katja, but not before he arranged to have the implant placed in himself. He wasn't going to make the same mistake Gottfried did. Gottfried had a friend at the hospital, Dr. Gedlhoff, who was reluctant but had promised Steffen he would provide Matthew with anything he needed. Matthew explained the precise location of the injection: through the soft bone at the base of the brain near the neck joint. He hated going under anesthesia but knew the pain would be too much to bear.

Lying on a massage table, with an IV inserted and oxygen placed on his nose, he felt the improvisations required due to the lack of proper equipment. He remembered lying there for just a few seconds, then drifting off.

Instead of going into an unconscious state like with a normal surgical anesthetic, Matthew went into a dream state. He was traveling through a tunnel toward a light, emerging in a place that looked familiar yet different. The air was swift, and a storm was heading his way. He felt the wind whipping around him and lightning strikes, much stronger than synaptic pulses, falling to the ground. He could feel the hair on his arms standing up. He looked for Id but couldn't find him. He was running up a hill toward a lone tree, the same tree he had seen Id under before.

He drifted toward it and stopped. Id was not there. He thought he even yelled for him, but there was no answer. The storm was now upon him. The sky began to swirl in a circular motion, the clouds turning from white and gray to black and red. He heard several strikes around him, then a bolt of lightning was hurled toward the tree. It sounded like a bombshell screaming through the air, and when it hit, it split the tree in two. The blast knocked Matthew to the ground. When he stood up, he saw three figures: Id and two others. They both looked like Id but were different. One looked very evil, and the other very serene and calming. Id turned to Matthew like God and pointed his finger down at him.

"I cannot control them now! You have released them both. You will be the harbinger of whatever may come from your pronouncement." A funnel cloud broke from the swirling mass above and plucked them from the air. They turned into dust and disappeared into the sky. With a loud clap, Matthew saw a flash of light. It went dark again. He heard another loud clap of lightning, and his eyes opened to see light. A third clap, and he saw the light on the ceiling in the operating room.

"Matthew… Matthew, it is done. We are done," a voice said. He sat up, feeling a little groggy, his head swimming from the drugs. He tried to see if he could feel anything, but couldn't.

"You should stay here overnight, Matthew. We have security. We can observe you and make sure everything is okay." He didn't want to, but he knew they were right. They left a sandwich and a pitcher of water on a stand next to him. He took a bite of the sandwich, but it was all he could do to swallow it. He poured a cup of water and sipped on it. He tried to fall asleep but couldn't. All he could do was worry about Mare. He sat there for some time with his eyes closed and eventually fell into a dream that felt so real. He could hear himself breathing, feel his heart beating, and his knee even ached like it did after walking too much. He was going back up the hill towards the tree again, but this time, the grass was green and there were leaves on the tree. All the other times, the tree had looked lifeless and dead.

Below the tree was a figure. It appeared to be Id, but it wasn't exactly him; it looked like him but felt different. The surroundings were calm, and the sky was blue. The figure was trying to play a wooden mouth flute, but he would only play a few pleasant notes before abruptly stopping and playing another. It felt like a spring day but was very warm. Matthew walked up to the Id-like figure and introduced himself. "I am Matthew. What is your name?"

"You know me very well, don't you, Matthew."

"I can't say that I do. Who are you?"

"Yes, you know me very well." He smiled eerily, his teeth yellowed and his gums black. His eye teeth seemed abnormally longer. "Matthew, you know me all too well." He played a few notes and ignored Matthew.

"Where is Id?" Matthew demanded.

"He is around, everywhere, nowhere." He smiled again and went back to incoherently playing the flute.

"I demand to know where Id is! What have you done with him?" Matthew was inflamed. He felt an overwhelming feeling of rage, a desire to destroy or kill something, and a sense that he was losing control.

"What is your name? Tell me now or I will..."

"Or you will what, Matthew?"

The figure stood, and his flute disappeared. Matthew just wanted to strike him down. A mace appeared in his hand out of thin air. He pointed it at him. "Tell me your name or die." He smiled again, further infuriating Matthew. He drew the mace in the air and swung it down. Just before it struck his head, he heard the name Cerebrus. He disappeared, and the ground fell away from Matthew's feet. He fell through darkness, the weightlessness of the trip feeling real. He hit the ground, but it was somewhat soft like sand. He picked up the soil, and as the light brightened, he could see the black sand falling from between his fingers. He was in a desert that was completely black. It was very bright but not hot.

He began to walk in the direction he thought he should go. The sand was deep, and it felt like he was walking in heavy, wet snow. He kept going, but when he looked behind him, his tracks were gone. On the horizon, he could see a pair of eyes becoming clearer with each step. The only reason he noticed them was because they blinked at him. He began hearing a growing noise that sounded like a waterfall. It grew louder as if it were echoing in a canyon. With a few more steps, he could see the eyes clearly. They were part of Cerberus's face. He smiled again, and Matthew felt enraged once more. The whites of his eyes matched the color of his teeth: yellow. He pointed behind Matthew, and he saw a ripple in the sand grow into a wave.

The wave moved toward and away from him at the same time. He ran toward Cerebrus and hit an invisible wall that tinged like a champagne glass. The sand rushed from around his feet, and he fell down, beginning to slide. He could hear him laugh. Matthew could not control his anger when he saw him. He was a prankster, a trickster, and Matthew hated him. He slid down, seeing the last few grains of sand disappear through a hole in the bottom of the glass floor. He caught himself on the sides with his feet and hands. Cerebrus shook the glass and tapped it, but Matthew would not go down. He could hear screams of torture and see heat rising from the hole in the glass bottom.

Cerebrus picked up the glass and looked down inside at Matthew's pathetic, tiny stature, clinging to the sides of the glass tunnel like a scared child. He laughed as he poured champagne into the glass. It hit Matthew in the face hard, and he lost his grip. Instead of going down, he caught himself on a bubble and floated up to the top of the glass. He grabbed the rim. Cerebrus was laughing as if playing with a child's toy. Matthew coughed, trying to capture oxygen in the carbonated atmosphere. If he could have jumped out, he would have killed him. He was a bully, a thug, and a punk. Matthew felt he was losing his grip, not just on the glass but on reality. This dream was so vividly real that it was frightening.

Cerebrus swirled the glass to make a vortex, and Matthew watched all the liquid draining through the bottom just like the sand. He took his finger and flicked the side of the glass, and Matthew fell into the swirling hole. He was being sucked down. He screamed for help, but no one came. He was sucked down through the hole, free-falling toward the screams. He looked up and saw Cerebrus looking at him with one huge, floating face. He blinked, and Matthew landed flat on his back in his hospital bed.

He was alive and well, but his bed was drenched in sweat. He was so relieved it was just a dream. The anger and rage he felt were slowly going away. He had never felt so out of control and so enraged in his life.

He looked around for his water glass. He wanted a drink very badly. As he stared at it, the glass began to vibrate. He focused on it more, and it moved and rattled on the table without falling over. He felt as if he could make it come to him, but couldn't. The glass began to make a high-pitched ringing noise. He reached for it, and it exploded, startling him.

A nurse came into the room, having heard the glass shatter. She was speaking German, but Matthew clearly heard every word in English. It was as if his brain were an automatic translation filter. Something had changed inside him. Even though he could learn a language, he had always had to concentrate and dig through his memory banks to find the words and their meaning. This time, it was effortless. He knew then the stems must be working. He could feel it. He could feel a whole range of emotions welling up inside him. He was not an emotional person, but it was like he was being plugged into something more. It's hard to describe, but when you have never experienced many emotions, encountering a new one is truly amazing. He felt an overwhelming urge to cry, but held it off.

The nurse cleaned up the glass and gave him a plastic cup. She helped him change the sheets, and he lay back down. He knew he was different, but by how much, no one knew. He happened to look at the clock, and it had only been half an hour since the doctor left the room. It felt like he had been in the dream for hours. It was as if time had slowed down or was not a factor where he had been. He poured a cup of water, took a few drinks, and tried to rest his eyes again. His head still felt weird, as if he had just been in an adrenaline rush that wouldn't stop. His body was exhausted, and his head felt pressured or swelled, similar to what you feel when you dive in over fifty feet of water or a plane climbs too quickly in the air after takeoff. He yawned to try to pop his ears, but it didn't work. So, he took a deep breath and pushed it against his lips like he was blowing up a balloon. His ears popped, and the pressure in his head seemed to relieve itself. His blood pressure must have been elevated. He could hear his heart beating and a ringing noise in his ears, a sound like blood flowing rapidly through his head. He heard a leaking noise inside his skull as if cerebral fluid were draining. The stem cells must be generating new growth. He must have been generating new synaptic paths by the dozens. His body felt tired, and an overwhelming sensation to sleep came over him.

He fell back asleep and began to dream again. He had the same feeling that the dream was not a dream at all but an altered state of reality. He was beginning to feel more comfortable going into them, but he still felt no control over the outcome. He was walking back up the hill toward the tree again. The tree had been lifeless, then green and lush. This time, it had multicolored leaves and was filled with some unusual fruit he had never seen before. He saw a figure under the tree again. It was not Id or Cerebrus; he could feel the difference between them. On this occasion, it was someone new. The figure looked similar, but again, he was different. Matthew felt fanciful, free, and without repose. His mind felt free. He wanted to write, sculpt, sing, and dance simultaneously. He felt good, just as he had with Mare. He could stay here with him for a very long time. The figure was smiling and looking at him. He sat at the base of the tree just like Cerebrus. Id had floated above the tree, which seemed strange to Matthew now. Who was this figure, this figment of his imagination? What did he want?

Imagination, fiction, and fancy are only fragments of our minds until we release them and give them life. His thoughts were growing. He felt like the wise man on the mountain or the tree dwellers who seek enlightenment. He felt like anything he could think of would happen and could be set free. It was as if this place were a workshop, and when he completed something, he could pull it out of this place into reality. The epiphany of his thoughts, every single emotion, was real here. He sat down and crossed his legs directly in front of the figure. They stared into each other's eyes. When he looked deep within him, he saw the clouds racing by. It looked like time-lapse photography in motion.

The figure was abstract, yet Matthew knew he could understand it. Without words, he asked him, "What is your name?" He looked up, and with his thoughts, he replied, "Caprice." Matthew was relieved. The last time he asked that question, he wanted to kill the entity immediately.

"Do you know of Id or Cerebrus?"

"Yes, I know of them."

"Where are they?"

"They are here, and yet they are not?"

"How do I know which one will show up?"

"That is up to you to decide."

"How is that? I cannot control anything."

"He smiled. You are in control of all that is and all that will be in this place."

"What is this place?"

"This is you."

"How is this me?"

"This place is you and yet it is not."

"Is there anyone else here?"

"Not at the moment."

"What do you mean, not at the moment?"

"You are new to this place. You must learn the rules."

"So, there are others here in this place?"

"There can be, but there is not."

"What are the rules? Tell me then."

"There are no rules."

"But you just said I must learn the rules?"

"Yes, you make up the rules. So how can I know what they are?"

Caprice spoke in riddles. Matthew could not follow his riddles very well, but he began to become more enlightened. As he said before, he could spend considerable time here, but that was something he had not been able to control.

"How long can I stay here, Caprice?"

"As long as you like, Matthew."

"How do you know my name?"

"Everyone knows the name of their creator."

"Then who created me?"

"You tell me, Matthew."

"A master designer created the heavens and the Earth, I believe, God."

"Then I would seek him out. He is your creator."

"You can't talk to God directly. You can only pray."

"That depends… Matthew."

"Depends on what?"

"How strong your faith and your will are in here."

"Are you saying I can talk with God?"

"I am saying in here you will discover and can do anything you can imagine."

"Can I do it outside of here as well?"

"I suppose it is possible."

"I have much to learn."

"Matthew, try to imagine the most fantastical thing you can and make it happen now."

"Now?"

"Yes, Matthew, now." Matthew tried to concentrate, and they lifted off the ground, beginning to hover above the grass. Caprice took two fruits from the tree and handed one to him. They both ate the fruit, and Matthew's mind went into a new dimension. He imagined they were in a famous painting. The first one that came to mind was a Brown & Bigelow advertisement by C.M. Coolidge featuring dogs playing poker.

Looking down at his hand, Matthew had two Kings and three sevens. A dog with a cigar in his mouth took a long draw and blew smoke in his face. "Are you in or out, Bub?"

"I'm in."

"Look at the new breed, pup boys, he says he's in." They all laughed, so Matthew slid all his chips across the table. "I'm all in."

They called his small pot. "Who does this guy think he is? Okay, boys, show him what you got." They all had really good hands, but no one could beat him.

The dog looked at him again. "Well, lay 'em down, pup, and let's see what you've been barking about." Matthew showed his hand. There was a long moment of silence, and then they all burst out laughing. "Here, we cheated, and the honest pup still beat us." He tried to laugh with them. This was a very strange game. The dog pulled out a gun and said, "We don't like honesty."

Matthew looked around, and Caprice was floating just behind him, invisible to the others. He closed his eyes and concentrated very hard. The noise of the card game and music faded away. He heard birds and felt a light breeze on his face. When he opened his eyes, he was part of Monet's *Poppies Blooming*. He heard a little boy talking to his mother. "Mommy, look, I picked you some flowers."

"That's nice, dear. Hold on to them, and we will put them in some water later."

On the hill above him were a woman and her daughter. Matthew was sitting in the tall grass, but this time, they could not see him. He tried to move and slipped. The painting consisted of tiny dots, millions of them. They were like little snowballs of paint in his hand. He spun his arm around, and the paint went flying, hitting the young woman and her son, staining her dress. She turned and scowled. He picked up several, made a big colored ball, and threw it at her. It hit her in the midsection, and she exploded into thousands of dots. The little boy began crying. "Mommy, mommy… where's my mommy?" The woman on the hill ran away with her daughter. Matthew threw another ball, hitting the boy, and he exploded as well. The little paint balls would roll and scatter like dust behind a car. He heard a mob of loud voices getting closer and saw several French police officers and men in suits standing on top of the hill, pointing at him. He started to concentrate very hard again.

He could hear seagulls squawking and the gentle sound of the surf. When he opened his eyes, he saw a black table and a dead tree. They were out of place. What was even stranger was the clocks hanging and dripping all around. The symbolism was clear. His mind, or Salvador Dalí, was telling him that it was time to get back. He walked over and picked up one of the clocks. It was pliable like paper but firm like plastic. The clock was still ticking. He looked around for Caprice, but he was gone.

He began to get a familiar feeling he did not like. Matthew started to feel upset and even nervous. He felt like Cerebrus was nearby. He started concentrating on the fruit tree, trying to get back, but it wasn't working. He began to run along the beach. There were clocks floating out of the surf like smelt on the ocean shore. He saw clocks flying out of the water with wings like a flying fish. On the horizon behind him, a storm was moving in fast. The surf began to take on a more defined shape, and the waves grew significantly larger. He ran faster and stopped suddenly, nearly falling off a rock cliff. He was standing right on the edge. He heard a large bird the size of a pelican. He turned to look behind him, and coming straight at him was a huge grandfather clock with wings. It hit him, and he fell over the cliff, screaming as he went down.

He fell for some time, kicking and screaming. He landed forcefully on the floor next to his hospital bed. He must have fallen from the bed this time, and the jarring awoke him. He was having some of the most outrageous, psychedelic dreams he had ever had. He was almost afraid of going to sleep. His mind was expanding rapidly, and the more it expanded, the stranger he felt. He knew it had worked. He felt like he was in another dimension of reality, yet in the same place he was before. He felt like he could accomplish anything he set his mind to.

He saw a piece of paint peeling from the wall. He walked over to it. Behind it were more layers of old paint, followed by plaster. He focused on the small crack beside it. He could actually see the individual granules of powder in the plaster. He focused harder, and he could see the construct behind the crack: the slatted wood, then a void space behind that. As he focused, it moved through the insulation and onto a block wall, then through the brick outer wall. He focused harder, and the wall became invisible to him, looking like a mirage of water. He stuck his hand out, and as it extended toward the wall, it became invisible as well and went right through it to the outdoors. He looked down, and his arm was still at his side. He could feel the cold night air on his arm, but how? He even felt the wall surrounding his arm like a second skin. He heard a noise in the hall and quickly pulled his hand back. He lost concentration, and the last few inches of his wrist felt like it was stuck between the slatted wood. He pulled hard and knocked a small hole in the wall.

He ran over and jumped into bed like nothing had occurred. The nurse walked in and asked how he was doing. Time was crawling by. It felt as if the entire world had slowed down and he had somehow sped up. Matthew was thinking faster and doing things at two or three times the speed of an average person. There was no doubt now that he was different. He would have to hide his talents from the world or suffer becoming a sideshow freak again. After the nurse left, he got his clothes on, went down the hall, and found Katja's room. He knew Eve would make her better now.

When he entered the room, Katja was asleep. He was in a hurry and had no choice. She was mute, so screaming was not possible. He knew it was cruel, but he turned her over gently and positioned her head off the side of the bed. He pulled Eve out and placed her in the syringe. He took some alcohol with a cotton ball, rubbed the base of her neck, and cleaned it. He put the long needle against her neck and concentrated. He began to see her skin in detail, right down to the hair follicles at the root. He traveled through the layers of her skin, through the muscle to the soft bone at the base of her skull. The base was very porous, so he chose a spot and began to insert the needle. He felt her body flinch and kept pushing, hoping the needle would not break off. He watched the tip of the needle make it through the bone into the fluid around her brain. He saw it enter the grey tissue and slide into the location the seed needed to reside. He pushed down on the syringe and watched as Eve traveled down, through the needle, and out of the tip.

He removed the needle from Katja's neck, still staring at the seed of Eve. He could see the stems drifting out from the pores of the shell. They were migrating toward the damaged areas of Katja's brain. He saw a synaptic pulse flicker where none had been before. The flash of light let him know it was working. He got off her back and rolled her over. He was looking at her when her eyes opened. He said to her, "You will thank me in the morning." She looked at him with a blank stare, then closed her eyes. He pulled the blanket up to her neck and slid out of the room. He needed to get home and was in a hurry. He went to the train station and took the night train to Paris so he could fly home. He checked his phone several times on the way, but with the time difference, it was late at night there. His thoughts turned to Mare.

27 PERSISTENCE OF TIME

Walking through the airport was torture. Not only could Matthew hear every conversation around him, but he could also hear every thought within ten feet. He tried not to walk near anyone; it was too depressing. Most of these people were miserable at best, their minds filled with vitriol. He heard a barrage of conversations all self-serving: "Dave is such a backstabbing prick. I wish I could just kill his ass and stuff him in a drum." "I don't know if I can take his mental abuse anymore, but I don't have anywhere else to go." "I wish just once I knew what to say when Joyce comes at me in meetings. She's always trying to make me look bad." "I can't tell Nicci I cheated on her; she will go apeshit and never trust me again." "One of these days I'm gonna take an axe and drive it through his big, fat, thick skull in front of everyone." "If I could only get a decent raise at this place, I would be able to get ahead in life." "I wish this old bag would finally die. I am tired of lugging her fat ass through every airport in the country." "Why does God hate me so much? I was perfect for that job, and they gave it to that brownnoser Brent."

Matthew didn't think he heard one good thought the entire time he was walking. The cab driver was a bit surprising, though. He was humming with his mouth but singing in his head. It was a nice change, but even in his mind, he could not carry a tune very well on key. It was like being in downtown Manhattan with no cell phone or Wi-Fi connection while everyone around you was talking or texting. He had a hard time concentrating on what was important: Mare. Mare was the only thing on his mind right now. He knew Lawrence would not hurt her as long as he needed something from him. He was not sure about Mrs. Werner. She was much older than her brother, and Matthew didn't think she really knew what he was up to. He didn't think she knew she was involved with a psychopathic savant trying to enlighten himself.

Matthew arrived at the building and paid the cab driver. He took his bag and briefcase and went through the security gate. There was no guard outside. Security levels must have been lowered. He entered the lobby and saw a security guard. "Good day, Mr. Le'Dain," the guard said as Matthew passed toward the elevator. He rode the elevator to the fifth floor and got off. He went to 5D, and before he slid his security card, he looked across the hall. Mrs. Werner's door caught his senses for some reason. He paused to study it. The carpet touched the base of the door, so he could not see any shadows. He looked at the peephole and saw a faint image of an eyeball and the blinking of an eyelash. It moved back quickly.

Matthew began concentrating very hard on the door, and the paint on the door began to dissolve. He started to hear her thoughts, but they were garbled and indistinguishable. He could hear fast breathing and a faint heartbeat. He saw the grains of wood disperse. Through the door, he saw Mrs. Werner holding a knife as if she were frightened to death. She looked prepared for a psychotic attacker. Maybe she knew about her brother. Maybe she was afraid of him. He tried very hard to read her thoughts, but he still could not make them out. She was shaking and frightened. "What am I going to find on the other side of my door?" he thought to himself.

He was worried for a moment but was also optimistic. He was logical and understood how people thought, even those with irrational tendencies. Erik Lawrence Kaiser wanted something from him. He would not throw out his only bargaining chip and hope he could obtain it. If he were as smart as Matthew had been led to believe, he would take good care of her. He scanned his card and opened the door.

When he entered the apartment, it was nice and clean. There were not even dirty dishes in the sink. Everything was in its place. The apartment looked like no one had been there for a few days. Lawrence had a jump on him. What was his plan? What was he up to? Where was Mare? Matthew set down his briefcase, bag, and overcoat. He walked into the living room after checking the apartment for thugs. He didn't think that would be Lawrence's style. Matthew was not even sure he would be able to conceal Mare anywhere in Washington, D.C. He couldn't take her to the laboratories; someone there would get suspicious, and there were too many cameras and security to cover it up. He would not be at the Education Center. Matthew sat in the chair, running hundreds of scenarios through his mind, knowing that the persistence of time was upon him.

Having a brilliant mind also presented a major issue. He had to rule out all options that were not plausible before he could concentrate on the ones that were logical and made sense. When you factored in the irrational thinking of someone who may be mentally unstable, it was very difficult to narrow it down to one solution. Things that he did know were these: Lawrence would have to keep her sedated without harming the baby. She would require constant supervision from a nurse or doctor. Since he was a doctor, all he would need was a comparable nurse he could trust. Lastly, he would want to be on his own turf, somewhere he could have the upper hand. He was taking Mare back to Berlin. "How stupid of me!" Matthew yelled aloud without realizing it. The notebook was his only bargaining chip.

Something about the room kept bothering him the entire time he was sitting there. A little obsessive-compulsive issue was creeping up in his time of duress. He stood up and walked over to an oil painting he loved. It was by an unknown artist, one who sells paintings for a few hundred dollars each and probably does hundreds a year. Mare and he had picked it up at an art festival on the street. It was of a lone boat moored to a post, resting on the ground because the tide was out. He wasn't sure why he liked it; it was depressing in a way, but calming. He saw the tide receding as the crowds and the hustle and bustle of people were gone. He liked his solitude, and Mare was the only one to be able to share it with him. She was the only one who understood him. He reached out to straighten the frame, and an envelope fell from behind it. Clever, Lawrence knew him very well. He knew Matthew could not resist straightening that painting. No one else would notice it, even if the police came and searched the place. He opened the envelope and took out a single sheet of paper. It had a cryptic message inside and some numbers from Rosetta's Project.

With authority, I request the presence of a superlative bequest. Solitude must be assured to protect our accord. 3489 Wolfsschanze (Wolfs-Lair) Lane Spandau, Germany

Matthew gathered from the request, with so few words, the following: Lawrence wanted him to bring the notebook alone and, of course, not involve any authorities. He would exchange Mare for the book. He wanted Matthew to meet him at his home in the Spandau Forest at Wolfs Lair Lane. This was fabulous, another Hitler tie-in. This guy was either off his rocker or had an affinity to finish the work his hero began. No matter, Matthew had to save Mare and his unborn son.

He decided it was time to confront Mrs. Werner. He went over to her apartment and knocked on the door. She was standing about three feet from the door, her hands clutching a carving knife. "Go away, you monsters; I don't have anything you need! Go away, I said!"

"It's me, Matthew, Mrs. Werner. I am not going to hurt you. I just need to talk to you. Lawrence…where has he taken Mare?"

"You're a monster, an abomination just like him. Go away!"

"Please open the door, Mrs. Werner. I just want to talk with you." She was shaking like a leaf in a windstorm. He knew if he forced his way in, she would panic. He stared at the keypad on the door.

Their doors had a card slot and a keypad with a four-digit code. He looked very closely at the keypad and saw four numbers with oil and dirt stains. The numbers were 4, 7, 2, and 0. He concentrated on the direction of the oil-stained marks, the depth of the buildup, the length of time a finger would be on the key, and some basic characteristics of Mrs. Werner's personality. Since there are ten thousand different combinations, he could be here all day. He narrowed it down drastically to about five or six. You only have three attempts to enter it correctly. The fourth sets off a silent alarm downstairs.

Entering the first set of digits had no effect. He tried the second choice, and again, nothing. He tried the third set, and again, it did not work. If this fourth set had not been the combination, there would have been a problem. He knew two and seven had the heaviest oil buildup;

they had to be the first and last numbers. He pushed seven, then zero, four, and two. The door latch made a noise, and the magnetic lock released. He pushed the door open slowly, and Mrs. Werner was whipping the knife around at him. "Please, Mrs. Werner…I just want to talk with you, that's all."

"Stay away, stay away, you monster!"

"Mrs. Werner, Lawrence has Mare. He's taken her to his home near Berlin. Please, I am begging you, please help me?" He backed her into the living room. "Mrs. Werner, if you cared for Mare at all, you have to help me?" Tears started to stream down her face. She began to break down and cry.

"He was always a handful. My parents, God bless their souls, had trouble with him. He became mixed up after the war with a small group of loyalists. They vowed to complete Hitler's genetic dream, to develop a genetically altered superhuman, elite in intelligence, strength, and superiority. I blame my father for that. Erik fell into them deep after the trials were over, and our family name was mud in Germany. I was married and moved here. He changed his name, moved to Oslo, and completed medical school. That is where he met Dr. Helmet Stupak. He was working on his PHD to become a professor at the university. They shared many political views and had a love-hate relationship. The two of them developed a mind-altering stem cell therapy, but it was a one-off. It was not sustainable. When Erik got the taste of knowledge beyond all his expectations, he wanted more. It changed him."

"Helmet had no idea he had tested it on himself. Erik has a laboratory in his home. He confined himself there until he regained his sanity. He was calling himself Cerebrus for the longest time. He developed some unusual side effects. He claimed he could read minds, move objects, and see through walls. I was the only one he would let in his room. They strapped him down, and once I arrived, all the people he trusted fled. Later on, each one died from some type of physical ailment, strokes, heart attacks, or something else, including Dr. Stupak."

"Mrs. Werner, what else can you tell me?"

"His home is built over a hidden research facility. Even after the country was occupied, the Spandau Forest Research Facility was never discovered. Our father worked there during the war. People are so frightened by just the terror of that place that they will not talk about it. It has an expansive underground maze of rooms and test areas. She is there, I bet."

"Is there any way to get in, maybe a secret entrance?"

"Yes…but don't you think he will have them guarded?"

"Yes…I suppose you're right?"

"I am not sure how smart you really are, but he is smarter. He is demented and twisted now. He is lusting for knowledge. He hurt me, Matthew." She started crying again. "His own sister, he hurt me. My head hurt so badly." He must have been trying to see what she knew. "Is there anything else you can tell me?"

"Yes, the house only has a few guards. He does not trust anyone. Since no one knows about the laboratories below, he does not guard them. Be careful, Matthew, he has killed people before. I could see it in his eyes."

As Matthew entered the bank, he noticed two men following him. They could have been two of Kaiser's men, possibly, who knows? He went to his vault and opened the door. He slid out the box, and when he opened the metal door on top, the book was gone. Just for a second, his heart skipped a beat. He tilted the box up, and the leather-bound journal slid to him. He reached in and picked it up. He had a hidden pocket inside his suit. He pulled open the liner and slid it in. He checked to see if it was noticeable. He pulled another identical journal from his breast pocket as a decoy and checked it. It contained a lot of older research and thoughts. They were unique, but many were written with symbols from the Rosetta Project. No average person would be able to read them anyway.

Matthew could feel time placing a grip hold on him, paralyzing all his thoughts and senses. He knew time was of the essence, and he needed to get out of the bank and on his way. The redeeming feature for him at this point was that he had a driver, and the two thugs outside would not confront him with him around. He called the driver on his cell phone and asked him to pull up to the front, so he wouldn't have to walk very far. When he left the bank's security, he looked for them. They were still in the sedan, watching him. He looked right at them, and they made no indications that they were intimidated by him. He called ahead to Reagan National and checked to see if they logged any private medical flights in the last forty-eight hours. Since he was not an immediate relative of Mare, they would not provide any further details, except that a private flight had left for Paris yesterday. He at least knew that was most likely the flight they had taken. Now it was time for him to step up.

28 *SPANDAU BALLET*

The flight over the Atlantic seemed to take longer than usual. Perhaps it was because Matthew was restless and knew the only thing that mattered to him right now was Mare. To help with the notebook and all this cat-and-mouse game. He just wanted some semblance of a normal life. If he had only stayed on the sideshow freak tour, this would not have happened. Mare would, unfortunately, still be stuck with these two clowns. He wasn't sure if it was divine providence that brought them together, but he would like to think so. He thought some music would relax him, so he put on some headphones and switched to the music channel. "*This Much Is True*" was playing, a song by an old '80s pop group. How fitting that he was heading for Spandau Forest.

This was a good time to practice blocking what people around him were thinking. The woman next to him was completely distraught about her boyfriend. The guy behind him was rehearsing an important speech over and over. Luckily, a few of the others were dreaming. He was starting to be able to focus on one thought at a time. The man sleeping in front of him was having an erotic dream. He thought he was just flying over everyone, but that was the symbolic meaning of erogenous stimulation in a dream. Even with headphones and music blaring in his ear, he could listen in on somebody's thoughts. This was good to know. The blocking technique was working. How could anyone or anything concentrate with millions of these people's thoughts all going on at once? It would take a master creator to handle it. He couldn't even handle five or six thoughts at once. Mrs. Werner had sketched a map of what she could remember of the Wolf's Lair. This was not the original one but the manor that Lawrence had created. What kind of sick person idolizes the philosophy and goals of a mass murderer? He was going to have to have some well-crafted dance moves like a ballerina to tiptoe out of the mess he was in.

He noticed two men on the train ride from Paris to Berlin. The two thugs sat opposite him at one end of the lounge car. Matthew asked for a cola and went toward them. He saw a young girl his age standing there. He decided to befriend her so he could eavesdrop on the thugs. "Bonjour madam," he said in his best accent.

"Hello, I am sorry... I'm not French. I am from West Virginia. I am going to Berlin to complete my linguistics training. Can you understand anything I am saying? Probably not?"

"Yes, I can. I am American also, from the D.C. area."

"Oh, it's such a small place when you think about it. The world, that is. Jessica...my name is Jessica."

"Matthew, it's nice to meet you."

"Same here."

"He is playing us," one thug was thinking to himself as they passed through a tunnel. He was thinking in Russian, but Matthew could clearly understand him in English. It was as if he were a human translator of tongues. He had noticed earlier that no matter what language anyone was speaking, he could hear it in English. "If we could get him alone or going to the John, we may have a chance," the second thug thought. "He thinks he's being clever, but he will get his soon enough."

Matthew knew he could not let himself be alone. As soon as the thought was created in his mind, he had to go to the bathroom. Several men had gotten up to go to their cars. He asked Jessica to come sit with him at the other end of the car at a table that had opened up. On trains, the constant thumping can become loud at times. The rest of the time, you ignore it. However, when the tracks are shifted, the inside wheel grinds on the track, making an unnerving scream in the night. There was no way he was letting himself end up as a scream in the night. Jessica was going to be his unwilling accomplice in this charade. He bought her a drink and continued a light conversation. She was a U.S. government employee, which was even better for him. He just told her he was a genetics research scientist and nothing more. He knew another tunnel was approaching. There was always a brief moment of darkness, so he waited. He let Jessica know he had to go so she would not get too concerned. They entered the tunnel, and he opened the end car door and went to the next car, a dining car. He was about to enter the next car when they left the tunnel, and the thugs noticed that he was no longer there.

He hurried to shut the car door. It was a sleeping car. He went onto the next one, bypassing the bathroom. He went to the next car, hid in a broom closet, and waited for them to pass. The broom closet had a small cast ring door handle that lifted up and turned. He lifted it up and held on to it just in case he needed to make it appear locked. He concentrated on the door in the dark, and as he did so, tiny rays of light began piercing the door. A hole opened in the center, and he could see the hall clearly. It was as if his face had left his skull, peaking through the door. The two men entered the car and took a look around. They banged on the bathroom door next to him, and some man came out grumbling in German about the lack of privacy on the train. One of them hit the door he was in, and the hand came right at his face. He flinched and lost concentration. He was holding the door ring as tight as he could. One of them must have tried to open it. He felt a momentary pressure as the door opened, then it subsided. He concentrated on the door again, and when the hole opened, he saw the back of one of them going on down the hall. He could hear them knocking on each locked door as they went, disturbing passengers. After they had left the car he was in, he returned to the lounge car. Jessica must have grown weary waiting for him and left. No matter, he went on down a few cars in the opposite direction and found an empty one. He went inside and locked the door. He could not sleep at all. Thump, thump...thump, thump...thump, thump...all night long. He tried to close his eyes, but he could not fall asleep. He fell in and out, and finally drifted off into a light sleep.

He was drifting toward the tree he had been having recurring dreams about, but his feet were not touching the grass. When he got there, the tree was lifeless and barren. He stood at the base and looked around in all directions. The sky was split into three distinct weather groupings. One direction was clear and calm, the next stormy and dark, and the last full of broad-spectrum lights bouncing off fluffy clouds, similar to a wide-banded rainbow. He surmised from his past experience which areas belonged to each entity. The dark, stormy clouds were rapidly consuming the other areas. He thought very hard about Id, hoping he would see him again.

With his head down and his eyes closed, he heard a voice say his name. When he opened his eyes, Id was floating above the ground in front of the tree as before. This time, the sky remained the same. The dark stormy clouds were at bay for now, but seemed to be fighting to consume the entire sky.

"Id, where have you been? What is going on here?"

"I have been here as always. Things are out of balance now."

"What do you mean, out of balance?"

"You have allowed Caprice and Cerebrus to escape. They are now fighting for control."

"Control of what?"

"Your psyche, Matthew."

"I am in control of my mind, not them. I will remain in control!"

"Are you sure?"

"Id, explain it to me. Quit talking in riddles."

"I had dominion over Caprice and Cerebrus when they were locked within the tree of knowledge. You released them, and now they will fight until one defeats the other. Then the victor will bind me."

"Why, Id…why would they do that?"

"One is controlled by darkness and the other by light. We are all connected by our designer. However, the designer has a rival. The rival thinks he should rule and plays on the vanity, greed, lust, and other infirmities of the soul to gain dominion. It is a war of numbers. As each mind is won over to one side or the other, the masters of good and evil prosper."

"Are you trying to tell me that by opening the door for these two, they are now battling for my soul?"

"In an obtuse manner, yes."

Matthew's feet hit the ground, and he sat there and crossed his legs. He was silent for some time. He could hear the crash of lightning and the wind pick up. He felt large, hard drops of rain begin hitting him. Leaves and grass were flying around, dancing like water tossed into a scalding hot pan. The air turned colder. A storm was upon them now. "Id, is there anything I can do to change this?"

"Yes, you must bind Caprice and Cerebrus."

"How do I do that?"

"You are not ready. You must master your thoughts, conquer your fears, and control your feelings."

"How much time do I have?" Id looked out at the approaching storm and said, "Not long."

There was a loud banging on his door, and it startled him. The conductor was trying to make sure everyone was off the train. He went to pick up his luggage at the baggage claim, and they were back —the two Russian thugs. One thug saw him, threw his cigarette down, and snuffed it out with the sole of his shoe. He blew the smoke into the air and appeared to smile ominously at him. Matthew went to the car rental window and picked up his keys. The two thugs followed him out. He went with a few other men, then they suddenly took off in another direction. Matthew saw a rental agent returning to the office, so he intercepted him and asked him to lead him to his car. The agent took him directly to it and even loaded his bags in the boot. The trunk was in the front, so as soon as the agent moved, he waved goodbye and took off. This tiny car was not going to outrun anyone. That's what you get for not planning ahead. He pulled onto the main road, leaving the airport, and they were right behind him.

He had set the navigation for the Excelsior hotel again. Maybe that was not the best place, but it was all he knew at the moment. He checked Mare's GPS on her phone. She was showing up slightly Northwest of Berlin in Spandau, or at least her phone was there. He had contemplated the scenario that Mare never left the States and was, in fact, back home somewhere. However, why would he give up his notes for a promise? He pulled into the valet area and got out of the car. He retrieved his bags and went inside. He kept looking over his shoulder every few minutes. The two thugs were nowhere around. He checked in and headed for the elevator. The clerk looked at him funny when he handed him his room key. Maybe he was being too paranoid. He got on the elevator and went up to the third floor. When the door opened, the two Russians were standing there. He was trapped. Nowhere to run and nowhere to hide. One of them grabbed his arm, and the other grabbed his bag. "What room number?"

"347," he replied. The thug scanned his key for him, and they went inside. Holding on to his arm, he tossed him into a chair and turned on the television.

Matthew had seen too many movies to know what happened next. He reached into his pocket, and one of them grabbed his wrist. "Slowly, very slowly. You know what we want. Your friend Dimment left you with a hefty debt to pay. I am not sure the original agreement still holds." Matthew pulled out the notebook, and before he could hand it to him, the thug snatched it. He studied through the pages and looked completely unimpressed. He tossed the book back in his lap. He stood up and walked by, rubbing his face. He was agitated at a minimum. His buddy was digging through Matthew's bag. "It's not here, Dmitry." He took his hand and swung it at Matthew's face, backhanding him. It hurt; it hurt a lot.

"What is this? You think we are playing games here. I want the stems. I want them now!"

"The notebook, it is all my research. Everything you need to perform the experiments yourself is in there."

"It's gibberish, it's a children's coloring book!"

"No…it's not. It is encrypted in a kind of symbolic language."

"How is this useful to me? Tell me!"

"The language is easily deciphered using the neurodivergent Rosetta Project key tablet. It has an application for it on any smartphone."

"You have put me in a very precarious situation. You don't have the stems, and Dimment is dead. You're connected to him somehow. You must be the little punk that he was trying to steal them from. We have no choice. You have to come with us."

"Dmitry…the General is not going to like this very much."

304

"So what? We will take him and the notebook. If he's done it once, he can do it again. In our laboratories, in Russia."

Matthew tried to object. "I can't go there; I have pressing business here. They will notice if I don't show up." Dmitry raised his hand like he was going to backhand him again and then pointed his finger at him. "You screw with me, and you will end up like your friend Dimment. Understood!"

"Let's go!" He took the notebook from Matthew and placed it inside his jacket pocket. They left the room without Matthew's bag, headed toward the elevator, and waited for it. They got into an empty car and pushed the ground floor. The car went down one floor to the second, and the door opened. Two large men got on the elevator. One stood in front of each of the Russian thugs and did not turn around. Dmitry barked at the one in front of him. "What…you have a problem?" Matthew heard two quick puffs of air, and that was it. The door opened on the ground floor, and Matthew was going to try to leave. The one guy shook his head no.

They were too busy leaning each dead Russian against the back wall. When one of them hit the button on the eighth floor, Matthew turned sideways and jumped out, making sure he did not trip the rubber pad that reopens the doors. Thank goodness, this was an old hotel. New elevators have sensor lights; they would reopen when they passed through the door. He saw the one guy trying to hit the button to open the door, but it was too late. He did not wait around to see where they stopped. He knew they would need to hide those bodies to prevent alerting security, so that gave him a jump-start. He retrieved his car from the valet, and just as he was getting in, he saw the two new thugs getting off the elevator. He floored it, but the small car was like taking off on a bicycle.

He turned down a side street, then another. He made a loop back around the hotel valet. He saw the two in front of him in the distance, driving off. Who were these two thugs? In all the excitement, he could not concentrate enough to read anyone's thoughts. This was yet another unknown circumstance. Evidently, under extreme duress, he cannot focus very well. He needed to work on conquering his fear and emotions better, just like Id had said. He set the destination to the address noted on the navigation system.

29 *WOLFS DEN*

The Berlin countryside was menacing at dusk. There was just enough daylight to see as the shrinking orange sky in the west gave way to the night. Matthew had only passed one car and a farm tractor on this road. Now, it seemed he was alone on this rural jaunt. He drove for some time without seeing a single home, but the navigation confirmed his destination. "Arriving at destination," the feminine voice rang out. He turned it off and pulled up to the gates. Just as he was about to push the button, the gates opened with an ominous screeching sound of bare, rusty metal grinding together like the gnashing of teeth. The nearly full moon provided some faint light as he drove up the long, narrow drive and came into an opening in the trees. He could finally see the huge house. This would have been an ideal location to conceal an underground laboratory, even without the house.

He had no plan and no real confidence he would even see Mare, much less get out of this place alive. The closer he drove to the house, the stronger the feeling became that Mare was nearby. It felt like déjà vu. He saw the car from the hotel, along with its two thuggish companions; they were both standing outside by the car, smoking. The one thug threw a smoke down and snuffed it out with his shoe. He walked over and opened Matthew's door. "Good to see you again, sir. I trust you had a safe trip. The drive here was pleasant, I hope?" he said with a smug, assuming tone. Matthew immediately tried to focus on his thoughts. "Ours is not to reason why, only to do or die," the thug kept repeating over and over. The other thug kept repeating in his mind, *London Bridge is falling down…falling down…London Bridge is falling down…my fair lady.* Lawrence had trained them already.

The house was magnificent, full of antiques, sculptures, and paintings. If he were here under different circumstances, Matthew would have been impressed. They took him into the study and left the room. A man sat in the dark room with a fire going behind his desk. Matthew sat down in the chair in front of the desk. A desk light turned on, and he could see the man's face. It was Lawrence. At least it looked like him. Matthew immediately sensed something was not quite right, but could not figure it out. Lawrence was looking through his notebook. "Impressive...very impressive. You seem to have developed a knack for spy games. Who would've thought? I applaud you. Quite remarkable, considering how backward you used to be." Only Lawrence would know something like that. "Still not many friends in the world to help you out? Thus, the life of one on the spectrum. Friends are beneficial, especially in moments like these. I don't mind...in fact, it makes life much simpler and less messy for me."

"Would you like a drink, Matthew...oh, that's right, you don't touch the stuff? Why so quiet?"

Matthew was trying to read his thoughts, but they were completely off-limits. Then he heard something.

"You're wasting your time. I have the knack as well."

Matthew looked at him, smiling like a pig in shit.

"I thought...perhaps you might keep an open mind and enjoy a tour of my laboratory. I spared no expense...and with my private donations, it is comparable to the D.C. offices. But of course...you want to make sure your lady is OK first." He gestured with his hands as if to say Matthew was an idiot. However, Matthew knew he had already planned this and everything else out down to the finest details. A bookcase moved down, and on top was a flat-screen monitor that came on. It showed a camera shot of Mare. She had an IV in and appeared to be sleeping. "It's remarkable, really...Dimment managed to save Mare but was unable to save his own sister. What a pity. Do you recognize the nurse?" Using a hand remote control, the camera zoomed in on a familiar face. Matthew could not believe his eyes. It was Sophie, Mare's trusted best friend.

"It's amazing how greedy some people are. It astonishes me every day what people are capable of. In some...or should I say in most cases, I know what they are capable of. I know what they are thinking. So do you, Matthew. Remarkable again how much we are alike. For such a smart guy, you are either naive or stupid. Did you really think you could invent something so extraordinary and keep it all to yourself? I hope you are naive for Mare's sake. She is such a stunning young woman. Well, enough criticizing you; there is plenty of time for that later. I want to show you around."

Something about this guy was bothering Matthew, and he couldn't put his finger on it. They left his study and went out into the foyer. His goons were there waiting. Lawrence led, and Matthew followed with his muscle close behind. Matthew took a mental picture of every painting, sconce, table, and door as they proceeded down the hall. This was a huge home. Passing by the grand stairway, he could not see anything upstairs. They went into a lounge room, probably for guests to have some privacy when he was entertaining. It was decorated with a lovers' chair, a few couches, and chairs. The fireplace was ornate. Maybe this is where his goons were going to soften him up. Matthew had made up his mind that he wasn't going down easily. Once in the room, they stood there looking at each other awkwardly in silence. The house had a musty, dusty odor. By the door was a gold rope. Surely, that wasn't a servant's bell. "Swen, if you please," Lawrence motioned to him. He pulled the tasseled rope.

Matthew almost lost his balance when the room began to move downward. Swen and the other thug never cracked a smile. They just stood there looking at him with a menacing scowl. "Who wears sunglasses at night anyway?" The wall behind them transformed from concrete to cut stone. They went down fifty-six feet. Matthew studied the speed of travel by focusing on abnormalities on the wall and counted the seconds it took to travel. At fifty-six feet, they stopped. It looked like they were stopped in a hallway. "Rene, the door, please?" He opened a glass door, and as soon as he moved, the lights in the hallway came on. They must have been sound or motion activated.

Right in front of them as they left the elevator, carved into the limestone like an ancient pyramid, were Nazi insignia. A bird with its wings open, with the Nazi insignia below, was as pristine as the day it was placed there. Matthew felt a cold chill remembering how innocent people were experimented on and used as test subjects for the demonic research his regime administered. "I sense you do not approve, Matthew?"

"No, I do not, Dr. Kaiser." He smiled, knowing Matthew had discovered his shady past. "You know as well as I do that no matter how distasteful the research was in this bunker, we have all benefited from its fruits."

"Not all fruit was intended to be eaten, Doctor." Matthew's reference to Eve was a private slap in his face. He had already set her free and rekindled the fire in a fading ember.

Their shoes echoed every scuff, scratch, and pop as they walked down the empty corridors. Matthew made sure he kept a mental map in his head. Lawrence knew what his capabilities were, or at least what they had been. They stopped at a door. Matthew stood there waiting for his lead. Lawrence held his left arm out, as if to welcome Matthew to lead now. "Well...go on in, Matthew." He opened the door, and inside was Mare. He lost all control of his emotions and ran to her, but she was out cold. "What have you done to her?"

"Nothing, Matthew. What would it benefit me to harm her now? She has something very special inside. As long as we understand each other's desires, nothing will happen to either of them. You have my word." Matthew did not like that look on his face at all.

"Mare...Mare, if you can hear me, I am here now. I love you so much, sweetie." He was stroking her head and rubbing her arm. This was the moment. He had an overwhelming desire to be with her. He was emboldened; his resolve was firm. He would do whatever it took to make her and his unborn child safe again. "She is not anesthetized; she is in a chemical-controlled coma. Much like she was before she was awakened. She and the baby will be unharmed. I am amazed that she has completely recovered and no longer requires stem treatment. In fact, the stems were having a degenerative effect on her. Dr. Dimment carried on her treatment for way too long, or he did not know the difference. No matter, she is under my care now." The Doctor did not know that Mare could hear when she was in a trance-like state.

Matthew leaned over and whispered in her ear. "Sophie served you up, Mare. Do not trust her. I will find a way to get us out of here, even if I have to give up the notebook." She moved slightly as if she were trying to lift her arm. Sophie came into the room. "I am sorry, Matthew, but I have to think about my family. My husband…well, he is helpless. I am tired of being broke all the time. I really do care for Mare and you. Dr. Meacham said he has no intention of hurting either of you."

"That's enough, Sophie. Administer her medication and leave us." Matthew looked at a clock by her bed. It was eight o'clock. The medicine must wear off around this time. He didn't know how often it was given, but at least this was beneficial information.

"Let's continue with the tour, shall we? I have much to show you." The next room they went into had a few scientists. It was a stem cell regeneration laboratory. There were embryonic sacs floating in glass vessels. This must be where they were harvesting stems from living, developing fetuses. "I am sure you are unimpressed. This practice is not for the faint of heart. However, German scientists have never been weak." A subtle jab, based on the fact that some scientists have morals. They stopped in several other rooms, all of which dealt with genetics research. However, this was the most disturbing room they visited. They had a live male with his skullcap removed, stimulating different parts of his brain and noting the reactions. He had literally hundreds of small electrical wires inserted into his brain. They watched a monitor on the wall, and it appeared to be picking up his thoughts.

"I thought this room might interest you. You are correct in your thinking. What's on the screen is what he is thinking. It needs much more work, and the technology, I'll admit, is crude at best, but the human brain is the most efficient living calculator in the world. No computer chip will ever match the speed or storage capacity, but you already know this, don't you? Just think, computers in the future may not even have to be plugged into a power source. They may have a human brain, and the only fuel you may need is food." This guy was mad beyond all reason. He was proud of his accomplishments. There were no subtle hints of remorse, shame, or a moral compass.

They came to a set of highly secured double doors. Lawrence paused before speaking on purpose. "I am not sure if I should let you see what's in here or not. However, I think since you will be living here, it is best to be open and honest." He placed his eyes in the retinal scan and his fingers on a green pad. Matthew saw the light from the scan. The doors opened, and they walked inside. He motioned for Swen and Rene to wait outside. This must be very important to him. With his ego, Matthew sensed he wanted to brag. He had a few secrets of his own that he would reveal when the time was right. The laboratory was very warm. When the doors opened, the heat was palpable. They were standing in a clean room.

Donning surgical masks, outerwear, shoe covers, hair covers, and gloves. "Precautionary, not for us but for the ones inside." Matthew could see through the glass, and the room was empty. There were just a bunch of huge cylindrical vessels. You couldn't even see inside them. Kaiser hit a button, and the inner door opened. The room felt like it was 98.6 degrees. They walked inside, and Matthew could feel him grinning right through his mask. He walked up to one of the tanks and typed in a code (7042). How ironic was that? The outside door opened, revealing a glass bubble. He waved for Matthew to come near. Matthew thought he had seen everything, but this was amazing beyond his wildest dreams. He walked over, and inside was a human. A full-grown adult male human. It looked just like Swen.

"Is that who I think it is?" Matthew said with much hesitation.

"Yes, that is a second-generation Swen. Rene is on his sixth regeneration. He is accident-prone and not very bright to boot."

"But how…humans. It's just not possible?"

"Oh, but it is, and I am living proof."

Matthew spoke aloud without realizing it, "I knew there was something not quite right when I met you!"

"Your intuition did not deceive you. You must listen to it when it calls upon you." He was talking with a clone the entire time. Matthew let his guard down for just a second, and he could feel him reading his thoughts. He winced from the pain. He stopped immediately. "Sorry, Matthew, old habits. I can answer the questions you were thinking. Savant, photographic memory, any of this ring a bell? With the brain scan technology and the ability to sort memories like data files, all Dr. Meacham has to do is send me a zip file across the World Wide Web. In about fifteen or twenty minutes, I have memorized every thought and experience he sends me. Impressed now?" Matthew could not speak, so he just shook his head.

"The scientists you met earlier are clones. Since I originally had some unwilling participants, I cloned them and then copied their memories. I trashed personal memories and kept their technical abilities. I released the scientists and paid them a great deal of hush money. Just think of the possibilities. With access to the right people and enough time, I can replace anyone at any time. I have had some recessed data slip through the filters, but for the most part, a success. Are you ready to go to work?"

"Me...work for you?"

"Yes, I am only asking to be polite. Maybe this will help convince you." He put in the code for the next tube, and it opened. Matthew was afraid to walk over, but Dr. Kaiser gently pulled him by the elbow. He pointed at the case, and inside was a fully developed Matthew. He was in shock; his body started to revolt. He felt a sudden rage come over him and could sense that Cerebrus was near. As he looked into the case, he was looking into his own face, just floating there in silence. He could not move his eyes; they were fixed on him. The body inside jerked, and his eyes opened and looked back at him. Matthew flinched and fell backward, trying to catch himself. He was so overcome with emotion and shock that he fainted like a debutant in a tight corset on a hot summer day.

30 *MIND OVER MATTER*

Matthew found himself standing at the barren tree, soaked to the bone. The leaves were flying off in all directions, and a full-blown storm raged directly overhead. He tried to concentrate on Id, but the roaring wind and the lightning arcing across the sky made it impossible. The tiny hair on his arms and neck stood on end. He felt lost and hopeless as small hailstones began to pelt him. He imagined an umbrella, and one appeared in his hand, but it was useless against the gale. The wind caught it, tearing the fabric and breaking the supports before ripping it from his grasp. The hailstones grew larger, striking him with increasing force, cutting through his shirt sleeve as he tried to deflect them.

In a moment of desperation, he imagined a shack. One materialized in the distance, and he ran toward it, its wooden porch creaking and cracking as he stepped inside. But the shack was no true shelter. The hail, now the size of golf balls, hammered against the walls, which began to disintegrate. The wind tore off pieces of the roof, and the hailstones, now misshapen chunks of ice with a blue flame surrounding them, broke through the windows. Everywhere they rolled on the floor, they left a trail of fire.

He ran to the back door, and when he opened it, the wind ripped the door from his hands, sending it flying away. The shack was engulfed in flames. He saw a cellar in the back, a last-ditch effort of his panicked imagination. He ran towards it, trying to open the ship-like hatch door. An ice ball hit his arm, setting his shirt on fire. He padded it out and continued turning the wheel. After seven turns, it finally opened. He went inside and pulled the door down, fighting the wind that tried to keep it open. Looking up, he saw the menacing yellow eyes of Cerebrus floating in the dark clouds. With all his might, he closed the door, spun the hand wheel seven times, and locked it. He went down the seven steps to the floor and collapsed on a bench, exhausted and out of energy.

There was a dim light overhead, and he took a moment to rub his hands through his hair, smelling the burnt clothes and hair. He felt a spot on his head where an ice ball had apparently struck him. Other than some red marks, he was fine.

"Rough out there, isn't it?" a voice said, startling him. The rage he had felt began to subside. "Cerebrus… he is very unpredictable."

"So are you!" Matthew barked. "I've already been on one of your 'love hippy trips.' You're both nonsensical. What is going on?"

"Cerebrus is trying to gain control. He will stop at nothing short of killing to get it."

"Where is Id?"

"I am not sure. He is my enemy as well, but very predictable, as you say."

"I never said that!"

"You said that Cerebrus and I are unpredictable, specifically excluding Id. I merely conjectured that he is, therefore… predictable."

"It doesn't matter now. I have my own Cerebrus to deal with in the real world."

"This world is not real. It is very real to me. It is very real to Cerebrus, and it is very real to you. We are a part of you, and yet we are separated and then all connected."

"You keep saying that, and none of you ever explain. How in the hell are we all connected?"

"Life connects us all. Even though we have no physical properties to speak of, we are very real. The enlightenment process takes some time for even a brilliant mind like yours to process."

Matthew sat in silence for a moment. "If this reality is real and the physical world reality is real, why can't I see them both when I'm awake?"

"Why can't you?" the figure countered.

"No, that's what I'm asking you."

"My reply is: why do you refuse to see them as one and the same?"

"Are you trying to say I can fight and kill Dr. Kaiser from in here?"

"No… you cannot kill a soul, a person's essence. You can only kill their physical body, but definitely not from in here. There are several dimensions of life. When your physical body dies, you live on. This is the basic premise of all religion. While you reside inside a physical body, you can still access the fifth dimension. I dare say it would be possible to reach the sixth, but not the seventh."

"So, you're telling me that there are seven dimensions of reality total between the physical and spiritual world?"

"In a sense, yes, but they are not dimensions to spiritual beings. Spiritual beings have no boundaries. That is why, spiritually, you can access other people's thoughts. The thoughts that annoy you in the airport are, " Are you actually connecting with these people spiritually?"

"So, if I imagine something in here or in the physical world, I can make it happen?"

"Possibly, yes."

"To be completely spiritual means I have to give up my physical boundaries?"

"Yes, that is definite."

"We are all connected spiritually, so I can go deep into my own spiritual world and connect to others like an internet superhighway?"

"Then yes, the spiritual connection is an internet superhighway."

"How do I 'dial up' Lawrence then?"

"Dial up? I am not sure what you're talking about. You're very nonsensical."

"What I am asking is, in the construct of the spiritual world, how do I connect to others?"

"This is a most difficult art to master. You have to open your psyche, for lack of a better term, to the fifth dimension. You will be lost to yourself, and if you cannot find your way back, then your physical body will not awaken. You could get trapped in here."

"And we are trapped in here right now, by the looks of things. The only way out is through that door, and Cerebrus is waiting. He will wait as long as it takes. Our only hope is that Id can bind him. He feeds on fear, anger, lust, vanity, and avarice."

"I do not subscribe to any of those notions, so why isn't he shrinking?"

"All physical creatures do. It doesn't take much, but he can also feed on others near you. Things you ignore, like the people in the airport that annoy you, he is feeding on now."

"How do I connect?"

"You must have a strong bond or connection in the physical world to begin with. If you go to the wrong door and open it, and that spiritual being is starving like Cerebrus, then it may feed off you for eternity."

"What about Mare? I have the strongest connection to her. It may be my only connection other than Dr. Kaiser."

"I would definitely start with your strongest connection first. And I may be able to help."

"You just said Id had to bind him."

"I did… I am Id." The figure stepped closer to the light, and Matthew could see him. It was Id. He had a golden rope tethered to his waist that bound Caprice. "When they are bound, I can help control them."

"I thought you hated them both."

"Hate is a very strong word. They are my brothers. I could never hate them. That would feed into Cerebrus." The storm outside was now subsiding, the winds had died down, and the constant banging of hail had ceased.

"I need you to open the door, Matthew. When we step out, I will have only a few seconds to tether Cerebrus. I am not even sure I can hold him down this time. When I do, you must leave as quickly as you can."

Matthew nodded in agreement. The door opened, and they stepped out. Lightning erupted in all directions. Id swept into the sky on a chariot of smoke and flames. Matthew saw Cerebrus look at him, then Id, and blink. Id lassoed Cerebrus with the golden rope. Cerebrus struggled, then closed his eyes. He sent a blue bolt down the golden rope, and Id lost control of the reins. Caprice was just standing there, holding on to the side of the chariot. Id was going down hard, but he did not let go of the reins. Just before they hit, Caprice reached out and pulled up the reins. The horse of fire and smoke began to turn up. The back of the chariot hit the ground with a thud and rose up. Id regained his footing, tightened his grip, and began to pull the rope in. The clouds began to swirl from the rope's epicenter. Ice balls erupted and fell to the ground, charged with blue static. They popped and cracked as they rolled on the ground. Matthew could smell ozone and mist in the air. In the distance, he could finally see the tree.

He ran for it. The harder he ran, the more the wind pulled at him, as if he were running in place. He felt his feet leave the ground. Cerebrus had him in his hand. The hand was made of clouds, dust, and smoke. He pulled Matthew up and looked him directly in the eyes. He was not pleased. He blinked, and Matthew fell.

When he landed and opened his eyes, he was staring directly into the face of **Dr. Kaiser**, who was leaning over his body. That startled him more than Cerebrus had.

"You fainted in there. Like a little girl." Kaiser laughed, a cold, dry sound. "It is very miraculous seeing your own face for the first time. I needed some insurance. They are there to ensure you follow through. You see, I live life like a chess match. I don't just look three moves ahead. I look ten. I knew every move you would make, and I never lifted an angry hand to get you here. You will do what I ask. I know you better than you know yourself. You can't help but be intrigued by what I have shown you here." He laid his arm on Matthew's chest as he looked into his eyes with a flashlight to check for a concussion. "This place is your clay. You are not restricted here. Do whatever you like. Have you ever been here before? Think very hard, Matthew, you have a photographic memory."

"You know the answer to that, Dr. Kaiser. I would never work here."

"Won't they miss you and me back home? Don't you think that will raise suspicions?"

"I know you are not that dense, my boy. Dr. Kaiser is home, working as usual. Mare was taken to the finest facility in Germany for treatment of her sudden illness. Her boyfriend is at her side and will remain there until she has recovered." He was walking out of the room, smiling.

"That won't hold up forever, and you know it," Matthew retorted.

"I have it covered. We will be fine for several months."

Matthew got off the bed and went to the door. It would not open. He tried the keypad and typed in 7042, but it did not work. A loudspeaker came on. "Matthew, you need to rest tonight. It's lights out. Tomorrow we will begin." The lights went out, and he was in complete darkness. He turned back toward the bed, and in his mind, he pictured everything in its place just before the lights went out. He walked eight steps, avoiding a couch, reached out, and picked up a glass. With his left hand, he picked up a pitcher of water, poured a cup, and stopped just below the top edge. He could hear the glass filling up and knew exactly when to stop. He took a drink and set the glass down.

He turned to the door and approached it. He fixated his thoughts on the door, concentrating as hard as he could. The door began to become clear in his mind, but the pitch-black darkness provided no contrast for him to work with. This would be a case of mind over matter. He concentrated again until he could shove his arm through the door. He felt himself stepping out of his body. It wasn't his physical arm reaching through the wall at the Hospital in Berlin at all. It was his inner being. He was able to leave his body and walk. It finally made sense. He strained even harder and stepped through the door. His body was still standing in place. He walked down the hall toward Mare's room and went in, stepping right through the door without opening it. She was lying there motionless. Light from the instrumentation and machines monitoring her vitals provided plenty of illumination, a stark contrast to the pitch-black darkness he had just left.

He leaned over her and gave her a hug. She was very warm. He stroked her head and decided to do as Id had suggested. Sitting down next to Mare, he held her hand. He just thought that would help for some reason. His spirit began ascending. He felt himself connected with her mind. After a few seconds, he found himself walking across a field covered with tall grass and wildflowers. The air smelled like an ocean breeze, even though there was no water in sight. He walked up a slight hill towards a large shade tree. Just underneath was a red and white checkered tablecloth, accompanied by a picnic basket. He could see a phonograph playing "Moonlight Serenade," a soothing, peaceful melody of perfect orchestration.

He did not see Mare immediately, but then her head appeared out of the tall grass on the other side of the hill. She made the picture complete; she made his life complete. Mare had on a light yellow sundress with flowers and an old white cloche hat. She was twirling a flower in her hand and smelling it as she came.

"I thought you were never going to come?" she said.

"I was held up for a while."

"Your clothes," she said, laughing and partially covering her mouth. He looked down and saw he was wearing dress shoes, knee-high socks, short pants to his knees, a sweater vest, and a short-sleeved shirt. Worst of all, he had on a flat cap as if he were going to play golf.

This reality must be what Mare dreams of as the perfect moment in time. They sat on the tablecloth and ate lunch, enjoying light conversation and laughing. He was feeling very melancholy. He reached into his pocket and pulled out a tiny box. When he opened it, inside was a sterling silver engagement ring set with a burst of small diamonds, featuring a large oval diamond at its center. The music box seemed to sense the moment and slowed down, then came to a complete stop. A breeze picked up.

"Mare, will you marry me?" The words hung in the air, and she just sat there motionless. For a moment, he thought she had frozen. She dropped the brownies in her lap, leaned over, and hugged him. He had never seen her this happy ever. He noticed she wasn't pregnant anymore.

He took the ring out of the box and slipped it on her hand. "Yes… Matthew Le'Dain, I will marry you." They kissed for some time. When they stopped, he had to bring her back down to earth with a dose of reality. He explained where she was, how they had arrived, and what was happening. She told him she had been listening to conversations between Sophie and Dr. Kaiser. They were never going to let them leave. She also told him he wanted their baby. He had some crazy idea that it would be a super savant. Matthew did not tell her his plans because he thought it would put her in danger. Lawrence could easily ravage her mind. He just told her that when he came, she should be ready.

31 *NIGHT OF THE LONG KNIVES*

The next few weeks were a living hell. Matthew seized every opportunity to meticulously log schedules, camera movements, personnel patrols, and the routine of feeding and lights-out. The one thing he desperately needed, and didn't have, was a way to enter the clone room. It seemed the only security was Dr. Kaiser himself. He left instructions for me each day in a file, sending me decoy notebooks with a sarcastic note: "Nice try." It was only a matter of time before he realized the real notebook was not in my vault box back in the States. The irony was suffocating—the very thing he desired the most, my real memories, were in a notebook hanging in his coat just a few feet away from him, and he had no clue.

The other unsettling concern was that this wasn't even the real Kaiser. The original was at home, living a free life. He had left a clone, with whom Matthew mentally dubbed K2, here to carry out his misguided plans. For days, Matthew observed the clone room. No one ever went in, and no one ever came out. He tried not to be obvious with his observations. The retinal scan would be impossible to overcome. Hacking into the security was an option, but Kaiser had banned me from all computer access. He wanted hard notes. Matthew proposed a new project: cleaning up some memory issues in the transcription application he'd designed. To his surprise, Dr. Kaiser granted him permission to work with it. At long last, Matthew had direct access to the system. The program worked by connecting fiber optic stimulators to the main neurosynaptic pathways running through the medulla oblongata, allowing a person to travel down any active or passive nodes. However, there were synaptic dead ends—pockets of memories that didn't loop back into the main synaptic highway. This was where the difficulty lay. When memories were transferred, the clone would retain some snapshots or personal pockets. Kaiser did not want this. So, he forced Matthew to work on a solution for his failures.

Matthew proposed a theory to Dimment, demonstrating it with an antiquated logic flow diagram model. He showed him a basic series of if-then statements that would evaluate the memories and determine their relevancy. He was sure Kaiser had tried some form of this, but his proposal used a learning script that, over time, as memories were scanned, would develop preferences based on Kaiser's desires. Kaiser approved the changes but made him use the two programmer clones assigned to the lab.

The clones were completely void of personality, with no memories or connections to love, empathy, or emotions of any kind. It was a bizarre feeling to be near them; they reminded him too much of how he once was. Kaiser was creating logically controlled sociopaths, devoid of emotions and empathy for others. The clones did not understand sarcasm, laugh, or joke. Their only redeeming quality was that they did not become upset, either. He decided to try an experiment. He made up names for them: Frick and Frack, after two old parody ice skaters. The names were ironic, seeing as this pair had no personality at all. They never noticed his sarcasm but followed instructions when called just the same. His plan to gain access to the computer system had worked, so he decided to move to the next phase.

He wanted to see what kind of psyche construct Frack had. He seemed to him to be the more vulnerable mind of the two. He was interested in checking up on his Id to see what these two looked like from the inside. He convinced Frack to sit in the stimulator chair, and he placed the non-penetrating neurotransmitter on his head—the device picked up electrical impulses at their generation point. This is why Kaiser had made all the clones bald. He told him it was out of calibration and he needed to reset the baseline. Lawrence had made their psyche the baseline for all cloned scientists in the building. He was surprised at how easy it was. He sent Frick to go get him another blank journal. After Frack had relaxed and closed his eyes, he placed an opposing neurotransmitter on his head instead of plugging him into the computer system. He sat down in a chair behind him and drifted into a controlled sleep.

When he opened his eyes, he was walking up the hill towards the tree. It was completely changed. The tree was covered in leaves and fruit and was void of any dead branches. When he reached full enlightenment, he thought aloud for Id. When he appeared, he had a golden belt over a white robe. Cerebrus adorned a black robe with a golden belt, and Caprice wore a purple robe with a golden belt. Id was tethered to both with a golden lead rope. No longer were Caprice and Cerebrus bound in the trunk of the tree nor were they roaming free to cause havoc. He had reached the door to the fifth dimension at last. The three brothers floated down to the base of the tree. They could sense what he was here for. A door formed on the tree, a symbol of course. All three pointed toward the door, and it opened. The light that shone from it was so white it blinded him temporarily. "This is the path; do not leave the road upon which you seek," was an instruction entrained with a stern warning. He was concentrating on Frack very hard as he entered through the door. He passed through the light and fell. The floor inside was an illusion. When he first stepped into the light, the floor rippled like touching the surface of water. How peculiar.

Falling rapidly, he was traveling as fast as a synaptic charge. He felt as if he were in a wormhole or a time machine. He could see a reflection of himself on the walls, and his face was drawn out and long as if it were melting. He felt weightless and began to feel off-balance. It felt like he had an inner-ear infection and could not hold his footing. A sick feeling came over him. He saw a wall coming up, and several paths coming from it. He did not know what to do. He was going to slam into it. All he could do was concentrate on Frack. The intersection looked like a white net or a spider's web. He threw his arms in front of his face, braced for the impact, and hit the wall. He rebounded from the netting like hitting a trampoline lying on its side. It threw him into another tunnel, and he dropped out of the end after a few more seconds of free-falling. He landed with a thump. Standing up, he could see a tree inside.

It looked like his psyche, only different. There was no grass at all. The ground was made up of a gray and white spongy material. It was also wet and sticky; he tried to wipe the goo onto his pants, but it was everywhere. He walked toward the tree as his shoes squished like they were full of water. He almost slipped as if wading across a mossy brook. When he got to the tree, he noticed it was lifeless and dead. The trunk was gray, and the bark was missing. There were termite holes all through the trunk. He did not see any signs of infestation, just a lifeless stump. The sky was still, with no movement. It was void… there was nothing going on inside here. He looked around for anything, as far as the eye could see—nothing, no stars, clouds, or even birds. This place was an emotionless wasteland.

  He tried to summon Id, and there was no sound, nothing. He tried to summon Cerebrus and Caprice, but nothing happened. Surely, they were here somewhere. He leaned against the tree, and he heard an echo. He tapped the tree again, and the same thing happened. The tree was hollow. He concentrated on the tree, and a door began to appear. He was not sure if he should go in or not, but his curiosity got the best of him, and he opened the door. Inside, it was dark and damp. There were stone steps inside disappearing into the darkness. He moved inside to the top step and accidentally hit a pebble. He stood and watched it roll down each step, echoing until it was out of sight. He moved carefully down the spiral stairs, hearing muffled sounds echoing from the depths below. He continued until he reached the bottom. It was a room similar to a seventeenth-century dungeon. He could see shackles and chains against the east wall. He called out, "Id." His voice echoed off the walls and then disappeared into the distance.

  A chain moved, and from the shadows crawled an emaciated body. He could see every bone on the frail, human-like creature. It was frightening to look upon. What was this thing at his feet? "Id," he called again. It was malnourished and looked like it was almost dead. The feeble creature spoke with a frail voice. "You must go from this place now and never return. Go now before it is too late." He began to recall what his Id had said before. Cerebrus and Caprice feed on infirmities. Cerebrus feeds on the deadly sins and Caprice on fancy, bliss, and thrill. He could hear something breathing in the darkness. Suddenly, Id was jerked back into the shadows with a mighty heave of the clanging chains. He groaned in agony. "Come to us, brother," a deep voice said, panting like a dog. He backed up toward the stairs. The room opened up, and the wall on the other side of the stairs was gone. A green figure stepped from the shadows. It was hunched over, and all the bones in its body were showing, but this human-like creature had muscle as well. The muscle bulged out of its thighs and arms. The hunched spine displayed the creature's ripe vertebrae running down its back. He stepped back onto the first step.

The sight of this gruesome beast distracted him. He heard a second voice behind him and felt its feet sliding on the stone floor. He could sense them feeding on his emotions already. It reminded him of maggots consuming a rotting carcass. His mind was torn with despair and overwhelming bliss at the same time. It confused and frightened him all at once. He could taste metal in his mouth. He had never experienced fear like this before. "Brother, what do we have here? Fresh meat. It has been so long since we have eaten." This creature looked the same except for a red tint to its skin. He knew this was a bad idea, so he turned and ran up the stairs. The creatures gave chase, fighting with each other to get to him. That was the advantage he needed. If they had cooperated, he would be, well… dead meat. Their claws tore away the steps at his feet. He ran as fast as he could, lunging for the door. He barely made it out with his life. He took his foot and kicked it closed. He could hear them beating and clawing from inside. The echoes from the trunk of the tree sounded like a pack of wolves fighting. He stood up and slipped as he tried to run several times. He ran into the distance, not knowing where to go. He looked up in the sky; there was a small white light emanating from it.

He wasn't sure how to reach the door out, so he just concentrated very hard and jumped toward it. He felt sick briefly and saw his body stretch as if he had accelerated too rapidly. He was drawn into it like a vacuum. He went back through the tunnel, bouncing off the walls like a ping-pong ball, finally landing in the chair where he was sitting. He took off the transmitter and dropped it. He stood up and walked around. He was sweating and knew that this had been a near miss. Frack was still lying there. He was twitching like he was running in his sleep. He went over, pulled the transmitter off, and shook him by the shoulders. He was not waking. He took his hand and slapped him as hard as he could. After the impact, his eyes opened. He jumped from the chair and shoved him off him. He had very good reflexes for a clone. "What are you doing, Dr. Le'Dain?"

"Nothing, you did not awaken, so I slapped you." He shoved him out of the way as if nothing had happened and went immediately back to work. "Did you calibrate the baseline, Dr. Le'Dain?"

"Yes, Frack, the baseline is still intact. No changes will be required."

That night, he sat in his darkened room. He did not go to Mare's happy place, even though they were having a better relationship there than in the real world. He felt empathy and sadness for Frick and Frack. They were bound and starving to be free. The only way to do it was to free Id first. There was no way he knew of to do that right now. That would have to be done at a later time. Right now, he had to focus on freeing himself and Mare.

Kaiser must have become suspicious of his activities. Over the next few days, he spent all his time in the laboratory complex. He asked Frack to come with him. They exited the door and went down the hall. He opened the door and followed behind. Frick was busy and did not notice his absence. In fact, the entire staff had gotten used to his presence and did not respond when they passed him in the hallway. He stood at the corner and watched Dr. Kaiser go into the clone room. Frack waited until the door closed. To his amazement, Frack leaned over and scanned in as well. He disappeared at the door. He went back to the laboratory so as not to arouse suspicion. He finally had a plan. It would include freeing Frack before he could free himself. Id would have to help him. Somehow, he had to obtain the binding rope.

The next day, he put his plans into motion. The computers in the genetics laboratory were not linked with any other system, a very clever move on Lawrence's part. He sabotaged the baseline again and convinced Frack to allow him to use him as a calibration model. Frick was already gone and would not return for a while. Kaiser had him harvesting stems from the adjacent laboratory. He had a little trouble relaxing and returning to a state of enlightenment; his adrenaline was running too high. However, he finally reached it, and once inside, he searched for Id. The three floated into his view at the tree just like harmony.

"Id, I need to obtain a binding rope. I want to bind Frack, I mean, his psyche. His Id is starving to death, and Cerebrus and Caprice are devouring him. They have him chained in the trunk of the tree." He noticed Cerebrus and Caprice look at each other and smile behind Id's back. "What are you two smiling about? I need your help."

Cerebrus spoke up, "We cannot help you."

"Cannot or will not help?"

"We cannot," Caprice said.

Id finished, "We cannot leave this place. We only exist here. They cannot kill Id, but they can keep him bound in pain, agony, and a state of weakness indefinitely. They do this to keep him from controlling them. I can provide you with binding rope and this advice." Id pulled on the tassel around his waist. He coiled the golden rope as he extended it from the belt. It was never-ending; the rope never shortened in length. "The binding rope is a tool and a weapon. They will shy away from it. It will protect you from their advances. However, should you lose control of it, they will be able to tether you to them. If this occurs, there is nothing we can do. You are not Id. You will eventually wither and die like the fruit on this tree."

"Anything else?" he inquired.

"Use your mind. It is your ultimate weapon. Be resourceful and cunning." Id took his index finger and shot a blue bolt of lightning at the rope, severing it from his waist. He heard the door open, walked over to it, and just before he stepped through, he said, "Thank you all."

He did not get ill traveling through the tunnel this time. When he fell from the sky, he landed on his feet, bending his knees to catch himself with the help of his hands. He went to the tree and opened the door. The echoes of water dripping and the cold, damp air caused goosebumps on his arms. The inside of the door was covered in claw marks. There was a long nail stuck in the wood. The steps were covered in blood, and he saw a broken tooth lying on one. Before he even made it down halfway, he heard the chains move, clinking through the loops on the wall slowly, one by one. The links made a menacing sound like a clock counting down at a military test site. It was possible they would be more resourceful and work together this time, but he doubted it. He walked all the way down into the dungeon. It was lit up, and there were sconces with flaming torches on four-sided stone columns all around.

Id was tethered to the wall tightly. They had taken most of his chain away. "Brother, I smell fear."

"No, Brother, I smell angst and can sense his happiness."

He replied, "I smell envy and greed."

They replied, "Mind your tongue, or we will cut it out and pour molten metal down your throat."

They were spaced apart from one another. He had concealed the golden rope behind him. He had backed up to Id. He continued to conceal the rope behind him as he wrapped it around his waist and tied a knot in it. "I am not afraid of you."

They replied, "That just makes you foolish." The other chimed in, "You will not leave here this time. I can assure you of that." They laughed and mocked him.

He took a few short breaths. His heart was beating so loudly he could hear it thumping. He relaxed some more, and it began to slow down. The metallic taste left his mouth, and he regained control of his fear. Id looked terrible. They had drained him to nothing, yet they were starving. He could sense one of them near him. Caprice lunged from his right side. It took him by surprise, and he knocked him to the ground. He held steadfast to the rope and did not lose his grip. He jumped on top of him and took a swipe at his face. His claws hit the stone floor, spilling sparks into the air. He moved just in time. He wrapped the rope around his waist once. He tried to pull free. "He has the binding rope," he screamed and moaned. "Ayye…ayyeeeeeeeeee!" He tied a single knot and let go. He was bound. In the struggle, he lost half of the rope. He could sense Cerebrus near. He made it to his feet. Caprice continued to writhe and scream in pain. His body was shrinking, and the color was leaving his skin.

He did the only thing he could: he made himself disappear. At the last second, Cerebrus lunged at him, and he stepped out of the way. "Brother… brother… help me," Caprice yelled.

"He is mine now. I will not share him. I may not be able to see you, but I can smell your fear. The stink of your weakness reeks and burns my nostrils." He stood up with his arms out and took a deep breath through his nose. The muscles on his chest flexed outward. He was almost to the rope, and he lunged, trying to pick it up. He shot flames from his mouth, knocking the rope out of the way. It did not hurt the rope or even discolor it. He had to overcome his fear, or he would not be able to find him. He ran toward the far side of the room and hid behind a column.

He closed his eyes and took deep breaths. He began to meditate. "That isn't working, I can still smell you," he said as he slowly moved toward him. "Brother… please… save me, and we can hunt him together." Cerebrus chided him, "Shut up!" He continued to taunt him, trying to distract his thoughts, but he was with great resolve. He took one last deep breath and pictured the perfect day with Mare in his mind. All his fear, angst, and doubt were removed. Mare had saved him once again. He stayed perfectly still and never moved. He walked right by him, sniffing the air. He became enraged and blew flames into the distance. He waited until he was as far from him as possible, then he ran for the rope.

As soon as his feet scuffed the floor, he turned. He jumped between the sides of the columns, gaining ground on him quickly. He lunged forward, becoming perpendicular with the ground, and grabbed the rope. He landed on him at the same time. He was very strong. He slapped the rope from his hands. He sat on top of him, holding his arms down like a playground bully. A look of greed and anger developed on his face. "I am going to enjoy this." He leaned back and roared like a lion. His mouth was dripping saliva. His teeth grew longer, and his face changed to look like a canine's. He threw his head back one last time and went for his throat. He waited with his eyes closed, but he never hit him.

He heard him struggling. Caprice and Id had him by the arms. "Get the rope!" Id yelled. They both looked normal, just like his did. Cerebrus was very strong, and they began to lose their grip. He threw Caprice off him and reached for Id, tearing the clothing from his arm and ripping his skin. He took the rope and wrapped it around his waist. He slapped at him with his free arm, cutting him up. He struggled to tie the knot that would bind him. Finally, he was in Id's control now. He fell to the side, lying in the fetal position, screaming and writhing in pain. His skin changed color, and his body shrank until it took a human form again.

Once Id had him in control, he took them up the stairs. The door was closed. He kicked it with his foot, and it flew off into the air. A rainstorm developed, then rapidly dried. The grass began to grow, and the wet, spongy ground receded. Leaves slowly sprouted from the tree, and fruit began to form. The tree healed. New bark formed on the trunk, and the termite holes disappeared. The tree's trunk was left with a dead spot running through the middle. It was scarred, but at least now, it could grow. The three brothers took fruit from the tree and ate it. They offered him a piece, but he declined.

"Thank you," Id paused. "Matthew… my name is Matthew."

"Thank you, Matthew. Is there any way we can repay you?" That was what he was waiting for. He asked them to help him when he regained consciousness. In the distance, he saw a figure resembling Frack spinning and dancing on the hillside in the meadow. He was ecstatic. He didn't think he even noticed they were there. "I will tell him when he is settled down a bit."

Frack was free. He was now his own man. He has no clue where his original was or how many copies were made, but he had a feeling he did not care. Have you ever wondered about what it means when someone comes up to you and talks to you like they know who you are? This is a plausible explanation. He awoke, took off the transmitter cap, and laid it down. This time, he gently shook Frack until he came to.

When his eyes opened, he smiled for the first time. He pulled him down to his chest and bear-hugged him. "Settle down, you cannot act this way when Frick returns. He will notice."

Frack's face dripped with joy. "I am so happy, he cannot control my emotions." He began to cry. He was all over the place emotionally. It took about an hour to settle him, but he was finally able to discuss his plans for an escape.

The first thing the next morning, Frack went up to retrieve his coat. He waited for Sophie to come in for Mare's sedative and surprised her with an ether mask. He took a soaked towel and held it over her mouth and nose until she passed out. He administered Mare a vitamin B shot to speed her recovery. Frack came in to help move Sophie into the closet. "We need to come back for her."

Frack looked puzzled. "Why? She is a clone." He moved the hair on the backside of her head, and there was a three-digit number, 111. It was very small in black ink, like a tattoo. Each clone has a three-digit number indicating how many times it was copied. The memory data becomes corrupted, and the clones are more unstable the higher the number. After nine, they are not even able to have memories copied. He held his head over to him, and it said 222.

"I am a second-generation."

The baseline or original is not numbered but is considered 000. That must mean the real Sophie is at home and has no clue she was copied. They bound and gagged her. He gave Mare a Vitamin B shot so she would start waking up. He needed Frack to get him into the clone room. He was going to destroy his clone and make sure there were no others. He went over to check on Mare and then checked the door. He was rubbing her head, and she rolled over. He did not see what he was doing. Frack saw something on her head, 111. "Matthew, you need to come see this."

He replied hastily, "Not now, this is our chance. You can tell me later." They walked down the hall, trying not to arouse suspicion. A woman walked by with a clipboard and looked at Frack. He froze in his steps. She huffed at him and went around. He thought she noticed his change, but she didn't.

Frack scanned his eyes and his prints, and they went in. There were ten vessels. They both went to the opposite ends and went around opening the doors. Most of the tanks were empty. Swen, Rene, himself, and an unknown were inside the chambers, still floating. He wasn't concerned with the others, only with himself. He began to drain the tank, and it opened its eyes. It put its hands on the glass, trying to touch him. He felt remorseful at what he was about to do. Frack spoke up, "Don't underestimate these things. They are void of feeling, emotion, and memory; they're unpredictable creatures, and if threatened, will kill you. They become frightened and scared, and their basic survival instincts activate."

He took a bottle filled with acid and dropped a cyanide pill into it. He opened a small pod door and placed it inside. The gas started drifting into the pod, and he saw himself banging the glass. He was an abomination, he kept telling himself. An alarm went off immediately. The other tanks began to drain, and all four doors opened, spilling fluid all over the floor. Frack and he ran for the door and hit the button to open it. The four abominations came straight for them. The door opened, and they quickly closed it. Red lights were flashing in the hallway. The loud, repeating buzzer was mind-numbing.

They went through the second door and left it open—no time to shut it. They headed for Mare. He heard them break through the glass door. The elevator had come down, and Swen and Rene got off as he turned down the hallway. He heard machine gun fire. Frack ran into a break room, placed a bottle with accelerant in the microwave, and turned it on. He hid in a door recess, sensing someone coming. It was a lone guard with a pistol. He tripped him as he passed by, and he hit the floor hard, striking his head. He grabbed his handgun and went to get Mare. When he went into the room, she was still groggy. He got her out of bed and wrapped his coat around her. Frack came into the room, startling him. "Mare, we have to go!" Frack and he each got under her arms. They carefully dragged her from the room. "I know an emergency escape to the west lawn." Sounds of gunfire and the buzzing alarm echoed through the halls.

They reached a door leading to a set of stairs. "Stay here while I go up and make sure we can get out." He had to jog up several flights of stairs. He ran as fast as he could to the top. There was a man-way hatch with a hand wheel. He tried to turn it, and it was stuck. He finally got it to move and turned the wheel until it opened. They were far away from the house. He could see no signs of any activity there. He ran back down the stairs, skipping on their edges. He slipped once, almost dropping the gun. When he got to the bottom of the stairs, he saw Frack standing there by Mare with a funny look.

Something behind him moved, and he fell to his knees, then face down. His clone had impaled him with a long knife. He grabbed Mare, and he screamed. Everything slowed down, and he could taste metal in his mouth once again. There was an explosion from inside, and the ground shook. Machine gun fire was getting closer. You could feel a pressure change, and he felt a rush of air come down the stairs. The fire and explosion were sucking air from up top. The door behind his clone blew off its hinges. With one quick pull of his hand, he snapped her neck, and she fell to the floor. Machine gun fire riddled his body with holes. He fell to the floor beside her. He shot back a few times into the smoke but did not hit anything. Swen and Rene opened fire again. He ran up the steps, and he could hear them coming.

Another loud explosion rocked the ground just as he made it to the ladder. It almost knocked him down. The wind was so strong through the hatch that he could barely climb out. He struggled to get to the top. He was crying and could not think at all. The machine gun fire ceased. He felt another loud explosion and almost fell back inside. He stuck his head out and could see the lawn. In the distance, coming toward him, he saw fire shoot up from the hidden exhaust vents, blowing the tops off. The air had stopped rushing through the tunnel and had reversed. He jumped clear of the opening, and a loud flame erupted from the hole. Lawrence must have set off a self-destruct sequence. The ground across the lawn began to drop and cave in. The noise continued, and the ground shook for several more minutes. Smoke billowed up into the sky. When it stopped, the laboratory was no more. Mare was no more. He lay on the lawn, curled in a fetal position, crying and coughing at the same time.

He tried to get up, and his body was in so much shock that he collapsed. He got to his feet and could hear sirens coming through the forest. The house suddenly erupted in flames and began to burn. He staggered forward, stopped, holding onto a small tree, and vomited. He has never felt this lost before, completely void of all hope. He was in no condition to walk. He tried to go toward the house and fell down and passed out.

The sirens are closing in on Matthew, but his escape has come at a terrible cost.

32 *SIDE SHOW FREAK RETURNS*

It was several days after the incident before Matthew awoke. It took several weeks before he could discuss it, and several months before the German authorities finally cleared him and allowed him to return home. He was sitting in a Paris airport security lockup when a man from the CIA walked in. "Matthew…I am Stedman, Jonathon Stedman. My friends call me Jack, among other things," the man said. It was a typical ploy, aimed at establishing a connection. "I understand you're a scientist, a very good one, I'm informed." Matthew just sat there, cold, beaten down, and lost, still mourning Mare. He had asked himself so many times what he could have done differently. He wished he had never listened to Meacham and Dimment. He was lost in his thoughts and had forgotten the man was still talking.

"Matthew, are you listening to me?" Jack snapped his fingers in Matthew's face, then looked at the other two men standing by the door and smirked. "Matthew, I hope you're listening. I am somewhat of a scientist myself." Matthew's mind, once again sharp and cynical, thought, *Yeah, I bet you are.* He had realized even before the accident that any signs of his autism had been slowly but systematically eliminated. The stem cell treatment from a morally responsible source, his own, had cured his social infirmities. "Matthew…I am part of a special group, a group that could greatly benefit from your talents. There are others like you." Matthew perked up a little and looked at him. "Oh…I see you are listening." He knew that comment was grating on Matthew's nerves.

Matthew noticed how the guard to his back left kept clearing his throat and sniffing. He was allergic to something. He also noticed that when the men came in, the other guard had a bad habit: he bit his fingernails down to the quick. His suit was not as tidy as the sniffler's. The sniffler was married; even though he had no ring on, he had gained some weight but still fit, and it left an indentation on his ring finger. He also owned a cat. The sniffler, a dog guy, had the slightest evidence of dandruff but treated it on a regular basis. Lastly, he had a poison ivy breakout on the back of his left hand that was almost healed.

"Matthew, what I am saying is your government, your country, needs a man like you. You are a quick study, but with our training, well… you could become a government agent." That was a big mistake. The government was too big and out of control. Why would he want to stop being a tax contributor and become part of the problem? Second, he loved his country, but this was not the season for it. He did not want anything. "No," Matthew said. "Jack… I said no… no thank you." Jack was visibly bothered by that response. He was not used to hearing it. Suddenly, a thought came into Matthew's mind, loud and booming. "You miserable little, ungrateful, unpatriotic bastard!" Matthew replied, not realizing he had read Jack's thoughts. "What's that, Jack?" Jack sat back in a rebuffing position. "I did not say anything, Matthew. Is there anything you want to tell me?" Matthew decided to humor him. "Yes… It's not my season. I am not ready. I will think about it, but right now, I have other things on my mind."

Jack leaned and clasped his hands together, resting his arms on the table. He had coffee breath but was not a smoker. Was Matthew imagining things, or were his senses becoming keener? "I may have something back home that will cheer you up." Matthew tried again to read Jack's mind and was surprised by his reaction. "Not this time, Matt," he heard from Jack's mind. "Like I said, you're not the only one who has abilities in this world." They stared at each other without saying anything aloud. "If you have the knack, then tell me what I am thinking," Matthew challenged. "I can't, but I can sense you trying to run your fingers through my mind. I am 160, how about you?" Matthew replied, "I am above charting." They were now comparing IQ scores. Jack stood up and extended his hand to shake Matthew's. "I understand, Matthew. When you change your mind, call me." He handed Matthew a card. Clever—it was a normal card, but also had artwork on the back. The phone number was from work on his Rosetta project.

They stepped onto a private plane. Hours later, they landed at Reagan and walked down the stairs. There were agents everywhere. When he reached the last step, Jack stopped him. "Before we go in here, two things; first, you are not permitted, due to national security concerns, to discuss anything that happened in Germany. Second, there is someone inside that loves you, and you may be shocked." He handed Matthew an envelope. It was a court order. He recognized the official monograms. Why would he be surprised to see his mom and dad? He would be upset if they were not there. When he went through the door, the first person he saw was his mother. She ran to him and hugged him. "We are so proud of Matthew." She kissed his cheek and wrapped her arms around him as if she would never let go. He hugged her back; for the first time in his life, he hugged her, and he meant it truly.

His dad patted his back, then hers, and squeezed his shoulder. "We are so glad to have you home, son. Stephan filled us in on some of it. Maybe you could fill in the blanks later when you're ready. What a wackadoo his brother is. Hey… don't let them suck you into their tribe." Matthew looked at him. "Dad." "I am just saying, son; now that they know, they will be knocking at your door." His father, God love him, for someone who had spent his life acting against the government and profiting from it, certainly went out of his way to kick it in the teeth. His mom stepped back and put her hands on his cheeks. She was all teary-eyed now.

"There is someone here to meet you. Please relax, it may shock you." Nothing his mom ever said surprised him. Everyone kept saying that, but he didn't think anything could surprise him again. Mom and Dad moved aside and looked at the back of a woman. He recognized the shape immediately. She turned, smiling, and ran to him. She was talking with a woman holding a young child. It was Sophie holding the child, but how… what? Matthew was in shock when Mare turned around. She began to hug him. He did not return the hug. In fact, he pushed her off, thinking he hurt her feelings. His mom grabbed his arm and hand, leading him back to her. "This is not Mare; she is a clone. I saw her…" His mother stopped him.

"Matthew, this is Mare. The woman in Berlin was the clone." Suddenly, Matthew remembered something Frack had tried to tell him. The vision became clearer. When Matthew looked back at them, Frack was staring at her head, right where a mark would have been if she were a clone. He said, "Matthew, you need to come see this." Matthew didn't respond because he was too distracted. Suddenly, he snapped back into the airport and noticed the dead silence. Then he heard a baby cooing. He was drawn to it as if he had some connection to it. He walked over and looked down at it. Sophie smiled at him. The real Sophie hadn't betrayed Mare, and Mare was still alive. He felt an overwhelming sense of joy. He almost lost his balance, but his father grabbed his arm. "Easy there, Matthew. She is yours." The eyes were just like his.

A small life, this innocent baby; how could anything want to hurt her? Mare came over to him. Sophie was gently bouncing the baby on her lap. She had extensive experience working with children. "We named her Madeline, but we call her Mattie. If you don't like it, we can change her name?" He looked at her, making a connection. "No, Mattie is fine. I like that name." The little babe squeezed his finger and yawned. She squirmed around, and her face started to turn red. She had a grip like a gorilla. "What's wrong with her?" he asked. They all laughed. Sophie spoke up. "It's time you learned some things about being a father." She handed him the baby. Mattie smelled just like lotion and baby powder. Then a pungent, unmistakable odor hit him. He knew what they were laughing about. Sophie reached down and laid a diaper on her. "Your turn now… dad."

Jack came up behind them. "Cute baby looks like her mother. I have one last thing, Matthew. Can I see you just for a moment?" His father whispered aloud, "Tell them no son." Jack and Matthew went to a private room just down the hall. "I need you to tell me what this means?" He showed Matthew some pictures of Dr. Meacham. The first was his face, and the second was a mark on his head. "This is Dr. Meacham, and this is a clone of him. This number indicates that it is the third one. See the 333 on the scalp." Jack looked concerned. "Any idea on how many clones there are?" "No...not really. He could make as many as he wanted. However, one of the laboratory scientists noted that at number nine, the memory data becomes corrupted, and they start experiencing issues with the clones. Genetically, they also start having mental issues or something around copy six." Jack paused, then said, "This one killed himself when we went after him. He poisoned himself with a cyanide capsule. Not very original for a German but effective nonetheless."

Matthew thought hard and remembered, "The scientist also said the first clone made for Kaiser had to be put down. Since most scientists' tests on themselves first, that would mean 111 was also gone. In all, that means Meacham has cloned himself at least three times." Jack paced, then turned around and said, "That we know of." Matthew agreed, "Yes, which we know of." He handed the pictures back to him and reached for the doorknob. "Matthew, this means he is still out there somewhere. Any chance you will help us find him?" Matthew stopped and thought, "Switzerland, I would start there." Jack smiled, "Already on it. That will be difficult. They won't even let us search bank records. They are an island unto themselves. Matthew turned to leave, and Jack got in one last jab. "Have a nice life, Matthew. I am sure you will be happy playing the domesticated father." Matthew winced at him and left the room.

Mare and Matthew were married. He did not want to raise a bastard child. His parents retired and moved to Washington, D.C., near them. They moved just outside of the metro area in a nice, gated subdivision. Into a real home for the first time. He wrote a book on what it's like to be a Savant, titled "Savant." The book sold well and landed on Oprah's desk. She loved it. He was invited to be on her new network, OWN, and the crowd loved him. Like so many authors she has on her show, he ended up as a best seller. Her network offered him a mid-morning slot at ten. It was a mix of talk show and his talents as a Savant. He also brought on the show many unusually talented people. He especially promoted his favorite charity, Autism Speaks. Many neurodivergent guests are also invited to appear on the show.

Now you know how Matthew ended up here. On the cover of Time Magazine, U.S. News, Popular Science, USA Today, and with his own daily show on OWN Network. As he said, what he naturally lacked in social skills, there is always a book that can teach you. However, now he is cured. He would like this for everyone, but today they are limited by resources, technology, and a lack of understanding. He knows what you're thinking. Why can't he just patent his creation of Adam and Eve and inject everyone? It's very simple; morally, he would be creating a super race. Not all autistic children will respond to that type of treatment. Lastly, until a better way to collect stems is developed, he does not want to be a part of that type of science anymore. He has seen how it can be twisted and turned for nefarious gains. Yeah, he has made it. He has it all, and he is helping people. What more could any man ask for?

Sequel Preview – Clones in the Light

1
FROM THE ASHES

In Spandau Forest, the BKA (Bundeskriminalamt) enters the burnt and battered exit hatch to the secret laboratories of Dr. Lawrence Meachum. Taking a flashlight along with two others down the stairs to the bottom. Inside a doorway to a collapsed shaft, he sees five bodies, four men, and one woman. They are badly burned. Other men who entered behind them joined them to collect the bodies. Placing them carefully into bags, they zip them up one by one.

They are donned in surgical masks, gloves, and white disposable HAZMAT coveralls. The two agents start up the stairs. The initial agent walks over to the collapsed hallway and tries to look in. It is completely blocked with debris and rubble. He turns to leave, and his toe hits something where the bodies were lying. He pulls out a handkerchief and picks it up.

The object is a leather notebook. He opens it, looks inside, and develops an evil smile on his face, laughing aloud. The two men halfway up the steps stop and listen, then continue on. He wraps it up in the handkerchief, stuffs it in his inside jacket pocket, and starts up the steps. When he exits the tunnel, his superior is there along with the German Military. "Did you see anything?" He replies, "No, the tunnel is completely blocked. I do not have much faith that there is anything left." The two superiors look at each other. "Nevertheless, we shall excavate this entire site to see if we can find anything. The research here could be very valuable."

They walked across the lawn and back to the drive. The agent got into his car and drove all the way back to Berlin. He left his car with the valet at the Excelsior Hotel and went inside to the lounge. At a familiar table was a man. He was incognito. He had a hat, sunglasses, and a scarf around his neck. The agent looked around and then pulled the leather notebook from his pocket. He slid it across the table. The man picked it up, looked inside, and smiled. He put the notebook in his breast pocket and pulled out a thick yellow envelope. He slid it across the table but did not lift his fingers from it. The agent reached to pick it up, and the man pressed down. The agent scowled at him and then made a funny groan. Inside his head, his blood vessels were swelling and pulsing with every heartbeat. They began to burst one by one until the whites of his eyes turned red. Blood oozed from his mouth, nose, tear ducts, and ears.

The man took his index finger and pushed the agent back in his seat. He picked up the yellow envelope, put it back into his pocket, and grabbed his glass. He drank the last bit of his bourbon and set the glass down. The ice inside clinked as it hit the table. He looked into the dead man's eyes, trying to read his mind before the oxygen left his brain and he was gone. He focused in, and the dead man looked back into the man's eyes. Before the last flicker of his light went out, he saw into the eyes of the man. They were filled with storm clouds and rage. The face looking back at him was Kaiser's. He stood up, looked around while buttoning his overcoat, and sauntered out the door as if he were on top of the world. In the background, Frank Sinatra's *"Devil Moon"* was booming from the lounge.

REQUEST

My son is a high-functioning spectrum child. My wife and I are very fortunate and blessed for that reason. He will have a pretty normal life with our assistance. It is very difficult, as you know, to speak with family and friends who are not around the child all the time and expect them to understand how much time and effort it takes to care for an autistic child. They also do not take the time to read and understand the symptoms and therapies for neurodivergent children, especially if they are high-functioning. Our son is very intelligent and suffers mainly from Asperger's Syndrome. I encourage you to take this opportunity to visit their website and learn more about autism and many other disorders at www.autismspeaks.org. Please support this wonderful organization by making a donation or sharing your story.

I wrote this book to raise awareness of the gifts that are possible with children with special needs. Granted, this is a fictional character that is completely healed by the end of the book, but it demonstrates the talents many neurodivergent children possess. This book is a testament and highlights many of the frustrations, needs, and future possibilities for children with autism. Many famous people, great scientists, and artists have been known to have autism or other behavioral disorders. Instead of rejecting and locking this talent away, I hope this book will encourage you to let it out and foster the growth and development of a neurodivergent child.

DEDICATION

I dedicate this book to my family: my wife, who loves and supports me; my gifted son; and my loving daughter. In addition to all the struggling families of autistic children who fight each day with the public schools to obtain the help their children desperately need and deserve. Lastly, thank you, Lord, for revealing to me my gifts of writing and giving me the courage to share them with others.

Made in the USA
Coppell, TX
06 November 2025

62587369R00190